My Little Pony

Friends Forever

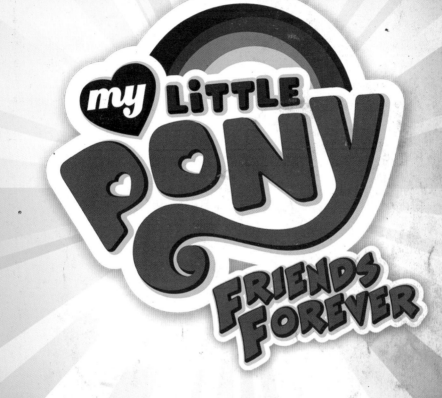

My Little Pony: Friends Forever

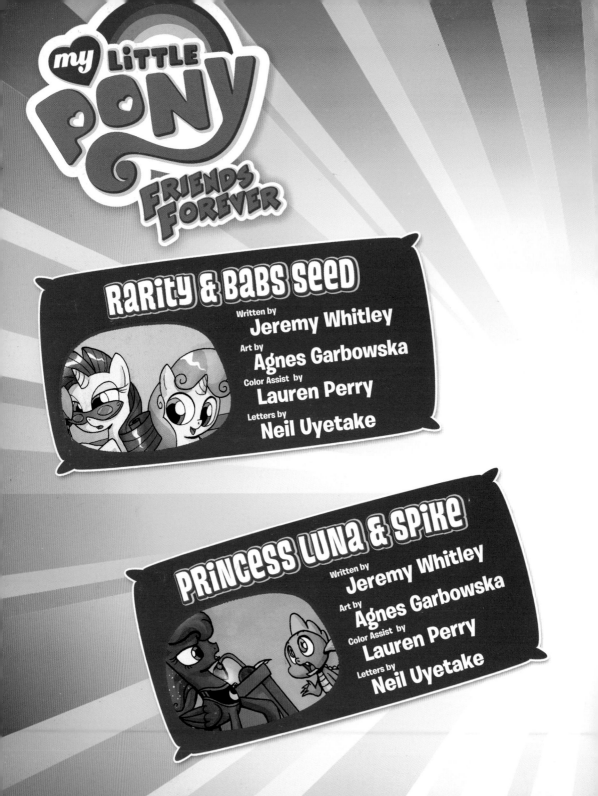

Rarity & Babs Seed

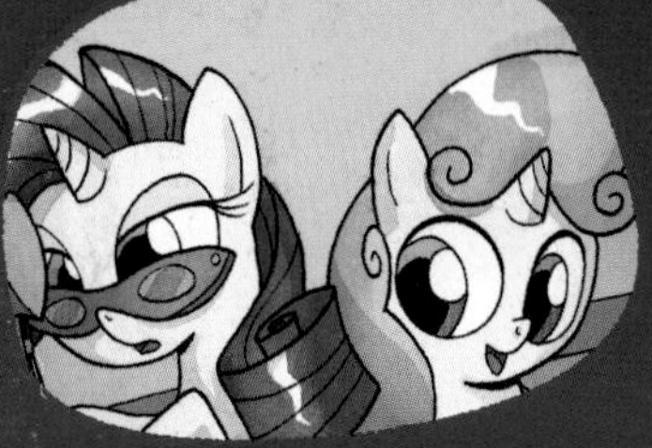

Written by
Jeremy Whitley

Art by
Agnes Garbowska

Color Assist by
Lauren Perry

Letters by
Neil Uyetake

Princess Luna & Spike

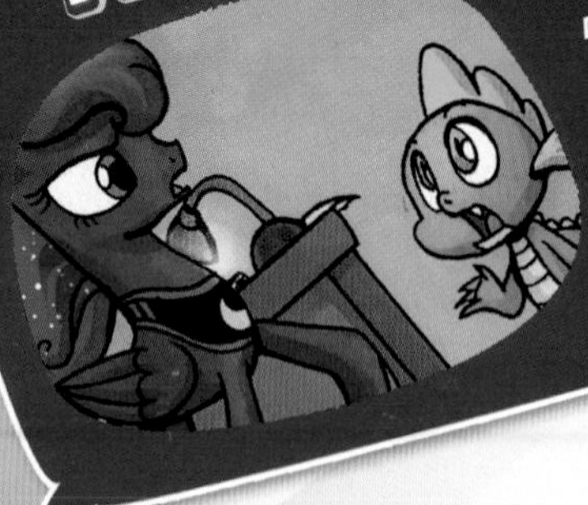

Written by
Jeremy Whitley

Art by
Agnes Garbowska

Color Assist by
Lauren Perry

Letters by
Neil Uyetake

Special thanks to Erin Comella, Robert Fewkes, Joe Furfaro, Heather Hopkins, Pat Jarret, Ed Lane, Brian Lenard, Marissa Mansolillo, Donna Tobin, Michael Vogel, and Michael Kelly for their invaluable assistance.

ISBN: 978-1-63140-377-4

19 18 17 16 2 3 4 5

IDW® Licensed By: Hasbro

www.IDWPUBLISHING.com
IDW founded by Ted Adams, Alex Garner, Kris Oprisko, and Robbie Robbins

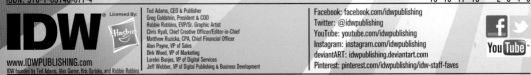

Ted Adams, CEO & Publisher
Greg Goldstein, President & COO
Robbie Robbins, EVP/Sr. Graphic Artist
Chris Ryall, Chief Creative Officer/Editor-in-Chief
Matthew Ruzicka, CPA, Chief Financial Officer
Alan Payne, VP of Sales
Dirk Wood, VP of Marketing
Lorelei Bunjes, VP of Digital Services
Jeff Webber, VP of Digital Publishing & Business Development

Facebook: facebook.com/idwpublishing
Twitter: @idwpublishing
YouTube: youtube.com/idwpublishing
Instagram: instagram.com/idwpublishing
deviantART: idwpublishing.deviantart.com
Pinterest: pinterest.com/idwpublishing/idw-staff-faves

Originally published as MY LITTLE PONY: FRIENDS FOREVER issues #13–16.

APPLEJACK & MAYOR MARE

Written by
Bobby Curnow

Art by
Brenda Hickey

Colors by
Heather Breckel

Letters by
Neil Uyetake

DIAMOND TIARA & SILVER SPOON

Written by
Jeremy Whitley

Art by
Jenn Blake

Colors by
Heather Breckel

Letters by
Neil Uyetake

Cover by
Amy Mebberson

Series Edits by
Bobby Curnow

Collection Edits by
Justin Eisinger & Alonzo Simon

Collection Design by
Thom Zahler

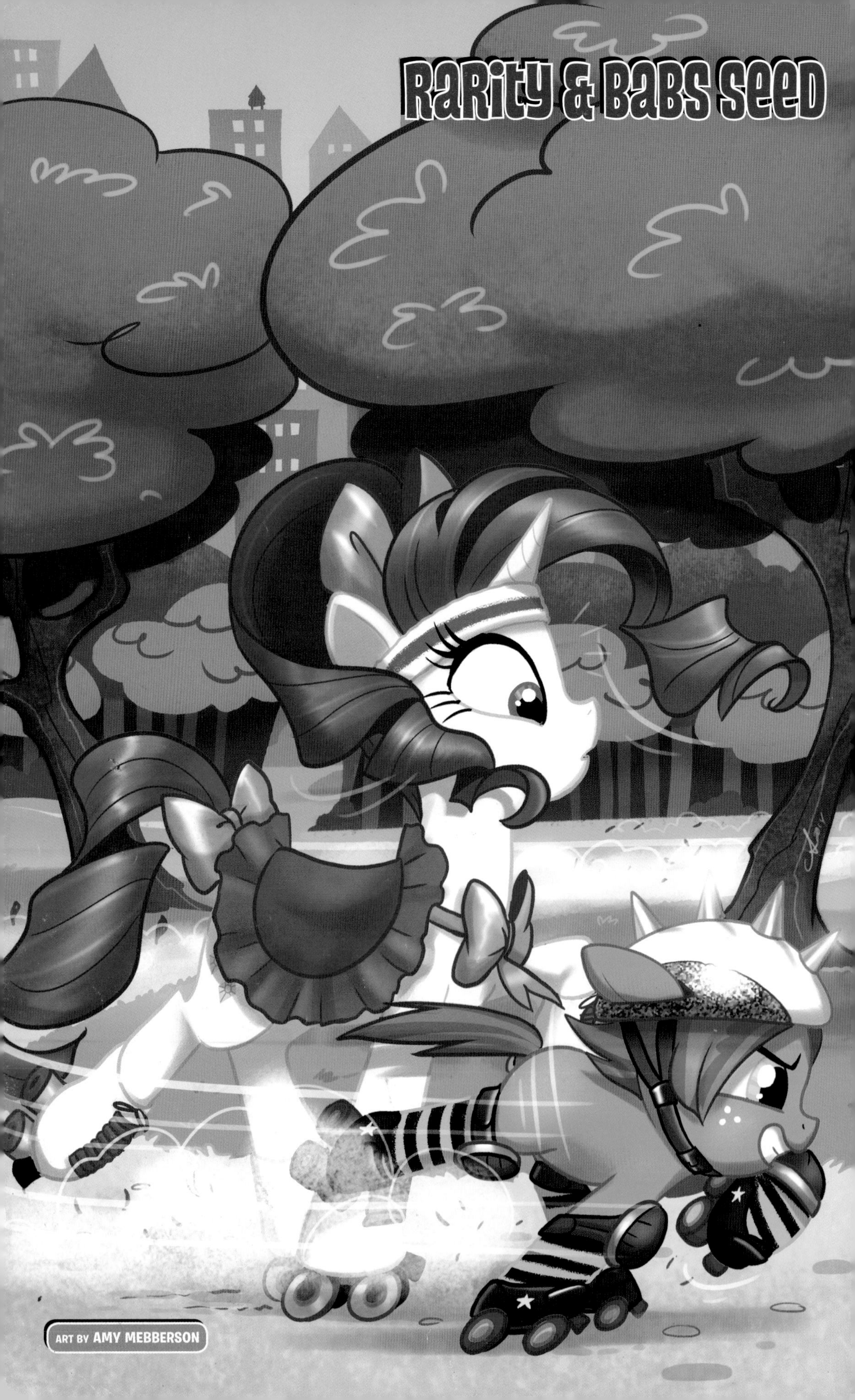
Rarity & Babs Seed
ART BY AMY MEBBERSON

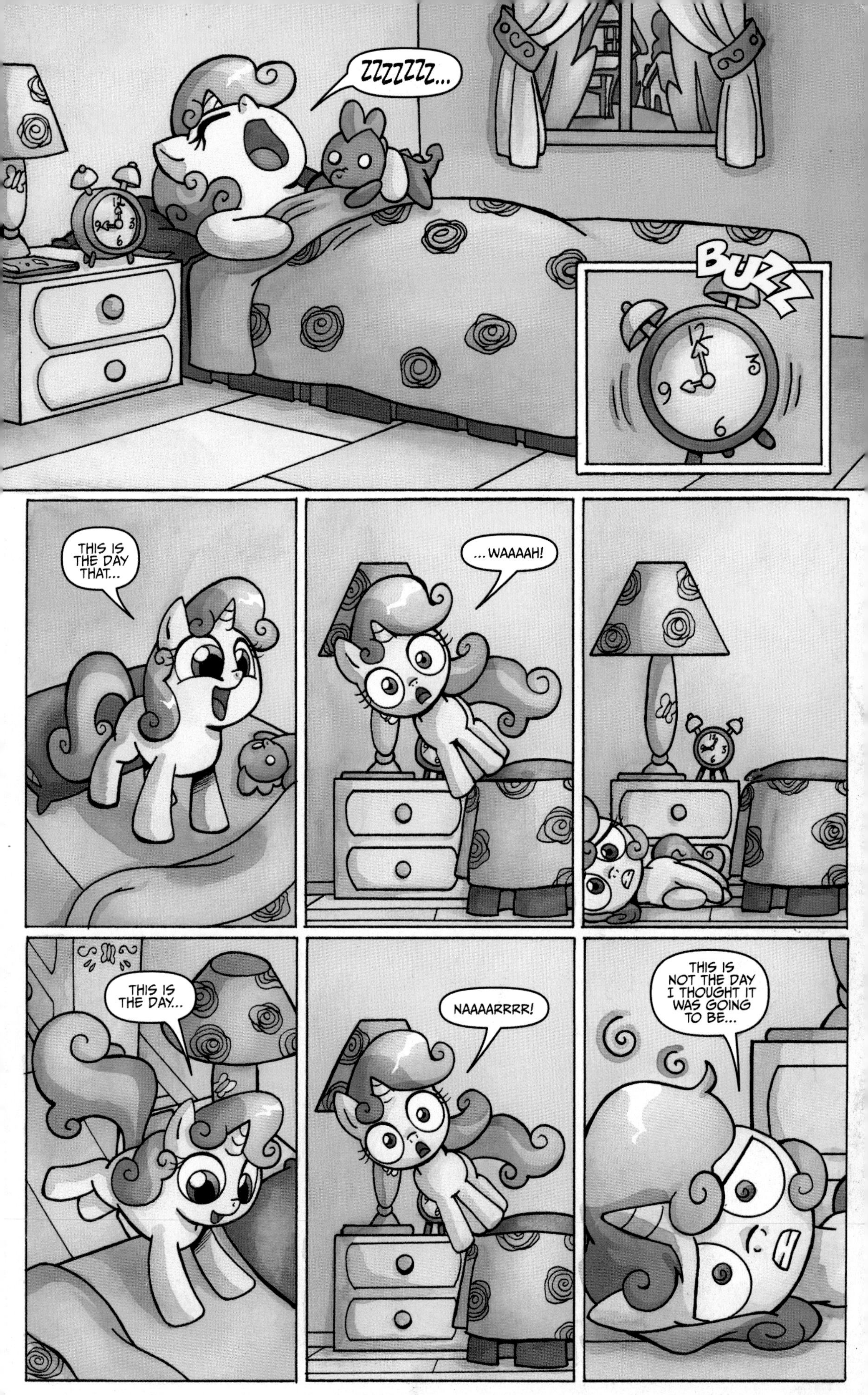
ZZZZZZZ...
BUZZ
THIS IS THE DAY THAT...
...WAAAAH!
THIS IS THE DAY...
NAAAARRRR!
THIS IS NOT THE DAY I THOUGHT IT WAS GOING TO BE...

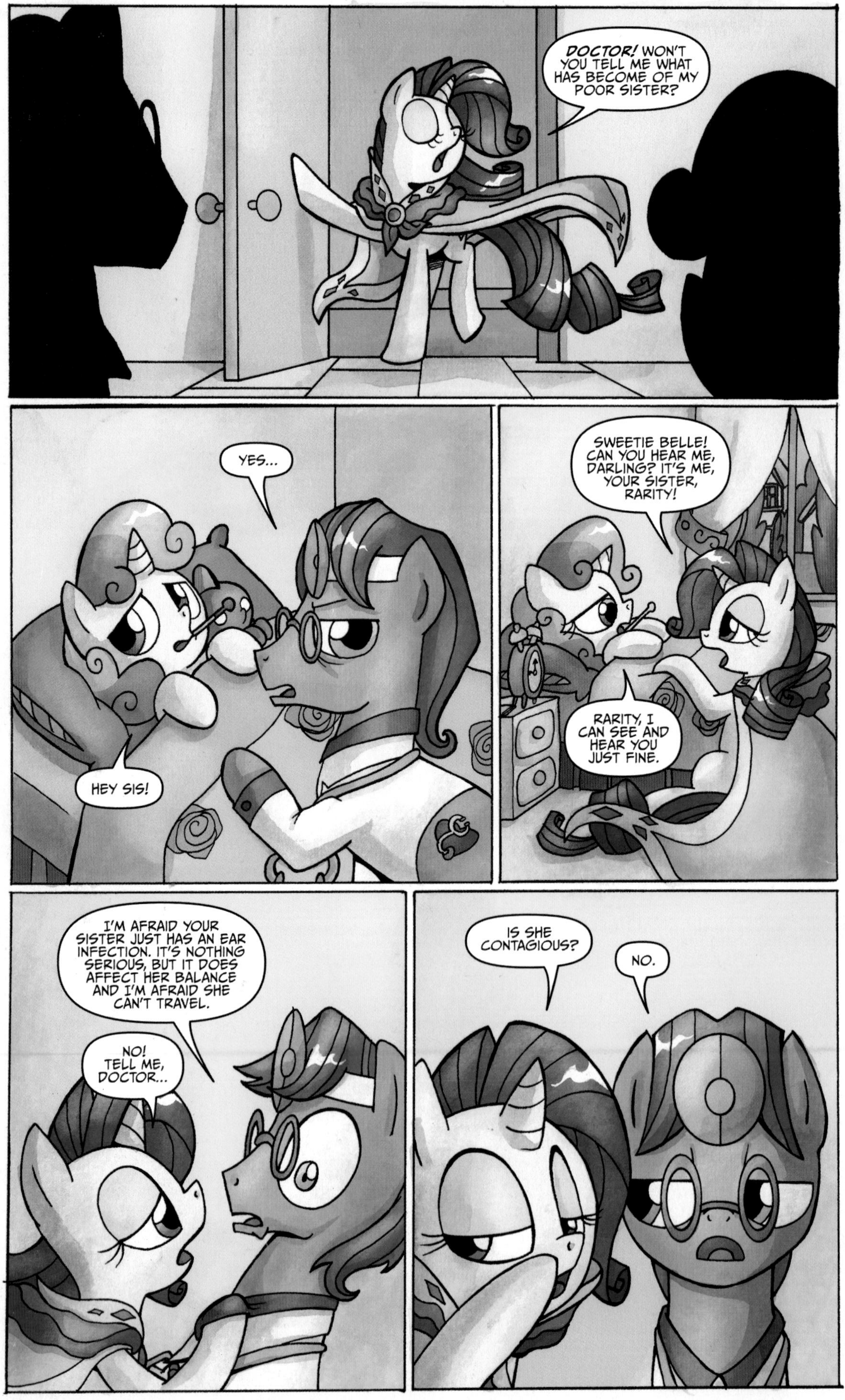
DOCTOR! WON'T YOU TELL ME WHAT HAS BECOME OF MY POOR SISTER?
YES...
HEY SIS!
SWEETIE BELLE! CAN YOU HEAR ME, DARLING? IT'S ME, YOUR SISTER, RARITY!
RARITY, I CAN SEE AND HEAR YOU JUST FINE.
I'M AFRAID YOUR SISTER JUST HAS AN EAR INFECTION. IT'S NOTHING SERIOUS, BUT IT DOES AFFECT HER BALANCE AND I'M AFRAID SHE CAN'T TRAVEL.
NO! TELL ME, DOCTOR...
IS SHE CONTAGIOUS?
NO.

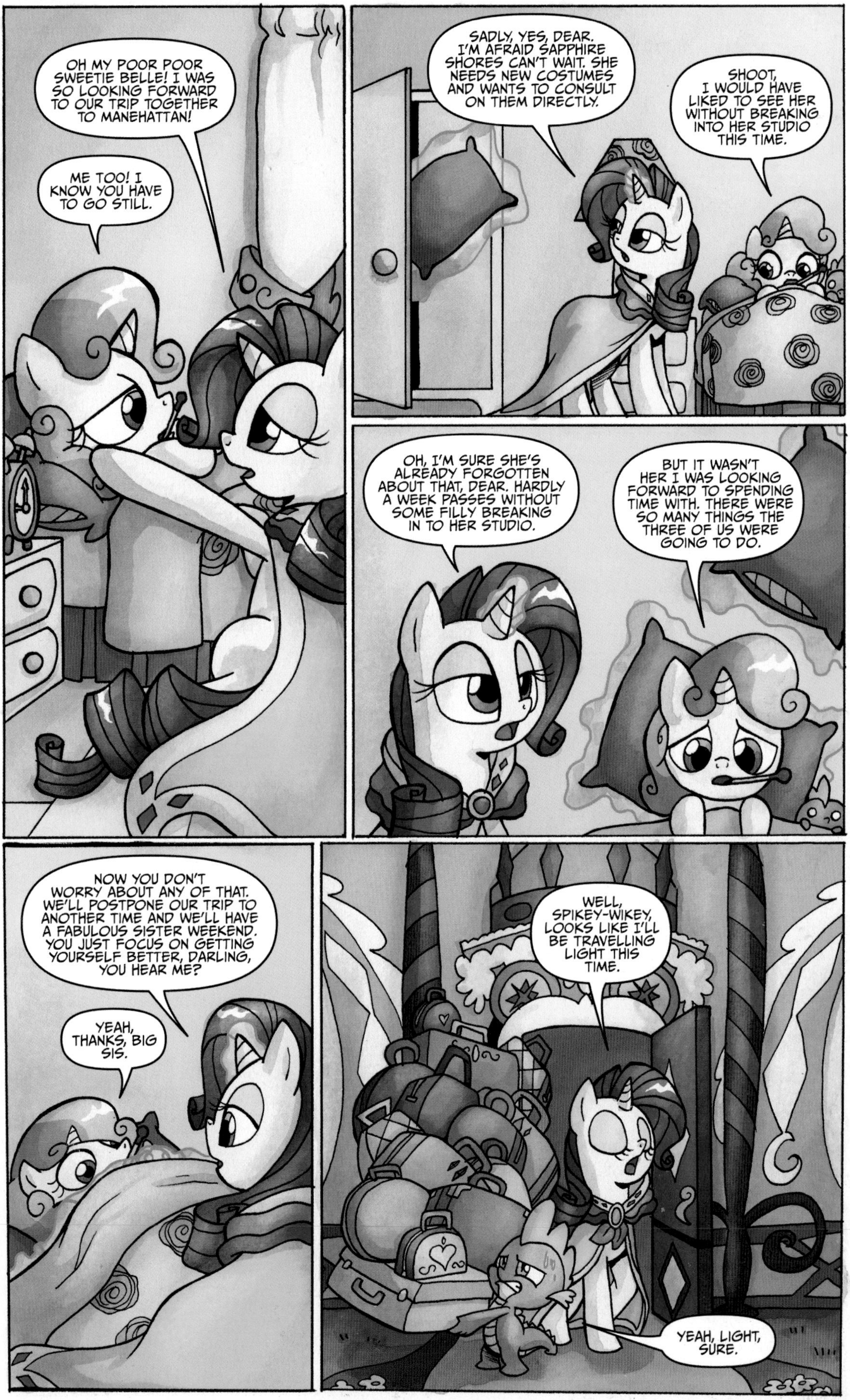

OH MY POOR POOR SWEETIE BELLE! I WAS SO LOOKING FORWARD TO OUR TRIP TOGETHER TO MANEHATTAN!
ME TOO! I KNOW YOU HAVE TO GO STILL.
SADLY, YES, DEAR. I'M AFRAID SAPPHIRE SHORES CAN'T WAIT. SHE NEEDS NEW COSTUMES AND WANTS TO CONSULT ON THEM DIRECTLY.
SHOOT, I WOULD HAVE LIKED TO SEE HER WITHOUT BREAKING INTO HER STUDIO THIS TIME.
OH, I'M SURE SHE'S ALREADY FORGOTTEN ABOUT THAT, DEAR. HARDLY A WEEK PASSES WITHOUT SOME FILLY BREAKING IN TO HER STUDIO.
BUT IT WASN'T HER I WAS LOOKING FORWARD TO SPENDING TIME WITH. THERE WERE SO MANY THINGS THE THREE OF US WERE GOING TO DO.
NOW YOU DON'T WORRY ABOUT ANY OF THAT. WE'LL POSTPONE OUR TRIP TO ANOTHER TIME AND WE'LL HAVE A FABULOUS SISTER WEEKEND. YOU JUST FOCUS ON GETTING YOURSELF BETTER, DARLING, YOU HEAR ME?
YEAH, THANKS, BIG SIS.
WELL, SPIKEY-WIKEY, LOOKS LIKE I'LL BE TRAVELLING LIGHT THIS TIME.
YEAH, LIGHT, SURE.

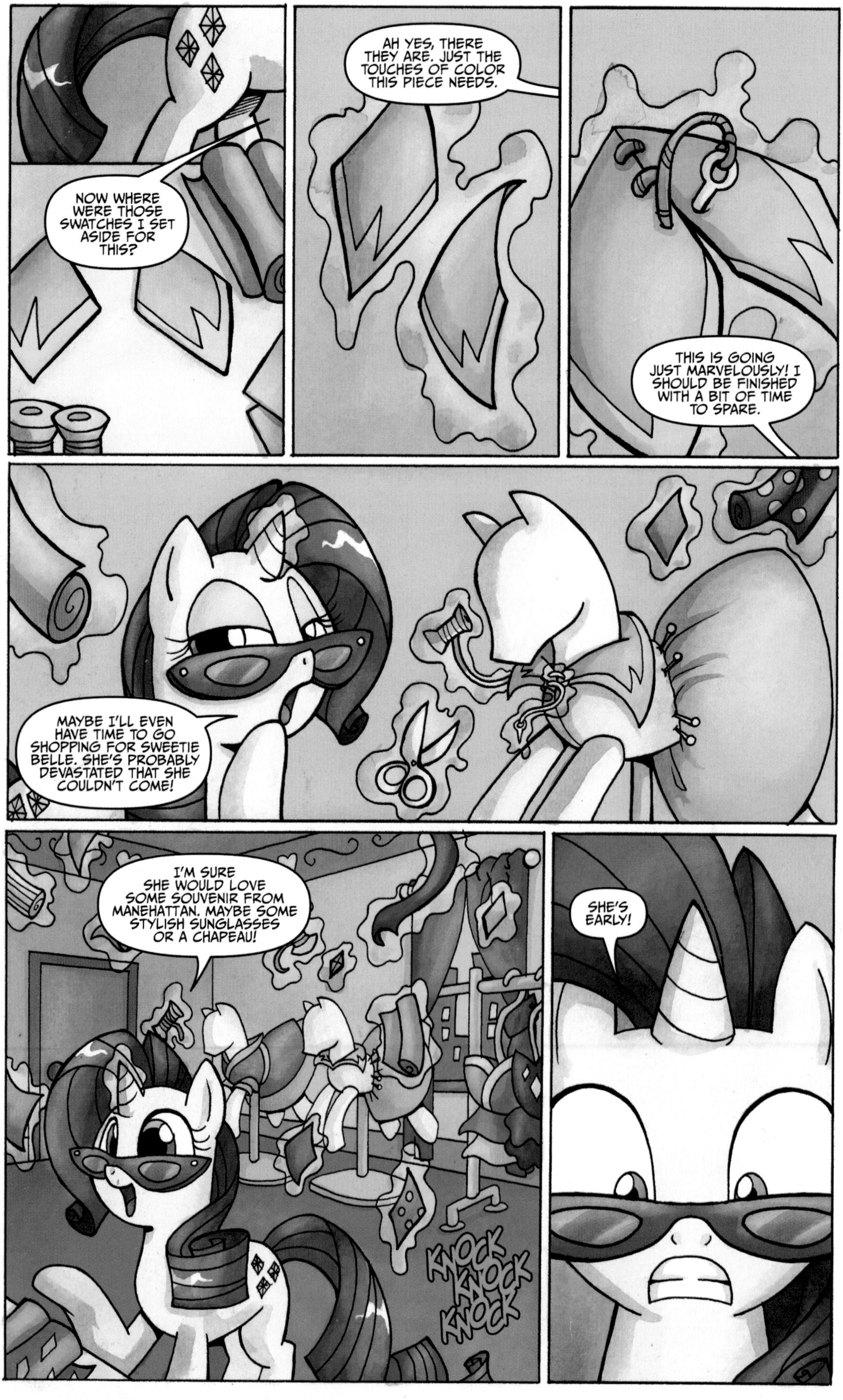
NOW WHERE WERE THOSE SWATCHES I SET ASIDE FOR THIS?
AH YES, THERE THEY ARE. JUST THE TOUCHES OF COLOR THIS PIECE NEEDS.
THIS IS GOING JUST MARVELOUSLY! I SHOULD BE FINISHED WITH A BIT OF TIME TO SPARE.
MAYBE I'LL EVEN HAVE TIME TO GO SHOPPING FOR SWEETIE BELLE. SHE'S PROBABLY DEVASTATED THAT SHE COULDN'T COME!
I'M SURE SHE WOULD LOVE SOME SOUVENIR FROM MANEHATTAN. MAYBE SOME STYLISH SUNGLASSES OR A CHAPEAU!
KNOCK KNOCK KNOCK
SHE'S EARLY!

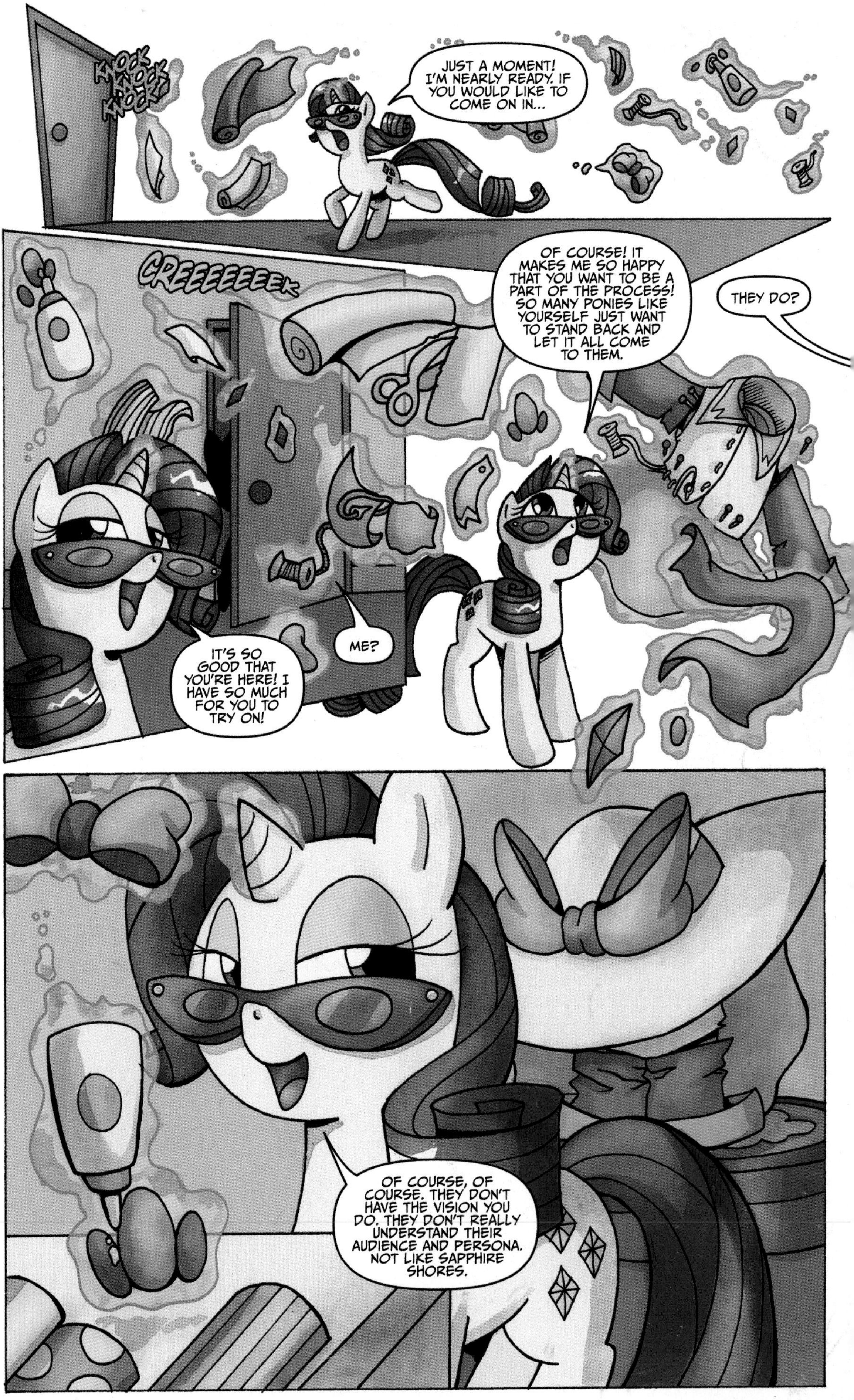
KNOCK KNOCK KNOCK
JUST A MOMENT! I'M NEARLY READY. IF YOU WOULD LIKE TO COME ON IN...
CREEEEEEEEK
IT'S SO GOOD THAT YOU'RE HERE! I HAVE SO MUCH FOR YOU TO TRY ON!
ME?
OF COURSE! IT MAKES ME SO HAPPY THAT YOU WANT TO BE A PART OF THE PROCESS! SO MANY PONIES LIKE YOURSELF JUST WANT TO STAND BACK AND LET IT ALL COME TO THEM.
THEY DO?
OF COURSE, OF COURSE. THEY DON'T HAVE THE VISION YOU DO. THEY DON'T REALLY UNDERSTAND THEIR AUDIENCE AND PERSONA. NOT LIKE SAPPHIRE SHORES.

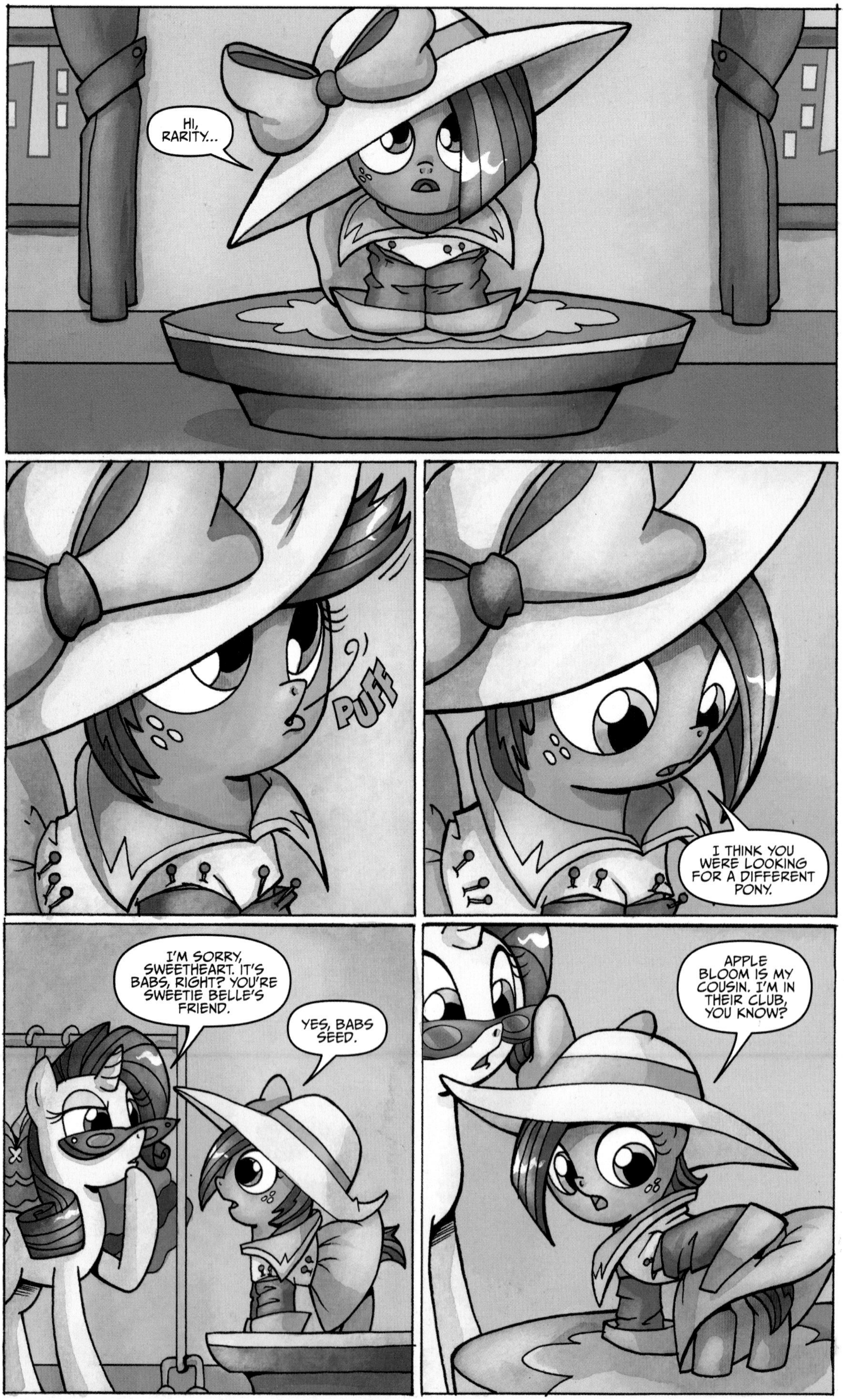
HI, RARITY...
PUFF
I THINK YOU WERE LOOKING FOR A DIFFERENT PONY.
I'M SORRY, SWEETHEART. IT'S BABS, RIGHT? YOU'RE SWEETIE BELLE'S FRIEND.
YES, BABS SEED.
APPLE BLOOM IS MY COUSIN. I'M IN THEIR CLUB, YOU KNOW?

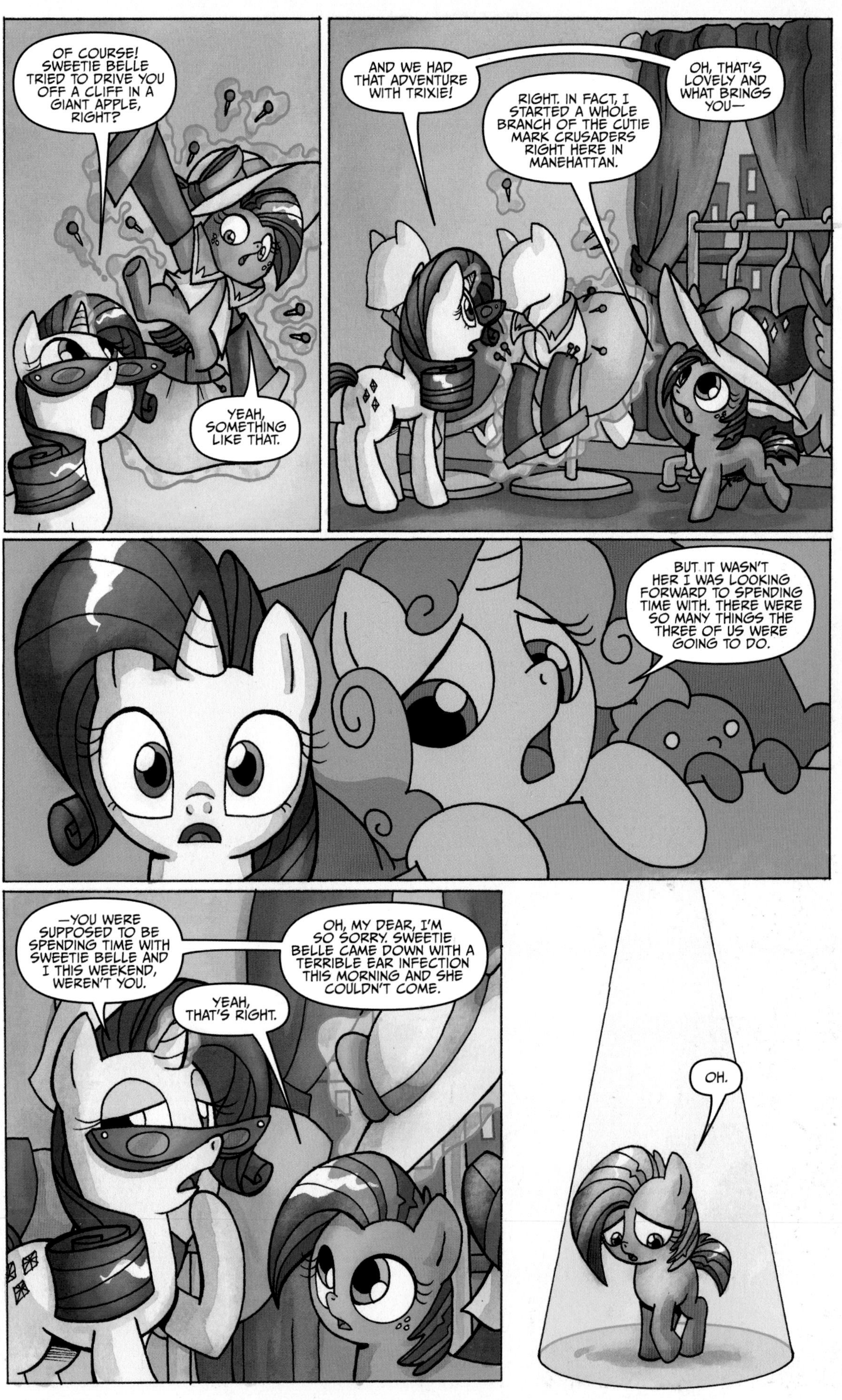
OF COURSE! SWEETIE BELLE TRIED TO DRIVE YOU OFF A CLIFF IN A GIANT APPLE, RIGHT?
YEAH, SOMETHING LIKE THAT.
AND WE HAD THAT ADVENTURE WITH TRIXIE!
OH, THAT'S LOVELY AND WHAT BRINGS YOU—
RIGHT. IN FACT, I STARTED A WHOLE BRANCH OF THE CUTIE MARK CRUSADERS RIGHT HERE IN MANEHATTAN.
BUT IT WASN'T HER I WAS LOOKING FORWARD TO SPENDING TIME WITH. THERE WERE SO MANY THINGS THE THREE OF US WERE GOING TO DO.
—YOU WERE SUPPOSED TO BE SPENDING TIME WITH SWEETIE BELLE AND I THIS WEEKEND, WEREN'T YOU.
YEAH, THAT'S RIGHT.
OH, MY DEAR, I'M SO SORRY. SWEETIE BELLE CAME DOWN WITH A TERRIBLE EAR INFECTION THIS MORNING AND SHE COULDN'T COME.
OH.

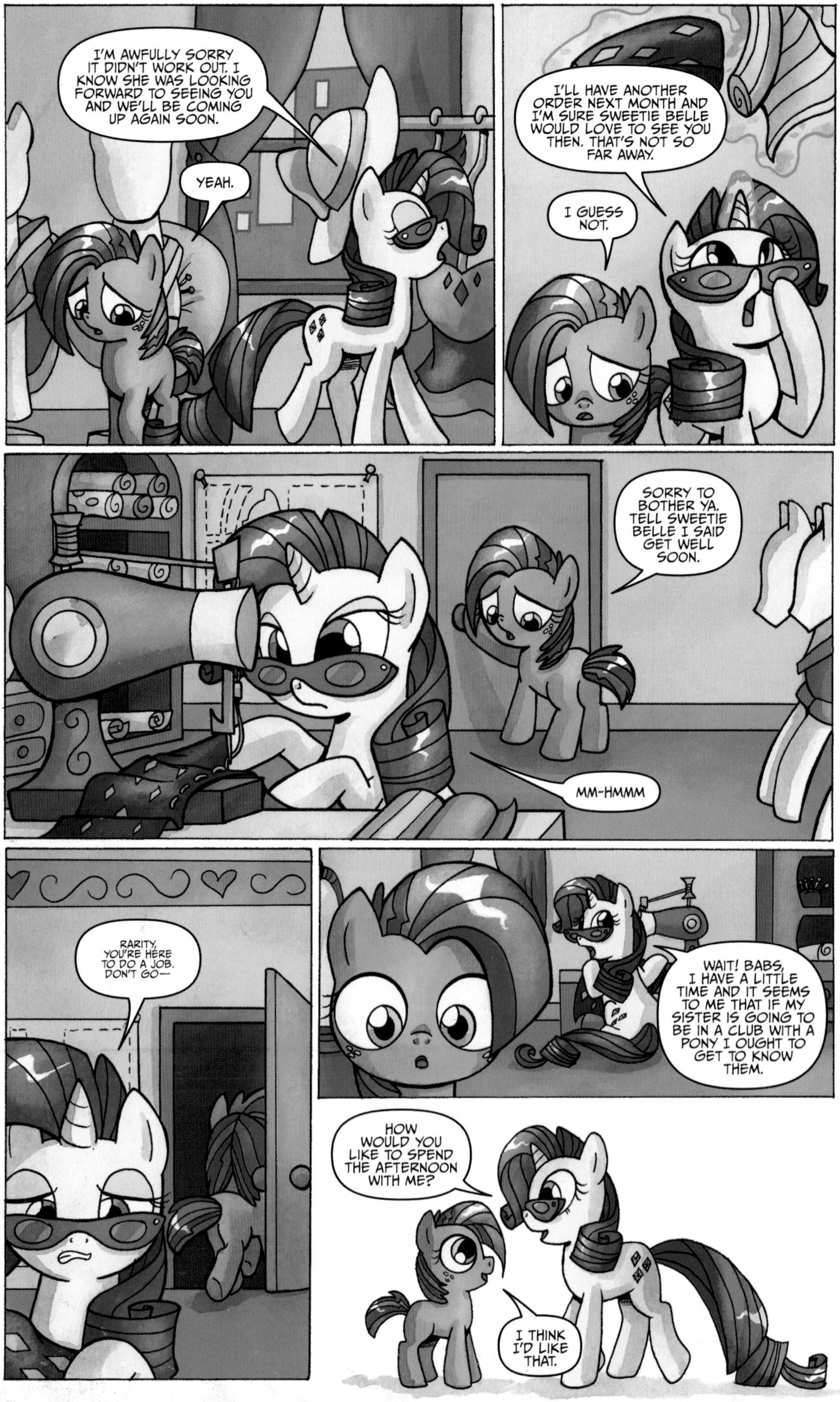
I'M AWFULLY SORRY IT DIDN'T WORK OUT. I KNOW SHE WAS LOOKING FORWARD TO SEEING YOU AND WE'LL BE COMING UP AGAIN SOON.
YEAH.
I'LL HAVE ANOTHER ORDER NEXT MONTH AND I'M SURE SWEETIE BELLE WOULD LOVE TO SEE YOU THEN. THAT'S NOT SO FAR AWAY.
I GUESS NOT.
SORRY TO BOTHER YA. TELL SWEETIE BELLE I SAID GET WELL SOON.
MM-HMMM
RARITY, YOU'RE HERE TO DO A JOB. DON'T GO—
WAIT! BABS, I HAVE A LITTLE TIME AND IT SEEMS TO ME THAT IF MY SISTER IS GOING TO BE IN A CLUB WITH A PONY I OUGHT TO GET TO KNOW THEM.
HOW WOULD YOU LIKE TO SPEND THE AFTERNOON WITH ME?
I THINK I'D LIKE THAT.

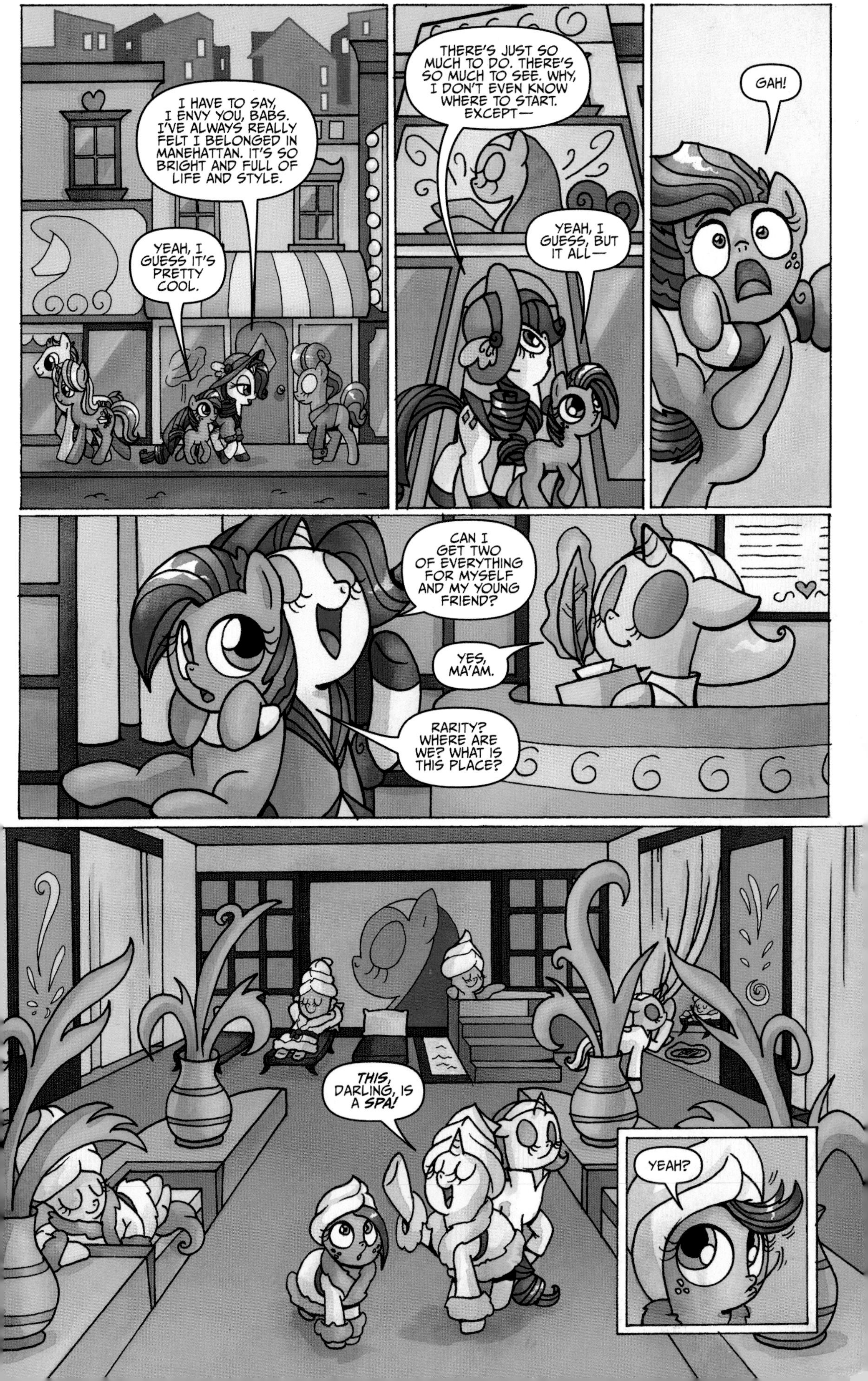
I HAVE TO SAY, I ENVY YOU, BABS. I'VE ALWAYS REALLY FELT I BELONGED IN MANEHATTAN. IT'S SO BRIGHT AND FULL OF LIFE AND STYLE.
YEAH, I GUESS IT'S PRETTY COOL.
THERE'S JUST SO MUCH TO DO. THERE'S SO MUCH TO SEE. WHY, I DON'T EVEN KNOW WHERE TO START. EXCEPT—
YEAH, I GUESS, BUT IT ALL—
GAH!
CAN I GET TWO OF EVERYTHING FOR MYSELF AND MY YOUNG FRIEND?
YES, MA'AM.
RARITY? WHERE ARE WE? WHAT IS THIS PLACE?
THIS, DARLING, IS A *SPA!*
YEAH?

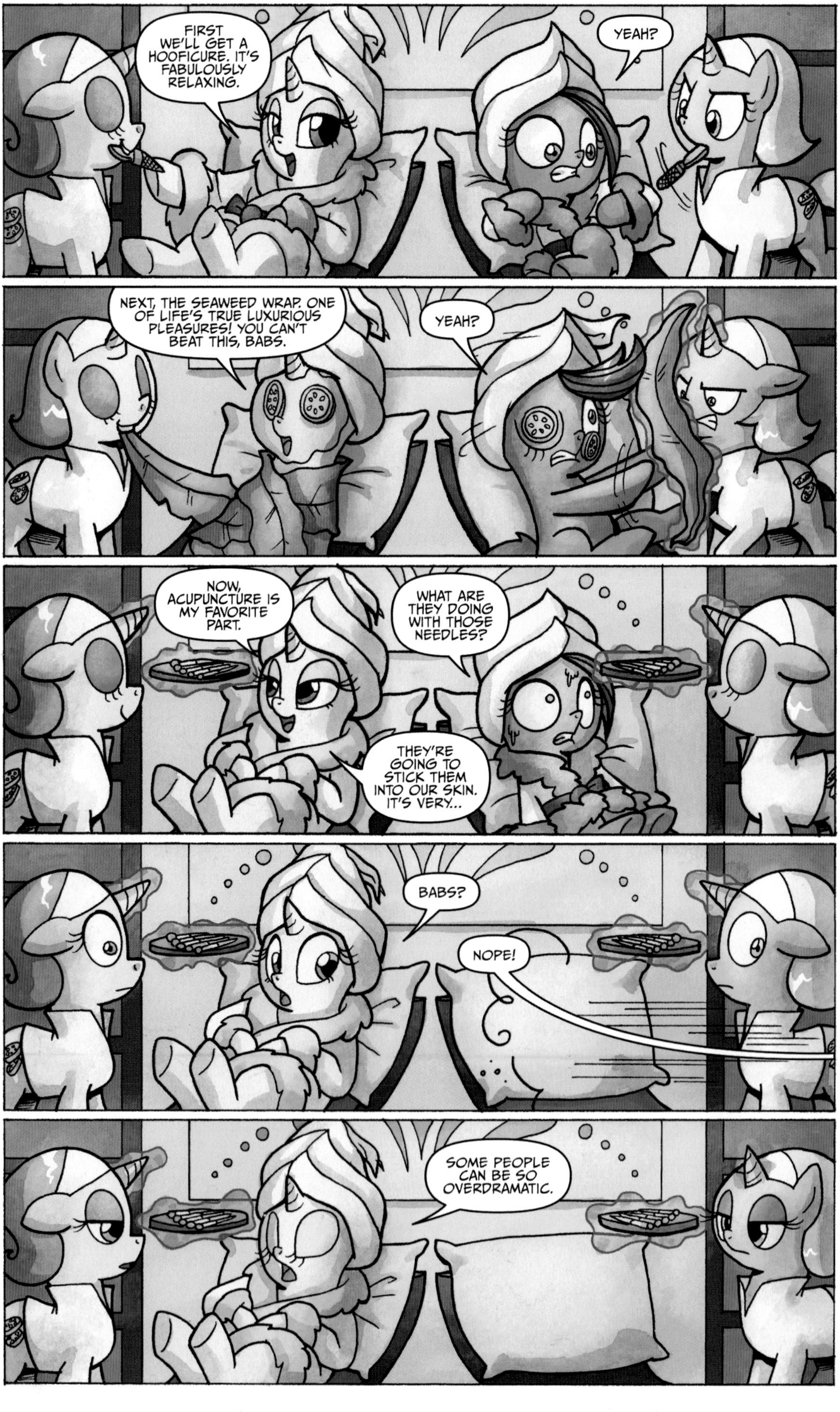
FIRST WE'LL GET A HOOFICURE. IT'S FABULOUSLY RELAXING.
YEAH?
NEXT, THE SEAWEED WRAP. ONE OF LIFE'S TRUE LUXURIOUS PLEASURES! YOU CAN'T BEAT THIS, BABS.
YEAH?
NOW, ACUPUNCTURE IS MY FAVORITE PART.
WHAT ARE THEY DOING WITH THOSE NEEDLES?
THEY'RE GOING TO STICK THEM INTO OUR SKIN. IT'S VERY...
BABS?
NOPE!
SOME PEOPLE CAN BE SO OVERDRAMATIC.

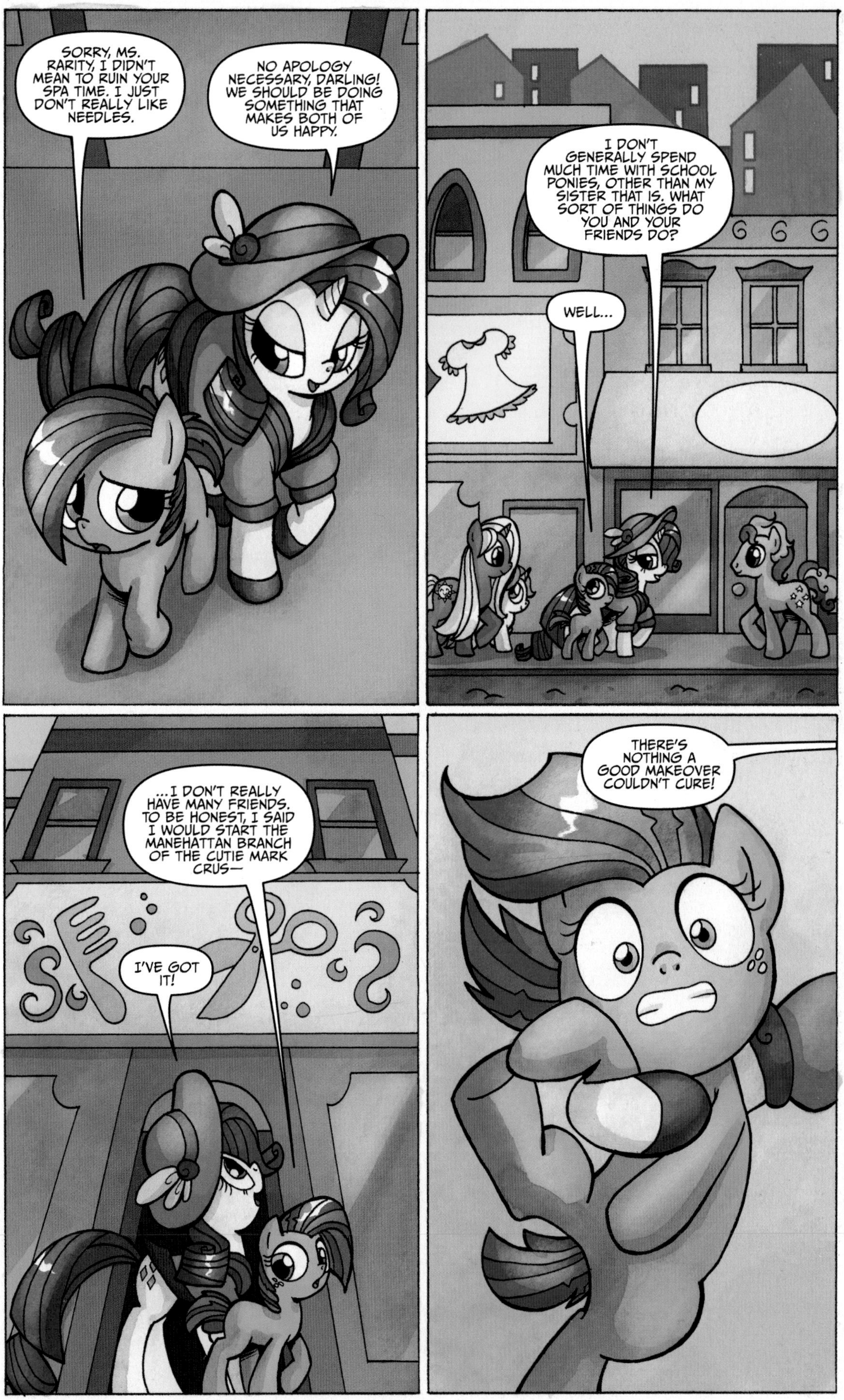
SORRY, MS. RARITY, I DIDN'T MEAN TO RUIN YOUR SPA TIME. I JUST DON'T REALLY LIKE NEEDLES.
NO APOLOGY NECESSARY, DARLING! WE SHOULD BE DOING SOMETHING THAT MAKES BOTH OF US HAPPY.
I DON'T GENERALLY SPEND MUCH TIME WITH SCHOOL PONIES, OTHER THAN MY SISTER THAT IS. WHAT SORT OF THINGS DO YOU AND YOUR FRIENDS DO?
WELL...
...I DON'T REALLY HAVE MANY FRIENDS. TO BE HONEST, I SAID I WOULD START THE MANEHATTAN BRANCH OF THE CUTIE MARK CRUS—
I'VE GOT IT!
THERE'S NOTHING A GOOD MAKEOVER COULDN'T CURE!

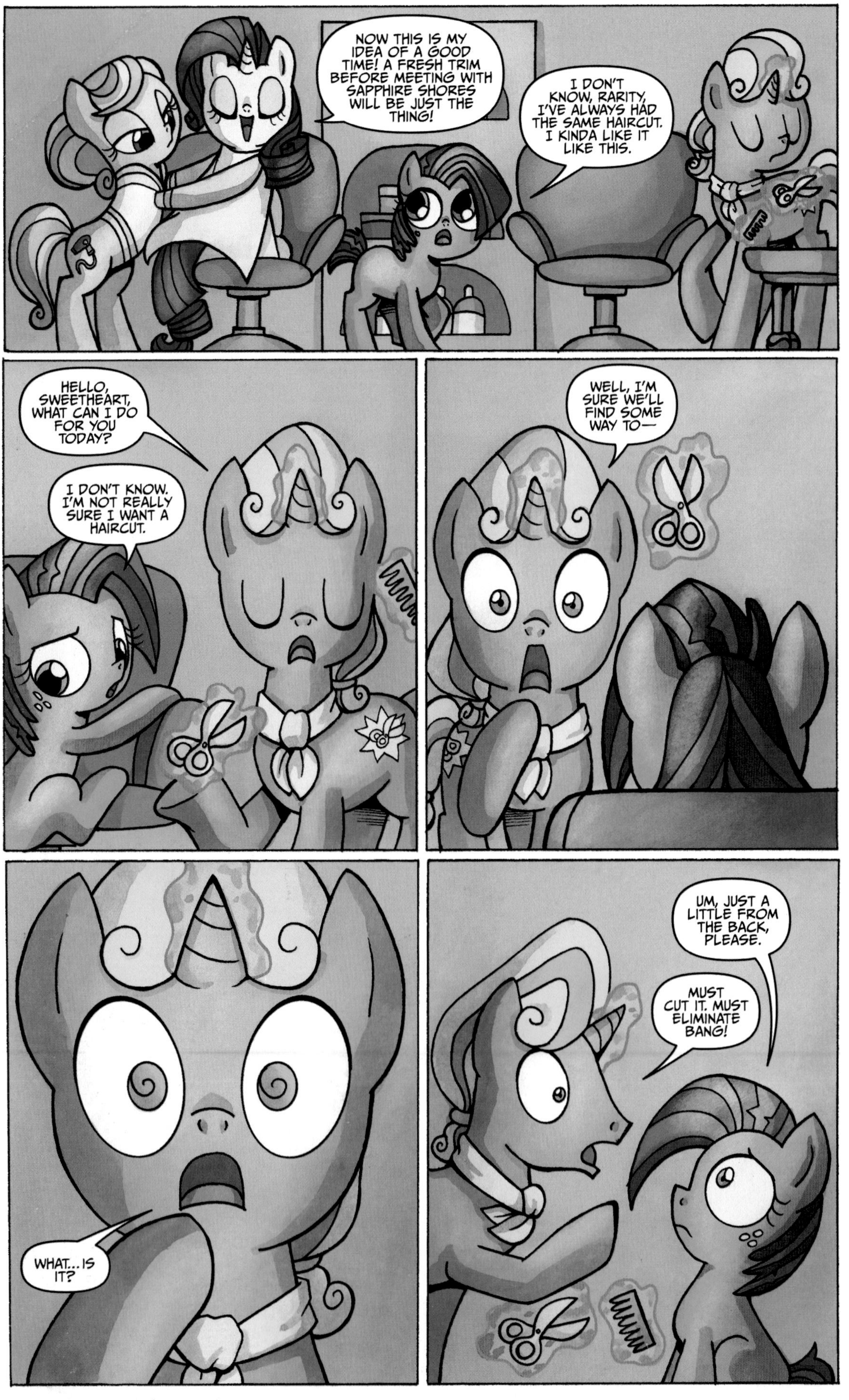
NOW THIS IS MY IDEA OF A GOOD TIME! A FRESH TRIM BEFORE MEETING WITH SAPPHIRE SHORES WILL BE JUST THE THING!
I DON'T KNOW, RARITY, I'VE ALWAYS HAD THE SAME HAIRCUT. I KINDA LIKE IT LIKE THIS.
HELLO, SWEETHEART, WHAT CAN I DO FOR YOU TODAY?
I DON'T KNOW. I'M NOT REALLY SURE I WANT A HAIRCUT.
WELL, I'M SURE WE'LL FIND SOME WAY TO—
WHAT... IS IT?
UM, JUST A LITTLE FROM THE BACK, PLEASE.
MUST CUT IT. MUST ELIMINATE BANG!

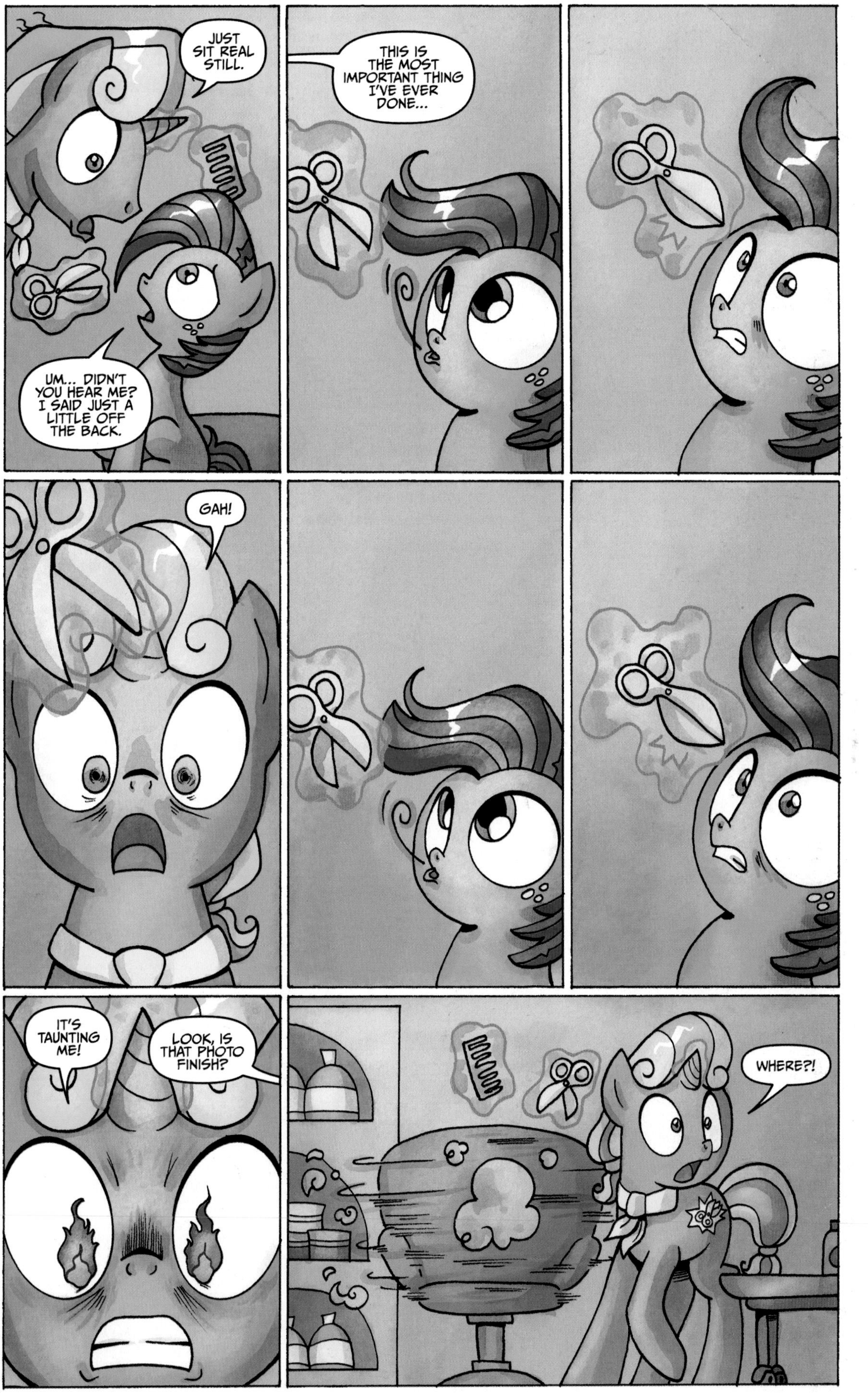
JUST SIT REAL STILL.
UM... DIDN'T YOU HEAR ME? I SAID JUST A LITTLE OFF THE BACK.
THIS IS THE MOST IMPORTANT THING I'VE EVER DONE...
GAH!
IT'S TAUNTING ME!
LOOK, IS THAT PHOTO FINISH?
WHERE?!

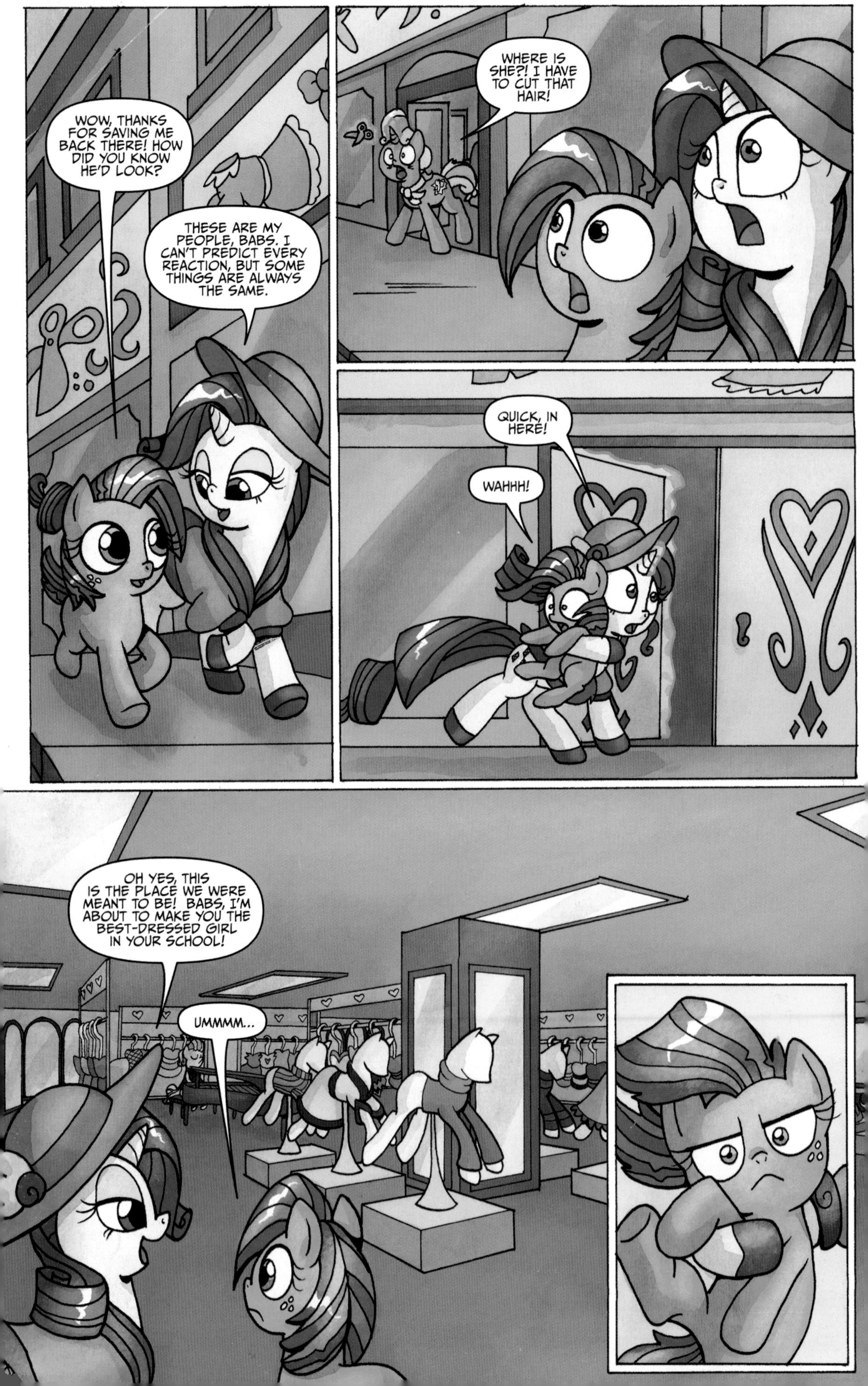
WOW, THANKS FOR SAVING ME BACK THERE! HOW DID YOU KNOW HE'D LOOK?
THESE ARE MY PEOPLE, BABS. I CAN'T PREDICT EVERY REACTION, BUT SOME THINGS ARE ALWAYS THE SAME.
WHERE IS SHE?! I HAVE TO CUT THAT HAIR!
QUICK, IN HERE!
WAHHH!
OH YES, THIS IS THE PLACE WE WERE MEANT TO BE! BABS, I'M ABOUT TO MAKE YOU THE BEST-DRESSED GIRL IN YOUR SCHOOL!
UMMMM...

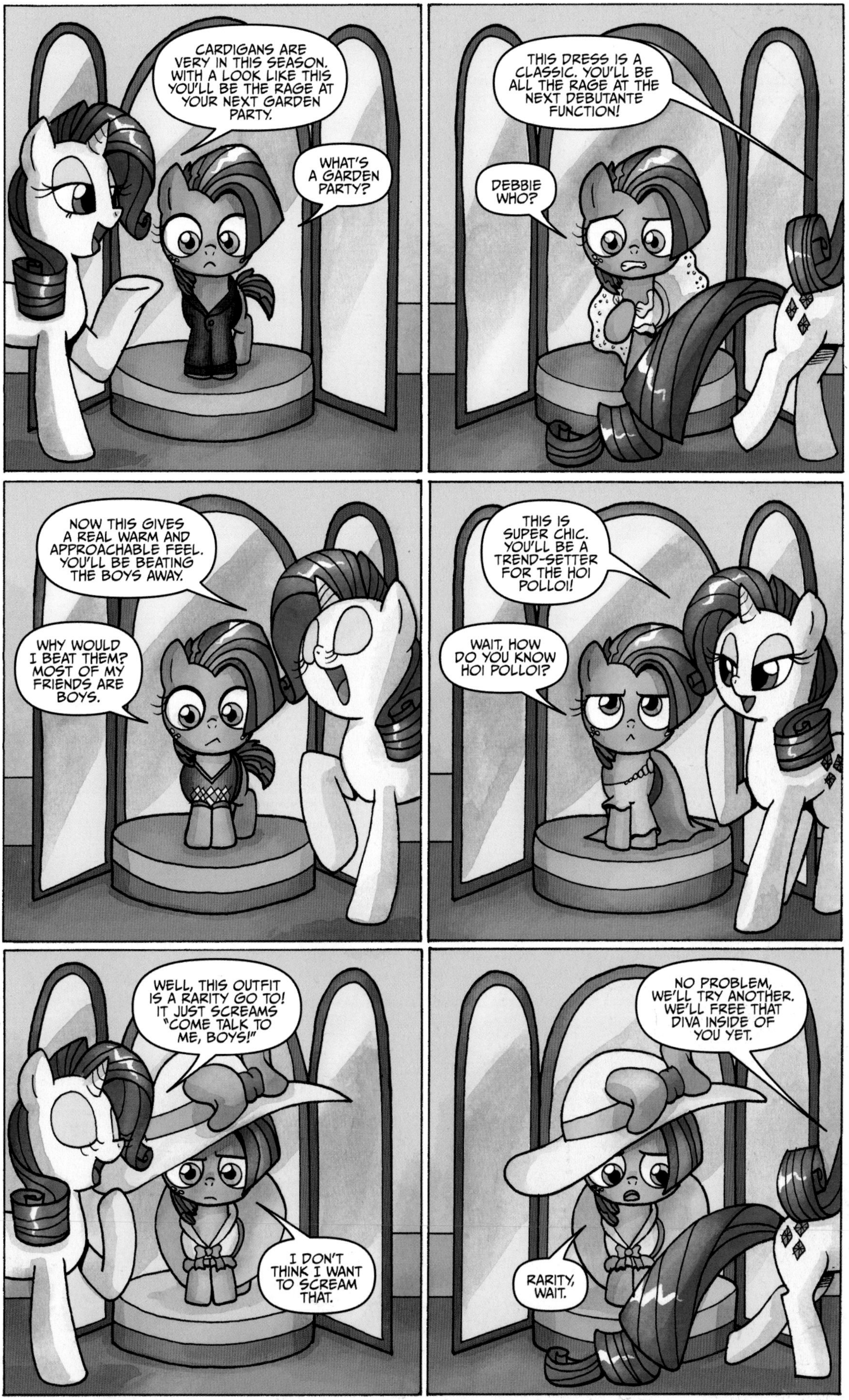
CARDIGANS ARE VERY IN THIS SEASON. WITH A LOOK LIKE THIS YOU'LL BE THE RAGE AT YOUR NEXT GARDEN PARTY.
WHAT'S A GARDEN PARTY?
THIS DRESS IS A CLASSIC. YOU'LL BE ALL THE RAGE AT THE NEXT DEBUTANTE FUNCTION!
DEBBIE WHO?
NOW THIS GIVES A REAL WARM AND APPROACHABLE FEEL. YOU'LL BE BEATING THE BOYS AWAY.
WHY WOULD I BEAT THEM? MOST OF MY FRIENDS ARE BOYS.
THIS IS SUPER CHIC. YOU'LL BE A TREND-SETTER FOR THE HOI POLLOI!
WAIT, HOW DO YOU KNOW HOI POLLOI?
WELL, THIS OUTFIT IS A RARITY GO TO! IT JUST SCREAMS "COME TALK TO ME, BOYS!"
I DON'T THINK I WANT TO SCREAM THAT.
NO PROBLEM, WE'LL TRY ANOTHER. WE'LL FREE THAT DIVA INSIDE OF YOU YET.
RARITY, WAIT.

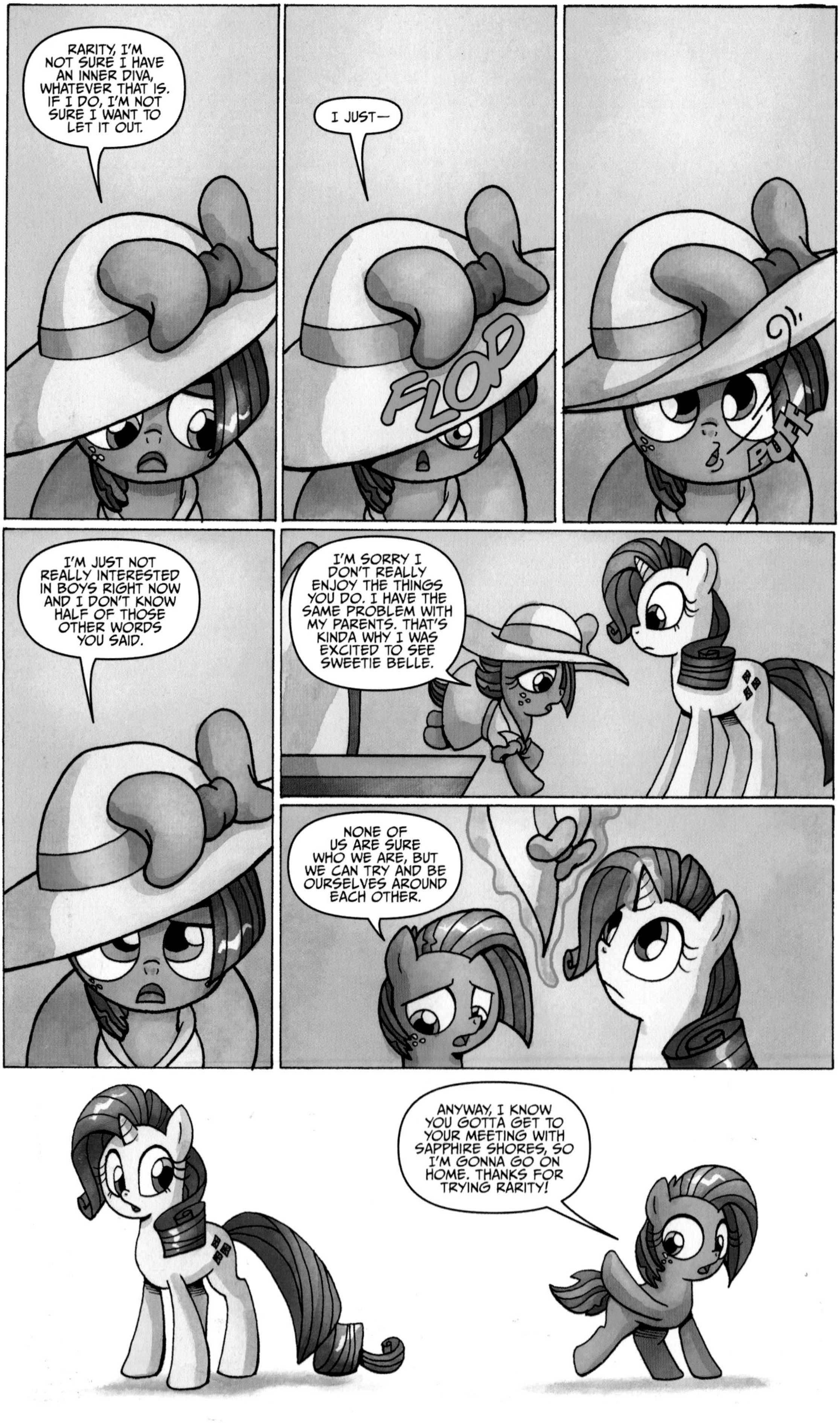
RARITY, I'M NOT SURE I HAVE AN INNER DIVA, WHATEVER THAT IS. IF I DO, I'M NOT SURE I WANT TO LET IT OUT.
I JUST—
FLOP
PUFF
I'M JUST NOT REALLY INTERESTED IN BOYS RIGHT NOW AND I DON'T KNOW HALF OF THOSE OTHER WORDS YOU SAID.
I'M SORRY I DON'T REALLY ENJOY THE THINGS YOU DO. I HAVE THE SAME PROBLEM WITH MY PARENTS. THAT'S KINDA WHY I WAS EXCITED TO SEE SWEETIE BELLE.
NONE OF US ARE SURE WHO WE ARE, BUT WE CAN TRY AND BE OURSELVES AROUND EACH OTHER.
ANYWAY, I KNOW YOU GOTTA GET TO YOUR MEETING WITH SAPPHIRE SHORES, SO I'M GONNA GO ON HOME. THANKS FOR TRYING RARITY!

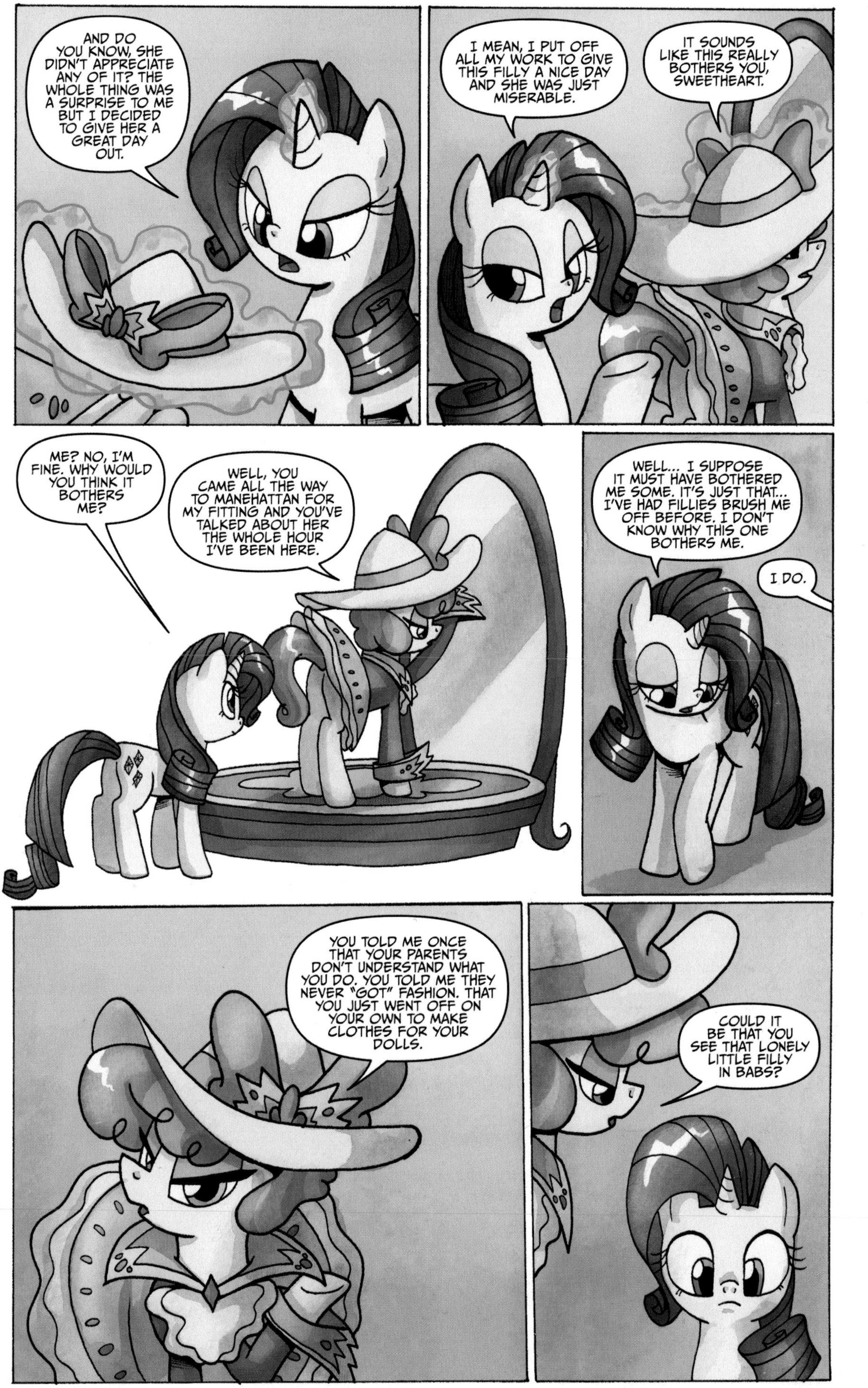
AND DO YOU KNOW, SHE DIDN'T APPRECIATE ANY OF IT? THE WHOLE THING WAS A SURPRISE TO ME BUT I DECIDED TO GIVE HER A GREAT DAY OUT.
I MEAN, I PUT OFF ALL MY WORK TO GIVE THIS FILLY A NICE DAY AND SHE WAS JUST MISERABLE.
IT SOUNDS LIKE THIS REALLY BOTHERS YOU, SWEETHEART.
ME? NO, I'M FINE. WHY WOULD YOU THINK IT BOTHERS ME?
WELL, YOU CAME ALL THE WAY TO MANEHATTAN FOR MY FITTING AND YOU'VE TALKED ABOUT HER THE WHOLE HOUR I'VE BEEN HERE.
WELL... I SUPPOSE IT MUST HAVE BOTHERED ME SOME. IT'S JUST THAT... I'VE HAD FILLIES BRUSH ME OFF BEFORE. I DON'T KNOW WHY THIS ONE BOTHERS ME.
I DO.
YOU TOLD ME ONCE THAT YOUR PARENTS DON'T UNDERSTAND WHAT YOU DO. YOU TOLD ME THEY NEVER "GOT" FASHION. THAT YOU JUST WENT OFF ON YOUR OWN TO MAKE CLOTHES FOR YOUR DOLLS.
COULD IT BE THAT YOU SEE THAT LONELY LITTLE FILLY IN BABS?

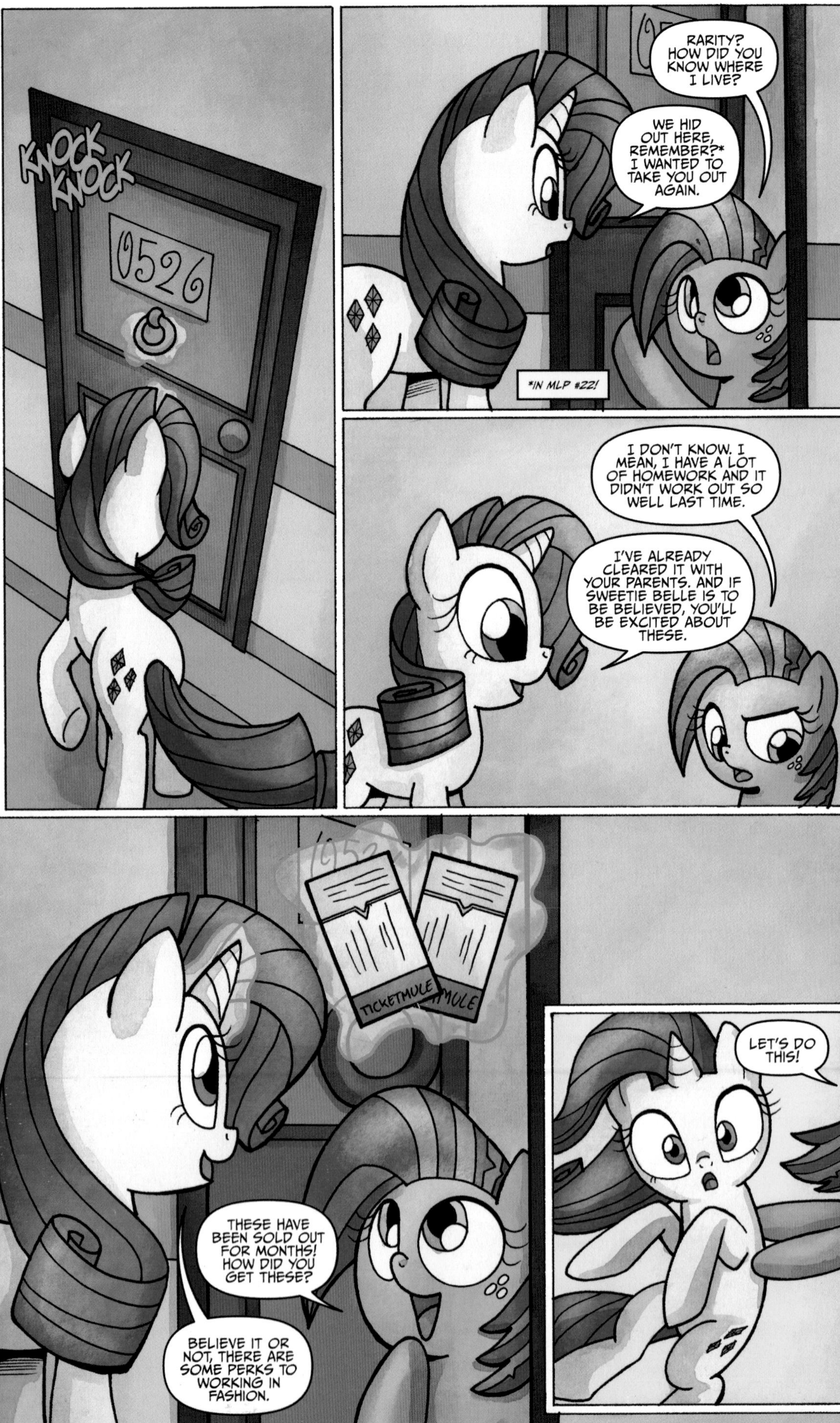
KNOCK KNOCK
0526
RARITY? HOW DID YOU KNOW WHERE I LIVE?
WE HID OUT HERE, REMEMBER?* I WANTED TO TAKE YOU OUT AGAIN.
*IN MLP #22!
I DON'T KNOW. I MEAN, I HAVE A LOT OF HOMEWORK AND IT DIDN'T WORK OUT SO WELL LAST TIME.
I'VE ALREADY CLEARED IT WITH YOUR PARENTS. AND IF SWEETIE BELLE IS TO BE BELIEVED, YOU'LL BE EXCITED ABOUT THESE.
TICKETMULE
THESE HAVE BEEN SOLD OUT FOR MONTHS! HOW DID YOU GET THESE?
BELIEVE IT OR NOT, THERE ARE SOME PERKS TO WORKING IN FASHION.
LET'S DO THIS!

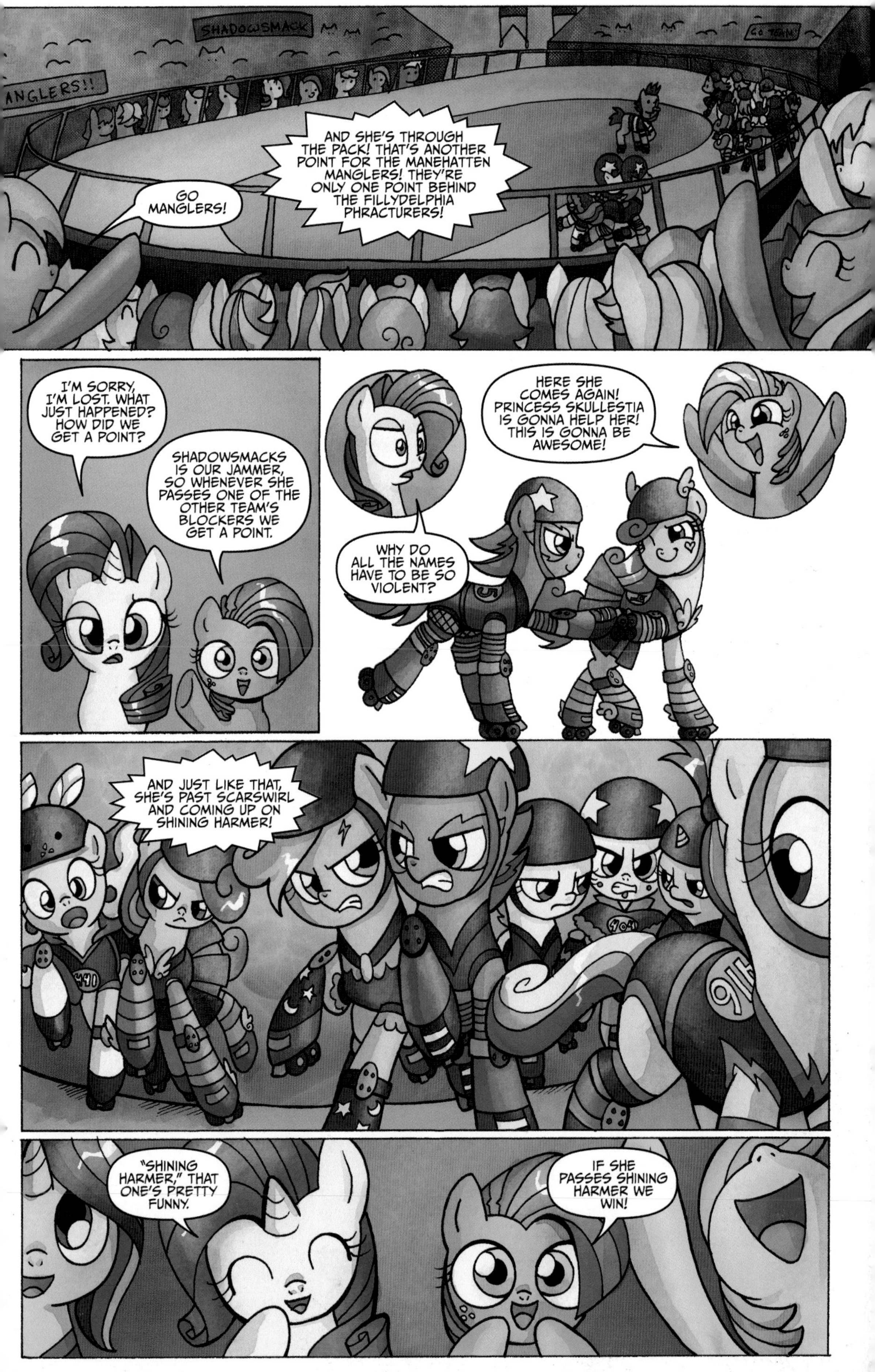
SHADOWSMACK
ANGLERS!!
GO TEAM!
AND SHE'S THROUGH THE PACK! THAT'S ANOTHER POINT FOR THE MANEHATTEN MANGLERS! THEY'RE ONLY ONE POINT BEHIND THE FILLYDELPHIA PHRACTURERS!
GO MANGLERS!
I'M SORRY, I'M LOST. WHAT JUST HAPPENED? HOW DID WE GET A POINT?
SHADOWSMACKS IS OUR JAMMER, SO WHENEVER SHE PASSES ONE OF THE OTHER TEAM'S BLOCKERS WE GET A POINT.
WHY DO ALL THE NAMES HAVE TO BE SO VIOLENT?
HERE SHE COMES AGAIN! PRINCESS SKULLESTIA IS GONNA HELP HER! THIS IS GONNA BE AWESOME!
AND JUST LIKE THAT, SHE'S PAST SCARSWIRL AND COMING UP ON SHINING HARMER!
"SHINING HARMER," THAT ONE'S PRETTY FUNNY.
IF SHE PASSES SHINING HARMER WE WIN!

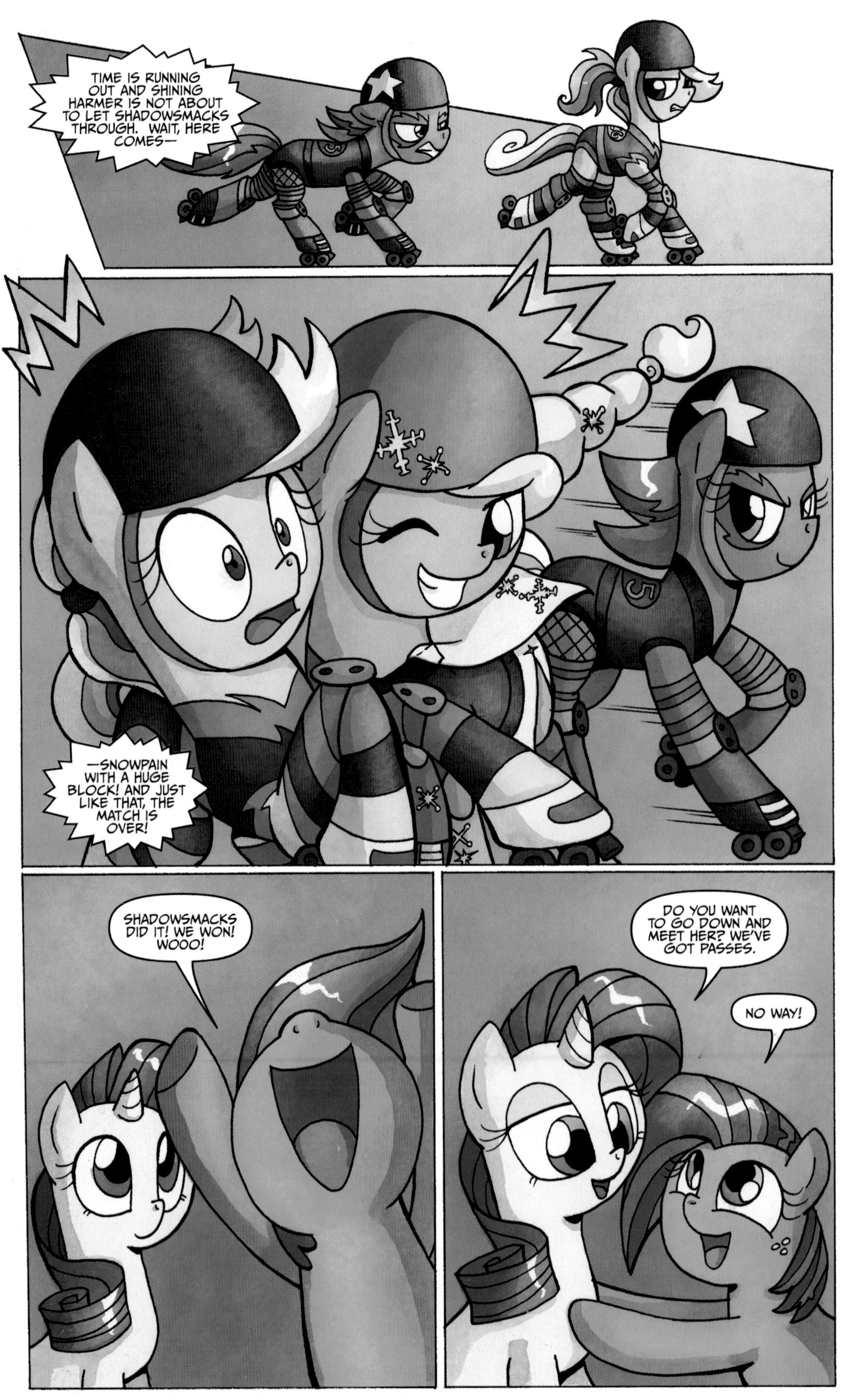
TIME IS RUNNING OUT AND SHINING HARMER IS NOT ABOUT TO LET SHADOWSMACKS THROUGH. WAIT, HERE COMES—
—SNOWPAIN WITH A HUGE BLOCK! AND JUST LIKE THAT, THE MATCH IS OVER!
SHADOWSMACKS DID IT! WE WON! WOOO!
DO YOU WANT TO GO DOWN AND MEET HER? WE'VE GOT PASSES.
NO WAY!

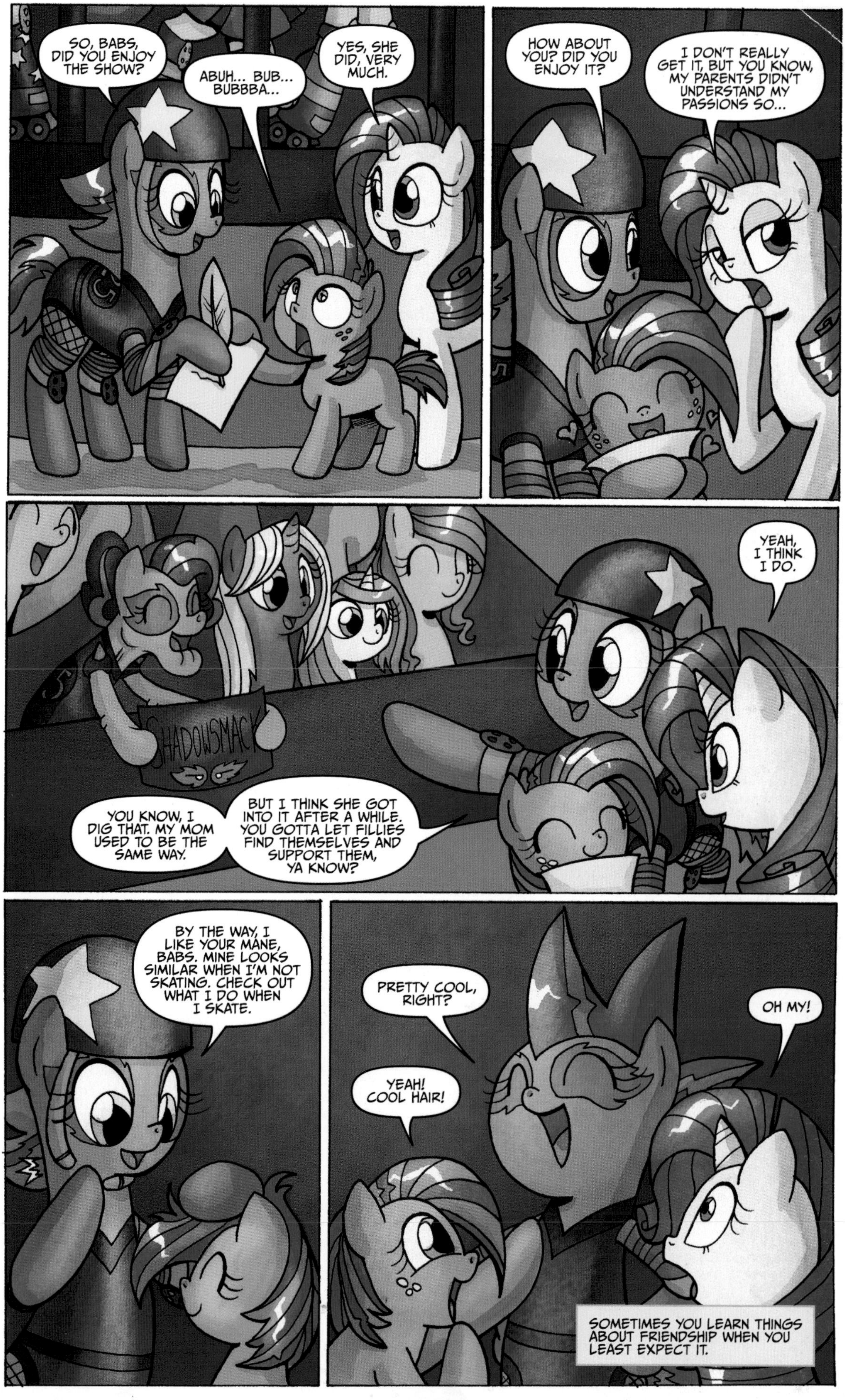
SO, BABS, DID YOU ENJOY THE SHOW?
ABUH... BUB... BUBBBA...
YES, SHE DID, VERY MUCH.
HOW ABOUT YOU? DID YOU ENJOY IT?
I DON'T REALLY GET IT, BUT YOU KNOW, MY PARENTS DIDN'T UNDERSTAND MY PASSIONS SO...
YEAH, I THINK I DO.
SHADOWSMACK
YOU KNOW, I DIG THAT. MY MOM USED TO BE THE SAME WAY.
BUT I THINK SHE GOT INTO IT AFTER A WHILE. YOU GOTTA LET FILLIES FIND THEMSELVES AND SUPPORT THEM, YA KNOW?
BY THE WAY, I LIKE YOUR MANE, BABS. MINE LOOKS SIMILAR WHEN I'M NOT SKATING. CHECK OUT WHAT I DO WHEN I SKATE.
PRETTY COOL, RIGHT?
OH MY!
YEAH! COOL HAIR!
SOMETIMES YOU LEARN THINGS ABOUT FRIENDSHIP WHEN YOU LEAST EXPECT IT.

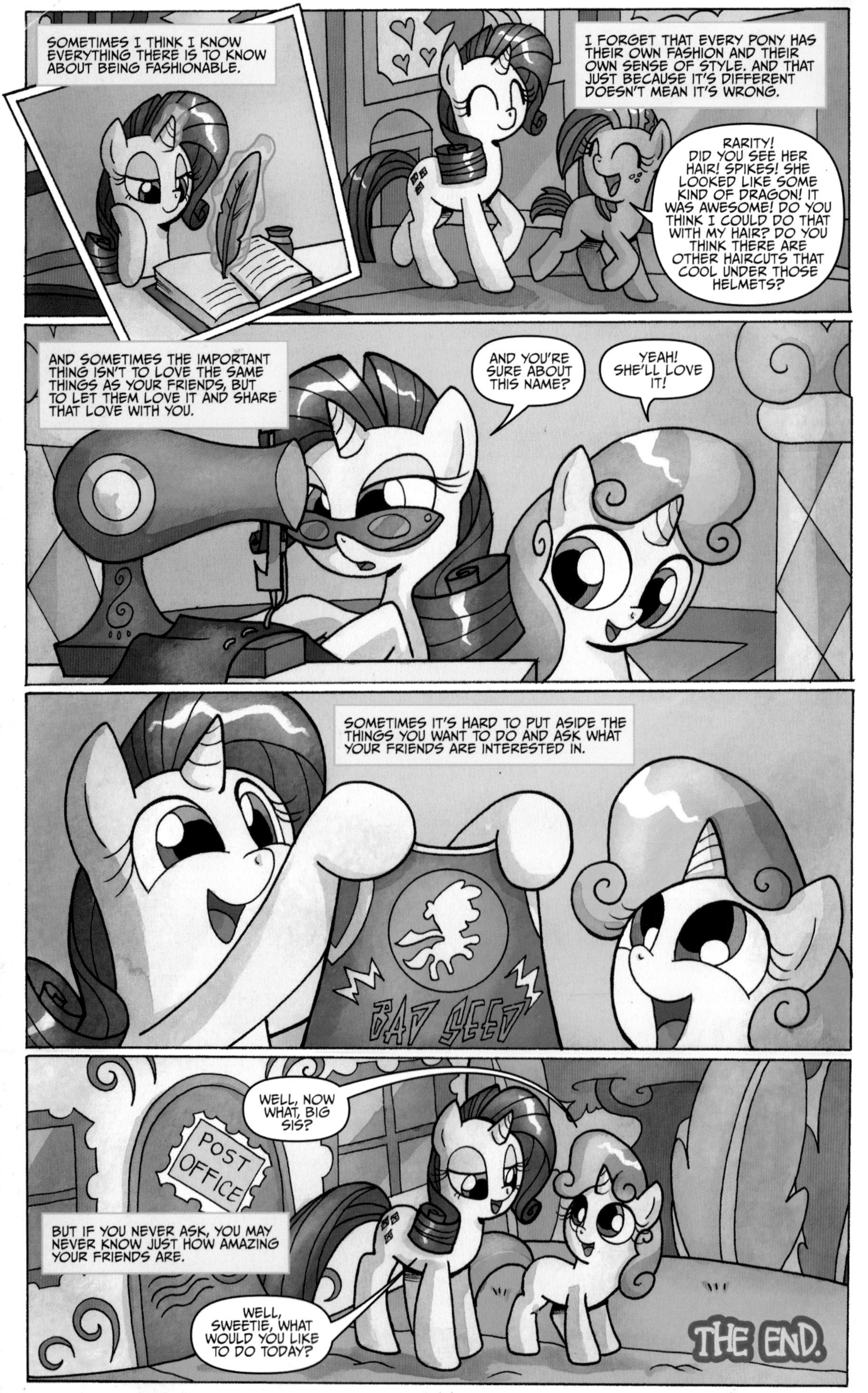
SOMETIMES I THINK I KNOW EVERYTHING THERE IS TO KNOW ABOUT BEING FASHIONABLE.
I FORGET THAT EVERY PONY HAS THEIR OWN FASHION AND THEIR OWN SENSE OF STYLE. AND THAT JUST BECAUSE IT'S DIFFERENT DOESN'T MEAN IT'S WRONG.
RARITY! DID YOU SEE HER HAIR! SPIKES! SHE LOOKED LIKE SOME KIND OF DRAGON! IT WAS AWESOME! DO YOU THINK I COULD DO THAT WITH MY HAIR? DO YOU THINK THERE ARE OTHER HAIRCUTS THAT COOL UNDER THOSE HELMETS?
AND SOMETIMES THE IMPORTANT THING ISN'T TO LOVE THE SAME THINGS AS YOUR FRIENDS, BUT TO LET THEM LOVE IT AND SHARE THAT LOVE WITH YOU.
AND YOU'RE SURE ABOUT THIS NAME?
YEAH! SHE'LL LOVE IT!
SOMETIMES IT'S HARD TO PUT ASIDE THE THINGS YOU WANT TO DO AND ASK WHAT YOUR FRIENDS ARE INTERESTED IN.
BAD SEED
WELL, NOW WHAT, BIG SIS?
POST OFFICE
BUT IF YOU NEVER ASK, YOU MAY NEVER KNOW JUST HOW AMAZING YOUR FRIENDS ARE.
WELL, SWEETIE, WHAT WOULD YOU LIKE TO DO TODAY?
THE END.

my LITTLE PONY

FRIENDS FOREVER

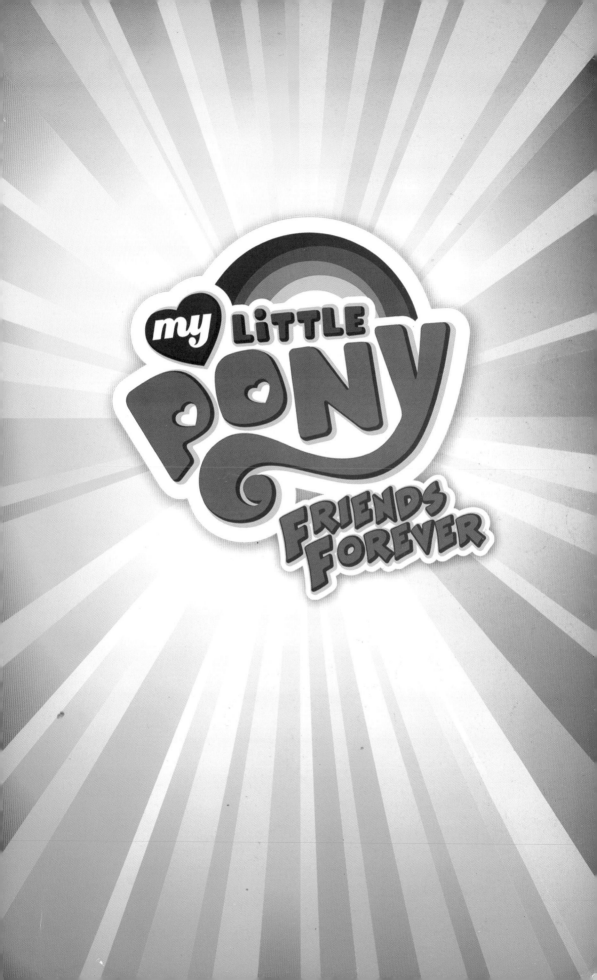

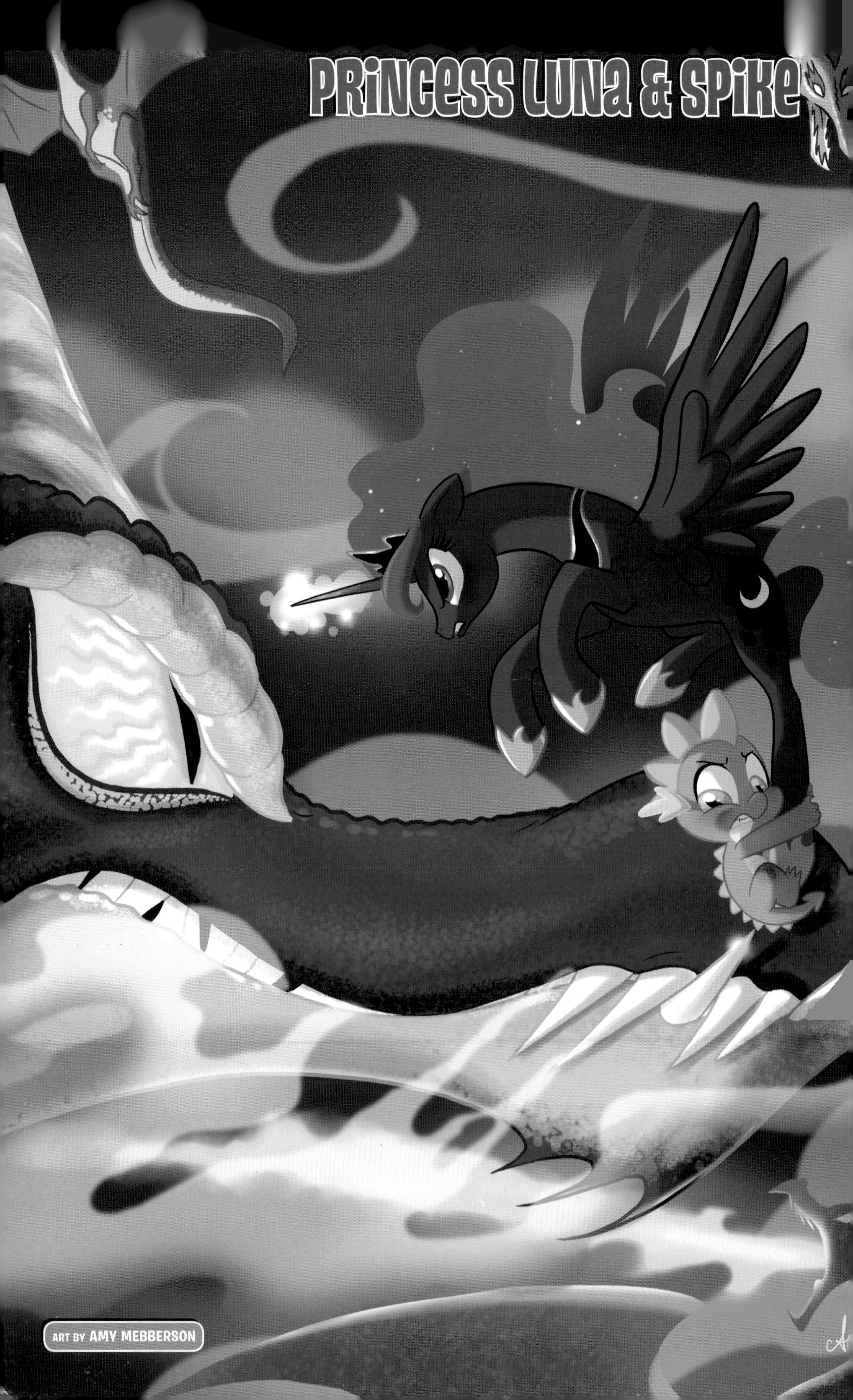
PRINCESS LUNA & SPIKE
ART BY AMY MEBBERSON

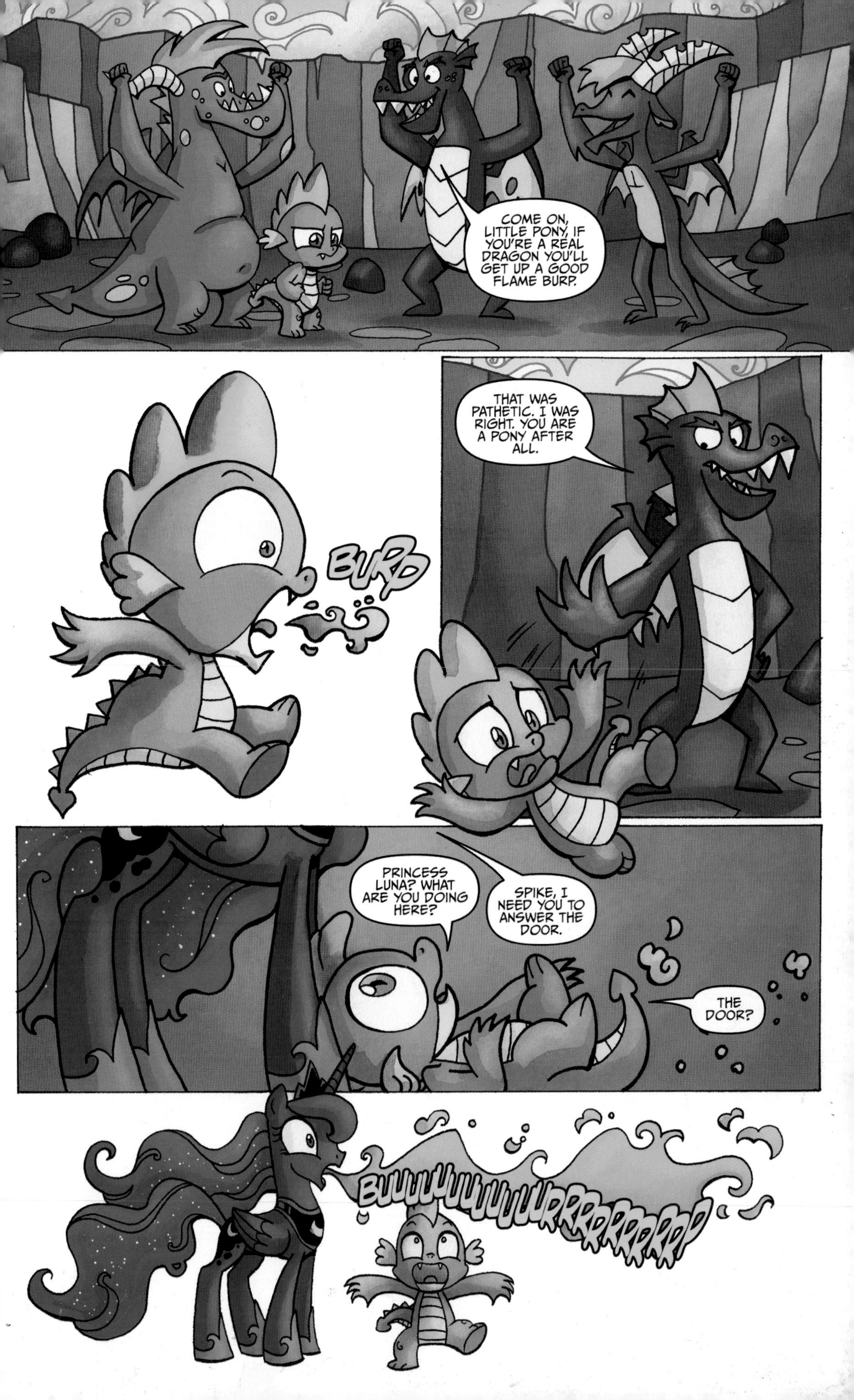
COME ON, LITTLE PONY, IF YOU'RE A REAL DRAGON YOU'LL GET UP A GOOD FLAME BURP.
BURP
THAT WAS PATHETIC. I WAS RIGHT. YOU ARE A PONY AFTER ALL.
PRINCESS LUNA? WHAT ARE YOU DOING HERE?
SPIKE, I NEED YOU TO ANSWER THE DOOR.
THE DOOR?
BUUUUUUUUUUURRRRRRRRRP

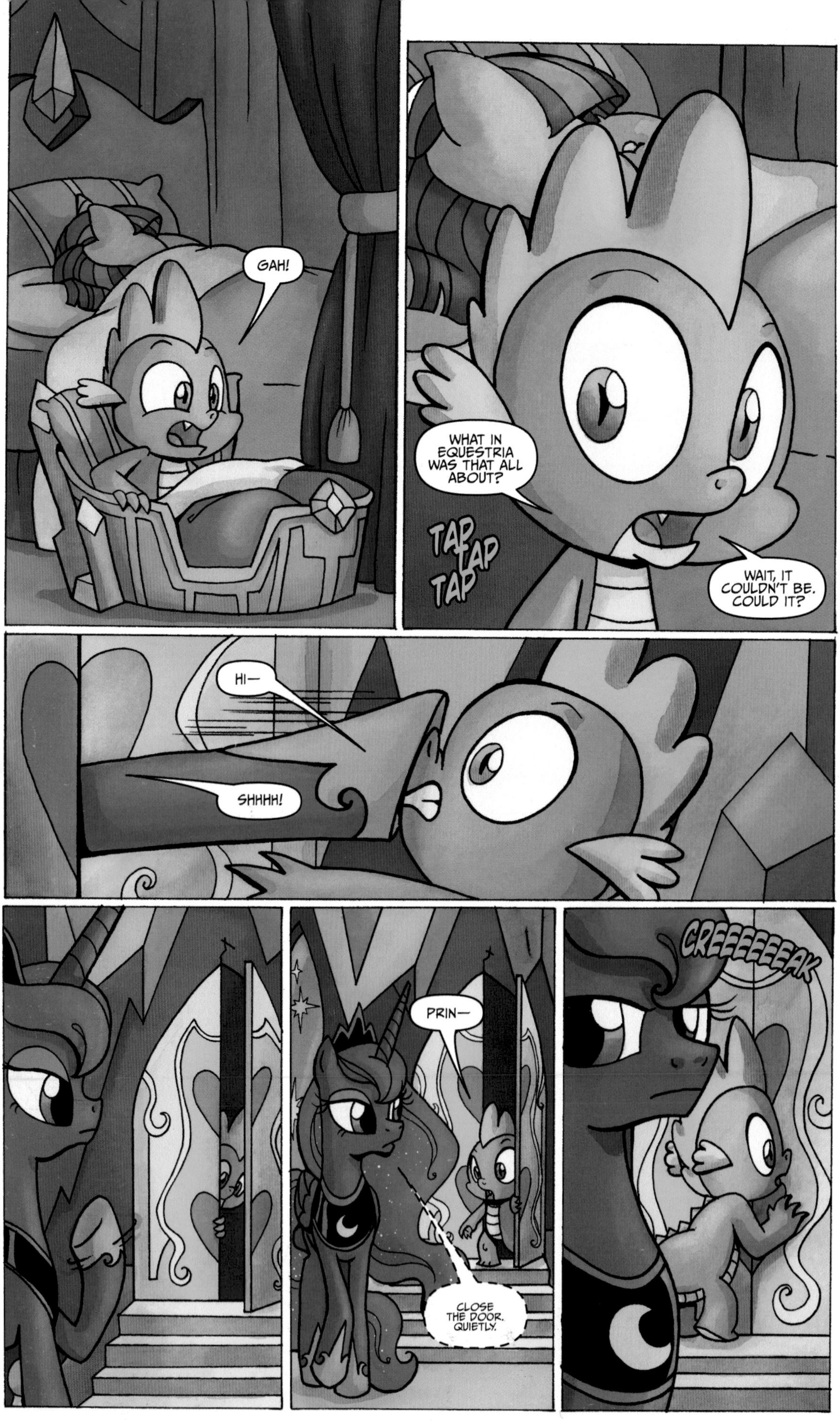
GAH!
WHAT IN EQUESTRIA WAS THAT ALL ABOUT?
TAP TAP TAP
WAIT, IT COULDN'T BE. COULD IT?
HI—
SHHHH!
PRIN—
CLOSE THE DOOR. QUIETLY.
CREEEEEEEAK

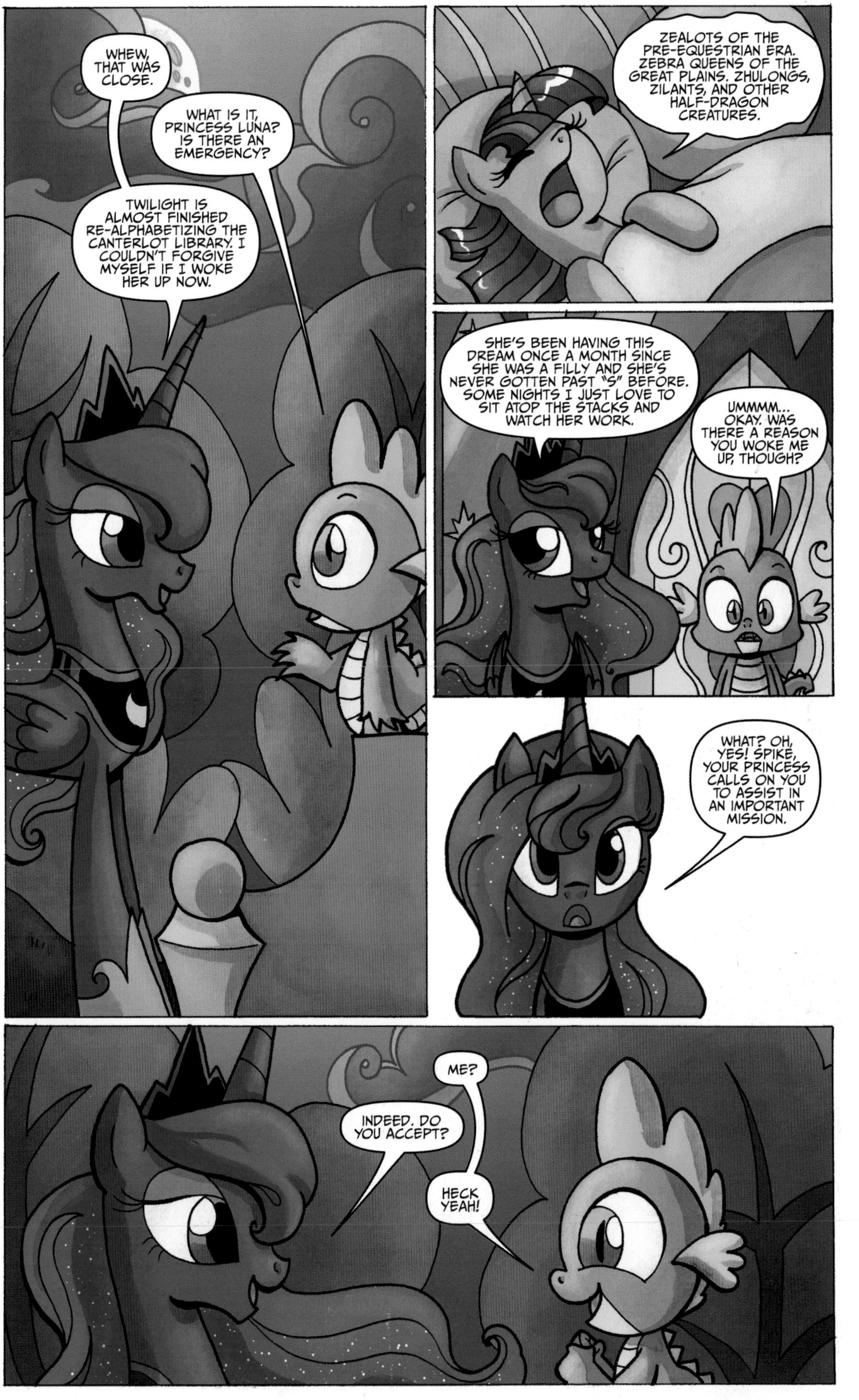
WHEW, THAT WAS CLOSE.
WHAT IS IT, PRINCESS LUNA? IS THERE AN EMERGENCY?
TWILIGHT IS ALMOST FINISHED RE-ALPHABETIZING THE CANTERLOT LIBRARY. I COULDN'T FORGIVE MYSELF IF I WOKE HER UP NOW.
ZEALOTS OF THE PRE-EQUESTRIAN ERA. ZEBRA QUEENS OF THE GREAT PLAINS. ZHULONGS, ZILANTS, AND OTHER HALF-DRAGON CREATURES.
SHE'S BEEN HAVING THIS DREAM ONCE A MONTH SINCE SHE WAS A FILLY AND SHE'S NEVER GOTTEN PAST "S" BEFORE. SOME NIGHTS I JUST LOVE TO SIT ATOP THE STACKS AND WATCH HER WORK.
UMMMM... OKAY. WAS THERE A REASON YOU WOKE ME UP, THOUGH?
WHAT? OH, YES! SPIKE, YOUR PRINCESS CALLS ON YOU TO ASSIST IN AN IMPORTANT MISSION.
ME?
INDEED. DO YOU ACCEPT?
HECK YEAH!

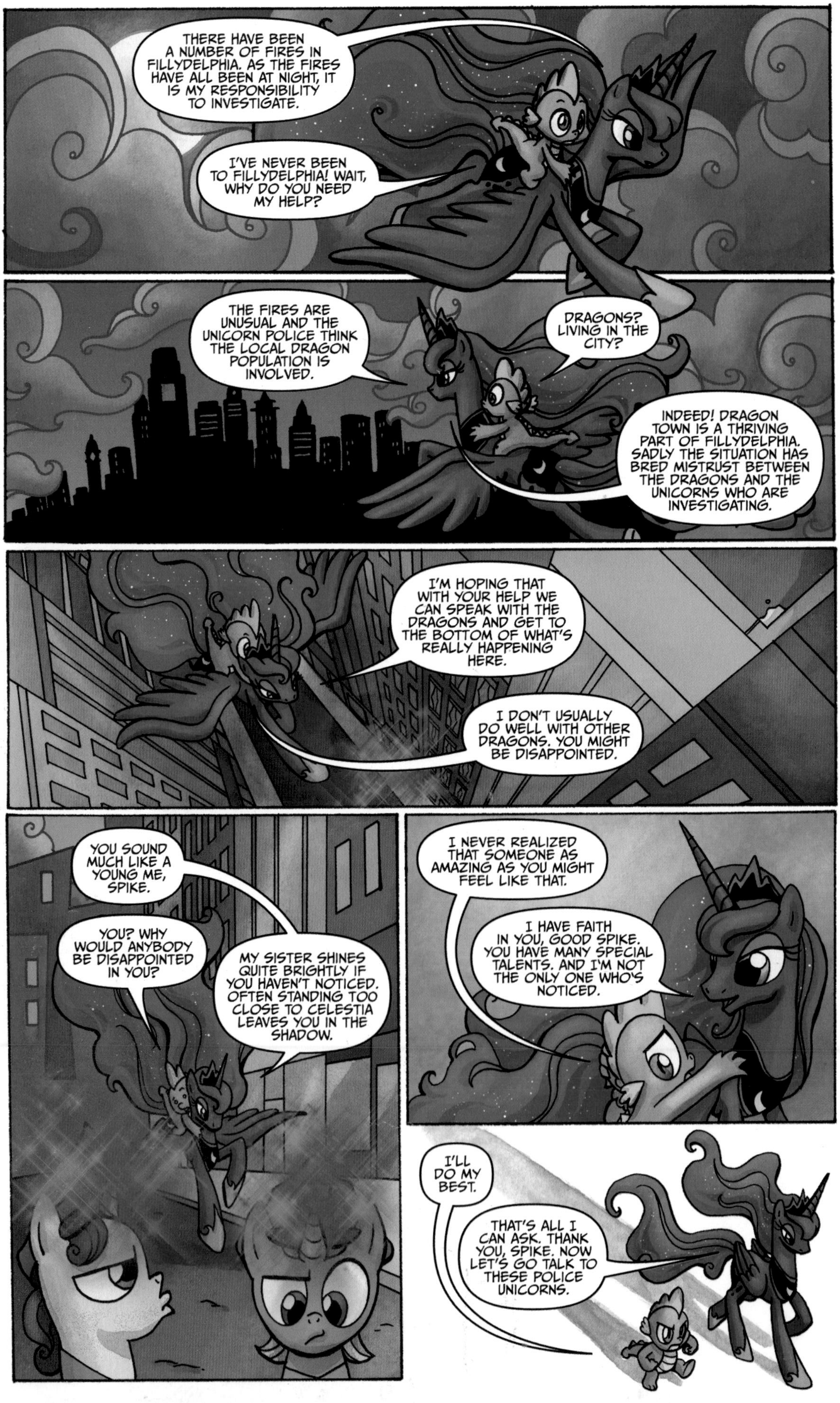
THERE HAVE BEEN A NUMBER OF FIRES IN FILLYDELPHIA. AS THE FIRES HAVE ALL BEEN AT NIGHT, IT IS MY RESPONSIBILITY TO INVESTIGATE.
I'VE NEVER BEEN TO FILLYDELPHIA! WAIT, WHY DO YOU NEED MY HELP?
THE FIRES ARE UNUSUAL AND THE UNICORN POLICE THINK THE LOCAL DRAGON POPULATION IS INVOLVED.
DRAGONS? LIVING IN THE CITY?
INDEED! DRAGON TOWN IS A THRIVING PART OF FILLYDELPHIA. SADLY THE SITUATION HAS BRED MISTRUST BETWEEN THE DRAGONS AND THE UNICORNS WHO ARE INVESTIGATING.
I'M HOPING THAT WITH YOUR HELP WE CAN SPEAK WITH THE DRAGONS AND GET TO THE BOTTOM OF WHAT'S REALLY HAPPENING HERE.
I DON'T USUALLY DO WELL WITH OTHER DRAGONS. YOU MIGHT BE DISAPPOINTED.
YOU SOUND MUCH LIKE A YOUNG ME, SPIKE.
YOU? WHY WOULD ANYBODY BE DISAPPOINTED IN YOU?
MY SISTER SHINES QUITE BRIGHTLY IF YOU HAVEN'T NOTICED. OFTEN STANDING TOO CLOSE TO CELESTIA LEAVES YOU IN THE SHADOW.
I NEVER REALIZED THAT SOMEONE AS AMAZING AS YOU MIGHT FEEL LIKE THAT.
I HAVE FAITH IN YOU, GOOD SPIKE. YOU HAVE MANY SPECIAL TALENTS. AND I'M NOT THE ONLY ONE WHO'S NOTICED.
I'LL DO MY BEST.
THAT'S ALL I CAN ASK. THANK YOU, SPIKE. NOW LET'S GO TALK TO THESE POLICE UNICORNS.

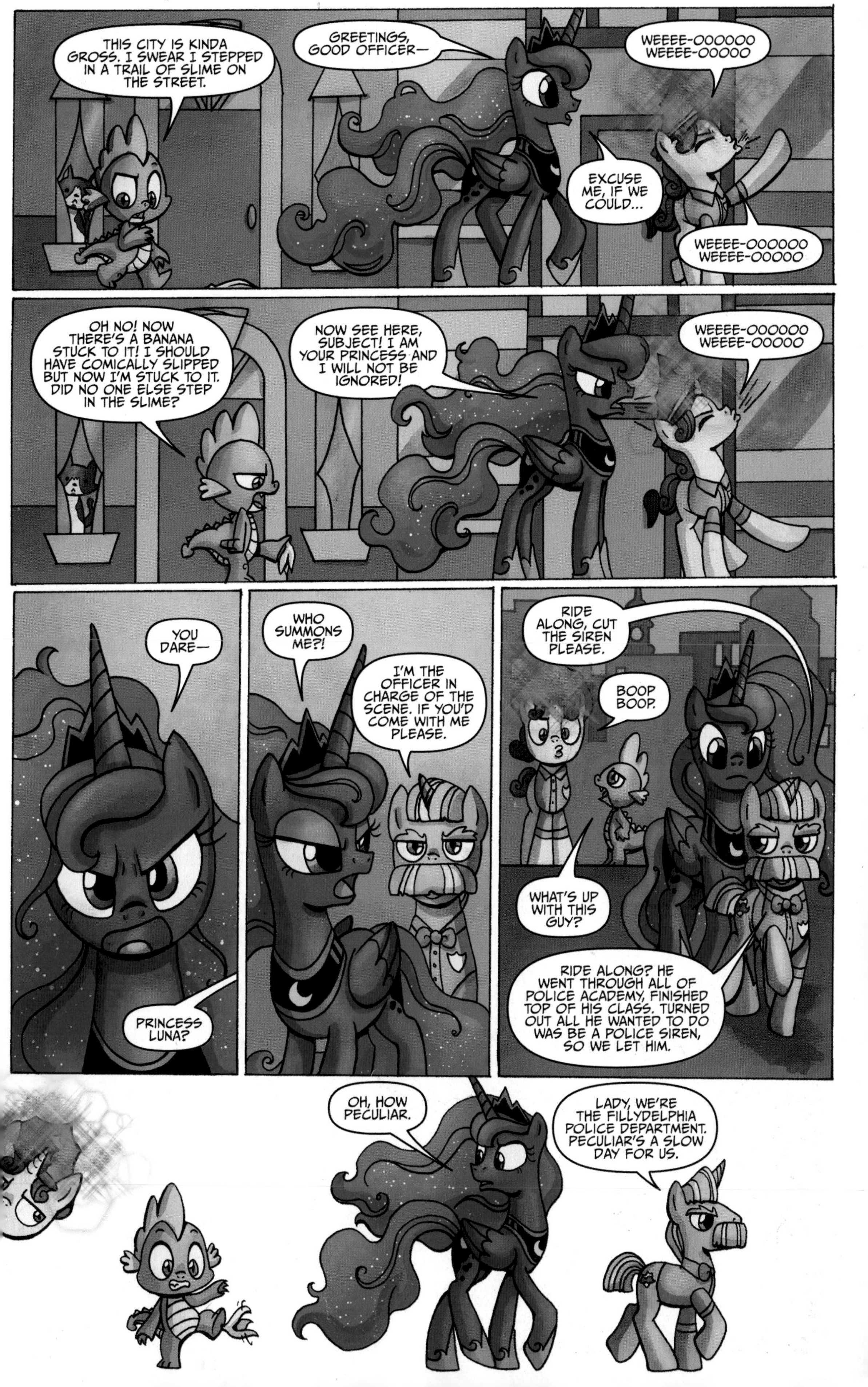
THIS CITY IS KINDA GROSS. I SWEAR I STEPPED IN A TRAIL OF SLIME ON THE STREET.
GREETINGS, GOOD OFFICER—
WEEEE-OOOOOO WEEEE-OOOOO
EXCUSE ME, IF WE COULD...
WEEEE-OOOOOO WEEEE-OOOOO
OH NO! NOW THERE'S A BANANA STUCK TO IT! I SHOULD HAVE COMICALLY SLIPPED BUT NOW I'M STUCK TO IT. DID NO ONE ELSE STEP IN THE SLIME?
NOW SEE HERE, SUBJECT! I AM YOUR PRINCESS AND I WILL NOT BE IGNORED!
WEEEE-OOOOOO WEEEE-OOOOO
YOU DARE—
PRINCESS LUNA?
WHO SUMMONS ME?!
I'M THE OFFICER IN CHARGE OF THE SCENE. IF YOU'D COME WITH ME PLEASE.
RIDE ALONG, CUT THE SIREN PLEASE.
BOOP BOOP.
WHAT'S UP WITH THIS GUY?
RIDE ALONG? HE WENT THROUGH ALL OF POLICE ACADEMY, FINISHED TOP OF HIS CLASS. TURNED OUT ALL HE WANTED TO DO WAS BE A POLICE SIREN, SO WE LET HIM.
OH, HOW PECULIAR.
LADY, WE'RE THE FILLYDELPHIA POLICE DEPARTMENT. PECULIAR'S A SLOW DAY FOR US.

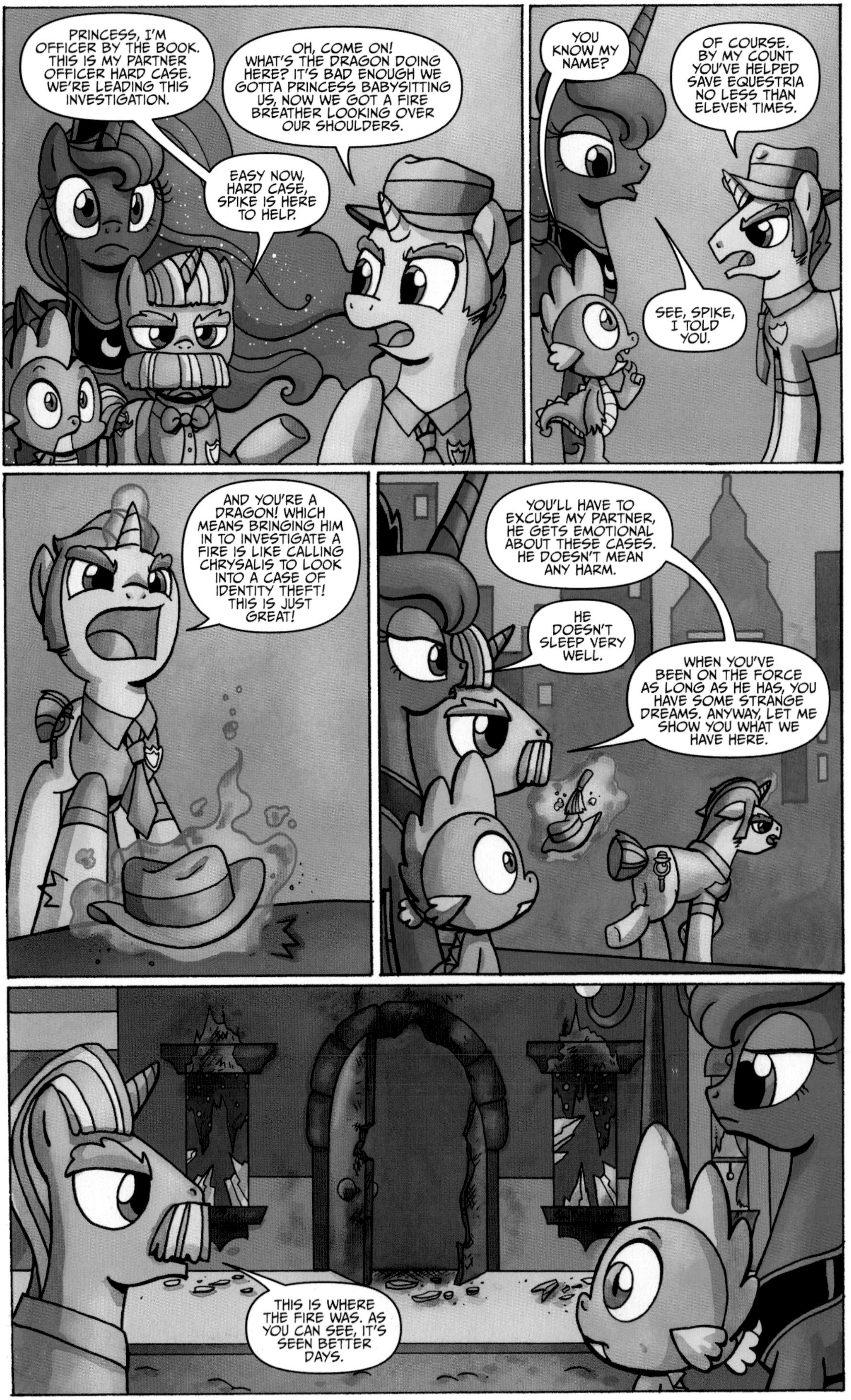

PRINCESS, I'M OFFICER BY THE BOOK. THIS IS MY PARTNER OFFICER HARD CASE. WE'RE LEADING THIS INVESTIGATION.
OH, COME ON! WHAT'S THE DRAGON DOING HERE? IT'S BAD ENOUGH WE GOTTA PRINCESS BABYSITTING US, NOW WE GOT A FIRE BREATHER LOOKING OVER OUR SHOULDERS.
EASY NOW, HARD CASE, SPIKE IS HERE TO HELP.
YOU KNOW MY NAME?
OF COURSE. BY MY COUNT YOU'VE HELPED SAVE EQUESTRIA NO LESS THAN ELEVEN TIMES.
SEE, SPIKE, I TOLD YOU.
AND YOU'RE A DRAGON! WHICH MEANS BRINGING HIM IN TO INVESTIGATE A FIRE IS LIKE CALLING CHRYSALIS TO LOOK INTO A CASE OF IDENTITY THEFT! THIS IS JUST GREAT!
YOU'LL HAVE TO EXCUSE MY PARTNER, HE GETS EMOTIONAL ABOUT THESE CASES. HE DOESN'T MEAN ANY HARM.
HE DOESN'T SLEEP VERY WELL.
WHEN YOU'VE BEEN ON THE FORCE AS LONG AS HE HAS, YOU HAVE SOME STRANGE DREAMS. ANYWAY, LET ME SHOW YOU WHAT WE HAVE HERE.
THIS IS WHERE THE FIRE WAS. AS YOU CAN SEE, IT'S SEEN BETTER DAYS.

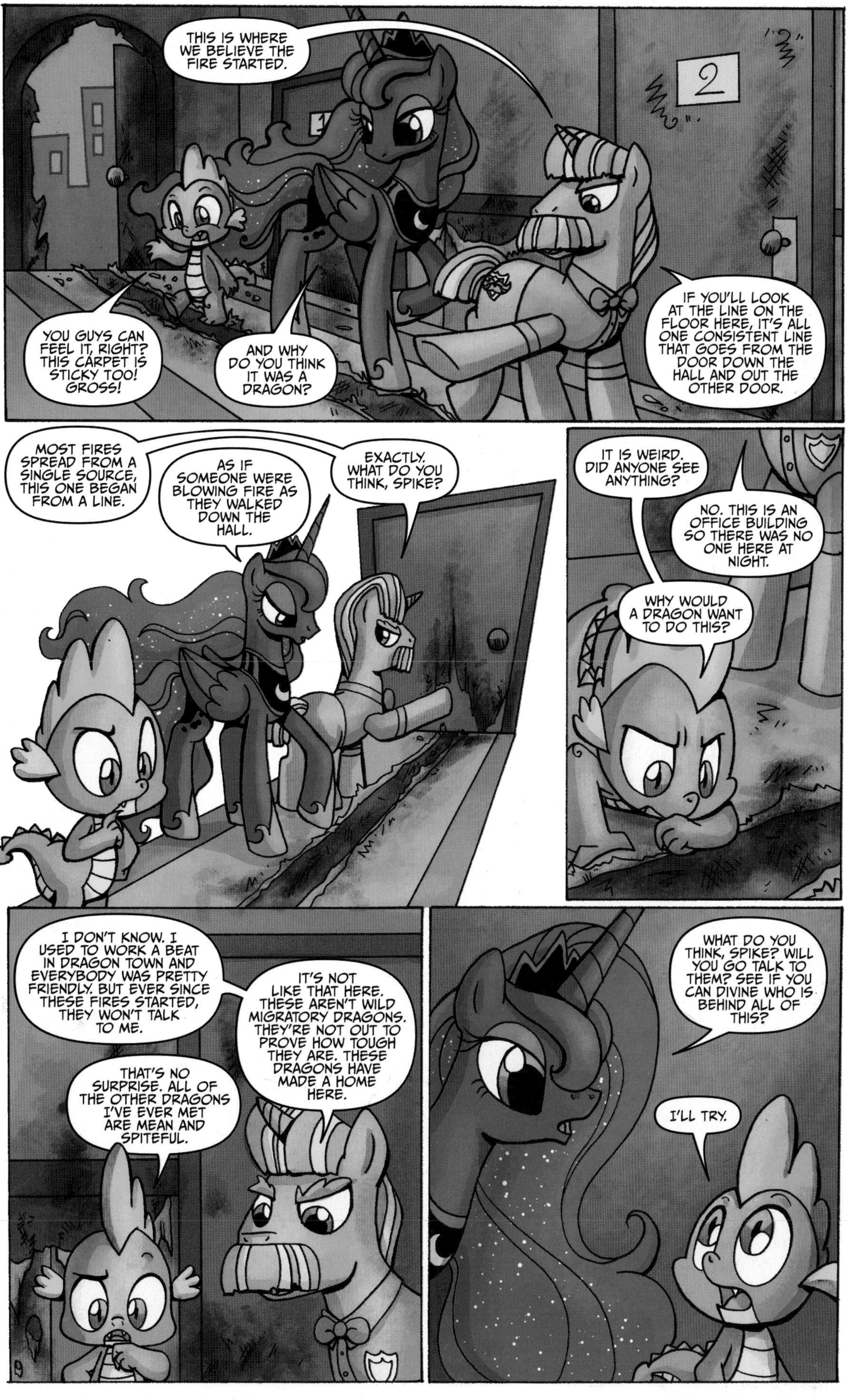
THIS IS WHERE WE BELIEVE THE FIRE STARTED.
YOU GUYS CAN FEEL IT, RIGHT? THIS CARPET IS STICKY TOO! GROSS!
AND WHY DO YOU THINK IT WAS A DRAGON?
IF YOU'LL LOOK AT THE LINE ON THE FLOOR HERE, IT'S ALL ONE CONSISTENT LINE THAT GOES FROM THE DOOR DOWN THE HALL AND OUT THE OTHER DOOR.
MOST FIRES SPREAD FROM A SINGLE SOURCE, THIS ONE BEGAN FROM A LINE.
AS IF SOMEONE WERE BLOWING FIRE AS THEY WALKED DOWN THE HALL.
EXACTLY. WHAT DO YOU THINK, SPIKE?
IT IS WEIRD. DID ANYONE SEE ANYTHING?
NO. THIS IS AN OFFICE BUILDING SO THERE WAS NO ONE HERE AT NIGHT.
WHY WOULD A DRAGON WANT TO DO THIS?
I DON'T KNOW. I USED TO WORK A BEAT IN DRAGON TOWN AND EVERYBODY WAS PRETTY FRIENDLY. BUT EVER SINCE THESE FIRES STARTED, THEY WON'T TALK TO ME.
THAT'S NO SURPRISE. ALL OF THE OTHER DRAGONS I'VE EVER MET ARE MEAN AND SPITEFUL.
IT'S NOT LIKE THAT HERE. THESE AREN'T WILD MIGRATORY DRAGONS. THEY'RE NOT OUT TO PROVE HOW TOUGH THEY ARE. THESE DRAGONS HAVE MADE A HOME HERE.
WHAT DO YOU THINK, SPIKE? WILL YOU GO TALK TO THEM? SEE IF YOU CAN DIVINE WHO IS BEHIND ALL OF THIS?
I'LL TRY.

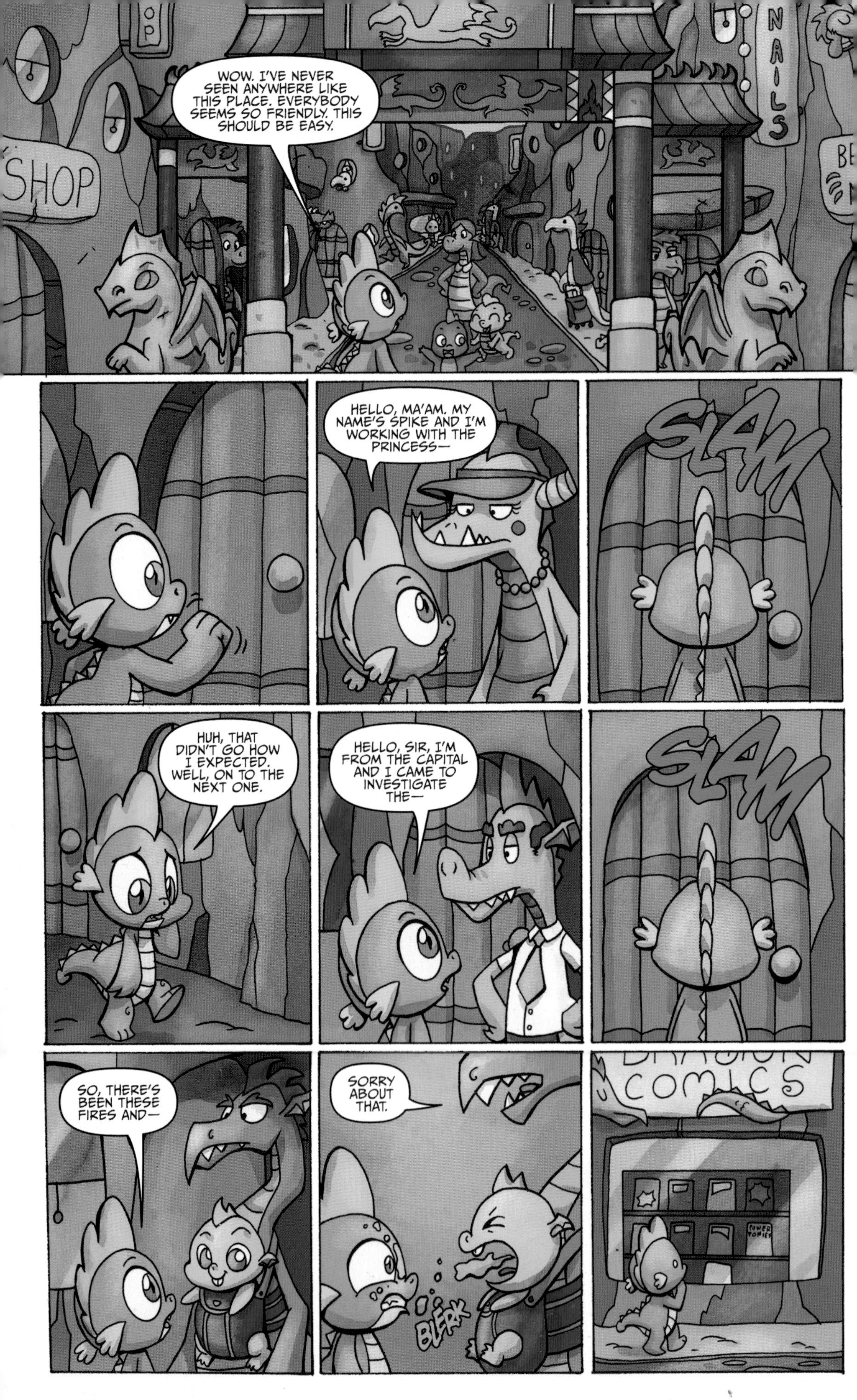
SHOP
NAILS
WOW. I'VE NEVER SEEN ANYWHERE LIKE THIS PLACE. EVERYBODY SEEMS SO FRIENDLY. THIS SHOULD BE EASY.
HELLO, MA'AM. MY NAME'S SPIKE AND I'M WORKING WITH THE PRINCESS—
SLAM
HUH, THAT DIDN'T GO HOW I EXPECTED. WELL, ON TO THE NEXT ONE.
HELLO, SIR, I'M FROM THE CAPITAL AND I CAME TO INVESTIGATE THE—
SLAM
SO, THERE'S BEEN THESE FIRES AND—
SORRY ABOUT THAT.
BLERK
COMICS

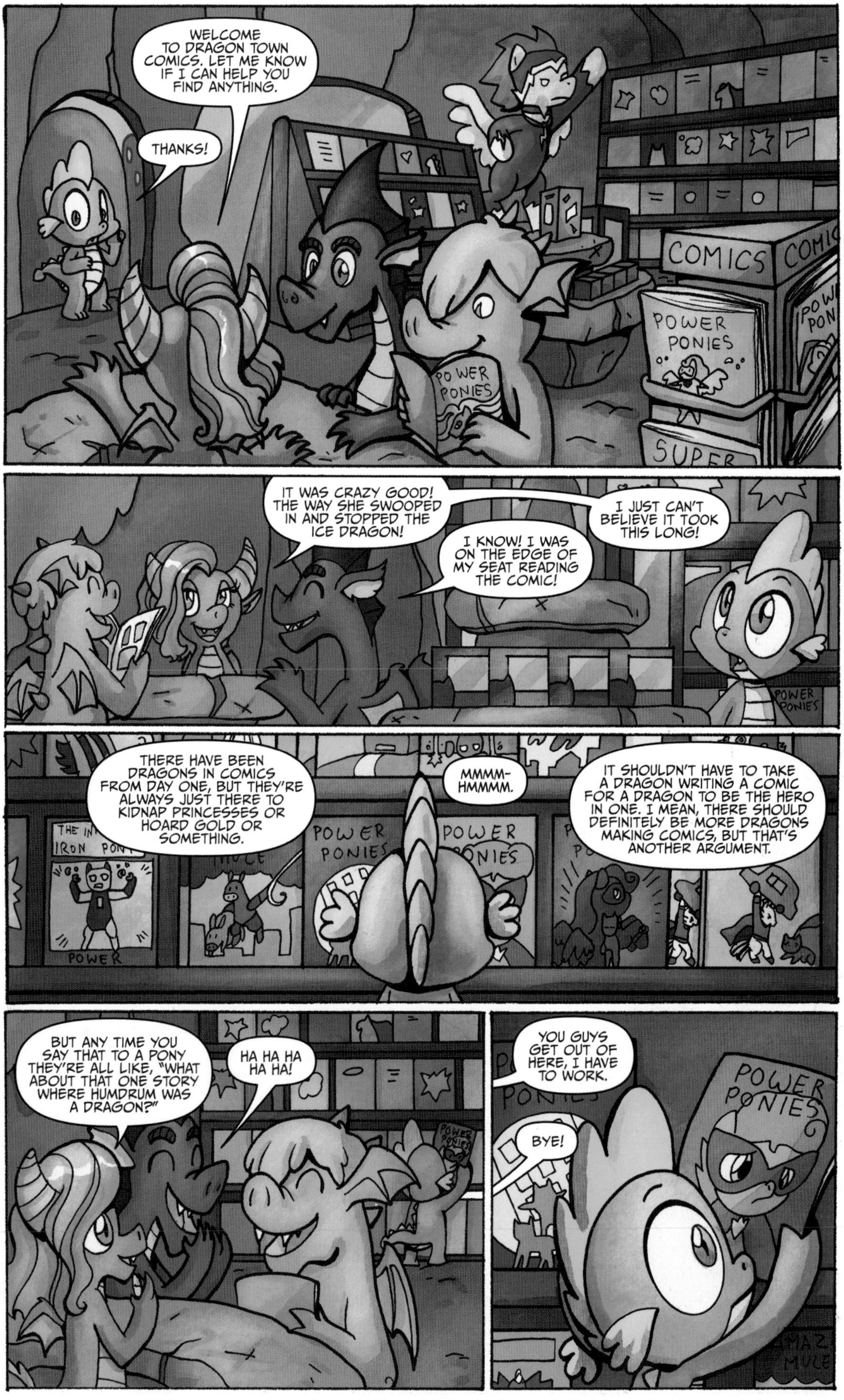
WELCOME TO DRAGON TOWN COMICS. LET ME KNOW IF I CAN HELP YOU FIND ANYTHING.
THANKS!
COMICS
COMICS
POWER PONIES
POWER PONIES
SUPER
IT WAS CRAZY GOOD! THE WAY SHE SWOOPED IN AND STOPPED THE ICE DRAGON!
I KNOW! I WAS ON THE EDGE OF MY SEAT READING THE COMIC!
I JUST CAN'T BELIEVE IT TOOK THIS LONG!
POWER PONIES
THERE HAVE BEEN DRAGONS IN COMICS FROM DAY ONE, BUT THEY'RE ALWAYS JUST THERE TO KIDNAP PRINCESSES OR HOARD GOLD OR SOMETHING.
MMMM-HMMMM.
IT SHOULDN'T HAVE TO TAKE A DRAGON WRITING A COMIC FOR A DRAGON TO BE THE HERO IN ONE. I MEAN, THERE SHOULD DEFINITELY BE MORE DRAGONS MAKING COMICS, BUT THAT'S ANOTHER ARGUMENT.
THE IRON PONY
POWER
POWER PONIES
POWER PONIES
BUT ANY TIME YOU SAY THAT TO A PONY THEY'RE ALL LIKE, "WHAT ABOUT THAT ONE STORY WHERE HUMDRUM WAS A DRAGON?"
HA HA HA HA HA!
YOU GUYS GET OUT OF HERE, I HAVE TO WORK.
BYE!
POWER PONIES

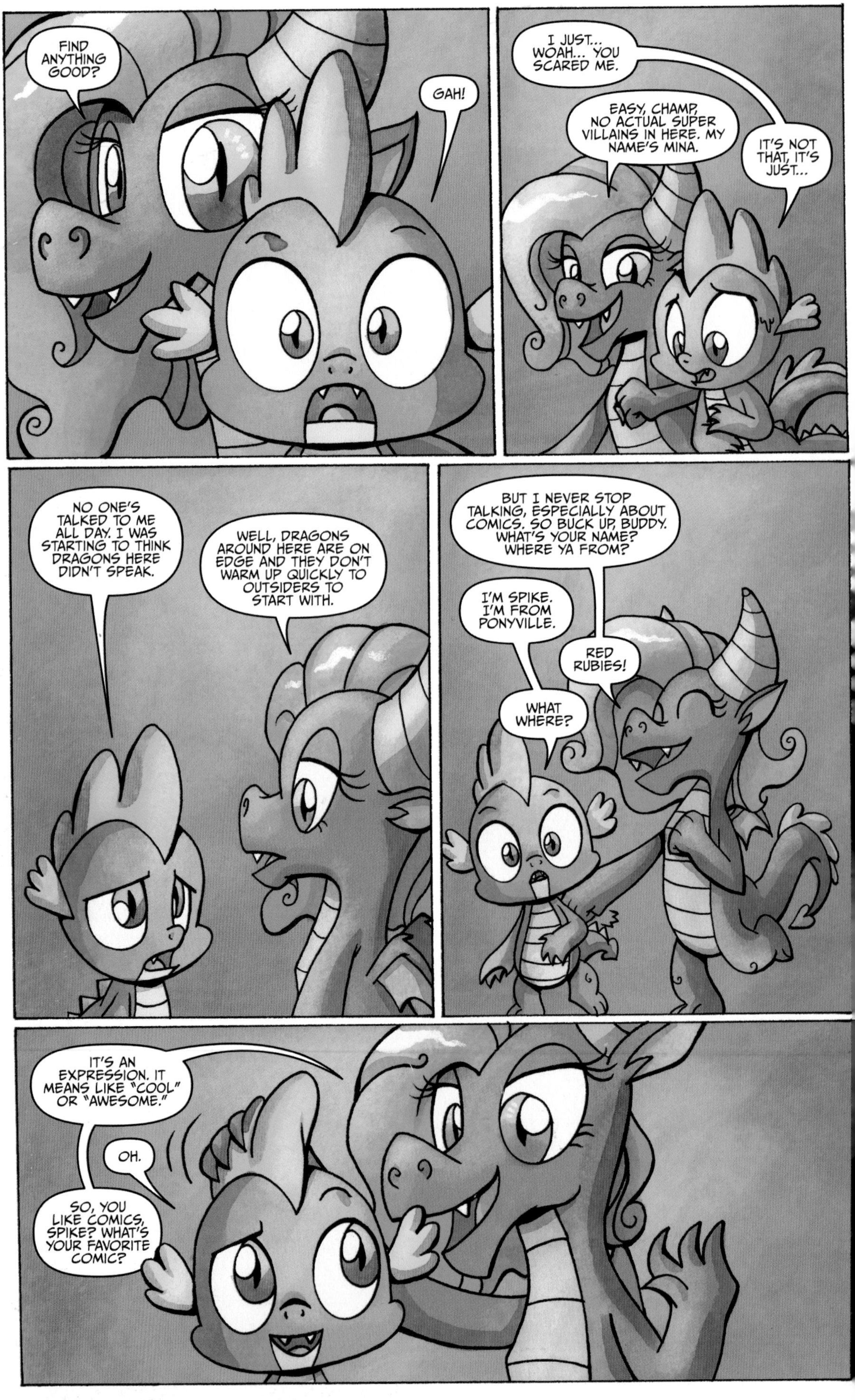
FIND ANYTHING GOOD?
GAH!
I JUST... WOAH... YOU SCARED ME.
EASY, CHAMP, NO ACTUAL SUPER VILLAINS IN HERE. MY NAME'S MINA.
IT'S NOT THAT, IT'S JUST...
NO ONE'S TALKED TO ME ALL DAY. I WAS STARTING TO THINK DRAGONS HERE DIDN'T SPEAK.
WELL, DRAGONS AROUND HERE ARE ON EDGE AND THEY DON'T WARM UP QUICKLY TO OUTSIDERS TO START WITH.
BUT I NEVER STOP TALKING, ESPECIALLY ABOUT COMICS. SO BUCK UP, BUDDY. WHAT'S YOUR NAME? WHERE YA FROM?
I'M SPIKE. I'M FROM PONYVILLE.
RED RUBIES!
WHAT WHERE?
IT'S AN EXPRESSION. IT MEANS LIKE "COOL" OR "AWESOME."
OH.
SO, YOU LIKE COMICS, SPIKE? WHAT'S YOUR FAVORITE COMIC?

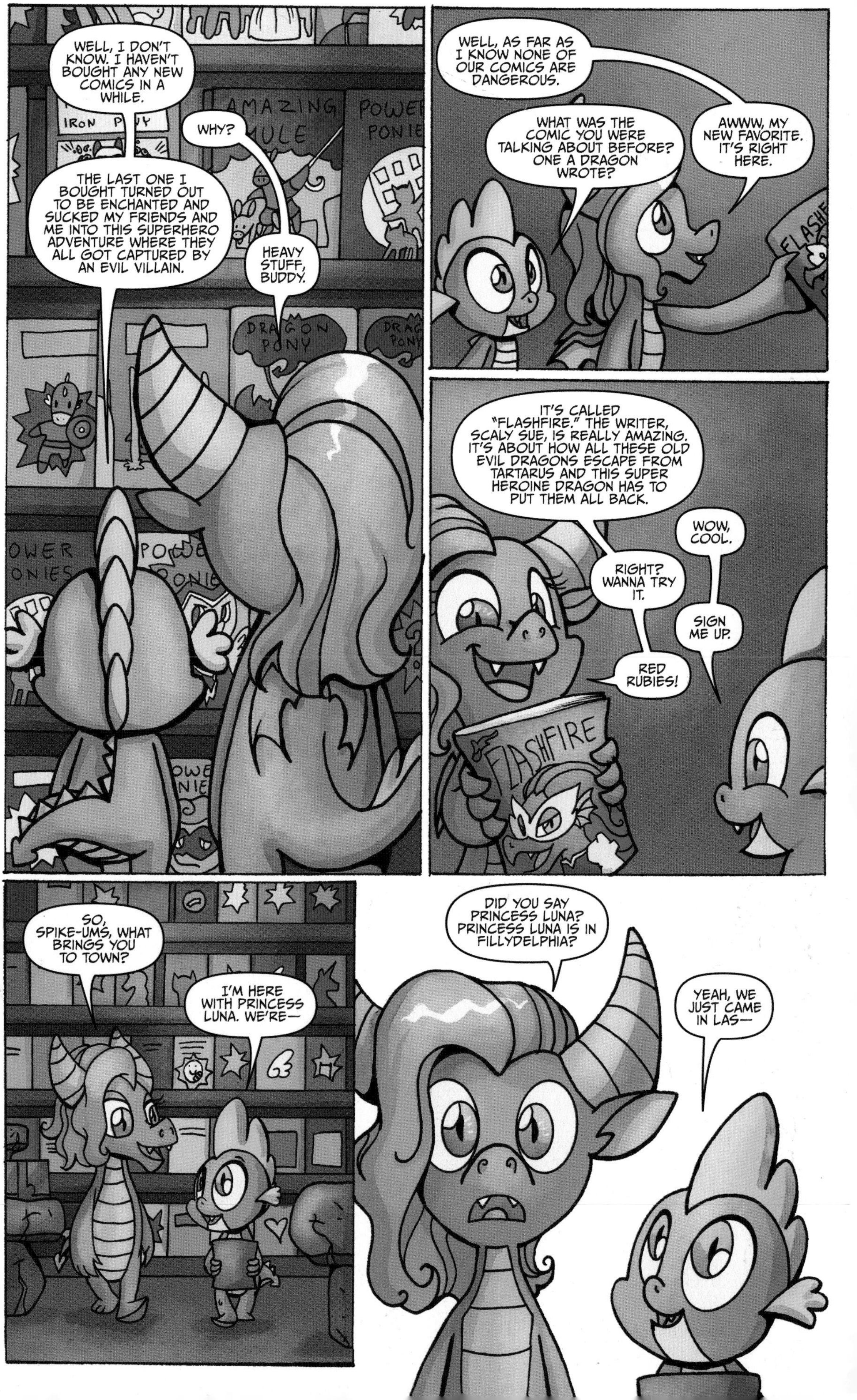
WELL, I DON'T KNOW. I HAVEN'T BOUGHT ANY NEW COMICS IN A WHILE.
THE LAST ONE I BOUGHT TURNED OUT TO BE ENCHANTED AND SUCKED MY FRIENDS AND ME INTO THIS SUPERHERO ADVENTURE WHERE THEY ALL GOT CAPTURED BY AN EVIL VILLAIN.
WHY?
HEAVY STUFF, BUDDY.
IRON PONY
AMAZING MULE
POWER PONIES
DRAGON PONY
WELL, AS FAR AS I KNOW NONE OF OUR COMICS ARE DANGEROUS.
WHAT WAS THE COMIC YOU WERE TALKING ABOUT BEFORE? ONE A DRAGON WROTE?
AWWW, MY NEW FAVORITE. IT'S RIGHT HERE.
IT'S CALLED "FLASHFIRE." THE WRITER, SCALY SUE, IS REALLY AMAZING. IT'S ABOUT HOW ALL THESE OLD EVIL DRAGONS ESCAPE FROM TARTARUS AND THIS SUPER HEROINE DRAGON HAS TO PUT THEM ALL BACK.
WOW, COOL.
RIGHT? WANNA TRY IT.
SIGN ME UP.
RED RUBIES!
FLASHFIRE
SO, SPIKE-UMS, WHAT BRINGS YOU TO TOWN?
I'M HERE WITH PRINCESS LUNA. WE'RE—
DID YOU SAY PRINCESS LUNA? PRINCESS LUNA IS IN FILLYDELPHIA?
YEAH, WE JUST CAME IN LAS—

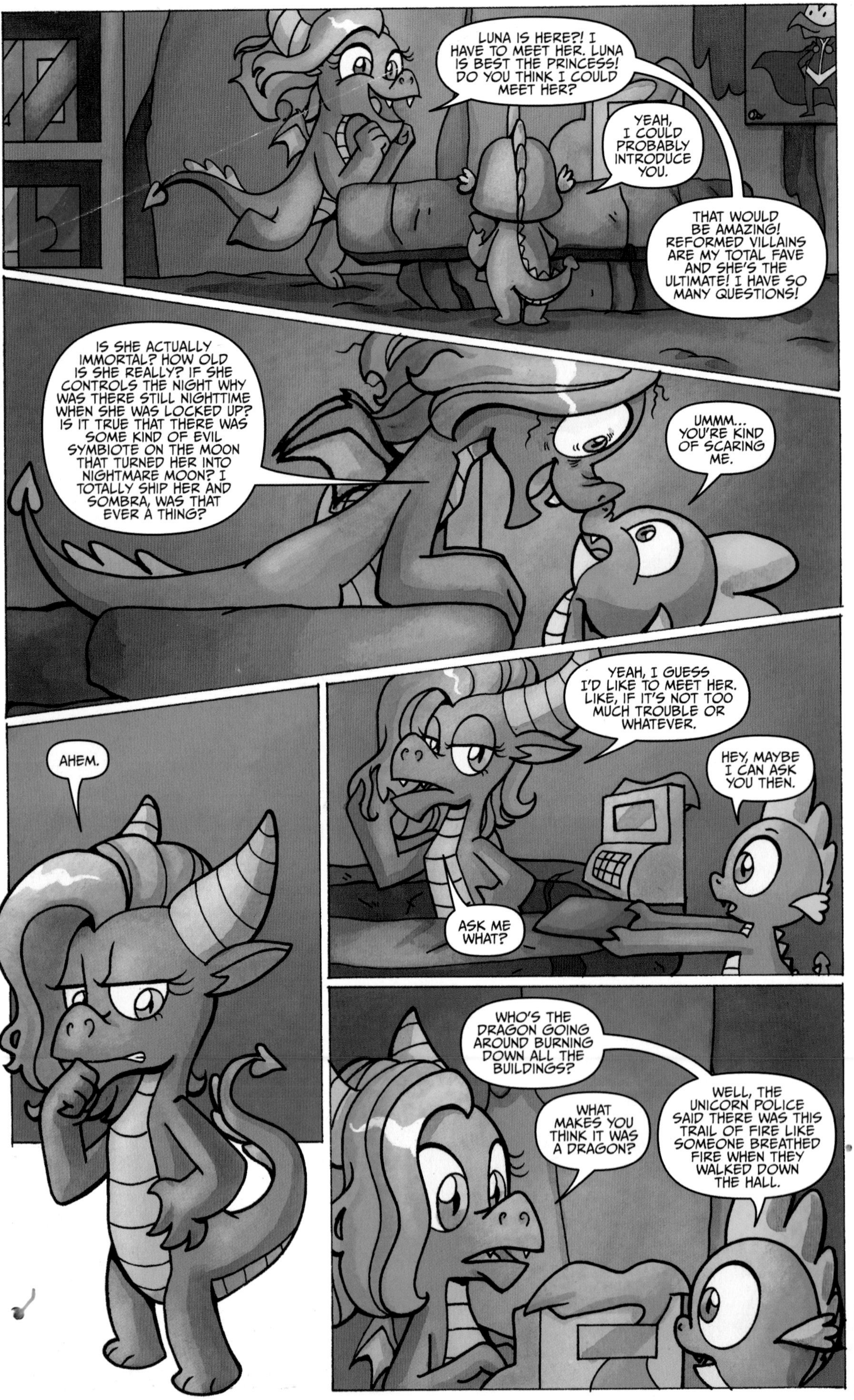
LUNA IS HERE?! I HAVE TO MEET HER. LUNA IS BEST THE PRINCESS! DO YOU THINK I COULD MEET HER?
YEAH, I COULD PROBABLY INTRODUCE YOU.
THAT WOULD BE AMAZING! REFORMED VILLAINS ARE MY TOTAL FAVE AND SHE'S THE ULTIMATE! I HAVE SO MANY QUESTIONS!
IS SHE ACTUALLY IMMORTAL? HOW OLD IS SHE REALLY? IF SHE CONTROLS THE NIGHT WHY WAS THERE STILL NIGHTTIME WHEN SHE WAS LOCKED UP? IS IT TRUE THAT THERE WAS SOME KIND OF EVIL SYMBIOTE ON THE MOON THAT TURNED HER INTO NIGHTMARE MOON? I TOTALLY SHIP HER AND SOMBRA, WAS THAT EVER A THING?
UMMM... YOU'RE KIND OF SCARING ME.
AHEM.
YEAH, I GUESS I'D LIKE TO MEET HER. LIKE, IF IT'S NOT TOO MUCH TROUBLE OR WHATEVER.
HEY, MAYBE I CAN ASK YOU THEN.
ASK ME WHAT?
WHO'S THE DRAGON GOING AROUND BURNING DOWN ALL THE BUILDINGS?
WHAT MAKES YOU THINK IT WAS A DRAGON?
WELL, THE UNICORN POLICE SAID THERE WAS THIS TRAIL OF FIRE LIKE SOMEONE BREATHED FIRE WHEN THEY WALKED DOWN THE HALL.

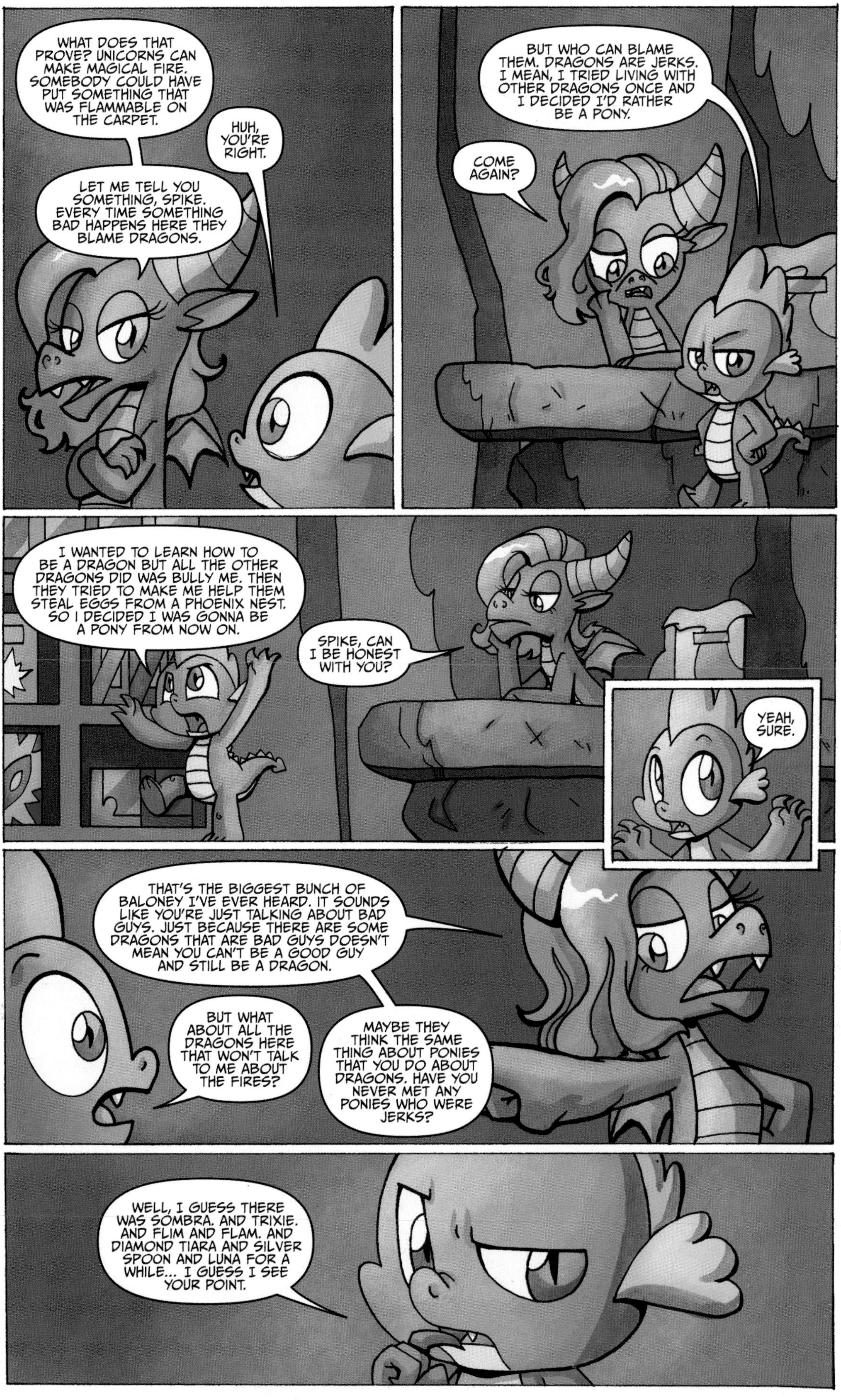
WHAT DOES THAT PROVE? UNICORNS CAN MAKE MAGICAL FIRE. SOMEBODY COULD HAVE PUT SOMETHING THAT WAS FLAMMABLE ON THE CARPET.
HUH, YOU'RE RIGHT.
LET ME TELL YOU SOMETHING, SPIKE. EVERY TIME SOMETHING BAD HAPPENS HERE THEY BLAME DRAGONS.
BUT WHO CAN BLAME THEM. DRAGONS ARE JERKS. I MEAN, I TRIED LIVING WITH OTHER DRAGONS ONCE AND I DECIDED I'D RATHER BE A PONY.
COME AGAIN?
I WANTED TO LEARN HOW TO BE A DRAGON BUT ALL THE OTHER DRAGONS DID WAS BULLY ME. THEN THEY TRIED TO MAKE ME HELP THEM STEAL EGGS FROM A PHOENIX NEST. SO I DECIDED I WAS GONNA BE A PONY FROM NOW ON.
SPIKE, CAN I BE HONEST WITH YOU?
YEAH, SURE.
THAT'S THE BIGGEST BUNCH OF BALONEY I'VE EVER HEARD. IT SOUNDS LIKE YOU'RE JUST TALKING ABOUT BAD GUYS. JUST BECAUSE THERE ARE SOME DRAGONS THAT ARE BAD GUYS DOESN'T MEAN YOU CAN'T BE A GOOD GUY AND STILL BE A DRAGON.
BUT WHAT ABOUT ALL THE DRAGONS HERE THAT WON'T TALK TO ME ABOUT THE FIRES?
MAYBE THEY THINK THE SAME THING ABOUT PONIES THAT YOU DO ABOUT DRAGONS. HAVE YOU NEVER MET ANY PONIES WHO WERE JERKS?
WELL, I GUESS THERE WAS SOMBRA. AND TRIXIE. AND FLIM AND FLAM. AND DIAMOND TIARA AND SILVER SPOON AND LUNA FOR A WHILE... I GUESS I SEE YOUR POINT.

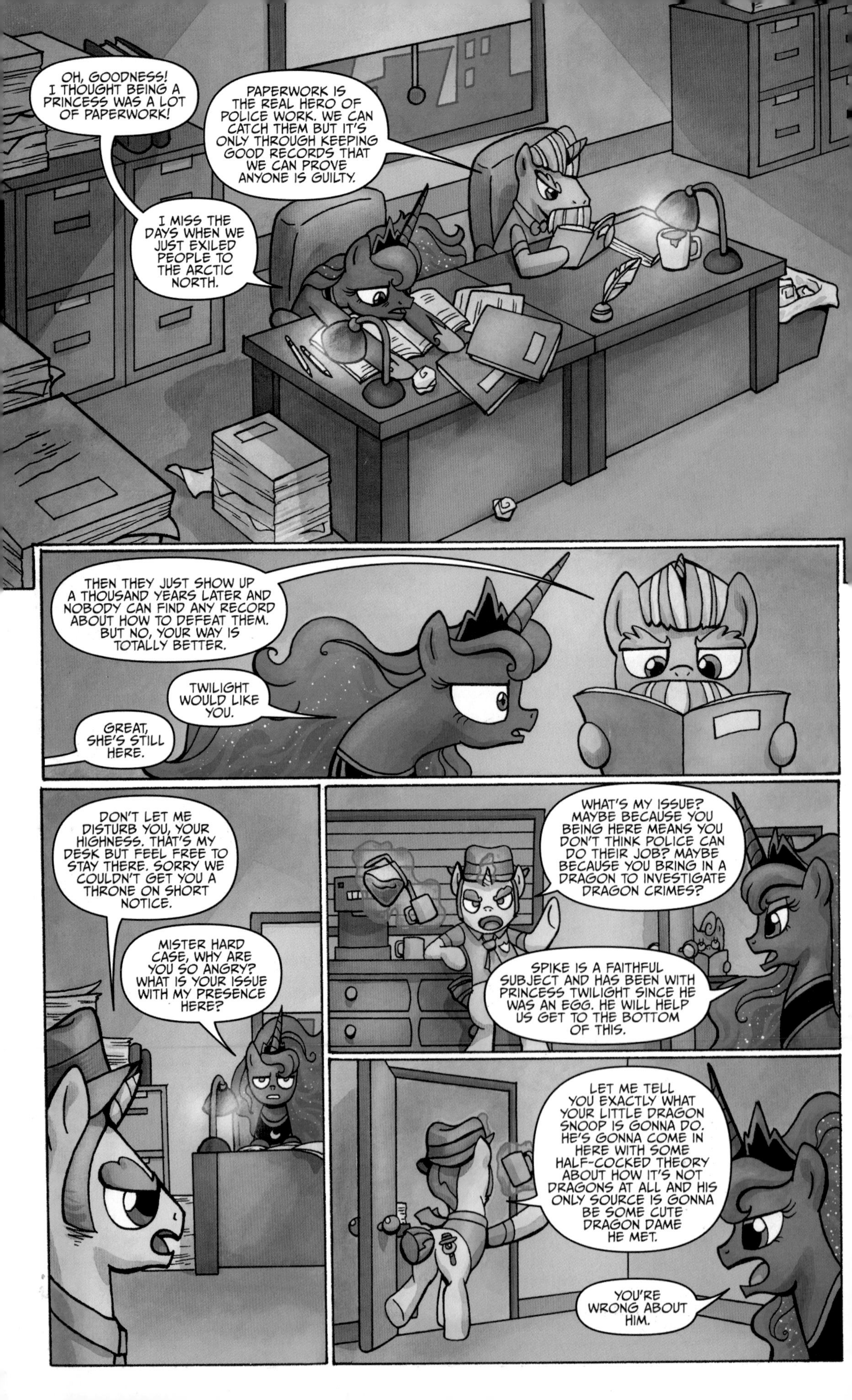
OH, GOODNESS! I THOUGHT BEING A PRINCESS WAS A LOT OF PAPERWORK!
PAPERWORK IS THE REAL HERO OF POLICE WORK. WE CAN CATCH THEM BUT IT'S ONLY THROUGH KEEPING GOOD RECORDS THAT WE CAN PROVE ANYONE IS GUILTY.
I MISS THE DAYS WHEN WE JUST EXILED PEOPLE TO THE ARCTIC NORTH.
THEN THEY JUST SHOW UP A THOUSAND YEARS LATER AND NOBODY CAN FIND ANY RECORD ABOUT HOW TO DEFEAT THEM. BUT NO, YOUR WAY IS TOTALLY BETTER.
TWILIGHT WOULD LIKE YOU.
GREAT, SHE'S STILL HERE.
DON'T LET ME DISTURB YOU, YOUR HIGHNESS. THAT'S MY DESK BUT FEEL FREE TO STAY THERE. SORRY WE COULDN'T GET YOU A THRONE ON SHORT NOTICE.
MISTER HARD CASE, WHY ARE YOU SO ANGRY? WHAT IS YOUR ISSUE WITH MY PRESENCE HERE?
WHAT'S MY ISSUE? MAYBE BECAUSE YOU BEING HERE MEANS YOU DON'T THINK POLICE CAN DO THEIR JOB? MAYBE BECAUSE YOU BRING IN A DRAGON TO INVESTIGATE DRAGON CRIMES?
SPIKE IS A FAITHFUL SUBJECT AND HAS BEEN WITH PRINCESS TWILIGHT SINCE HE WAS AN EGG. HE WILL HELP US GET TO THE BOTTOM OF THIS.
LET ME TELL YOU EXACTLY WHAT YOUR LITTLE DRAGON SNOOP IS GONNA DO. HE'S GONNA COME IN HERE WITH SOME HALF-COCKED THEORY ABOUT HOW IT'S NOT DRAGONS AT ALL AND HIS ONLY SOURCE IS GONNA BE SOME CUTE DRAGON DAME HE MET.
YOU'RE WRONG ABOUT HIM.

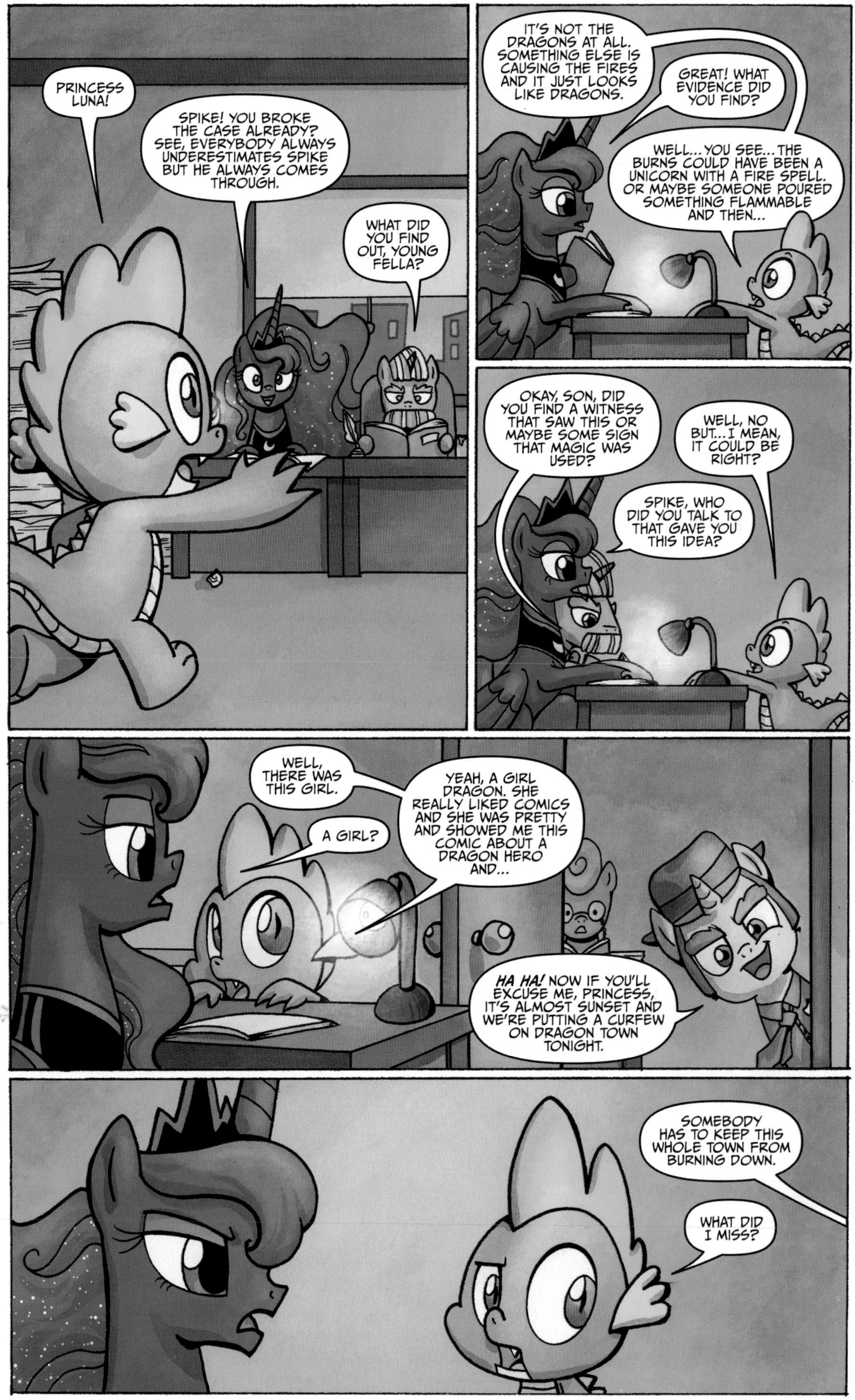
PRINCESS LUNA!
SPIKE! YOU BROKE THE CASE ALREADY? SEE, EVERYBODY ALWAYS UNDERESTIMATES SPIKE BUT HE ALWAYS COMES THROUGH.
WHAT DID YOU FIND OUT, YOUNG FELLA?
IT'S NOT THE DRAGONS AT ALL. SOMETHING ELSE IS CAUSING THE FIRES AND IT JUST LOOKS LIKE DRAGONS.
GREAT! WHAT EVIDENCE DID YOU FIND?
WELL... YOU SEE... THE BURNS COULD HAVE BEEN A UNICORN WITH A FIRE SPELL. OR MAYBE SOMEONE POURED SOMETHING FLAMMABLE AND THEN...
OKAY, SON, DID YOU FIND A WITNESS THAT SAW THIS OR MAYBE SOME SIGN THAT MAGIC WAS USED?
WELL, NO BUT... I MEAN, IT COULD BE RIGHT?
SPIKE, WHO DID YOU TALK TO THAT GAVE YOU THIS IDEA?
WELL, THERE WAS THIS GIRL.
A GIRL?
YEAH, A GIRL DRAGON. SHE REALLY LIKED COMICS AND SHE WAS PRETTY AND SHOWED ME THIS COMIC ABOUT A DRAGON HERO AND...
HA HA! NOW IF YOU'LL EXCUSE ME, PRINCESS, IT'S ALMOST SUNSET AND WE'RE PUTTING A CURFEW ON DRAGON TOWN TONIGHT.
SOMEBODY HAS TO KEEP THIS WHOLE TOWN FROM BURNING DOWN.
WHAT DID I MISS?

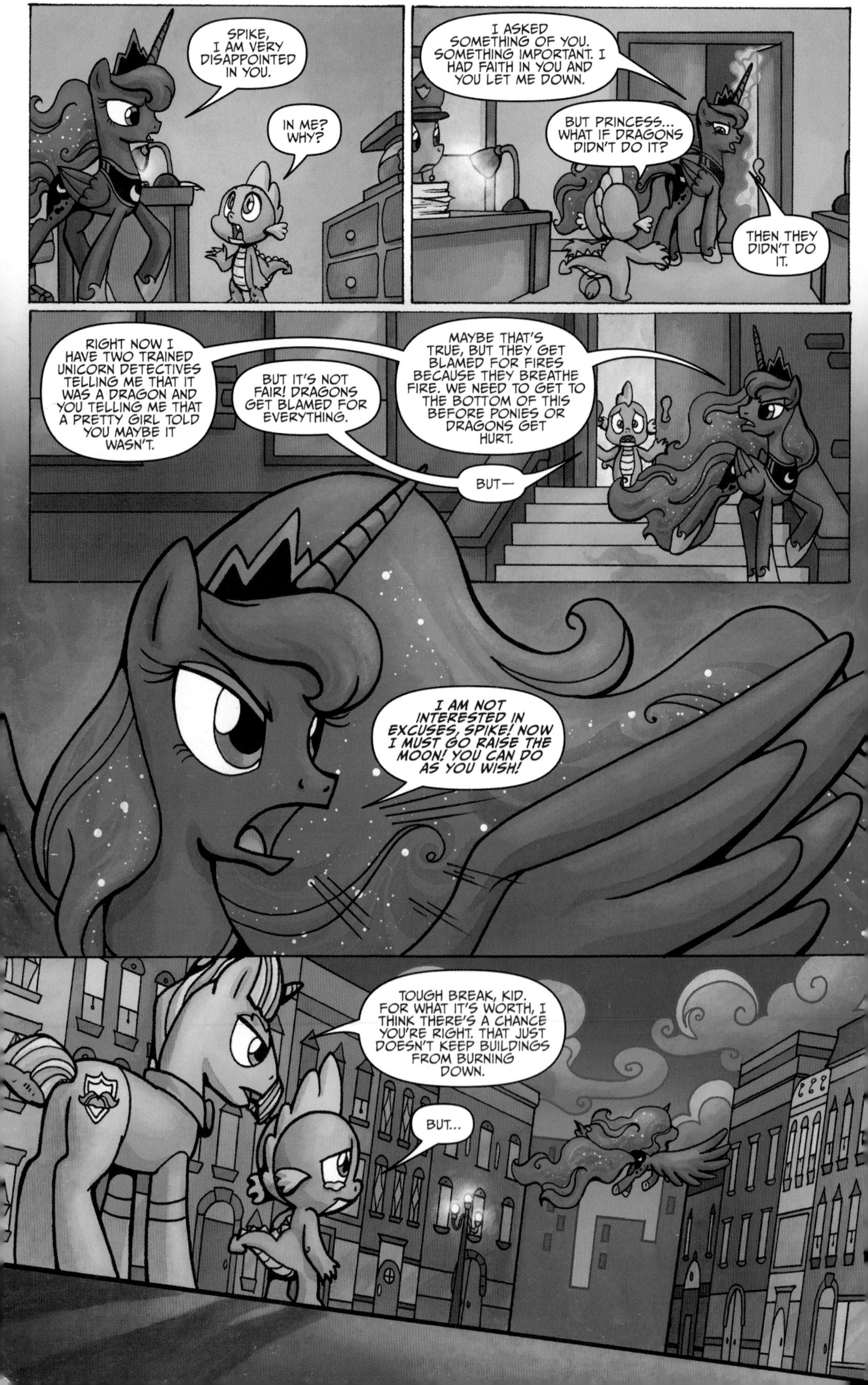
SPIKE, I AM VERY DISAPPOINTED IN YOU.
IN ME? WHY?
I ASKED SOMETHING OF YOU. SOMETHING IMPORTANT. I HAD FAITH IN YOU AND YOU LET ME DOWN.
BUT PRINCESS... WHAT IF DRAGONS DIDN'T DO IT?
THEN THEY DIDN'T DO IT.
RIGHT NOW I HAVE TWO TRAINED UNICORN DETECTIVES TELLING ME THAT IT WAS A DRAGON AND YOU TELLING ME THAT A PRETTY GIRL TOLD YOU MAYBE IT WASN'T.
BUT IT'S NOT FAIR! DRAGONS GET BLAMED FOR EVERYTHING.
MAYBE THAT'S TRUE, BUT THEY GET BLAMED FOR FIRES BECAUSE THEY BREATHE FIRE. WE NEED TO GET TO THE BOTTOM OF THIS BEFORE PONIES OR DRAGONS GET HURT.
BUT—
I AM NOT INTERESTED IN EXCUSES, SPIKE! NOW I MUST GO RAISE THE MOON! YOU CAN DO AS YOU WISH!
TOUGH BREAK, KID. FOR WHAT IT'S WORTH, I THINK THERE'S A CHANCE YOU'RE RIGHT. THAT JUST DOESN'T KEEP BUILDINGS FROM BURNING DOWN.
BUT...

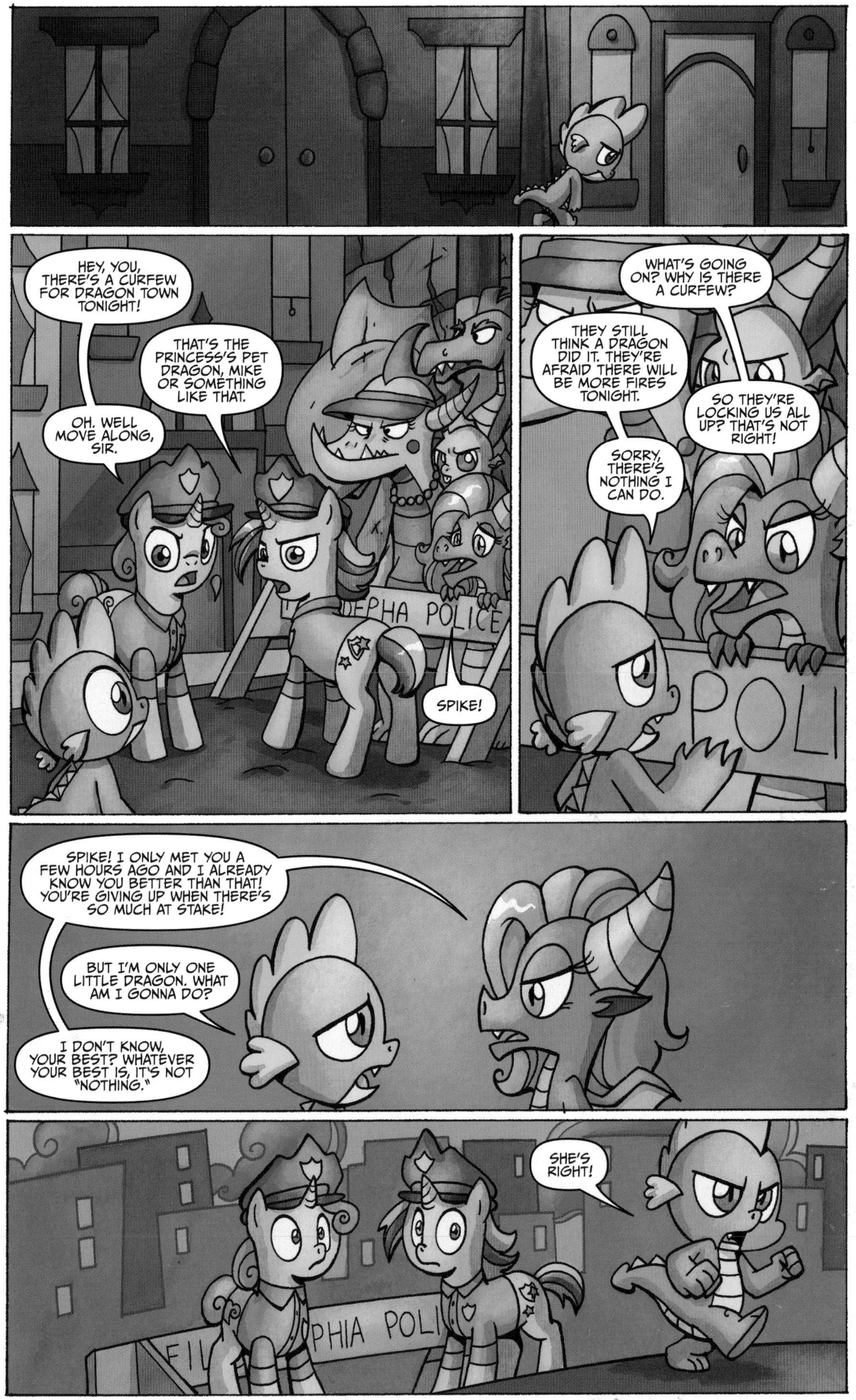

HEY, YOU, THERE'S A CURFEW FOR DRAGON TOWN TONIGHT!
THAT'S THE PRINCESS'S PET DRAGON, MIKE OR SOMETHING LIKE THAT.
OH. WELL MOVE ALONG, SIR.
PHA POLICE
SPIKE!
WHAT'S GOING ON? WHY IS THERE A CURFEW?
THEY STILL THINK A DRAGON DID IT. THEY'RE AFRAID THERE WILL BE MORE FIRES TONIGHT.
SO THEY'RE LOCKING US ALL UP? THAT'S NOT RIGHT!
SORRY, THERE'S NOTHING I CAN DO.
POLI
SPIKE! I ONLY MET YOU A FEW HOURS AGO AND I ALREADY KNOW YOU BETTER THAN THAT! YOU'RE GIVING UP WHEN THERE'S SO MUCH AT STAKE!
BUT I'M ONLY ONE LITTLE DRAGON. WHAT AM I GONNA DO?
I DON'T KNOW, YOUR BEST? WHATEVER YOUR BEST IS, IT'S NOT "NOTHING."
SHE'S RIGHT!
FIL PHIA POLI

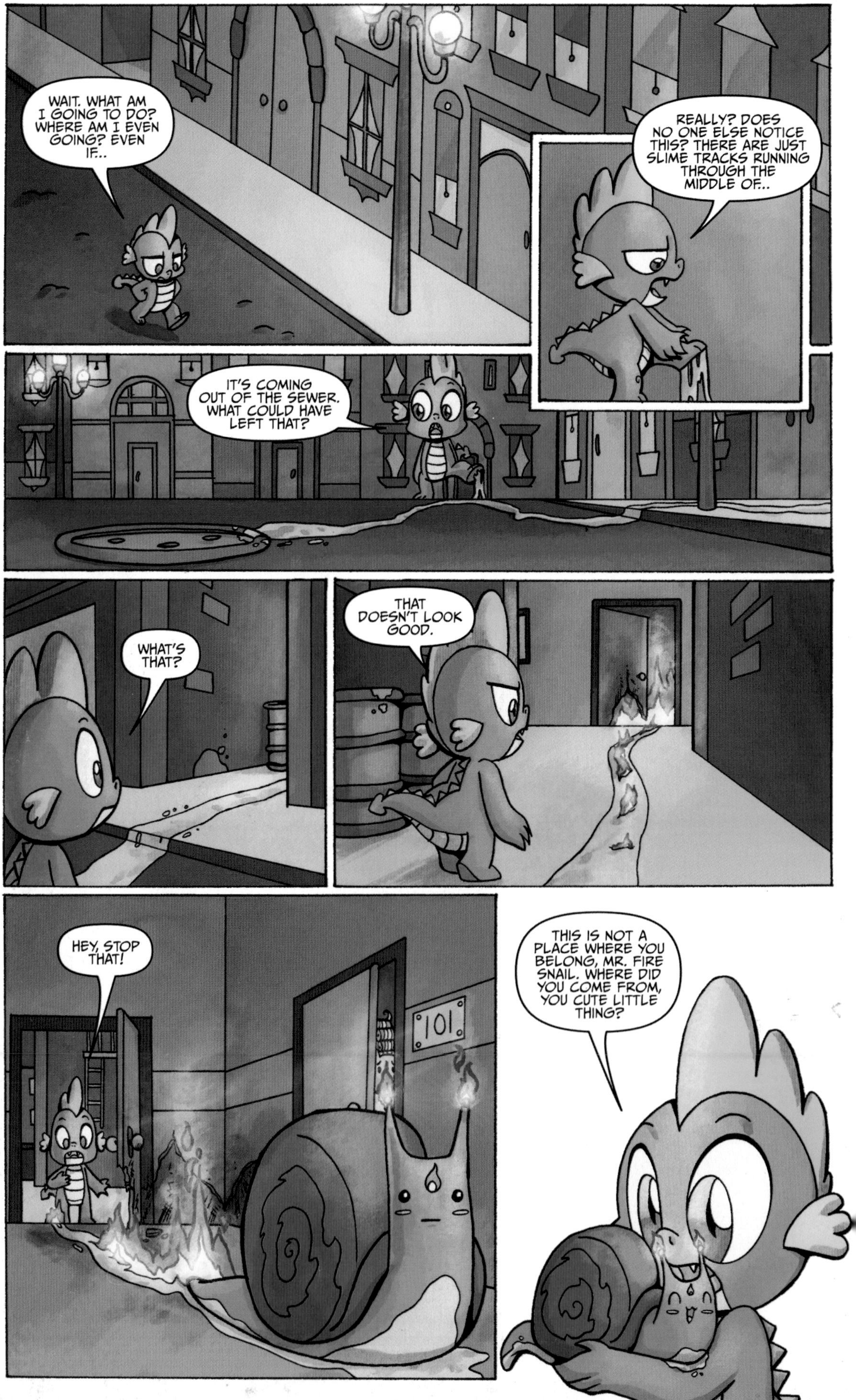
WAIT. WHAT AM I GOING TO DO? WHERE AM I EVEN GOING? EVEN IF...
REALLY? DOES NO ONE ELSE NOTICE THIS? THERE ARE JUST SLIME TRACKS RUNNING THROUGH THE MIDDLE OF...
IT'S COMING OUT OF THE SEWER. WHAT COULD HAVE LEFT THAT?
WHAT'S THAT?
THAT DOESN'T LOOK GOOD.
HEY, STOP THAT!
101
THIS IS NOT A PLACE WHERE YOU BELONG, MR. FIRE SNAIL. WHERE DID YOU COME FROM, YOU CUTE LITTLE THING?

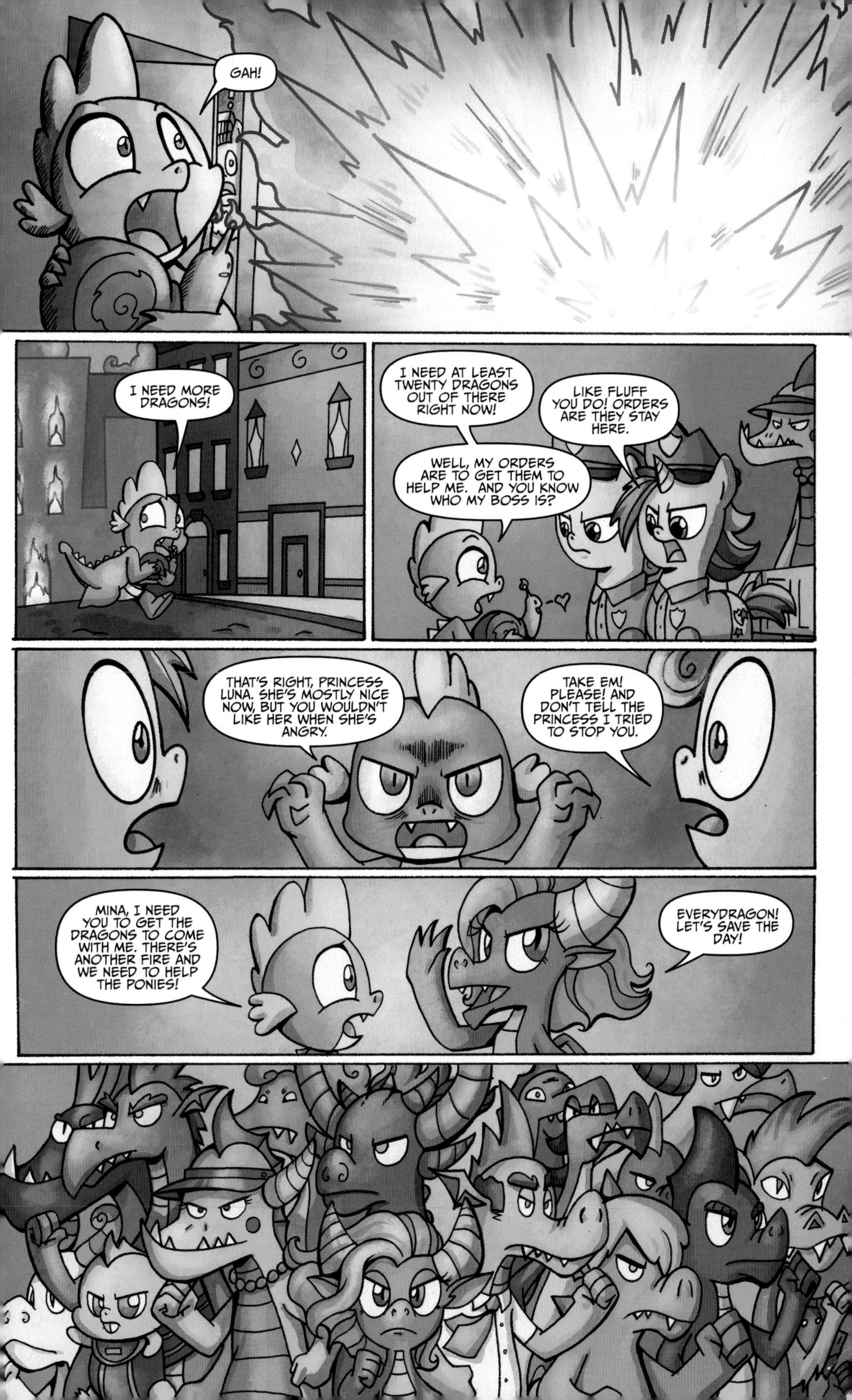
GAH!
I NEED MORE DRAGONS!
I NEED AT LEAST TWENTY DRAGONS OUT OF THERE RIGHT NOW!
LIKE FLUFF YOU DO! ORDERS ARE THEY STAY HERE.
WELL, MY ORDERS ARE TO GET THEM TO HELP ME. AND YOU KNOW WHO MY BOSS IS?
THAT'S RIGHT, PRINCESS LUNA. SHE'S MOSTLY NICE NOW, BUT YOU WOULDN'T LIKE HER WHEN SHE'S ANGRY.
TAKE EM! PLEASE! AND DON'T TELL THE PRINCESS I TRIED TO STOP YOU.
MINA, I NEED YOU TO GET THE DRAGONS TO COME WITH ME. THERE'S ANOTHER FIRE AND WE NEED TO HELP THE PONIES!
EVERYDRAGON! LET'S SAVE THE DAY!

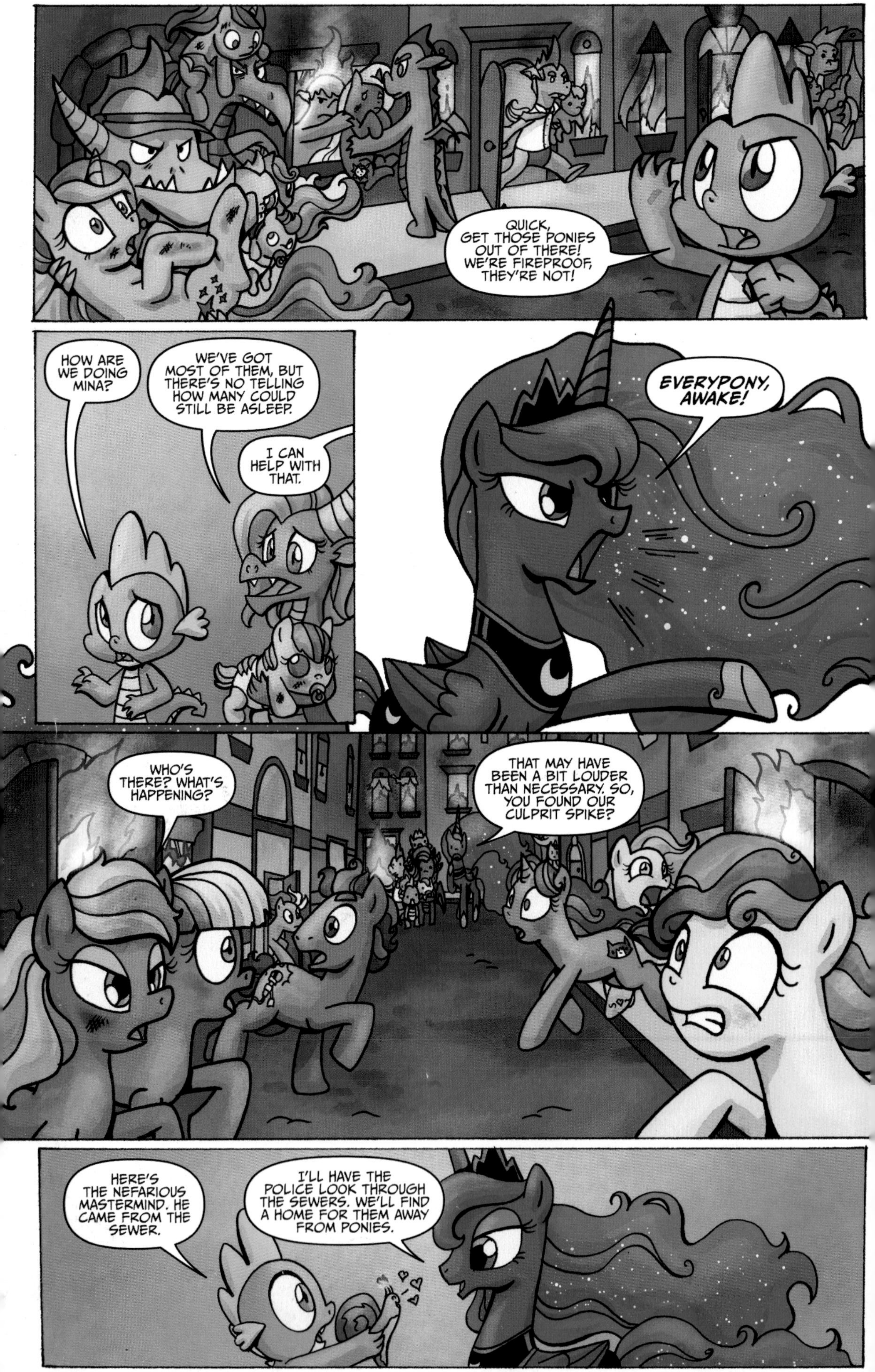
QUICK, GET THOSE PONIES OUT OF THERE! WE'RE FIREPROOF, THEY'RE NOT!
HOW ARE WE DOING MINA?
WE'VE GOT MOST OF THEM, BUT THERE'S NO TELLING HOW MANY COULD STILL BE ASLEEP.
I CAN HELP WITH THAT.
EVERYPONY, AWAKE!
WHO'S THERE? WHAT'S HAPPENING?
THAT MAY HAVE BEEN A BIT LOUDER THAN NECESSARY. SO, YOU FOUND OUR CULPRIT SPIKE?
HERE'S THE NEFARIOUS MASTERMIND. HE CAME FROM THE SEWER.
I'LL HAVE THE POLICE LOOK THROUGH THE SEWERS. WE'LL FIND A HOME FOR THEM AWAY FROM PONIES.

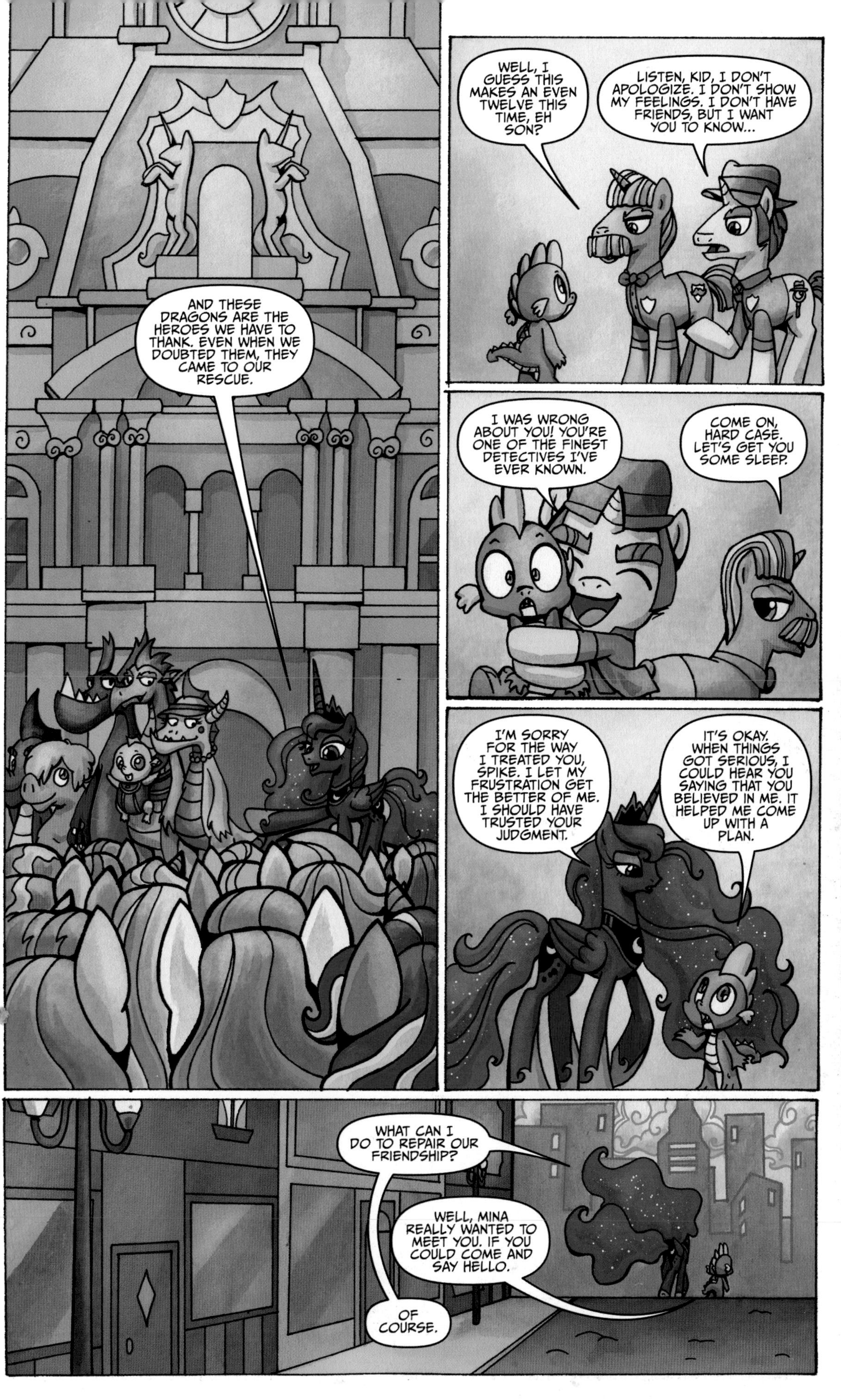
AND THESE DRAGONS ARE THE HEROES WE HAVE TO THANK. EVEN WHEN WE DOUBTED THEM, THEY CAME TO OUR RESCUE.
WELL, I GUESS THIS MAKES AN EVEN TWELVE THIS TIME, EH SON?
LISTEN, KID, I DON'T APOLOGIZE. I DON'T SHOW MY FEELINGS. I DON'T HAVE FRIENDS, BUT I WANT YOU TO KNOW...
I WAS WRONG ABOUT YOU! YOU'RE ONE OF THE FINEST DETECTIVES I'VE EVER KNOWN.
COME ON, HARD CASE. LET'S GET YOU SOME SLEEP.
I'M SORRY FOR THE WAY I TREATED YOU, SPIKE. I LET MY FRUSTRATION GET THE BETTER OF ME. I SHOULD HAVE TRUSTED YOUR JUDGMENT.
IT'S OKAY. WHEN THINGS GOT SERIOUS, I COULD HEAR YOU SAYING THAT YOU BELIEVED IN ME. IT HELPED ME COME UP WITH A PLAN.
WHAT CAN I DO TO REPAIR OUR FRIENDSHIP?
WELL, MINA REALLY WANTED TO MEET YOU. IF YOU COULD COME AND SAY HELLO.
OF COURSE.

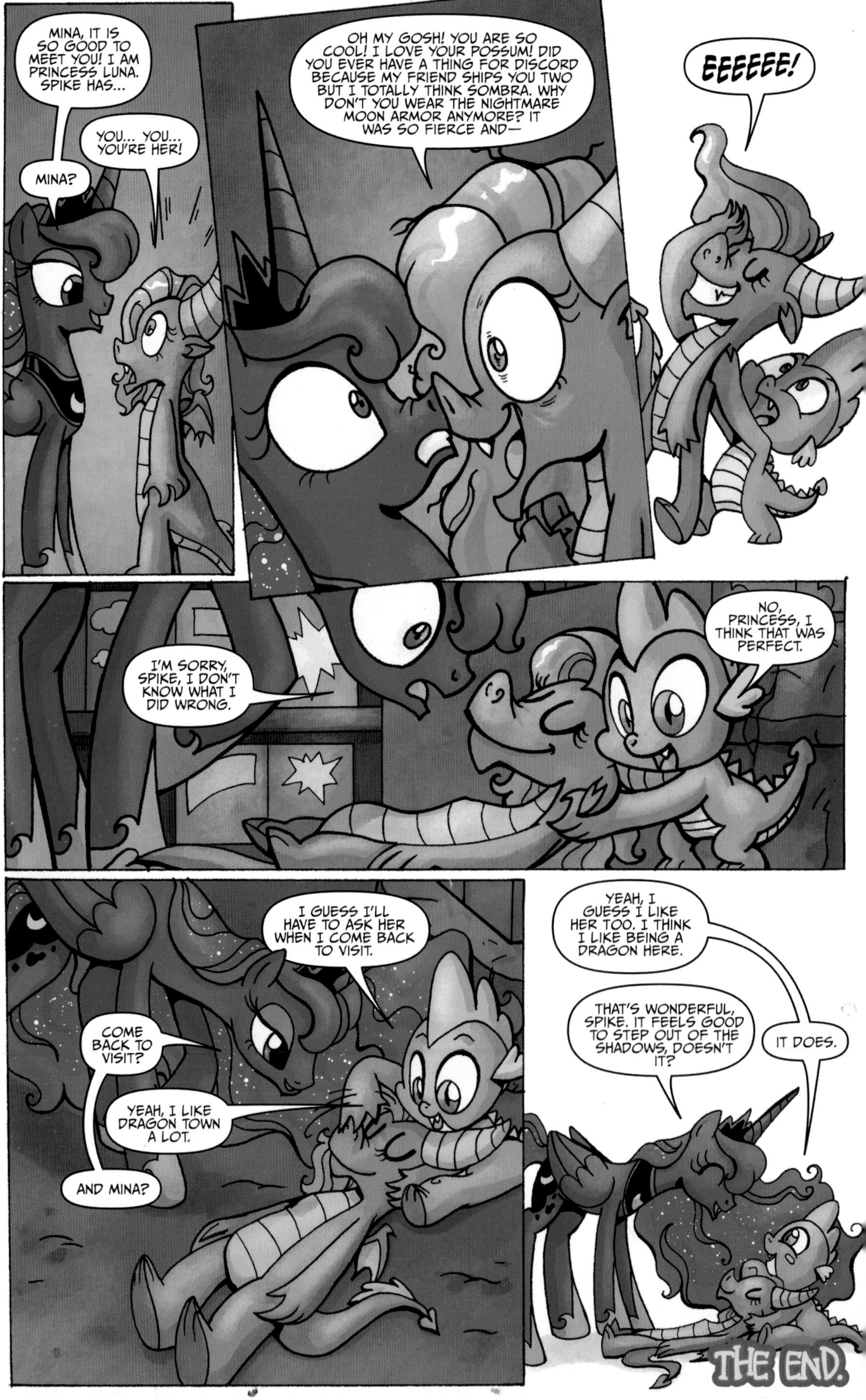
MINA, IT IS SO GOOD TO MEET YOU! I AM PRINCESS LUNA. SPIKE HAS...
MINA?
YOU... YOU... YOU'RE HER!
OH MY GOSH! YOU ARE SO COOL! I LOVE YOUR POSSUM! DID YOU EVER HAVE A THING FOR DISCORD BECAUSE MY FRIEND SHIPS YOU TWO BUT I TOTALLY THINK SOMBRA. WHY DON'T YOU WEAR THE NIGHTMARE MOON ARMOR ANYMORE? IT WAS SO FIERCE AND—
EEEEEE!
I'M SORRY, SPIKE, I DON'T KNOW WHAT I DID WRONG.
NO, PRINCESS, I THINK THAT WAS PERFECT.
I GUESS I'LL HAVE TO ASK HER WHEN I COME BACK TO VISIT.
COME BACK TO VISIT?
YEAH, I LIKE DRAGON TOWN A LOT.
AND MINA?
YEAH, I GUESS I LIKE HER TOO. I THINK I LIKE BEING A DRAGON HERE.
THAT'S WONDERFUL, SPIKE. IT FEELS GOOD TO STEP OUT OF THE SHADOWS, DOESN'T IT?
IT DOES.
THE END.

my LITTLE PONY

FRIENDS FOREVER

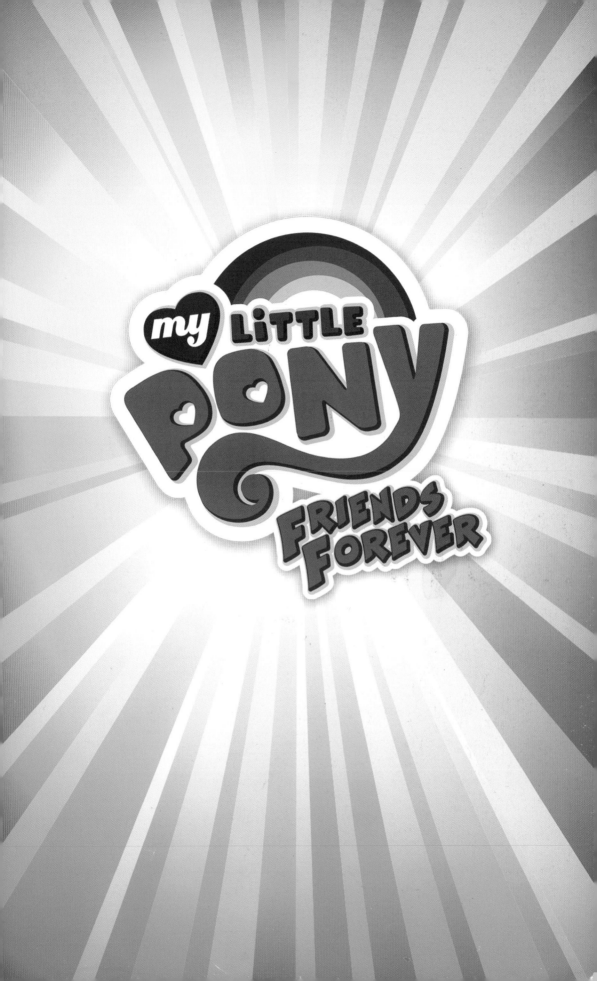

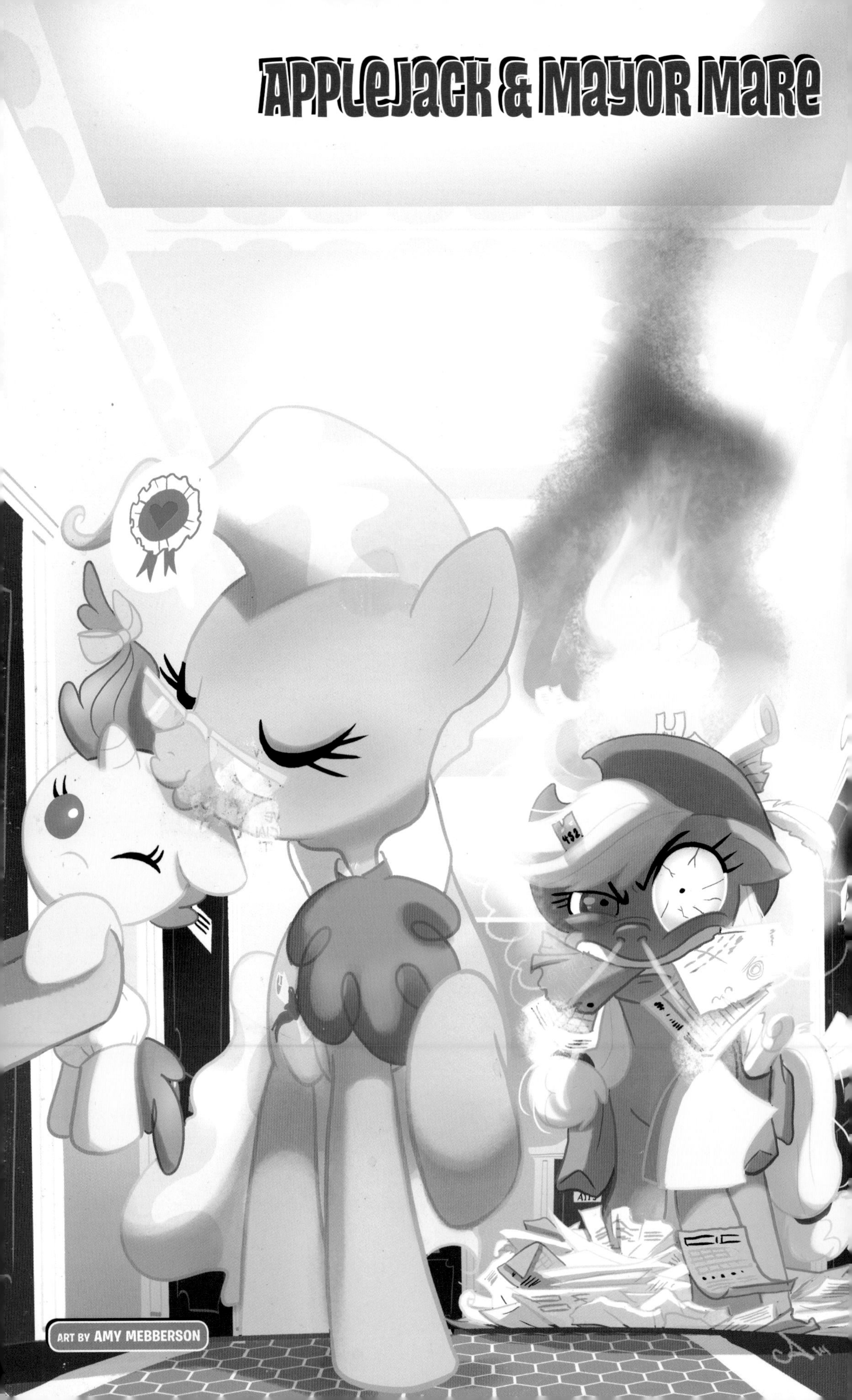
Applejack & Mayor Mare
ART BY AMY MEBBERSON

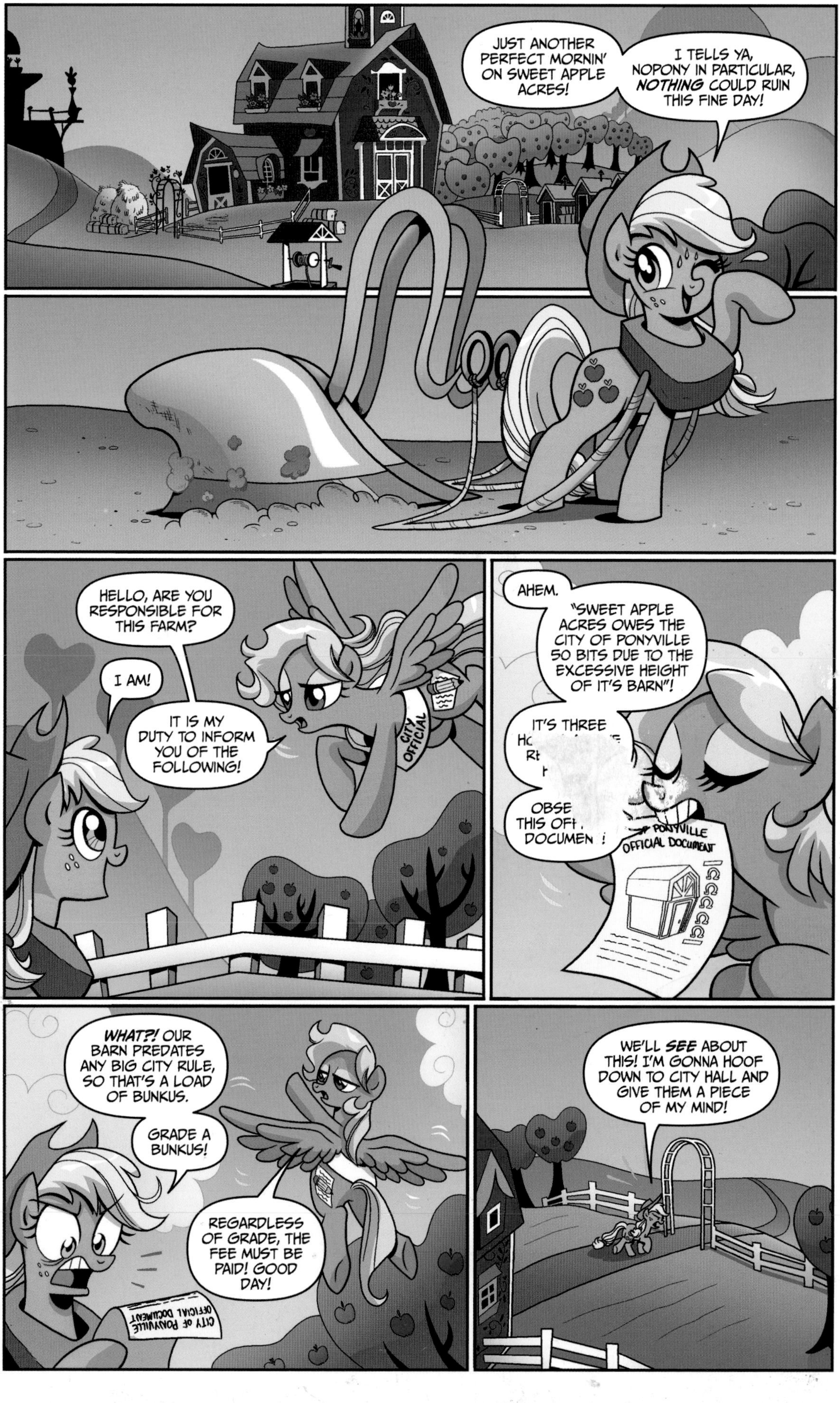
JUST ANOTHER PERFECT MORNIN' ON SWEET APPLE ACRES!
I TELLS YA, NOPONY IN PARTICULAR, ***NOTHING*** COULD RUIN THIS FINE DAY!
HELLO, ARE YOU RESPONSIBLE FOR THIS FARM?
I AM!
IT IS MY DUTY TO INFORM YOU OF THE FOLLOWING!
CITY OFFICIAL
AHEM.
"SWEET APPLE ACRES OWES THE CITY OF PONYVILLE 50 BITS DUE TO THE EXCESSIVE HEIGHT OF IT'S BARN"!
IT'S THREE
PONYVILLE OFFICIAL DOCUMENT
WHAT?! OUR BARN PREDATES ANY BIG CITY RULE, SO THAT'S A LOAD OF BUNKUS.
GRADE A BUNKUS!
REGARDLESS OF GRADE, THE FEE MUST BE PAID! GOOD DAY!
CITY OF PONYVILLE OFFICIAL DOCUMENT
WE'LL ***SEE*** ABOUT THIS! I'M GONNA HOOF DOWN TO CITY HALL AND GIVE THEM A PIECE OF MY MIND!

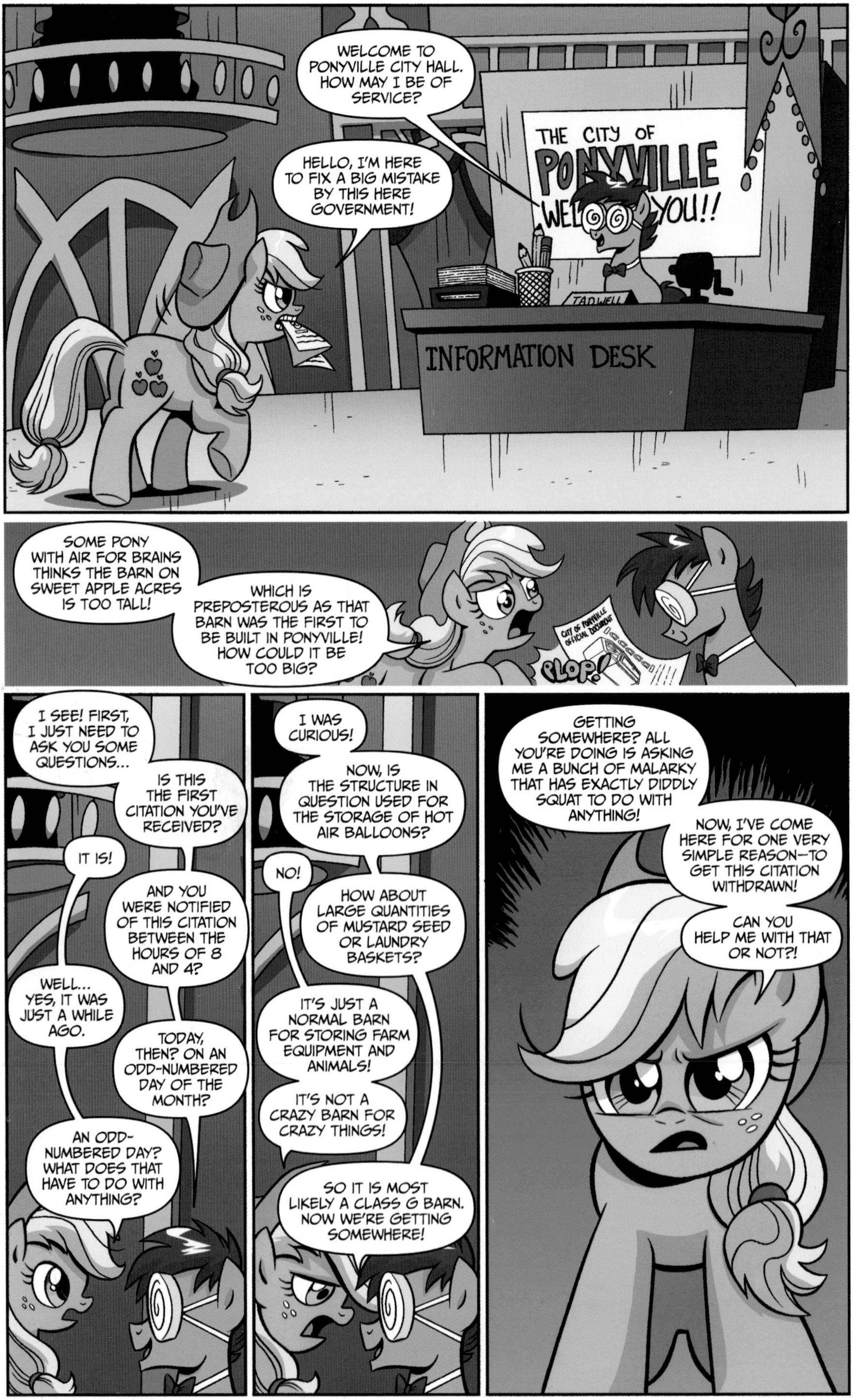
WELCOME TO PONYVILLE CITY HALL. HOW MAY I BE OF SERVICE?
HELLO, I'M HERE TO FIX A BIG MISTAKE BY THIS HERE GOVERNMENT!
THE CITY OF PONYVILLE
INFORMATION DESK
TADWELL
SOME PONY WITH AIR FOR BRAINS THINKS THE BARN ON SWEET APPLE ACRES IS TOO TALL!
WHICH IS PREPOSTEROUS AS THAT BARN WAS THE FIRST TO BE BUILT IN PONYVILLE! HOW COULD IT BE TOO BIG?
CITY OF PONYVILLE OFFICIAL DOCUMENT
PLOP!
I SEE! FIRST, I JUST NEED TO ASK YOU SOME QUESTIONS...
IS THIS THE FIRST CITATION YOU'VE RECEIVED?
IT IS!
AND YOU WERE NOTIFIED OF THIS CITATION BETWEEN THE HOURS OF 8 AND 4?
WELL... YES, IT WAS JUST A WHILE AGO.
TODAY, THEN? ON AN ODD-NUMBERED DAY OF THE MONTH?
AN ODD-NUMBERED DAY? WHAT DOES THAT HAVE TO DO WITH ANYTHING?
I WAS CURIOUS!
NOW, IS THE STRUCTURE IN QUESTION USED FOR THE STORAGE OF HOT AIR BALLOONS?
NO!
HOW ABOUT LARGE QUANTITIES OF MUSTARD SEED OR LAUNDRY BASKETS?
IT'S JUST A NORMAL BARN FOR STORING FARM EQUIPMENT AND ANIMALS!
IT'S NOT A CRAZY BARN FOR CRAZY THINGS!
SO IT IS MOST LIKELY A CLASS G BARN. NOW WE'RE GETTING SOMEWHERE!
GETTING SOMEWHERE? ALL YOU'RE DOING IS ASKING ME A BUNCH OF MALARKY THAT HAS EXACTLY DIDDLY SQUAT TO DO WITH ANYTHING!
NOW, I'VE COME HERE FOR ONE VERY SIMPLE REASON—TO GET THIS CITATION WITHDRAWN!
CAN YOU HELP ME WITH THAT OR NOT?!

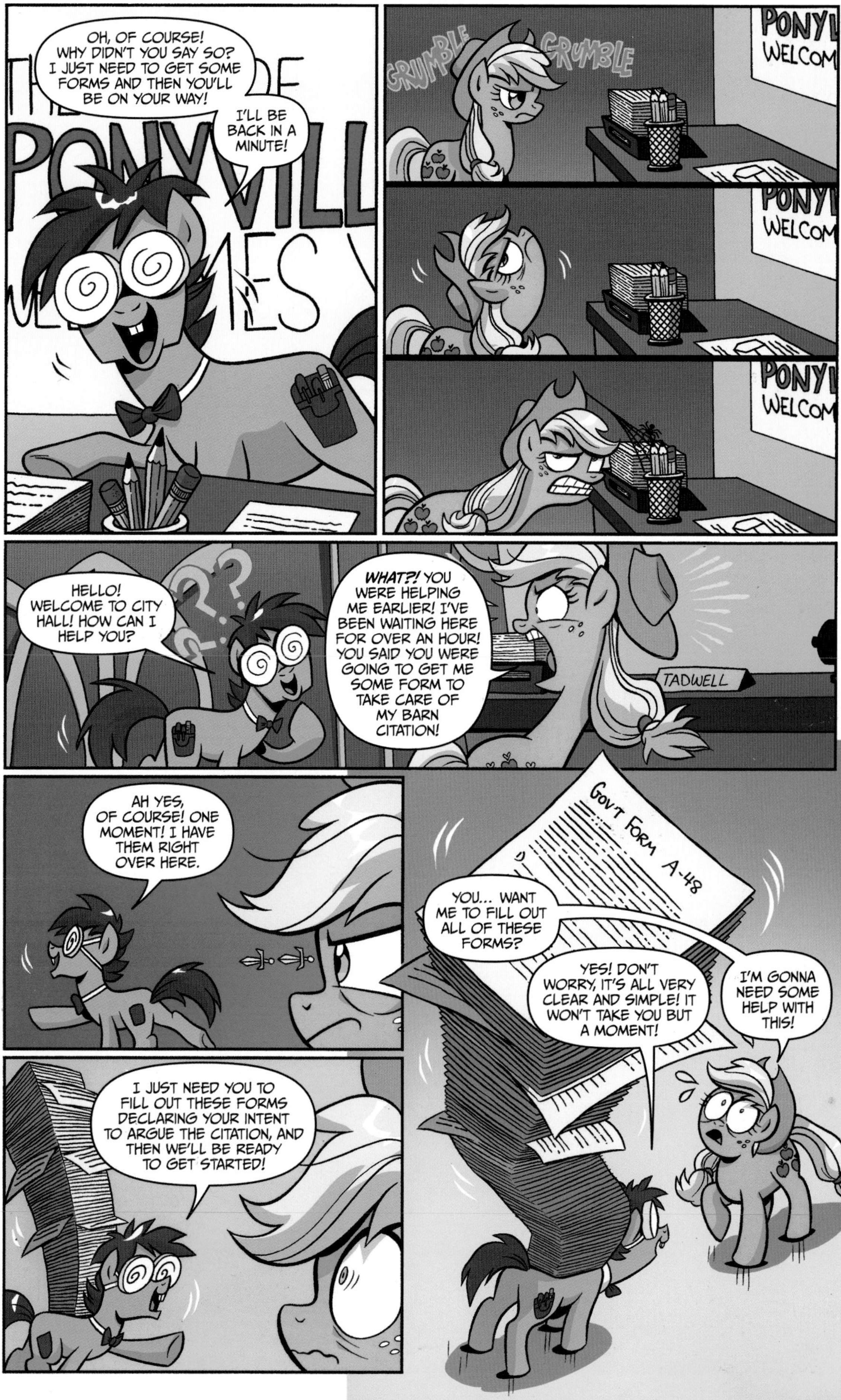
OH, OF COURSE! WHY DIDN'T YOU SAY SO? I JUST NEED TO GET SOME FORMS AND THEN YOU'LL BE ON YOUR WAY!
I'LL BE BACK IN A MINUTE!
GRUMBLE
GRUMBLE
HELLO! WELCOME TO CITY HALL! HOW CAN I HELP YOU?
WHAT?! YOU WERE HELPING ME EARLIER! I'VE BEEN WAITING HERE FOR OVER AN HOUR! YOU SAID YOU WERE GOING TO GET ME SOME FORM TO TAKE CARE OF MY BARN CITATION!
TADWELL
AH YES, OF COURSE! ONE MOMENT! I HAVE THEM RIGHT OVER HERE.
I JUST NEED YOU TO FILL OUT THESE FORMS DECLARING YOUR INTENT TO ARGUE THE CITATION, AND THEN WE'LL BE READY TO GET STARTED!
GOV'T FORM A-48
YOU... WANT ME TO FILL OUT ALL OF THESE FORMS?
YES! DON'T WORRY, IT'S ALL VERY CLEAR AND SIMPLE! IT WON'T TAKE YOU BUT A MOMENT!
I'M GONNA NEED SOME HELP WITH THIS!

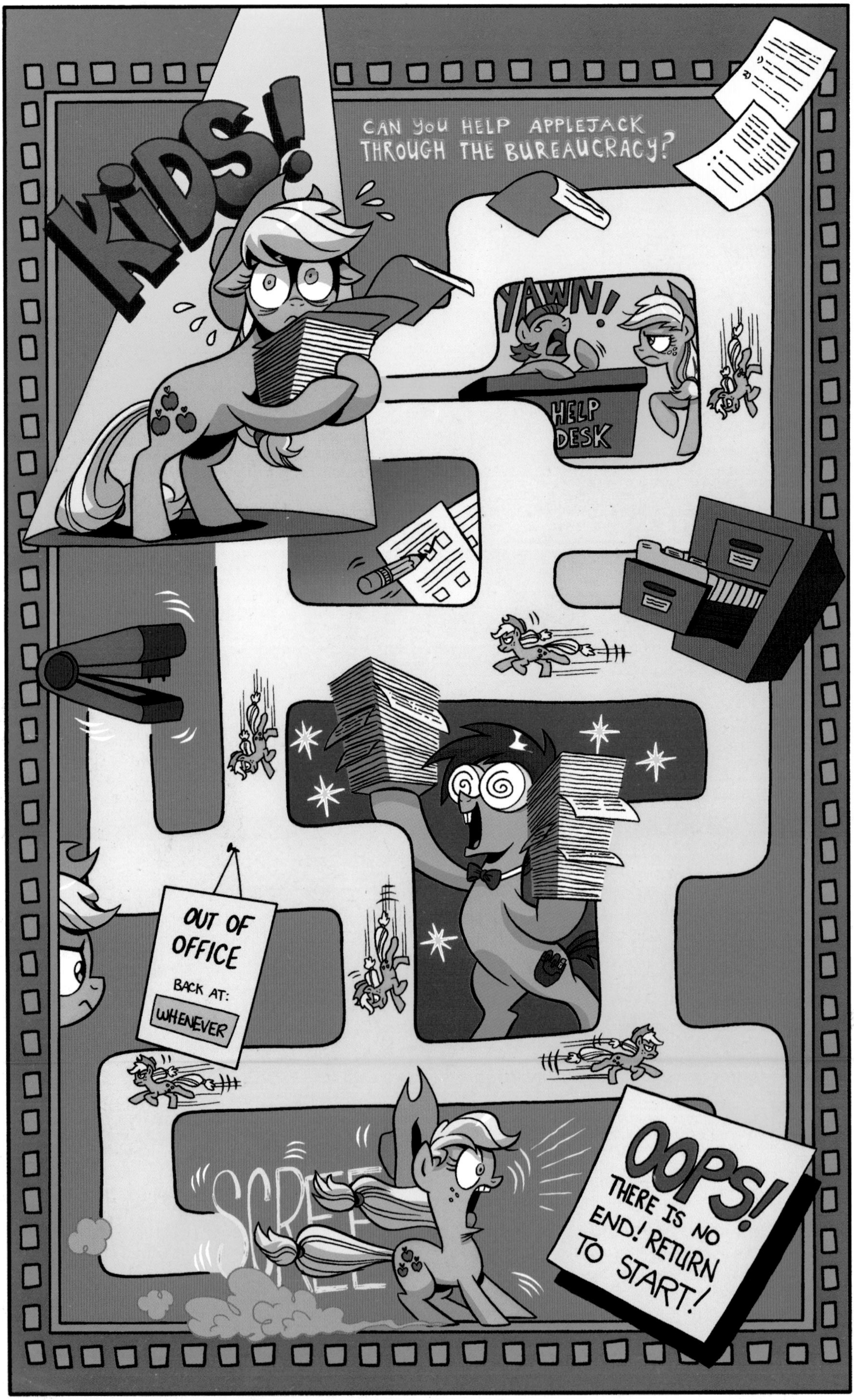
KIDS!
CAN YOU HELP APPLEJACK THROUGH THE BUREAUCRACY?
YAWN!
HELP DESK
OUT OF OFFICE
BACK AT:
WHENEVER
SCREEE
OOPS! THERE IS NO END! RETURN TO START!

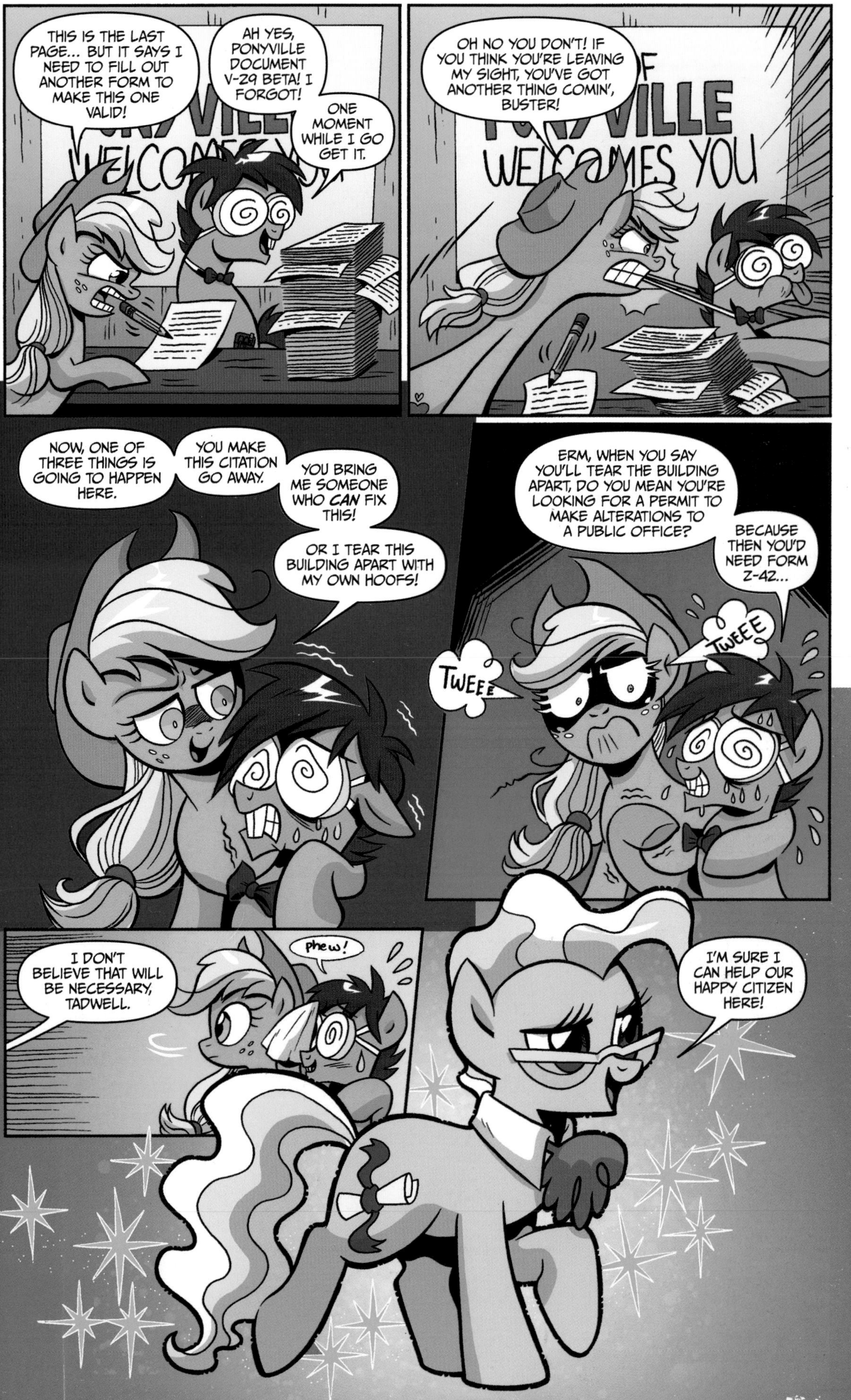
THIS IS THE LAST PAGE... BUT IT SAYS I NEED TO FILL OUT ANOTHER FORM TO MAKE THIS ONE VALID!
AH YES, PONYVILLE DOCUMENT V-29 BETA! I FORGOT!
ONE MOMENT WHILE I GO GET IT.
OH NO YOU DON'T! IF YOU THINK YOU'RE LEAVING MY SIGHT, YOU'VE GOT ANOTHER THING COMIN', BUSTER!
NOW, ONE OF THREE THINGS IS GOING TO HAPPEN HERE.
YOU MAKE THIS CITATION GO AWAY.
YOU BRING ME SOMEONE WHO CAN FIX THIS!
OR I TEAR THIS BUILDING APART WITH MY OWN HOOFS!
ERM, WHEN YOU SAY YOU'LL TEAR THE BUILDING APART, DO YOU MEAN YOU'RE LOOKING FOR A PERMIT TO MAKE ALTERATIONS TO A PUBLIC OFFICE?
BECAUSE THEN YOU'D NEED FORM Z-42...
TWEEE
TWEEE
I DON'T BELIEVE THAT WILL BE NECESSARY, TADWELL.
phew!
I'M SURE I CAN HELP OUR HAPPY CITIZEN HERE!

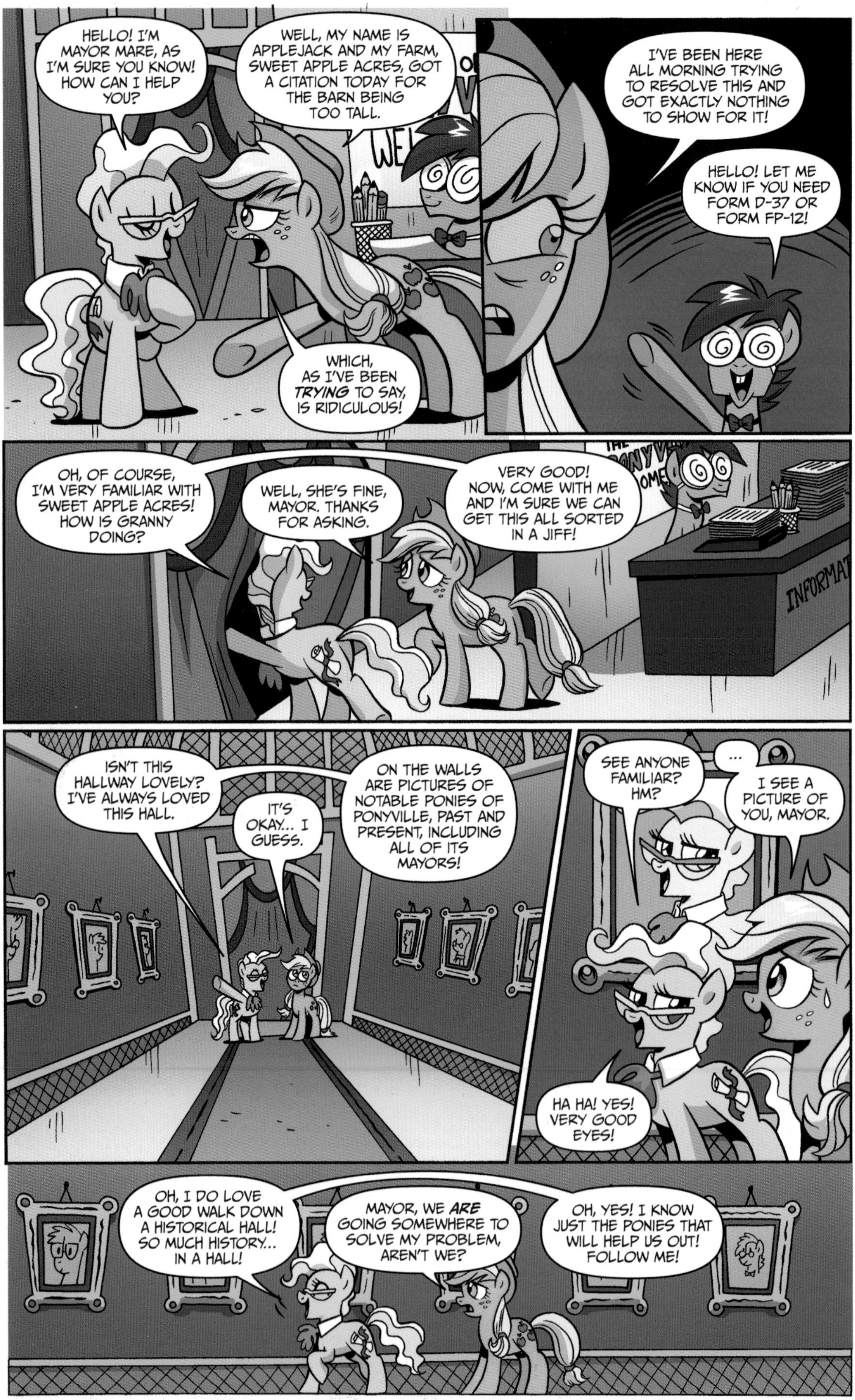
HELLO! I'M MAYOR MARE, AS I'M SURE YOU KNOW! HOW CAN I HELP YOU?
WELL, MY NAME IS APPLEJACK AND MY FARM, SWEET APPLE ACRES, GOT A CITATION TODAY FOR THE BARN BEING TOO TALL.
WHICH, AS I'VE BEEN *TRYING* TO SAY, IS RIDICULOUS!
I'VE BEEN HERE ALL MORNING TRYING TO RESOLVE THIS AND GOT EXACTLY NOTHING TO SHOW FOR IT!
HELLO! LET ME KNOW IF YOU NEED FORM D-37 OR FORM FP-12!
OH, OF COURSE, I'M VERY FAMILIAR WITH SWEET APPLE ACRES! HOW IS GRANNY DOING?
WELL, SHE'S FINE, MAYOR. THANKS FOR ASKING.
VERY GOOD! NOW, COME WITH ME AND I'M SURE WE CAN GET THIS ALL SORTED IN A JIFF!
INFORMAT
ISN'T THIS HALLWAY LOVELY? I'VE ALWAYS LOVED THIS HALL.
IT'S OKAY... I GUESS.
ON THE WALLS ARE PICTURES OF NOTABLE PONIES OF PONYVILLE, PAST AND PRESENT, INCLUDING ALL OF ITS MAYORS!
SEE ANYONE FAMILIAR? HM?
...
I SEE A PICTURE OF YOU, MAYOR.
HA HA! YES! VERY GOOD EYES!
OH, I DO LOVE A GOOD WALK DOWN A HISTORICAL HALL! SO MUCH HISTORY... IN A HALL!
MAYOR, WE *ARE* GOING SOMEWHERE TO SOLVE MY PROBLEM, AREN'T WE?
OH, YES! I KNOW JUST THE PONIES THAT WILL HELP US OUT! FOLLOW ME!

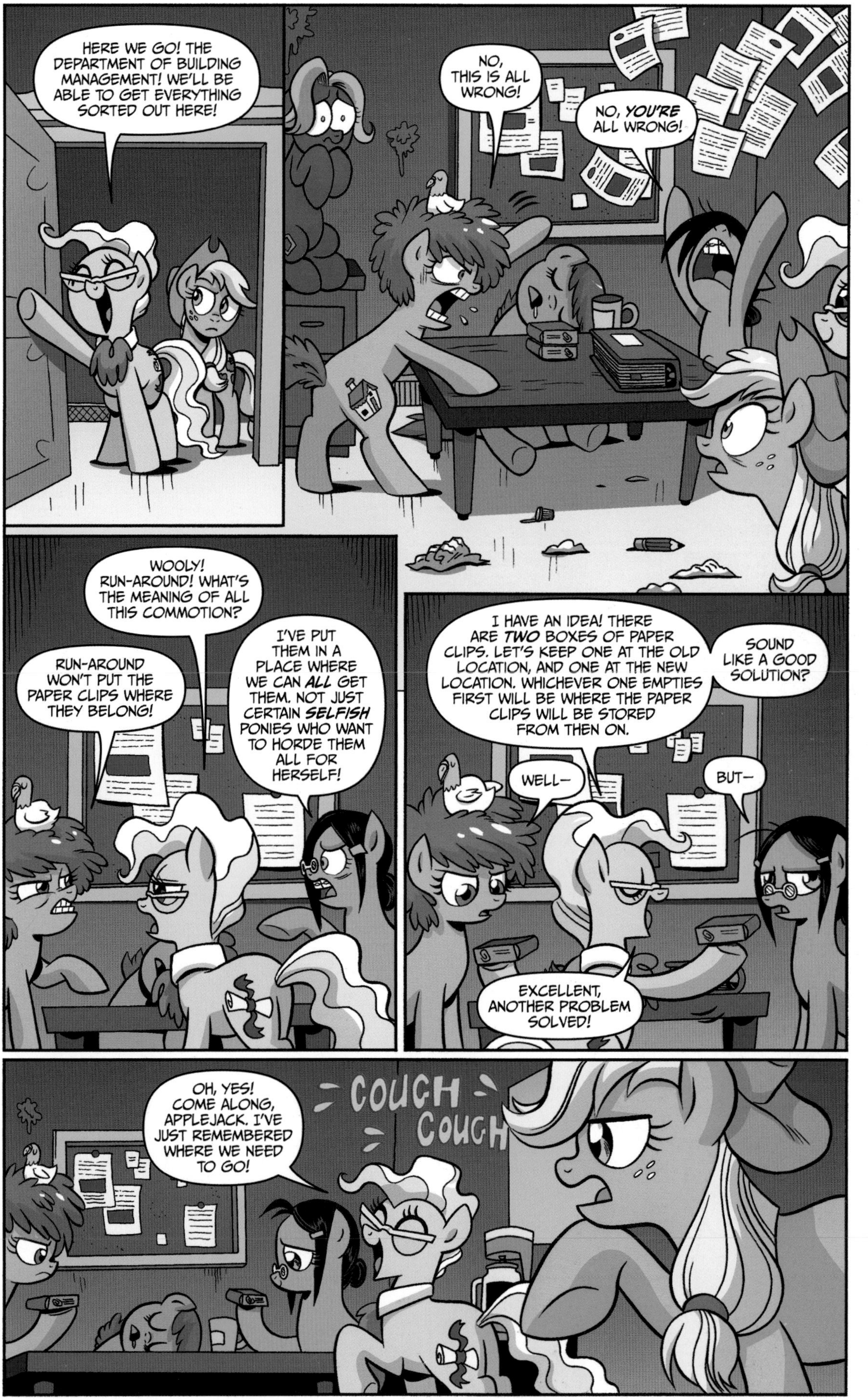
HERE WE GO! THE DEPARTMENT OF BUILDING MANAGEMENT! WE'LL BE ABLE TO GET EVERYTHING SORTED OUT HERE!
NO, THIS IS ALL WRONG!
NO, *YOU'RE* ALL WRONG!
WOOLY! RUN-AROUND! WHAT'S THE MEANING OF ALL THIS COMMOTION?
RUN-AROUND WON'T PUT THE PAPER CLIPS WHERE THEY BELONG!
I'VE PUT THEM IN A PLACE WHERE WE CAN *ALL* GET THEM. NOT JUST CERTAIN *SELFISH* PONIES WHO WANT TO HORDE THEM ALL FOR HERSELF!
I HAVE AN IDEA! THERE ARE *TWO* BOXES OF PAPER CLIPS. LET'S KEEP ONE AT THE OLD LOCATION, AND ONE AT THE NEW LOCATION. WHICHEVER ONE EMPTIES FIRST WILL BE WHERE THE PAPER CLIPS WILL BE STORED FROM THEN ON.
SOUND LIKE A GOOD SOLUTION?
WELL–
BUT–
EXCELLENT, ANOTHER PROBLEM SOLVED!
OH, YES! COME ALONG, APPLEJACK. I'VE JUST REMEMBERED WHERE WE NEED TO GO!
COUGH
COUGH

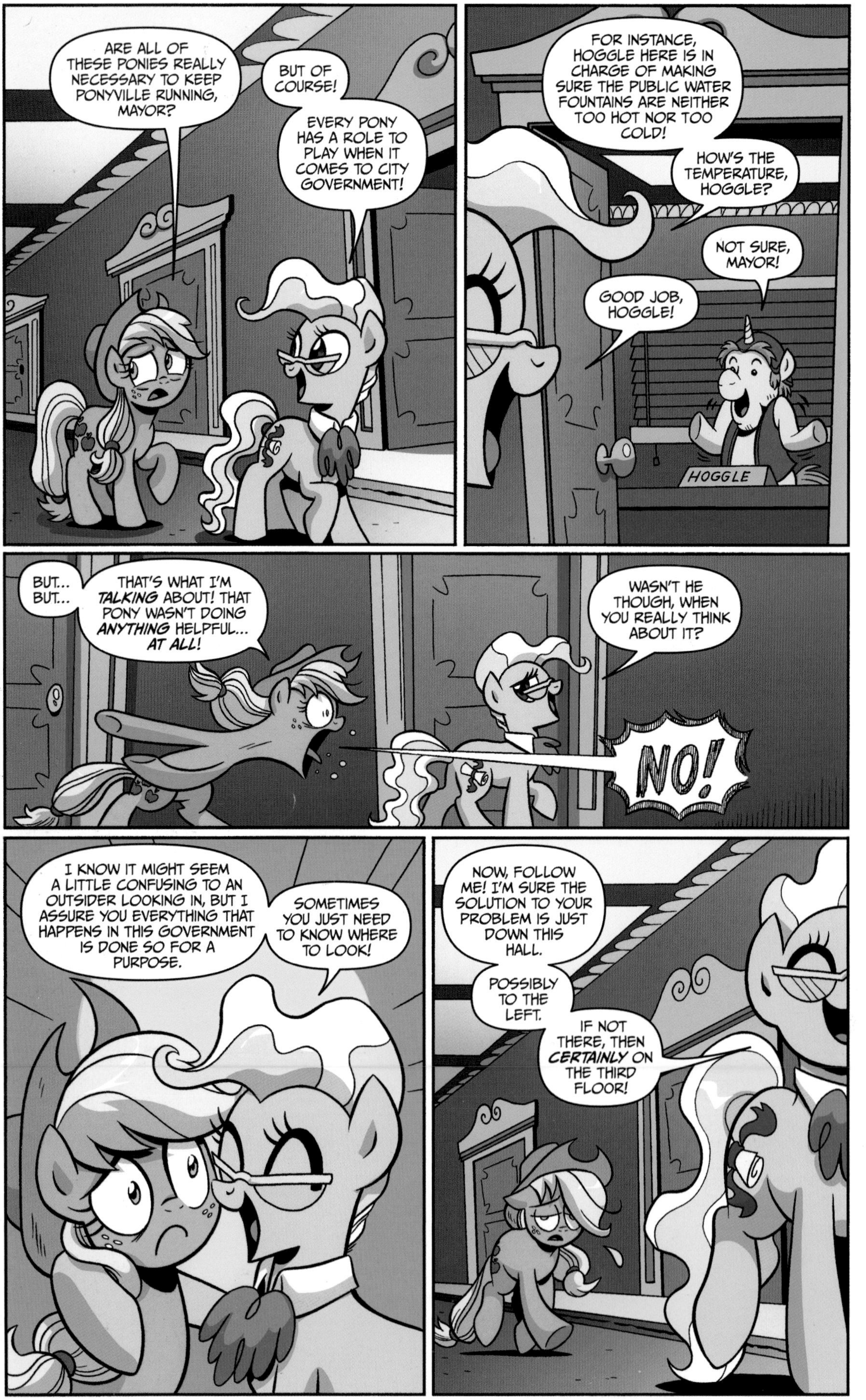
ARE ALL OF THESE PONIES REALLY NECESSARY TO KEEP PONYVILLE RUNNING, MAYOR?
BUT OF COURSE!
EVERY PONY HAS A ROLE TO PLAY WHEN IT COMES TO CITY GOVERNMENT!
FOR INSTANCE, HOGGLE HERE IS IN CHARGE OF MAKING SURE THE PUBLIC WATER FOUNTAINS ARE NEITHER TOO HOT NOR TOO COLD!
HOW'S THE TEMPERATURE, HOGGLE?
NOT SURE, MAYOR!
GOOD JOB, HOGGLE!
HOGGLE
BUT... BUT...
THAT'S WHAT I'M *TALKING* ABOUT! THAT PONY WASN'T DOING *ANYTHING* HELPFUL... *AT ALL*!
WASN'T HE THOUGH, WHEN YOU REALLY THINK ABOUT IT?
NO!
I KNOW IT MIGHT SEEM A LITTLE CONFUSING TO AN OUTSIDER LOOKING IN, BUT I ASSURE YOU EVERYTHING THAT HAPPENS IN THIS GOVERNMENT IS DONE SO FOR A PURPOSE.
SOMETIMES YOU JUST NEED TO KNOW WHERE TO LOOK!
NOW, FOLLOW ME! I'M SURE THE SOLUTION TO YOUR PROBLEM IS JUST DOWN THIS HALL.
POSSIBLY TO THE LEFT.
IF NOT THERE, THEN *CERTAINLY* ON THE THIRD FLOOR!

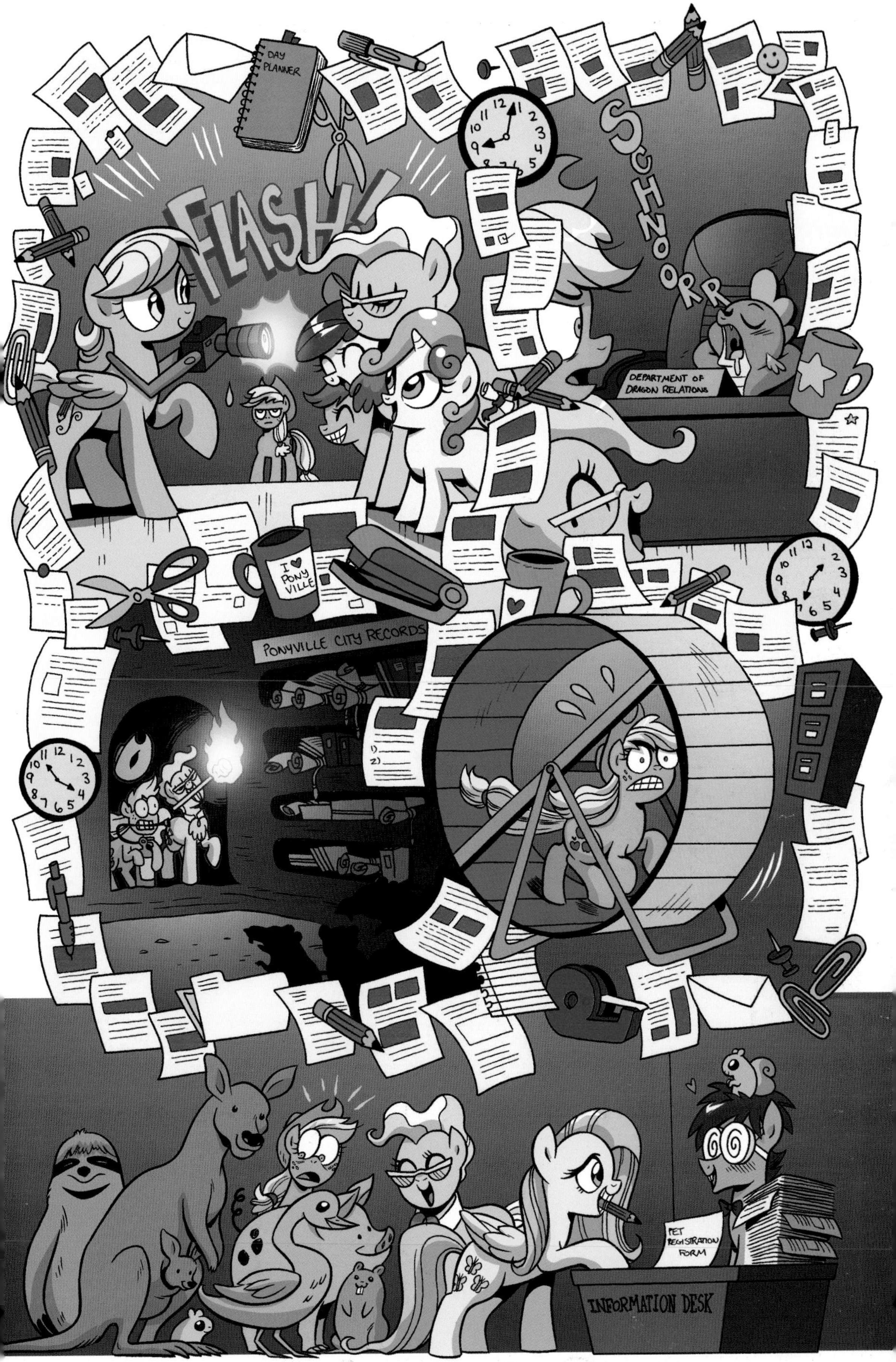

DAY PLANNER
FLASH!
SCHNOORR
DEPARTMENT OF DRAGON RELATIONS
I ♥ PONY VILLE
PONYVILLE CITY RECORDS
PET REGISTRATION FORM
INFORMATION DESK

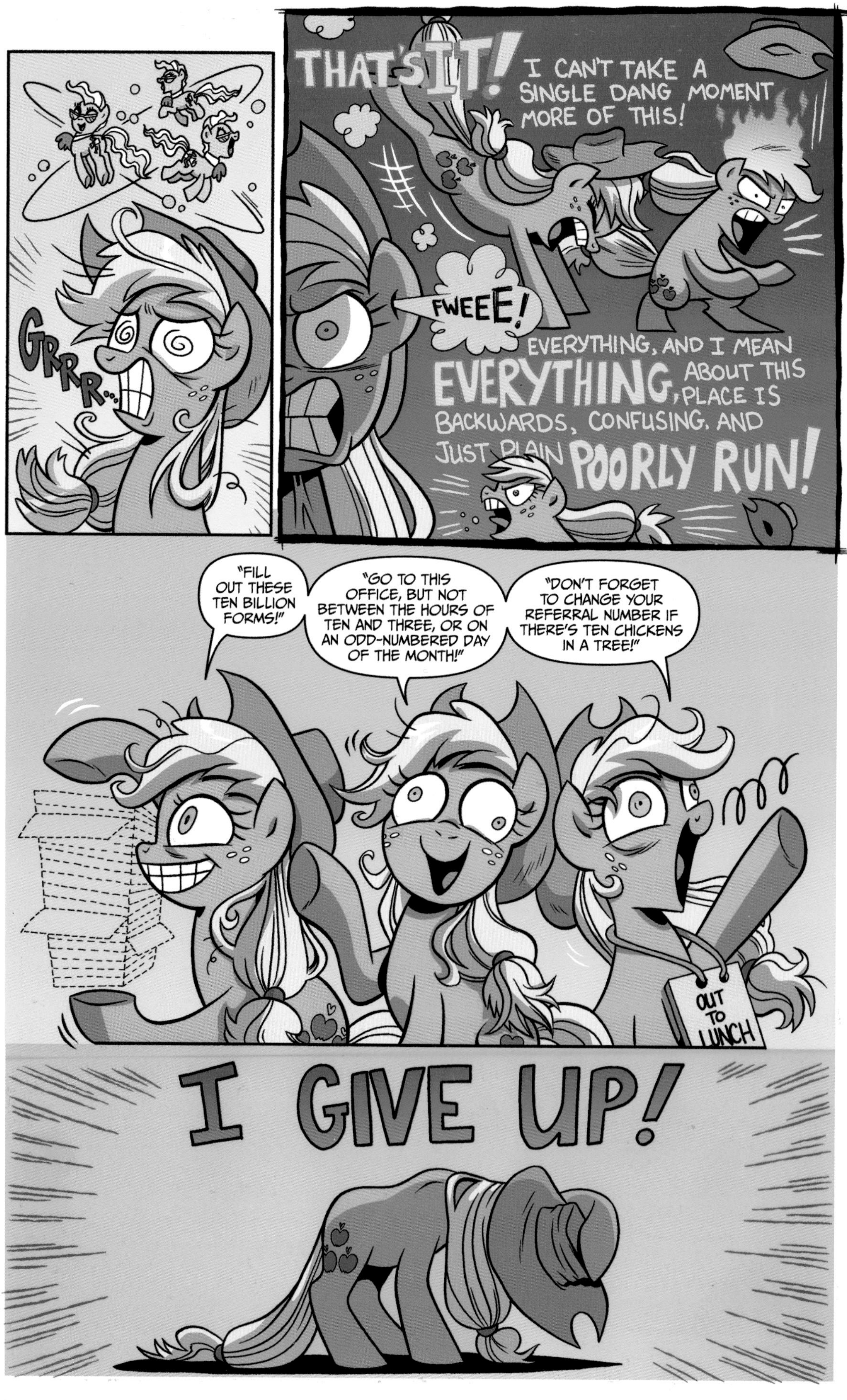
GRRRR...
THAT'S IT! I CAN'T TAKE A SINGLE DANG MOMENT MORE OF THIS!
FWEEEE!
EVERYTHING, AND I MEAN EVERYTHING, ABOUT THIS PLACE IS BACKWARDS, CONFUSING, AND JUST PLAIN POORLY RUN!
"FILL OUT THESE TEN BILLION FORMS!"
"GO TO THIS OFFICE, BUT NOT BETWEEN THE HOURS OF TEN AND THREE, OR ON AN ODD-NUMBERED DAY OF THE MONTH!"
"DON'T FORGET TO CHANGE YOUR REFERRAL NUMBER IF THERE'S TEN CHICKENS IN A TREE!"
OUT TO LUNCH
I GIVE UP!

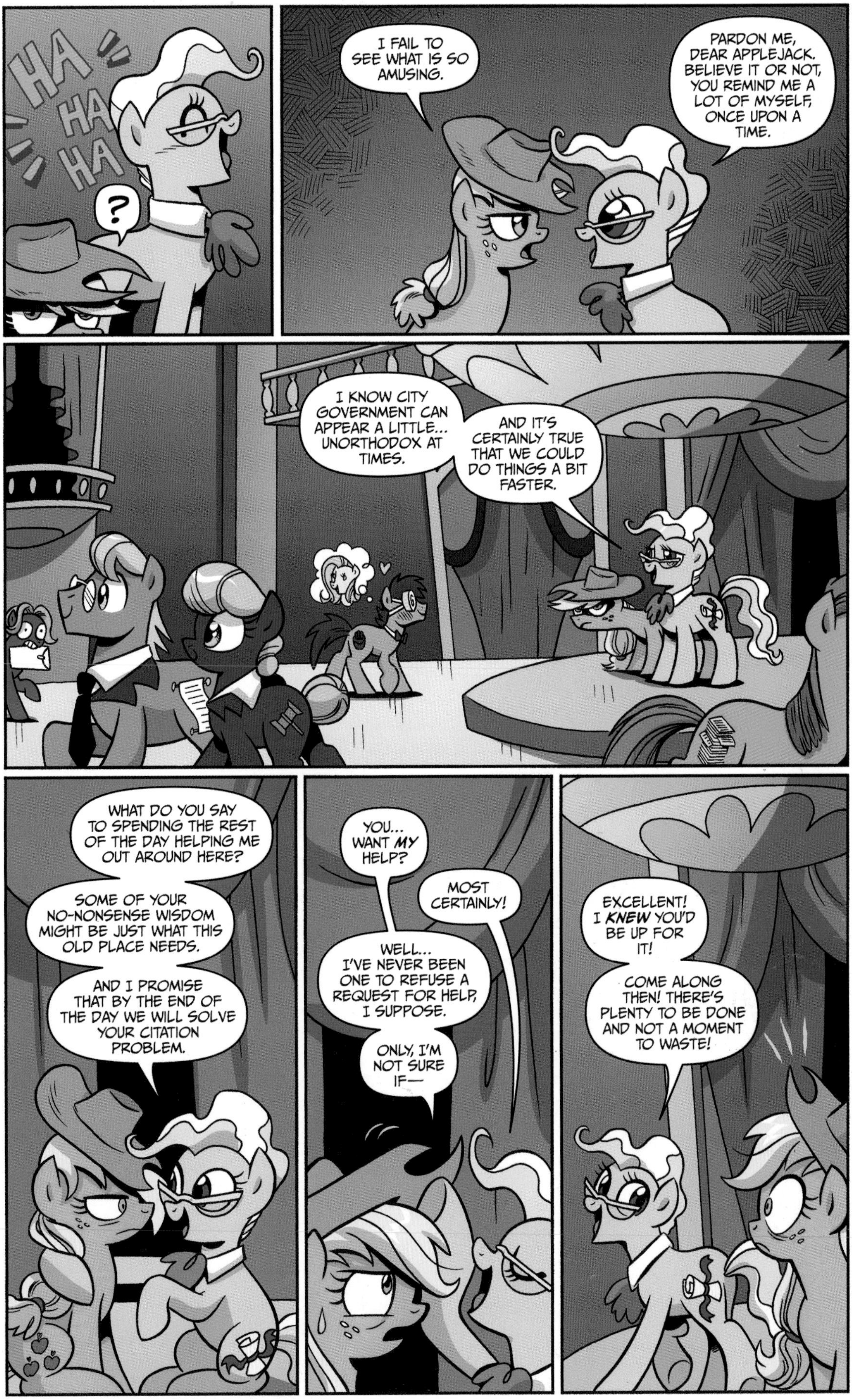
HA HA HA
?
I FAIL TO SEE WHAT IS SO AMUSING.
PARDON ME, DEAR APPLEJACK. BELIEVE IT OR NOT, YOU REMIND ME A LOT OF MYSELF, ONCE UPON A TIME.
I KNOW CITY GOVERNMENT CAN APPEAR A LITTLE... UNORTHODOX AT TIMES.
AND IT'S CERTAINLY TRUE THAT WE COULD DO THINGS A BIT FASTER.
WHAT DO YOU SAY TO SPENDING THE REST OF THE DAY HELPING ME OUT AROUND HERE?
SOME OF YOUR NO-NONSENSE WISDOM MIGHT BE JUST WHAT THIS OLD PLACE NEEDS.
AND I PROMISE THAT BY THE END OF THE DAY WE WILL SOLVE YOUR CITATION PROBLEM.
YOU... WANT MY HELP?
MOST CERTAINLY!
WELL... I'VE NEVER BEEN ONE TO REFUSE A REQUEST FOR HELP, I SUPPOSE.
ONLY, I'M NOT SURE IF—
EXCELLENT! I KNEW YOU'D BE UP FOR IT!
COME ALONG THEN! THERE'S PLENTY TO BE DONE AND NOT A MOMENT TO WASTE!

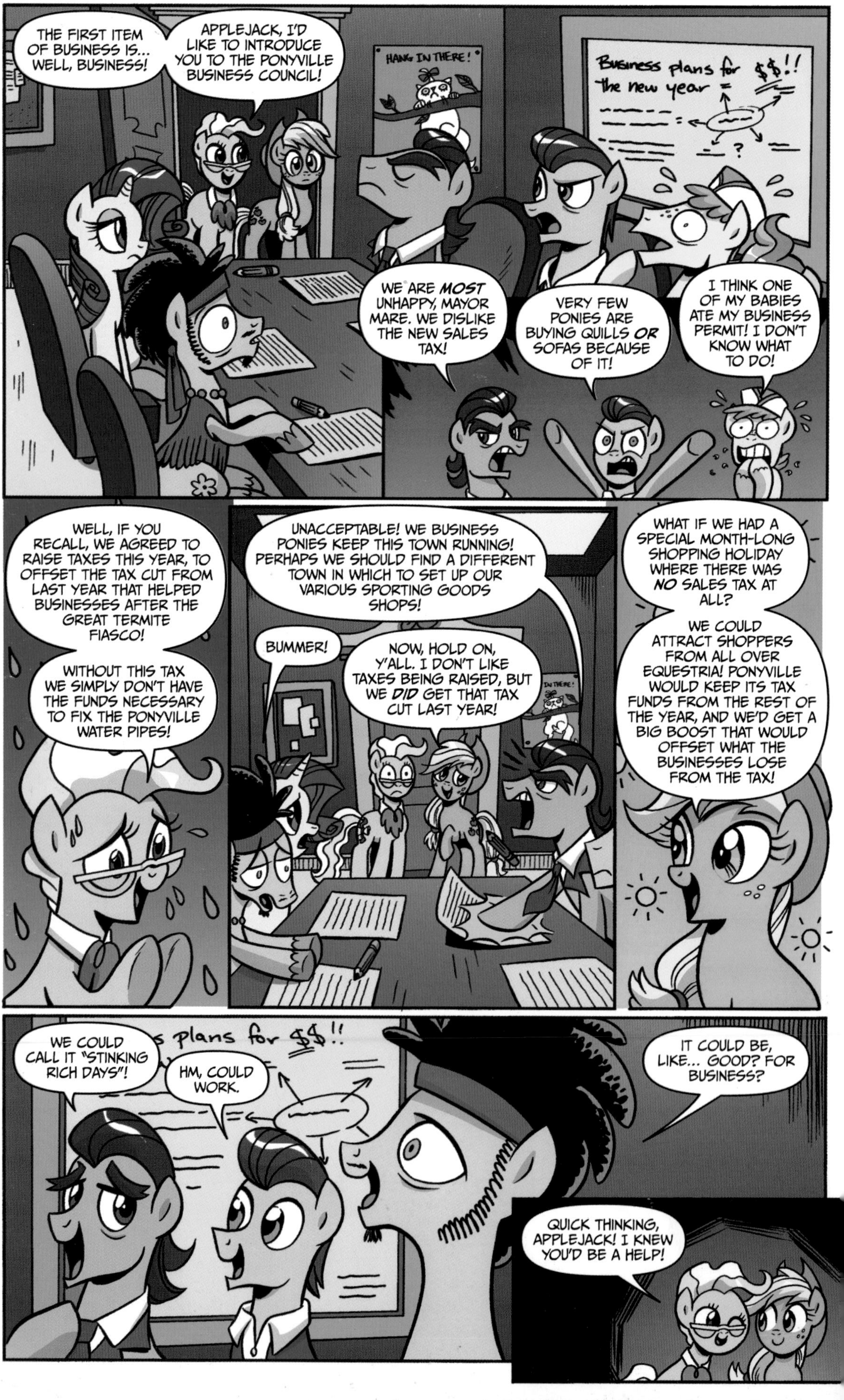
THE FIRST ITEM OF BUSINESS IS... WELL, BUSINESS!
APPLEJACK, I'D LIKE TO INTRODUCE YOU TO THE PONYVILLE BUSINESS COUNCIL!
HANG IN THERE!
Business plans for $$!! the new year =
WE ARE *MOST* UNHAPPY, MAYOR MARE. WE DISLIKE THE NEW SALES TAX!
VERY FEW PONIES ARE BUYING QUILLS *OR* SOFAS BECAUSE OF IT!
I THINK ONE OF MY BABIES ATE MY BUSINESS PERMIT! I DON'T KNOW WHAT TO DO!
WELL, IF YOU RECALL, WE AGREED TO RAISE TAXES THIS YEAR, TO OFFSET THE TAX CUT FROM LAST YEAR THAT HELPED BUSINESSES AFTER THE GREAT TERMITE FIASCO!
WITHOUT THIS TAX WE SIMPLY DON'T HAVE THE FUNDS NECESSARY TO FIX THE PONYVILLE WATER PIPES!
UNACCEPTABLE! WE BUSINESS PONIES KEEP THIS TOWN RUNNING! PERHAPS WE SHOULD FIND A DIFFERENT TOWN IN WHICH TO SET UP OUR VARIOUS SPORTING GOODS SHOPS!
BUMMER!
NOW, HOLD ON, Y'ALL. I DON'T LIKE TAXES BEING RAISED, BUT WE *DID* GET THAT TAX CUT LAST YEAR!
WHAT IF WE HAD A SPECIAL MONTH-LONG SHOPPING HOLIDAY WHERE THERE WAS *NO* SALES TAX AT ALL?
WE COULD ATTRACT SHOPPERS FROM ALL OVER EQUESTRIA! PONYVILLE WOULD KEEP ITS TAX FUNDS FROM THE REST OF THE YEAR, AND WE'D GET A BIG BOOST THAT WOULD OFFSET WHAT THE BUSINESSES LOSE FROM THE TAX!
WE COULD CALL IT "STINKING RICH DAYS"!
HM, COULD WORK.
IT COULD BE, LIKE... GOOD? FOR BUSINESS?
QUICK THINKING, APPLEJACK! I KNEW YOU'D BE A HELP!

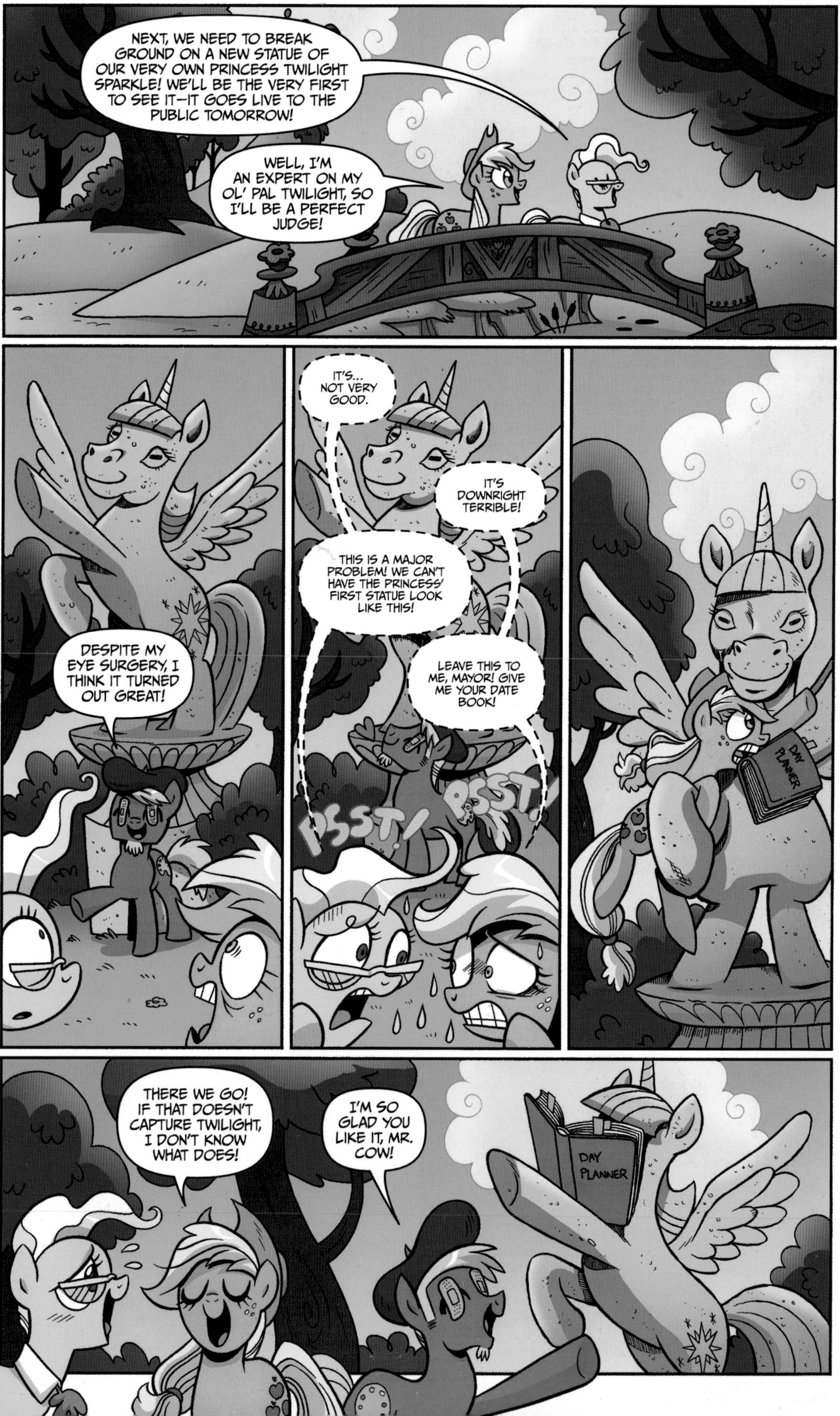
NEXT, WE NEED TO BREAK GROUND ON A NEW STATUE OF OUR VERY OWN PRINCESS TWILIGHT SPARKLE! WE'LL BE THE VERY FIRST TO SEE IT—IT GOES LIVE TO THE PUBLIC TOMORROW!
WELL, I'M AN EXPERT ON MY OL' PAL TWILIGHT, SO I'LL BE A PERFECT JUDGE!
DESPITE MY EYE SURGERY, I THINK IT TURNED OUT GREAT!
IT'S... NOT VERY GOOD.
IT'S DOWNRIGHT TERRIBLE!
THIS IS A MAJOR PROBLEM! WE CAN'T HAVE THE PRINCESS' FIRST STATUE LOOK LIKE THIS!
LEAVE THIS TO ME, MAYOR! GIVE ME YOUR DATE BOOK!
PSST!
PSST!
DAY PLANNER
THERE WE GO! IF THAT DOESN'T CAPTURE TWILIGHT, I DON'T KNOW WHAT DOES!
I'M SO GLAD YOU LIKE IT, MR. COW!
DAY PLANNER

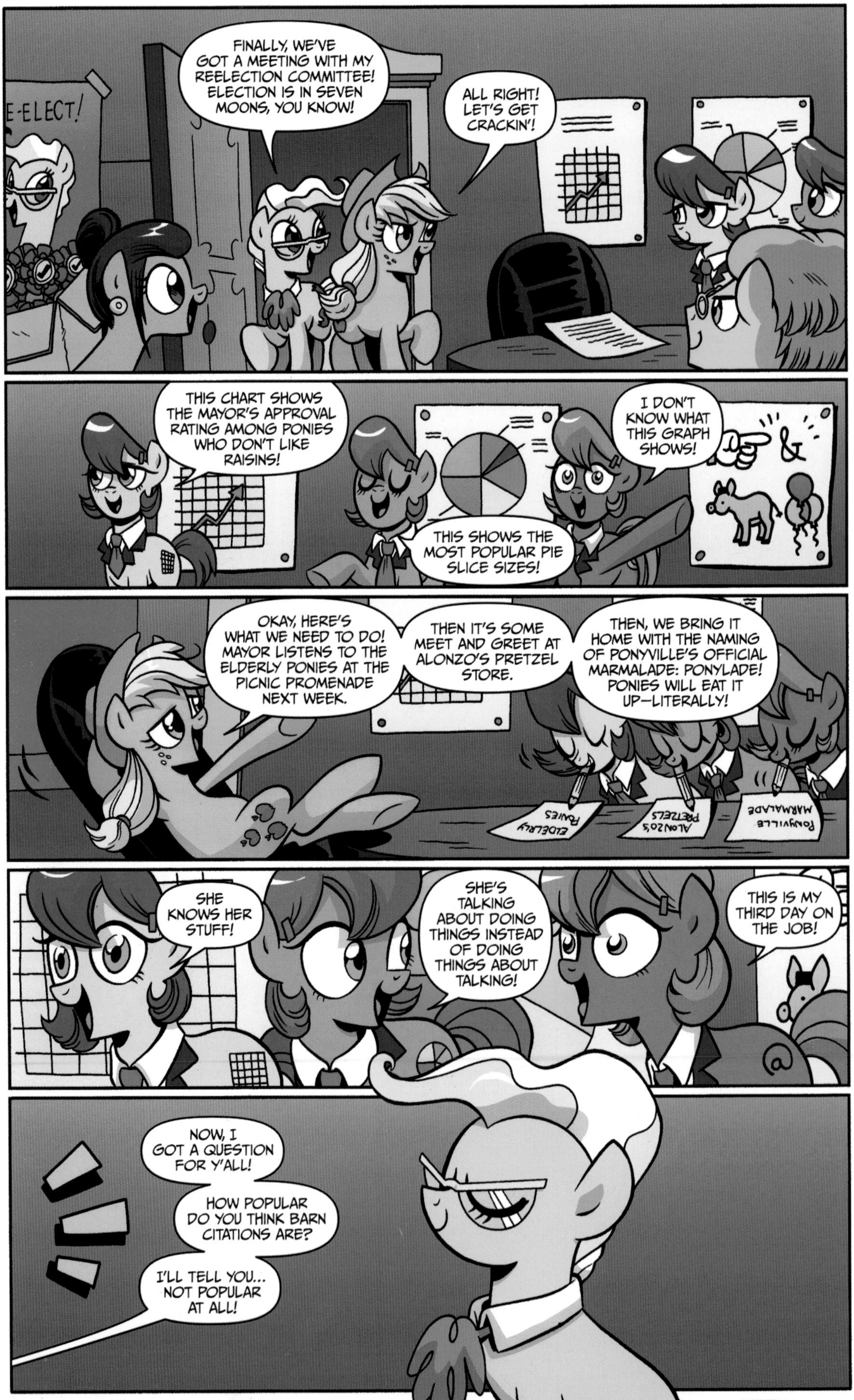
E-ELECT!
FINALLY, WE'VE GOT A MEETING WITH MY REELECTION COMMITTEE! ELECTION IS IN SEVEN MOONS, YOU KNOW!
ALL RIGHT! LET'S GET CRACKIN'!
THIS CHART SHOWS THE MAYOR'S APPROVAL RATING AMONG PONIES WHO DON'T LIKE RAISINS!
THIS SHOWS THE MOST POPULAR PIE SLICE SIZES!
I DON'T KNOW WHAT THIS GRAPH SHOWS!
&
OKAY, HERE'S WHAT WE NEED TO DO! MAYOR LISTENS TO THE ELDERLY PONIES AT THE PICNIC PROMENADE NEXT WEEK.
THEN IT'S SOME MEET AND GREET AT ALONZO'S PRETZEL STORE.
THEN, WE BRING IT HOME WITH THE NAMING OF PONYVILLE'S OFFICIAL MARMALADE: PONYLADE! PONIES WILL EAT IT UP—LITERALLY!
ELDERLY PONIES
ALONZO'S PRETZELS
PONYVILLE MARMALADE
SHE KNOWS HER STUFF!
SHE'S TALKING ABOUT DOING THINGS INSTEAD OF DOING THINGS ABOUT TALKING!
THIS IS MY THIRD DAY ON THE JOB!
NOW, I GOT A QUESTION FOR Y'ALL!
HOW POPULAR DO YOU THINK BARN CITATIONS ARE?
I'LL TELL YOU... NOT POPULAR AT ALL!

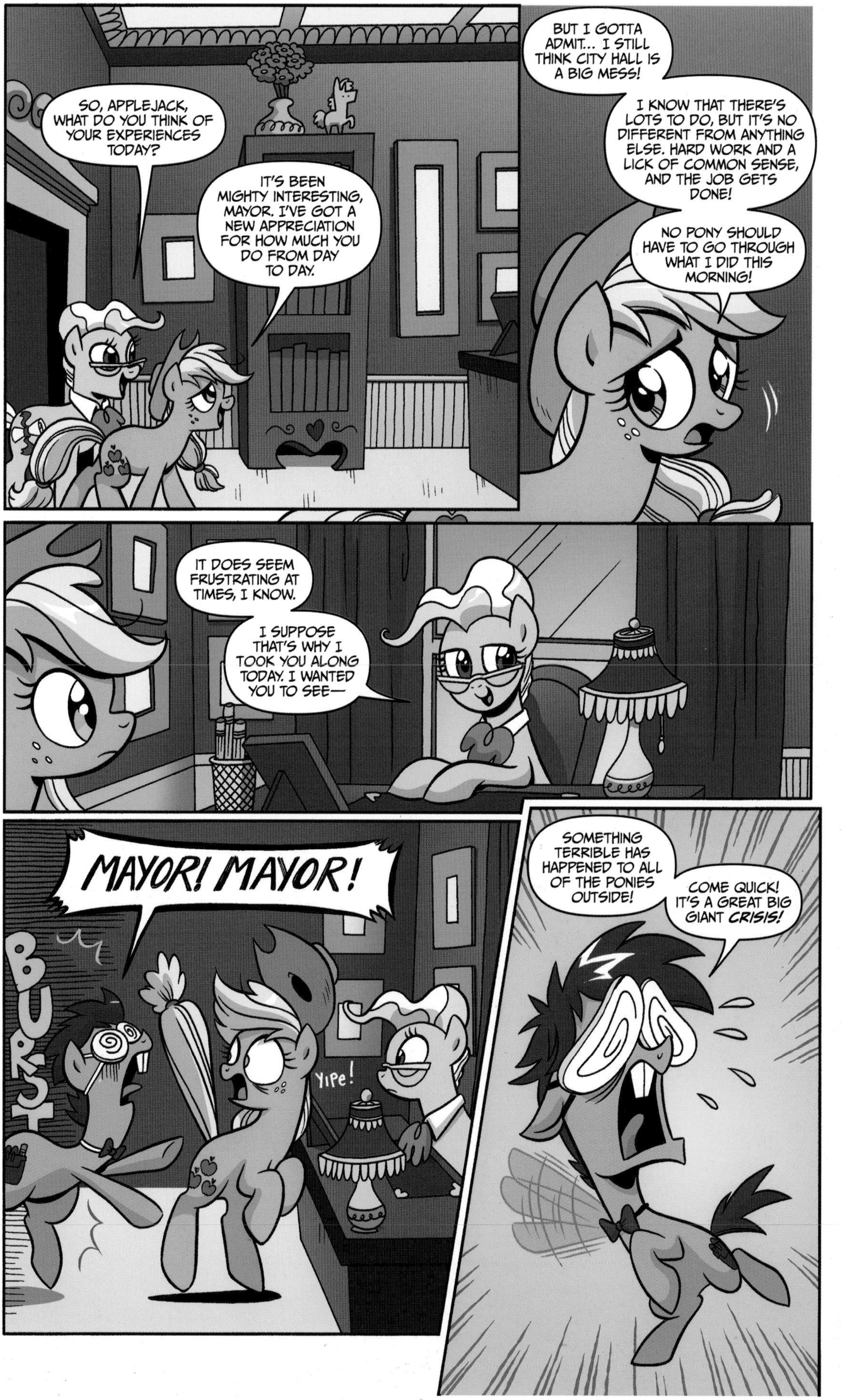
SO, APPLEJACK, WHAT DO YOU THINK OF YOUR EXPERIENCES TODAY?
IT'S BEEN MIGHTY INTERESTING, MAYOR. I'VE GOT A NEW APPRECIATION FOR HOW MUCH YOU DO FROM DAY TO DAY.
BUT I GOTTA ADMIT... I STILL THINK CITY HALL IS A BIG MESS!
I KNOW THAT THERE'S LOTS TO DO, BUT IT'S NO DIFFERENT FROM ANYTHING ELSE. HARD WORK AND A LICK OF COMMON SENSE, AND THE JOB GETS DONE!
NO PONY SHOULD HAVE TO GO THROUGH WHAT I DID THIS MORNING!
IT DOES SEEM FRUSTRATING AT TIMES, I KNOW.
I SUPPOSE THAT'S WHY I TOOK YOU ALONG TODAY. I WANTED YOU TO SEE—
MAYOR! MAYOR!
BURST
YIPE!
SOMETHING TERRIBLE HAS HAPPENED TO ALL OF THE PONIES OUTSIDE!
COME QUICK! IT'S A GREAT BIG GIANT *CRISIS!*

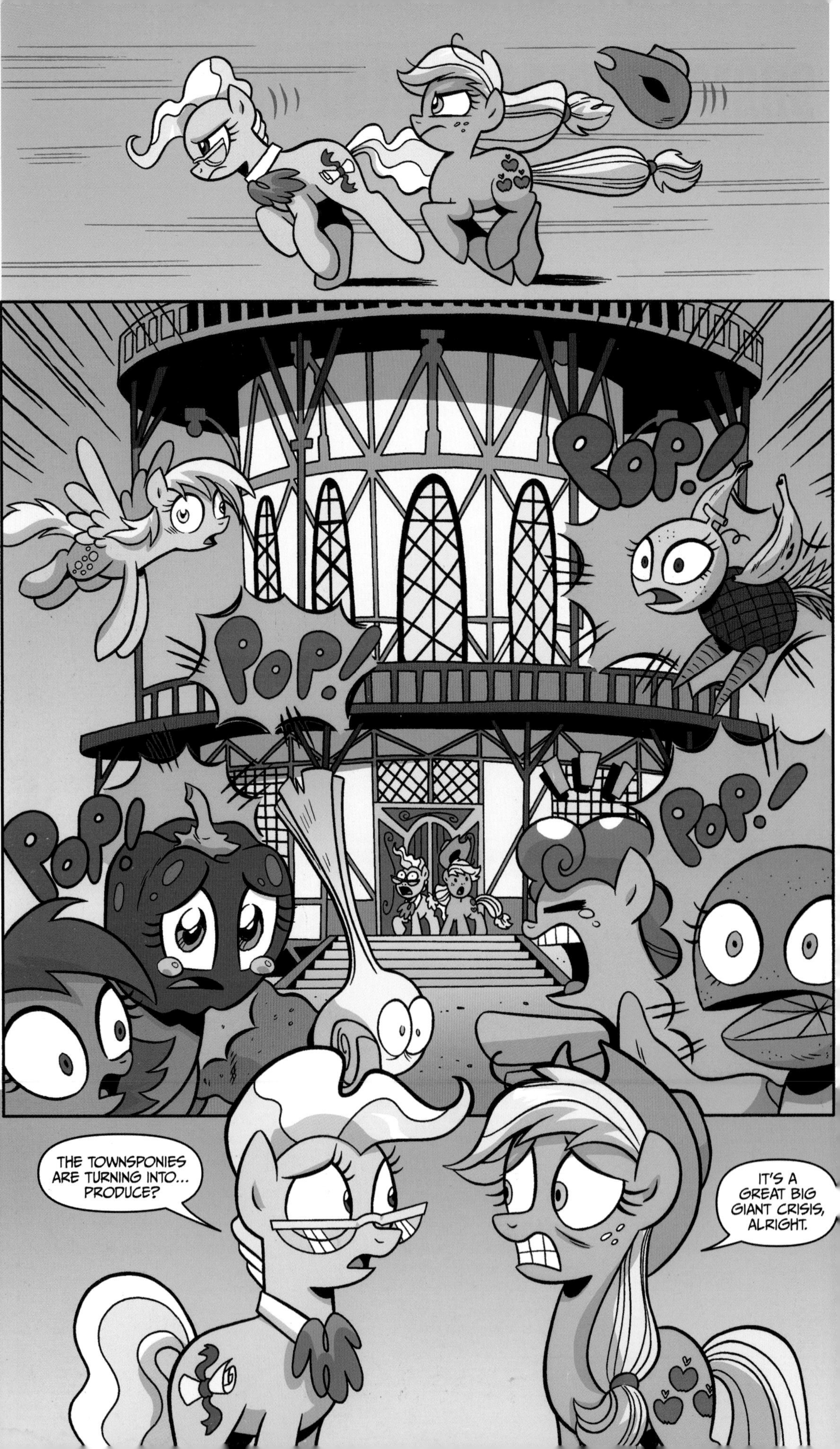

POP!
POP!
POP!
POP!
THE TOWNSPONIES ARE TURNING INTO... PRODUCE?
IT'S A GREAT BIG GIANT CRISIS, ALRIGHT.

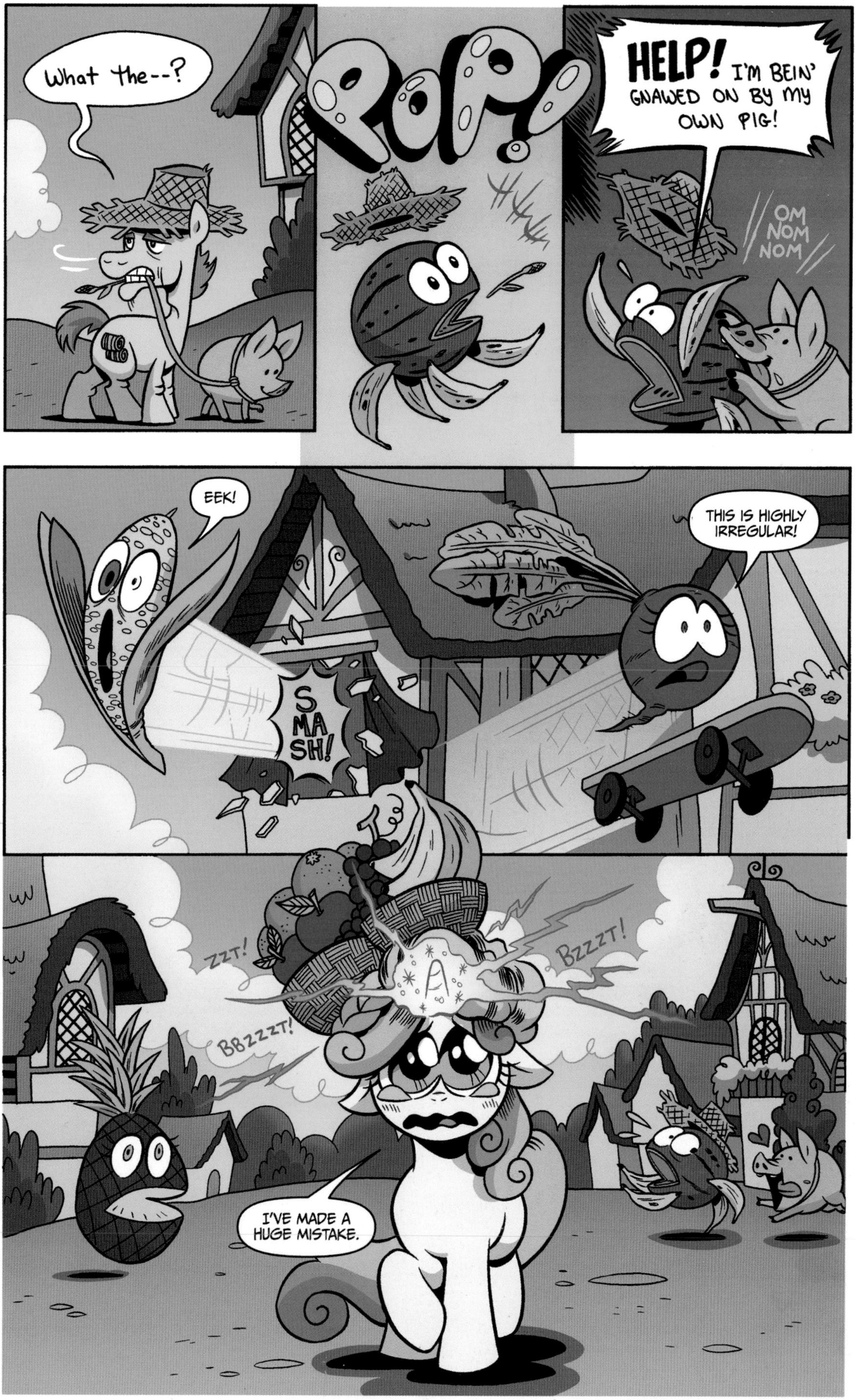
What the--?
POP!
HELP! I'M BEIN' GNAWED ON BY MY OWN PIG!
OM NOM NOM
EEK!
SMASH!
THIS IS HIGHLY IRREGULAR!
ZZT!
BZZZT!
BZZZZT!
I'VE MADE A HUGE MISTAKE.

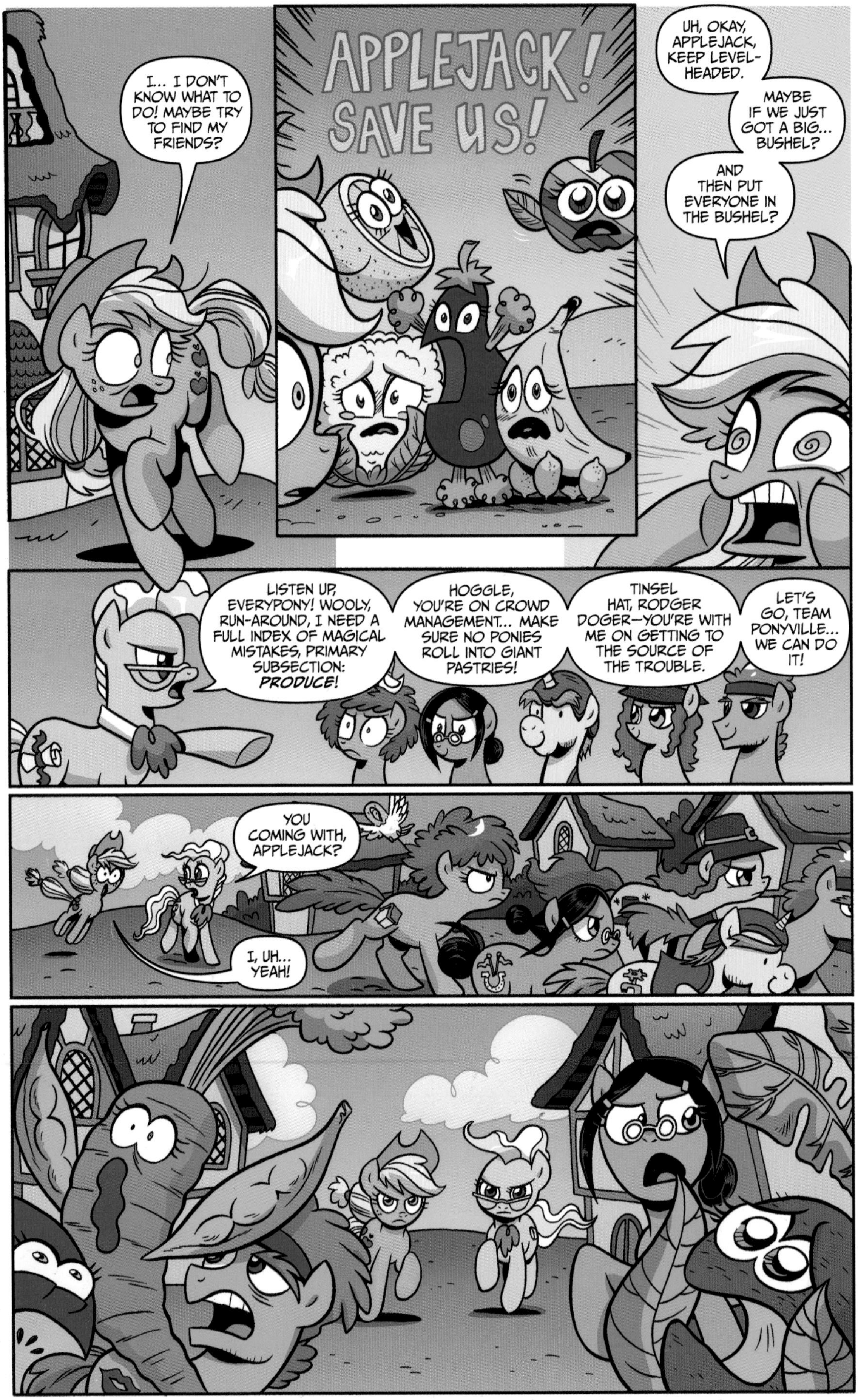
I... I DON'T KNOW WHAT TO DO! MAYBE TRY TO FIND MY FRIENDS?
APPLEJACK! SAVE US!
UH, OKAY, APPLEJACK, KEEP LEVEL-HEADED.
MAYBE IF WE JUST GOT A BIG... BUSHEL?
AND THEN PUT EVERYONE IN THE BUSHEL?
LISTEN UP, EVERYPONY! WOOLY, RUN-AROUND, I NEED A FULL INDEX OF MAGICAL MISTAKES, PRIMARY SUBSECTION: *PRODUCE*!
HOGGLE, YOU'RE ON CROWD MANAGEMENT... MAKE SURE NO PONIES ROLL INTO GIANT PASTRIES!
TINSEL HAT, RODGER DOGER—YOU'RE WITH ME ON GETTING TO THE SOURCE OF THE TROUBLE.
LET'S GO, TEAM PONYVILLE... WE CAN DO IT!
YOU COMING WITH, APPLEJACK?
I, UH... YEAH!

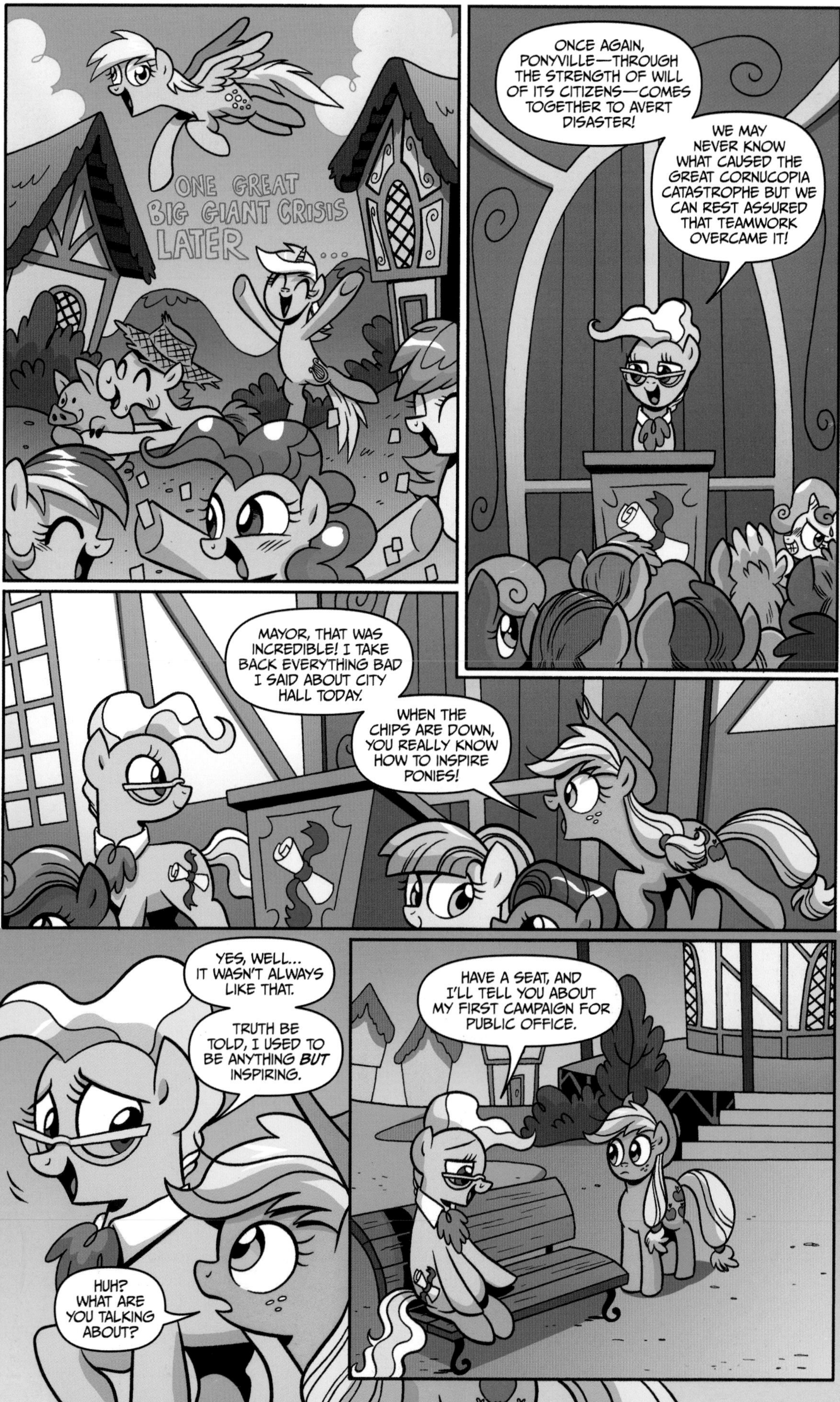
ONE GREAT BIG GIANT CRISIS LATER...
ONCE AGAIN, PONYVILLE—THROUGH THE STRENGTH OF WILL OF ITS CITIZENS—COMES TOGETHER TO AVERT DISASTER!
WE MAY NEVER KNOW WHAT CAUSED THE GREAT CORNUCOPIA CATASTROPHE BUT WE CAN REST ASSURED THAT TEAMWORK OVERCAME IT!
MAYOR, THAT WAS INCREDIBLE! I TAKE BACK EVERYTHING BAD I SAID ABOUT CITY HALL TODAY.
WHEN THE CHIPS ARE DOWN, YOU REALLY KNOW HOW TO INSPIRE PONIES!
YES, WELL... IT WASN'T ALWAYS LIKE THAT.
TRUTH BE TOLD, I USED TO BE ANYTHING *BUT* INSPIRING.
HUH? WHAT ARE YOU TALKING ABOUT?
HAVE A SEAT, AND I'LL TELL YOU ABOUT MY FIRST CAMPAIGN FOR PUBLIC OFFICE.

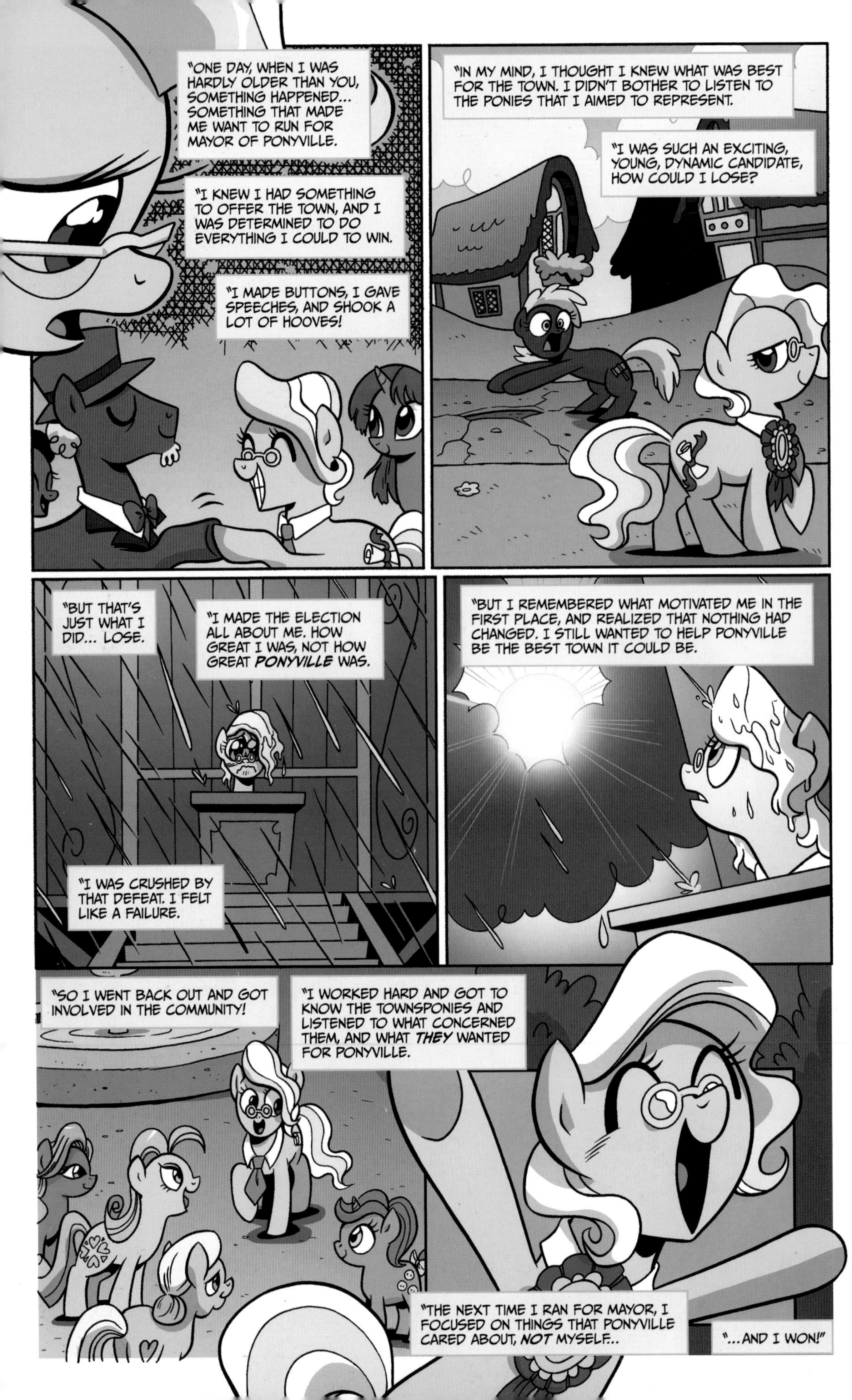
"ONE DAY, WHEN I WAS HARDLY OLDER THAN YOU, SOMETHING HAPPENED... SOMETHING THAT MADE ME WANT TO RUN FOR MAYOR OF PONYVILLE.
"I KNEW I HAD SOMETHING TO OFFER THE TOWN, AND I WAS DETERMINED TO DO EVERYTHING I COULD TO WIN.
"I MADE BUTTONS, I GAVE SPEECHES, AND SHOOK A LOT OF HOOVES!
"IN MY MIND, I THOUGHT I KNEW WHAT WAS BEST FOR THE TOWN. I DIDN'T BOTHER TO LISTEN TO THE PONIES THAT I AIMED TO REPRESENT.
"I WAS SUCH AN EXCITING, YOUNG, DYNAMIC CANDIDATE, HOW COULD I LOSE?
"BUT THAT'S JUST WHAT I DID... LOSE.
"I MADE THE ELECTION ALL ABOUT ME. HOW GREAT I WAS, NOT HOW GREAT *PONYVILLE* WAS.
"I WAS CRUSHED BY THAT DEFEAT. I FELT LIKE A FAILURE.
"BUT I REMEMBERED WHAT MOTIVATED ME IN THE FIRST PLACE, AND REALIZED THAT NOTHING HAD CHANGED. I STILL WANTED TO HELP PONYVILLE BE THE BEST TOWN IT COULD BE.
"SO I WENT BACK OUT AND GOT INVOLVED IN THE COMMUNITY!
"I WORKED HARD AND GOT TO KNOW THE TOWNSPONIES AND LISTENED TO WHAT CONCERNED THEM, AND WHAT *THEY* WANTED FOR PONYVILLE.
"THE NEXT TIME I RAN FOR MAYOR, I FOCUSED ON THINGS THAT PONYVILLE CARED ABOUT, *NOT* MYSELF...
"...AND I WON!"

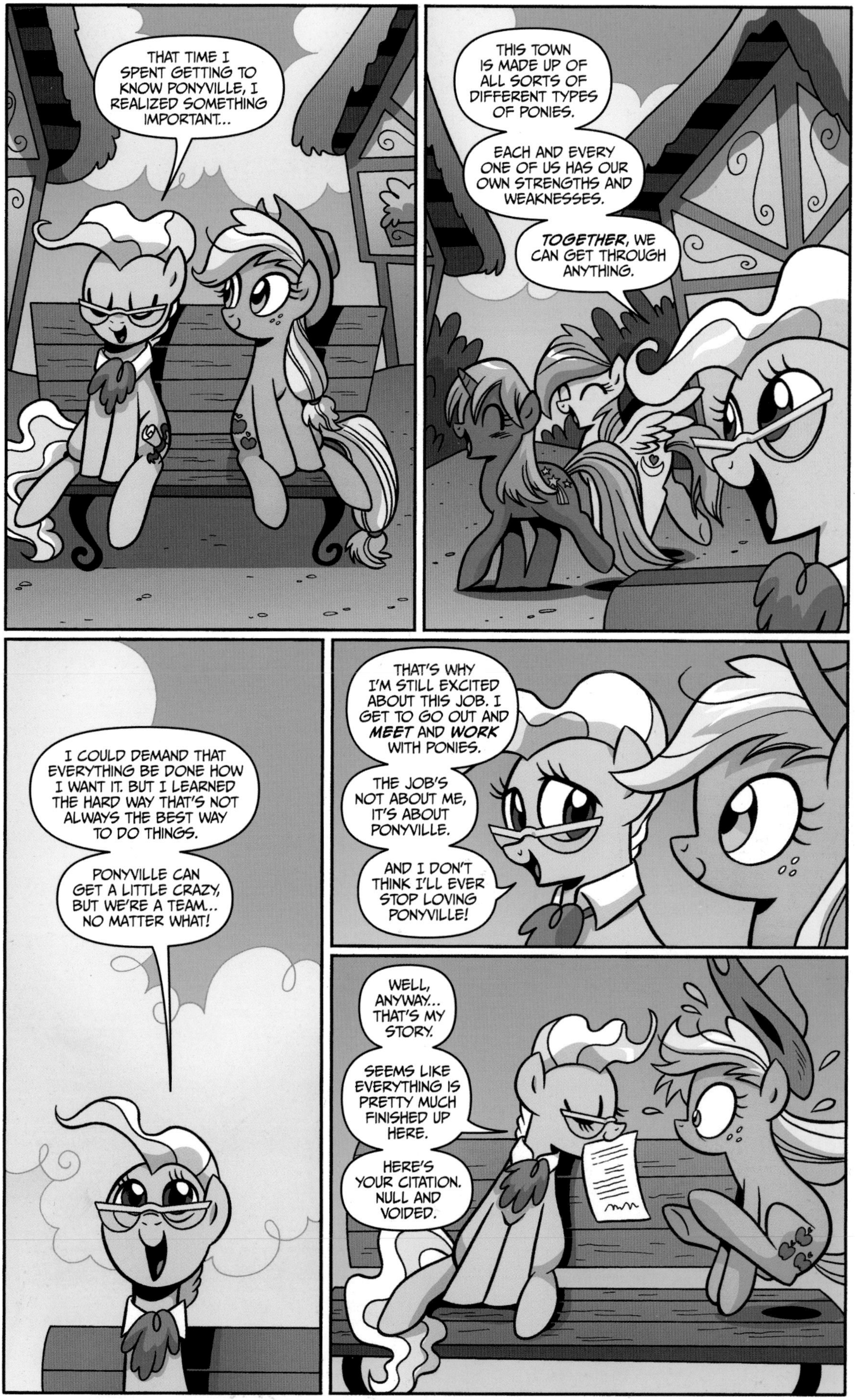
THAT TIME I SPENT GETTING TO KNOW PONYVILLE, I REALIZED SOMETHING IMPORTANT...
THIS TOWN IS MADE UP OF ALL SORTS OF DIFFERENT TYPES OF PONIES.
EACH AND EVERY ONE OF US HAS OUR OWN STRENGTHS AND WEAKNESSES.
TOGETHER, WE CAN GET THROUGH ANYTHING.
I COULD DEMAND THAT EVERYTHING BE DONE HOW I WANT IT. BUT I LEARNED THE HARD WAY THAT'S NOT ALWAYS THE BEST WAY TO DO THINGS.
PONYVILLE CAN GET A LITTLE CRAZY, BUT WE'RE A TEAM... NO MATTER WHAT!
THAT'S WHY I'M STILL EXCITED ABOUT THIS JOB. I GET TO GO OUT AND *MEET* AND *WORK* WITH PONIES.
THE JOB'S NOT ABOUT ME, IT'S ABOUT PONYVILLE.
AND I DON'T THINK I'LL EVER STOP LOVING PONYVILLE!
WELL, ANYWAY... THAT'S MY STORY.
SEEMS LIKE EVERYTHING IS PRETTY MUCH FINISHED UP HERE.
HERE'S YOUR CITATION. NULL AND VOIDED.

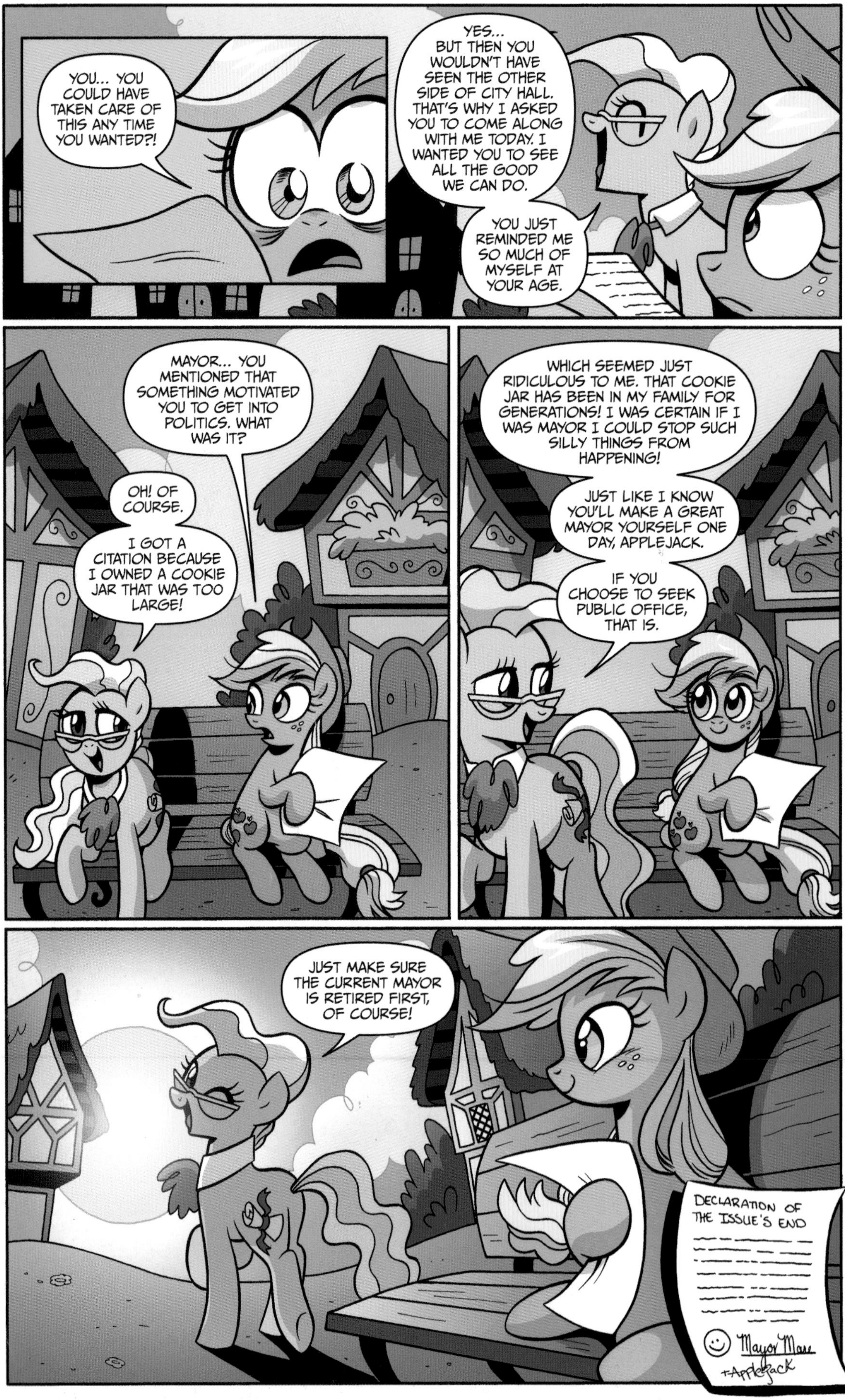
YOU... YOU COULD HAVE TAKEN CARE OF THIS ANY TIME YOU WANTED?!
YES... BUT THEN YOU WOULDN'T HAVE SEEN THE OTHER SIDE OF CITY HALL. THAT'S WHY I ASKED YOU TO COME ALONG WITH ME TODAY. I WANTED YOU TO SEE ALL THE GOOD WE CAN DO.
YOU JUST REMINDED ME SO MUCH OF MYSELF AT YOUR AGE.
MAYOR... YOU MENTIONED THAT SOMETHING MOTIVATED YOU TO GET INTO POLITICS. WHAT WAS IT?
OH! OF COURSE.
I GOT A CITATION BECAUSE I OWNED A COOKIE JAR THAT WAS TOO LARGE!
WHICH SEEMED JUST RIDICULOUS TO ME. THAT COOKIE JAR HAS BEEN IN MY FAMILY FOR GENERATIONS! I WAS CERTAIN IF I WAS MAYOR I COULD STOP SUCH SILLY THINGS FROM HAPPENING!
JUST LIKE I KNOW YOU'LL MAKE A GREAT MAYOR YOURSELF ONE DAY, APPLEJACK.
IF YOU CHOOSE TO SEEK PUBLIC OFFICE, THAT IS.
JUST MAKE SURE THE CURRENT MAYOR IS RETIRED FIRST, OF COURSE!
DECLARATION OF THE ISSUE'S END
Mayor Mare
+Applejack

My Little Pony

Friends Forever

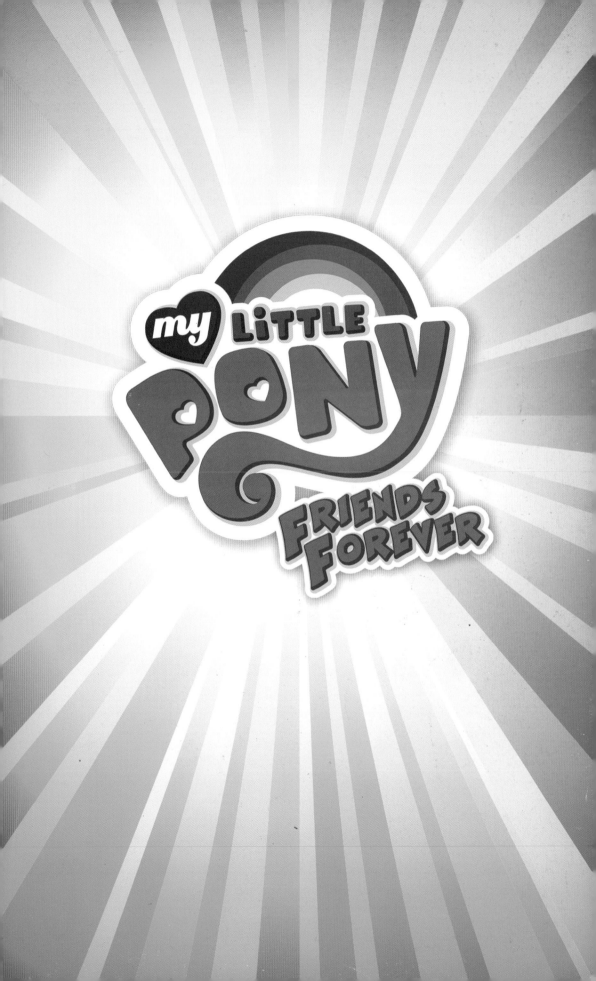

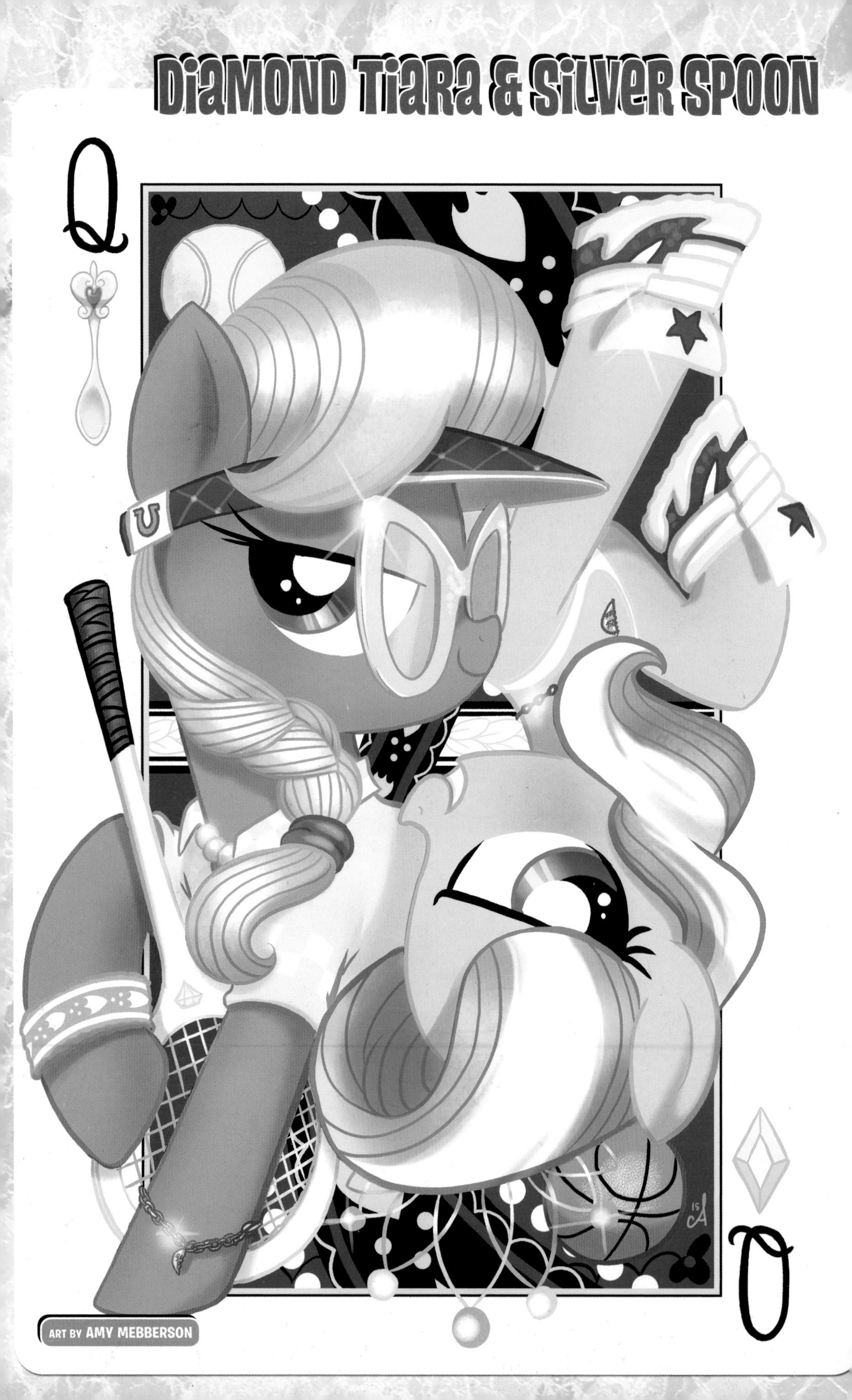
DIAMOND TIARA & SILVER SPOON
Q
U
15
A
Q
ART BY AMY MEBBERSON

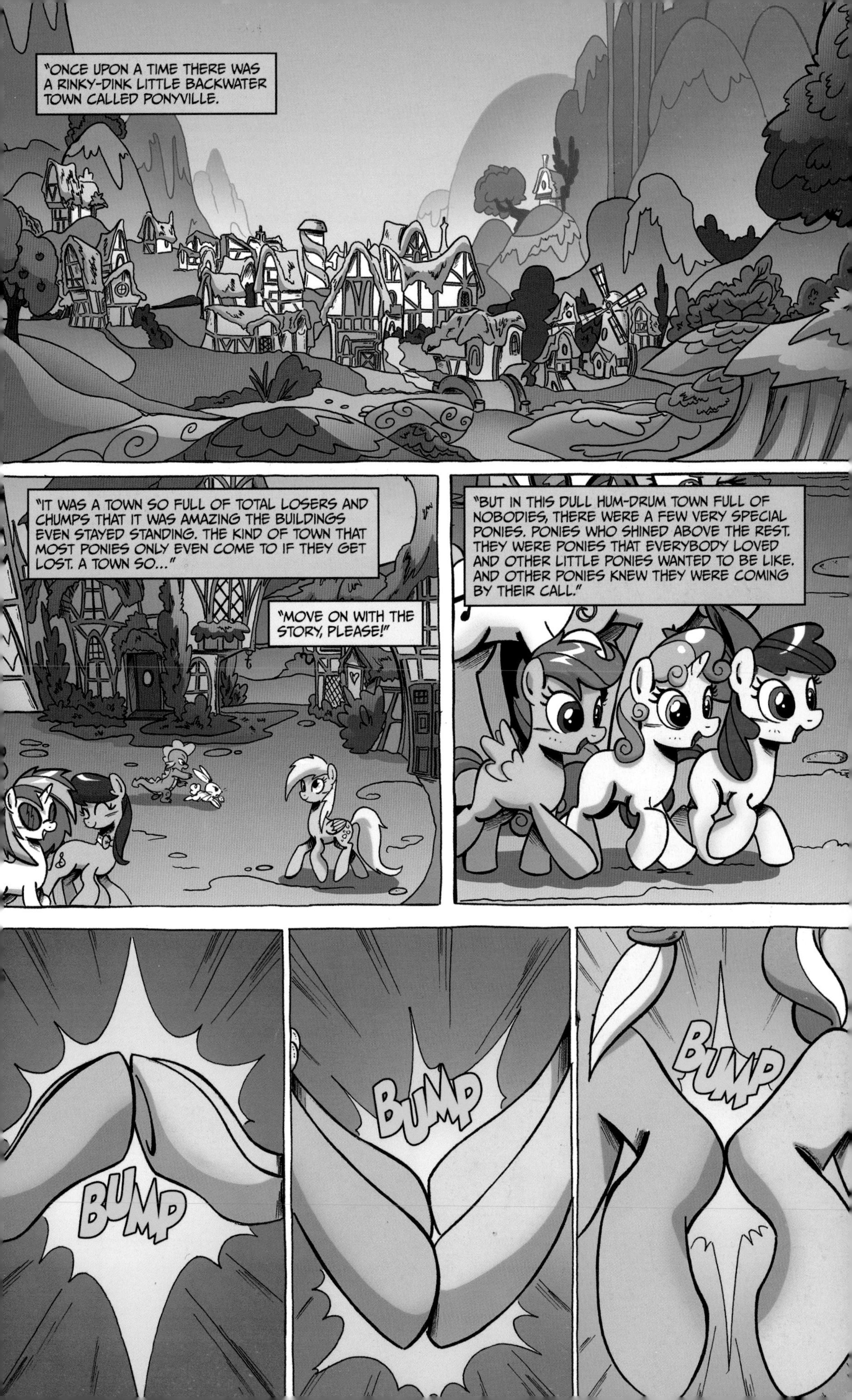
"ONCE UPON A TIME THERE WAS A RINKY-DINK LITTLE BACKWATER TOWN CALLED PONYVILLE.
"IT WAS A TOWN SO FULL OF TOTAL LOSERS AND CHUMPS THAT IT WAS AMAZING THE BUILDINGS EVEN STAYED STANDING. THE KIND OF TOWN THAT MOST PONIES ONLY EVEN COME TO IF THEY GET LOST. A TOWN SO..."
"MOVE ON WITH THE STORY, PLEASE!"
"BUT IN THIS DULL HUM-DRUM TOWN FULL OF NOBODIES, THERE WERE A FEW VERY SPECIAL PONIES. PONIES WHO SHINED ABOVE THE REST. THEY WERE PONIES THAT EVERYBODY LOVED AND OTHER LITTLE PONIES WANTED TO BE LIKE. AND OTHER PONIES KNEW THEY WERE COMING BY THEIR CALL."
BUMP
BUMP
BUMP

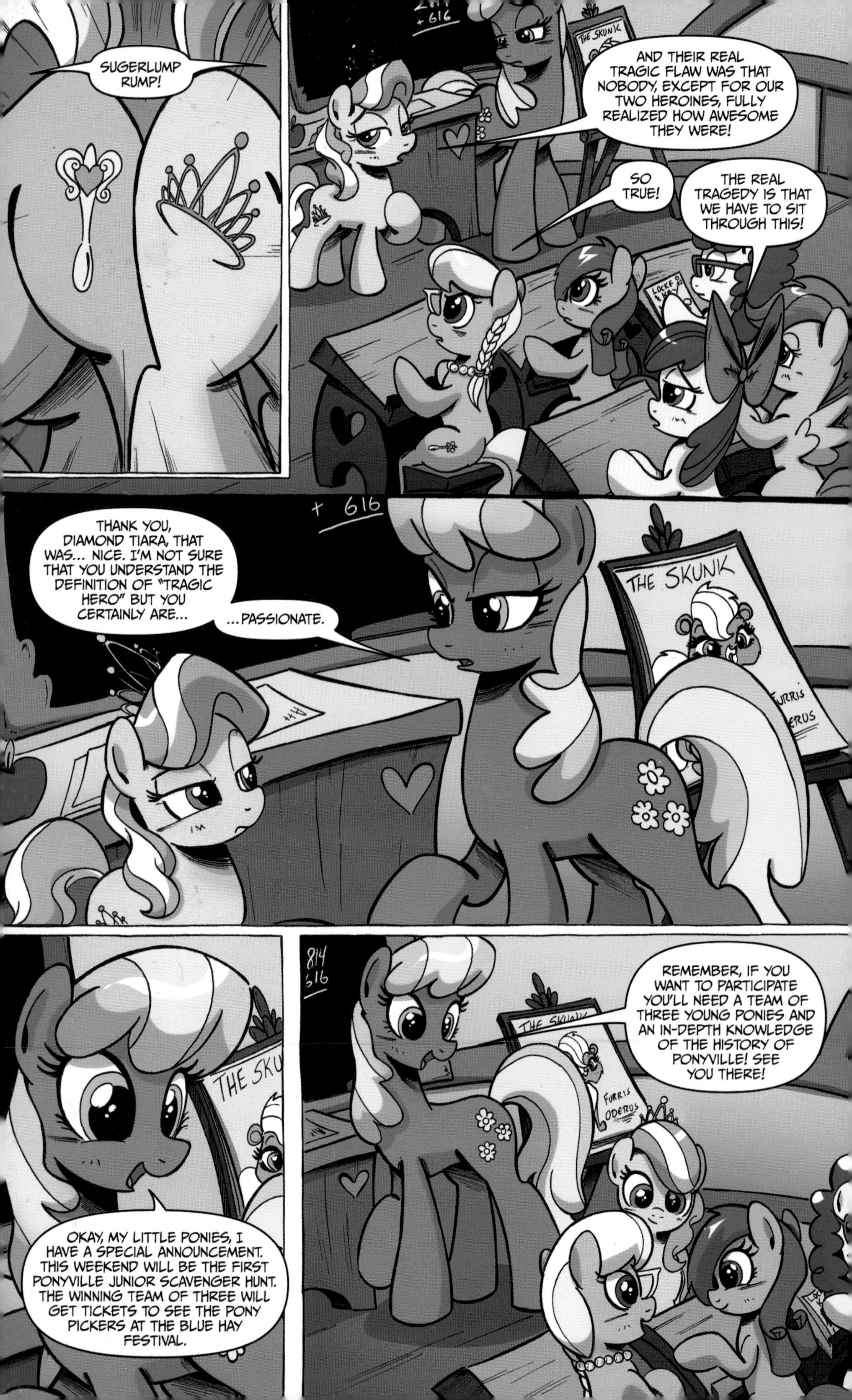
SUGERLUMP RUMP!
AND THEIR REAL TRAGIC FLAW WAS THAT NOBODY, EXCEPT FOR OUR TWO HEROINES, FULLY REALIZED HOW AWESOME THEY WERE!
SO TRUE!
THE REAL TRAGEDY IS THAT WE HAVE TO SIT THROUGH THIS!
THE SKUNK
+ 616
THANK YOU, DIAMOND TIARA, THAT WAS... NICE. I'M NOT SURE THAT YOU UNDERSTAND THE DEFINITION OF "TRAGIC HERO" BUT YOU CERTAINLY ARE...
...PASSIONATE.
THE SKUNK
FURRIS ODERUS
OKAY, MY LITTLE PONIES, I HAVE A SPECIAL ANNOUNCEMENT. THIS WEEKEND WILL BE THE FIRST PONYVILLE JUNIOR SCAVENGER HUNT. THE WINNING TEAM OF THREE WILL GET TICKETS TO SEE THE PONY PICKERS AT THE BLUE HAY FESTIVAL.
814
616
REMEMBER, IF YOU WANT TO PARTICIPATE YOU'LL NEED A TEAM OF THREE YOUNG PONIES AND AN IN-DEPTH KNOWLEDGE OF THE HISTORY OF PONYVILLE! SEE YOU THERE!
FURRIS ODERUS

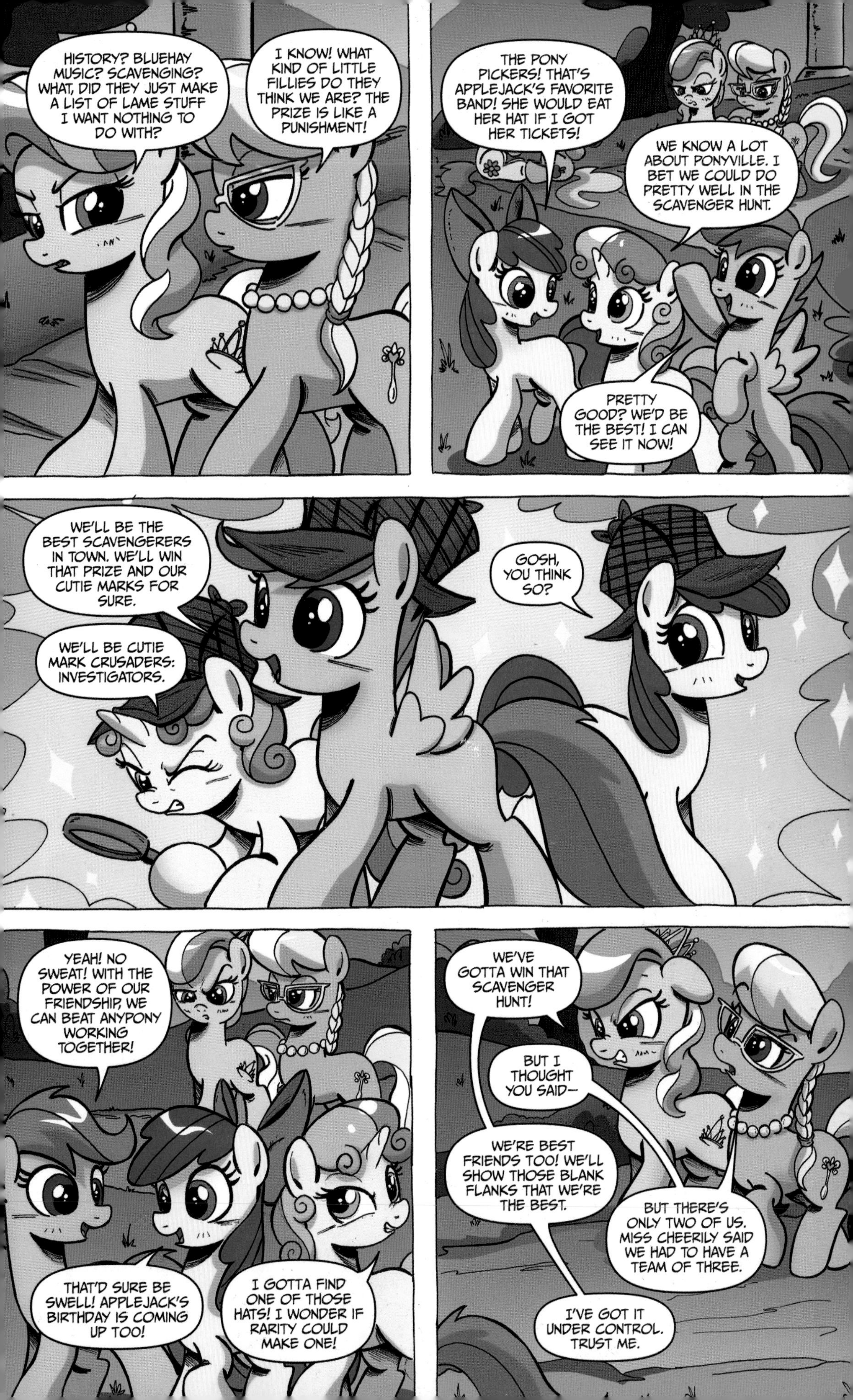
HISTORY? BLUEHAY MUSIC? SCAVENGING? WHAT, DID THEY JUST MAKE A LIST OF LAME STUFF I WANT NOTHING TO DO WITH?
I KNOW! WHAT KIND OF LITTLE FILLIES DO THEY THINK WE ARE? THE PRIZE IS LIKE A PUNISHMENT!
THE PONY PICKERS! THAT'S APPLEJACK'S FAVORITE BAND! SHE WOULD EAT HER HAT IF I GOT HER TICKETS!
WE KNOW A LOT ABOUT PONYVILLE. I BET WE COULD DO PRETTY WELL IN THE SCAVENGER HUNT.
PRETTY GOOD? WE'D BE THE BEST! I CAN SEE IT NOW!
WE'LL BE THE BEST SCAVENGERERS IN TOWN. WE'LL WIN THAT PRIZE AND OUR CUTIE MARKS FOR SURE.
WE'LL BE CUTIE MARK CRUSADERS: INVESTIGATORS.
GOSH, YOU THINK SO?
YEAH! NO SWEAT! WITH THE POWER OF OUR FRIENDSHIP, WE CAN BEAT ANYPONY WORKING TOGETHER!
THAT'D SURE BE SWELL! APPLEJACK'S BIRTHDAY IS COMING UP TOO!
I GOTTA FIND ONE OF THOSE HATS! I WONDER IF RARITY COULD MAKE ONE!
WE'VE GOTTA WIN THAT SCAVENGER HUNT!
BUT I THOUGHT YOU SAID—
WE'RE BEST FRIENDS TOO! WE'LL SHOW THOSE BLANK FLANKS THAT WE'RE THE BEST.
BUT THERE'S ONLY TWO OF US. MISS CHEERILY SAID WE HAD TO HAVE A TEAM OF THREE.
I'VE GOT IT UNDER CONTROL. TRUST ME.

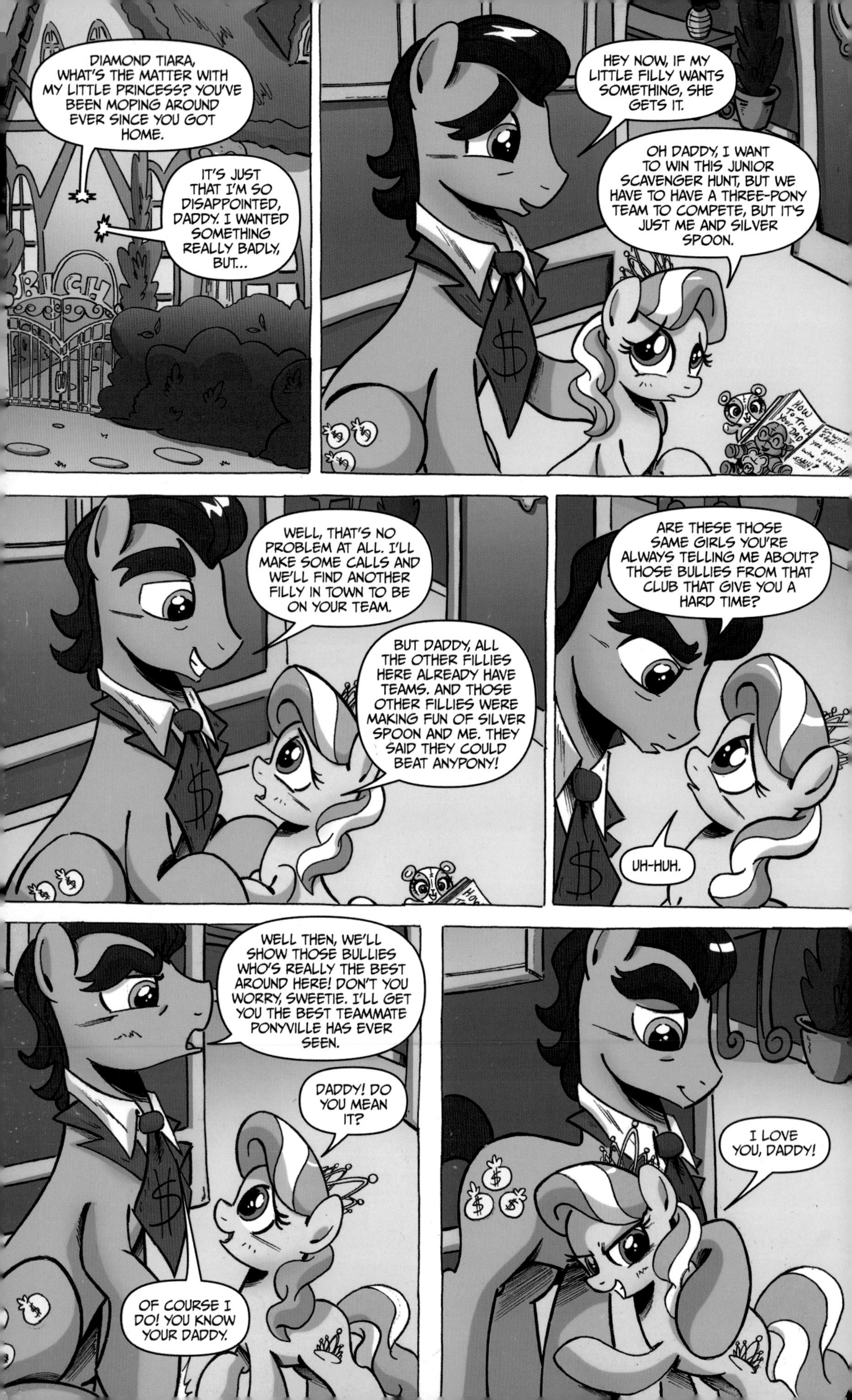
DIAMOND TIARA, WHAT'S THE MATTER WITH MY LITTLE PRINCESS? YOU'VE BEEN MOPING AROUND EVER SINCE YOU GOT HOME.
IT'S JUST THAT I'M SO DISAPPOINTED, DADDY. I WANTED SOMETHING REALLY BADLY, BUT...
RICH
HEY NOW, IF MY LITTLE FILLY WANTS SOMETHING, SHE GETS IT.
OH DADDY, I WANT TO WIN THIS JUNIOR SCAVENGER HUNT, BUT WE HAVE TO HAVE A THREE-PONY TEAM TO COMPETE, BUT IT'S JUST ME AND SILVER SPOON.
How To Trick Your DAD
WELL, THAT'S NO PROBLEM AT ALL. I'LL MAKE SOME CALLS AND WE'LL FIND ANOTHER FILLY IN TOWN TO BE ON YOUR TEAM.
BUT DADDY, ALL THE OTHER FILLIES HERE ALREADY HAVE TEAMS. AND THOSE OTHER FILLIES WERE MAKING FUN OF SILVER SPOON AND ME. THEY SAID THEY COULD BEAT ANYPONY!
ARE THESE THOSE SAME GIRLS YOU'RE ALWAYS TELLING ME ABOUT? THOSE BULLIES FROM THAT CLUB THAT GIVE YOU A HARD TIME?
UH-HUH.
WELL THEN, WE'LL SHOW THOSE BULLIES WHO'S REALLY THE BEST AROUND HERE! DON'T YOU WORRY, SWEETIE. I'LL GET YOU THE BEST TEAMMATE PONYVILLE HAS EVER SEEN.
DADDY! DO YOU MEAN IT?
OF COURSE I DO! YOU KNOW YOUR DADDY.
I LOVE YOU, DADDY!

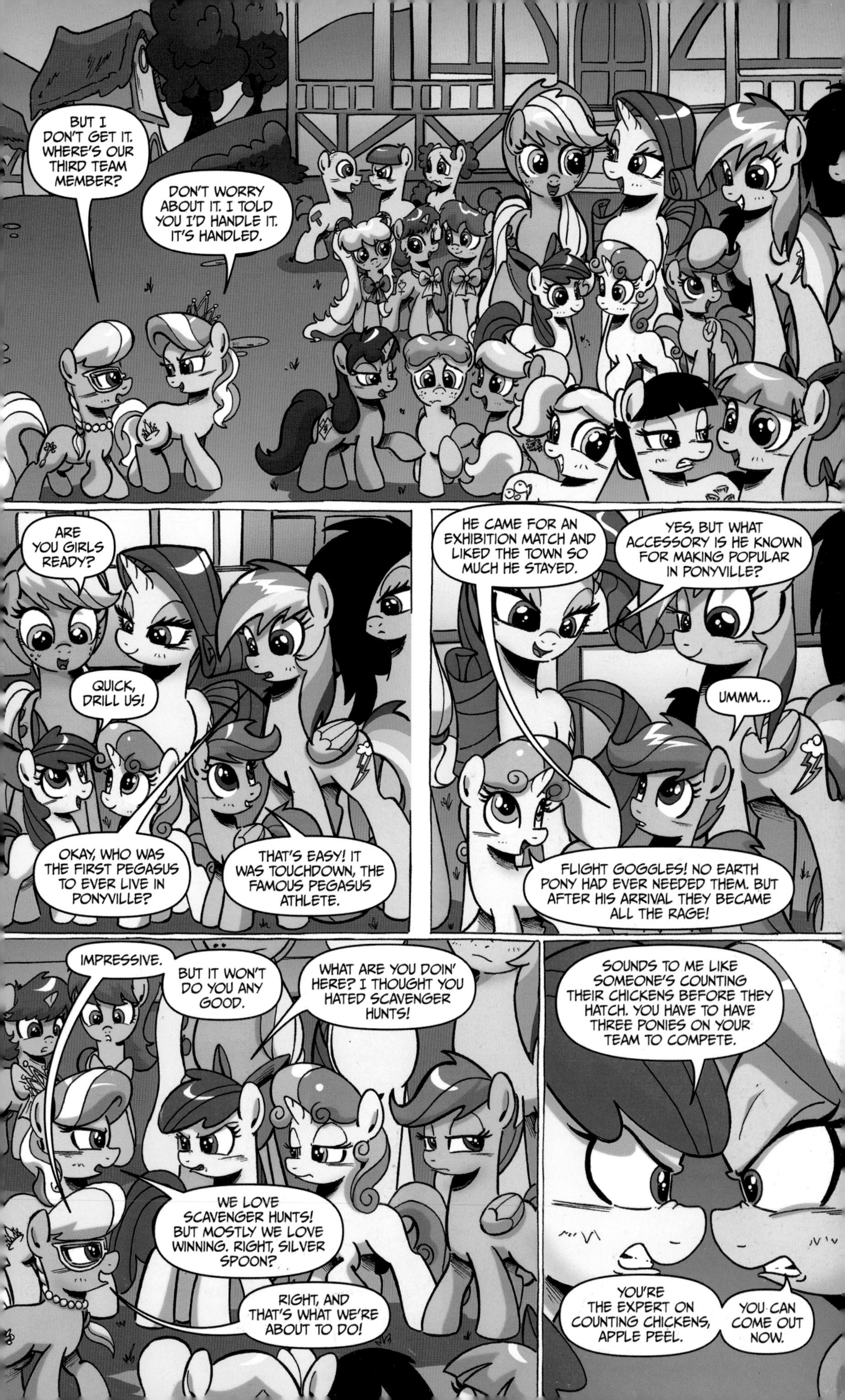

BUT I DON'T GET IT. WHERE'S OUR THIRD TEAM MEMBER?
DON'T WORRY ABOUT IT. I TOLD YOU I'D HANDLE IT. IT'S HANDLED.
ARE YOU GIRLS READY?
QUICK, DRILL US!
OKAY, WHO WAS THE FIRST PEGASUS TO EVER LIVE IN PONYVILLE?
THAT'S EASY! IT WAS TOUCHDOWN, THE FAMOUS PEGASUS ATHLETE.
HE CAME FOR AN EXHIBITION MATCH AND LIKED THE TOWN SO MUCH HE STAYED.
YES, BUT WHAT ACCESSORY IS HE KNOWN FOR MAKING POPULAR IN PONYVILLE?
UMMM...
FLIGHT GOGGLES! NO EARTH PONY HAD EVER NEEDED THEM. BUT AFTER HIS ARRIVAL THEY BECAME ALL THE RAGE!
IMPRESSIVE.
BUT IT WON'T DO YOU ANY GOOD.
WHAT ARE YOU DOIN' HERE? I THOUGHT YOU HATED SCAVENGER HUNTS!
WE LOVE SCAVENGER HUNTS! BUT MOSTLY WE LOVE WINNING. RIGHT, SILVER SPOON?
RIGHT, AND THAT'S WHAT WE'RE ABOUT TO DO!
SOUNDS TO ME LIKE SOMEONE'S COUNTING THEIR CHICKENS BEFORE THEY HATCH. YOU HAVE TO HAVE THREE PONIES ON YOUR TEAM TO COMPETE.
YOU'RE THE EXPERT ON COUNTING CHICKENS, APPLE PEEL.
YOU CAN COME OUT NOW.

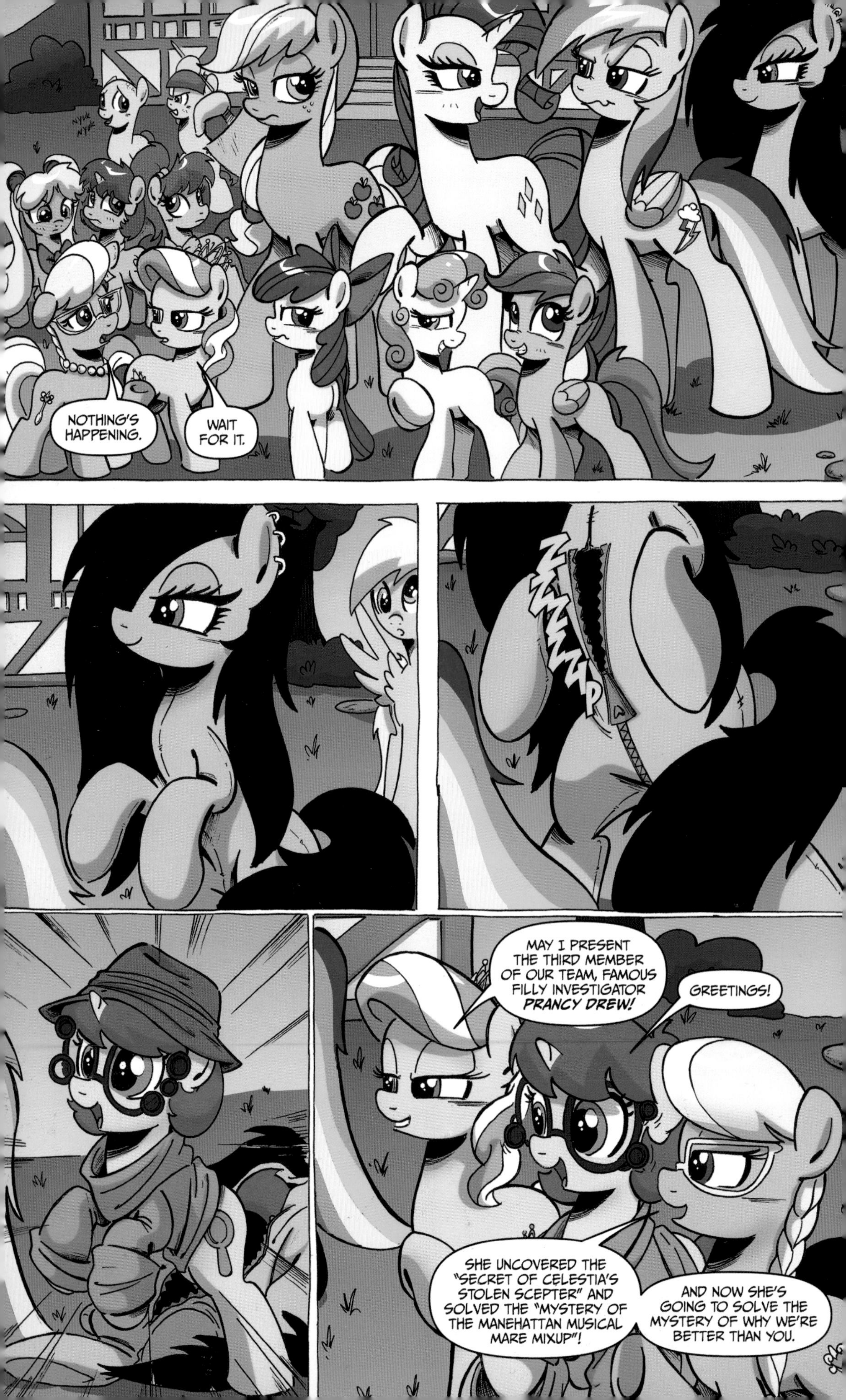
NYUK NYUK
NOTHING'S HAPPENING.
WAIT FOR IT.
MAY I PRESENT THE THIRD MEMBER OF OUR TEAM, FAMOUS FILLY INVESTIGATOR *PRANCY DREW!*
GREETINGS!
SHE UNCOVERED THE "SECRET OF CELESTIA'S STOLEN SCEPTER" AND SOLVED THE "MYSTERY OF THE MANEHATTAN MUSICAL MARE MIXUP"!
AND NOW SHE'S GOING TO SOLVE THE MYSTERY OF WHY WE'RE BETTER THAN YOU.

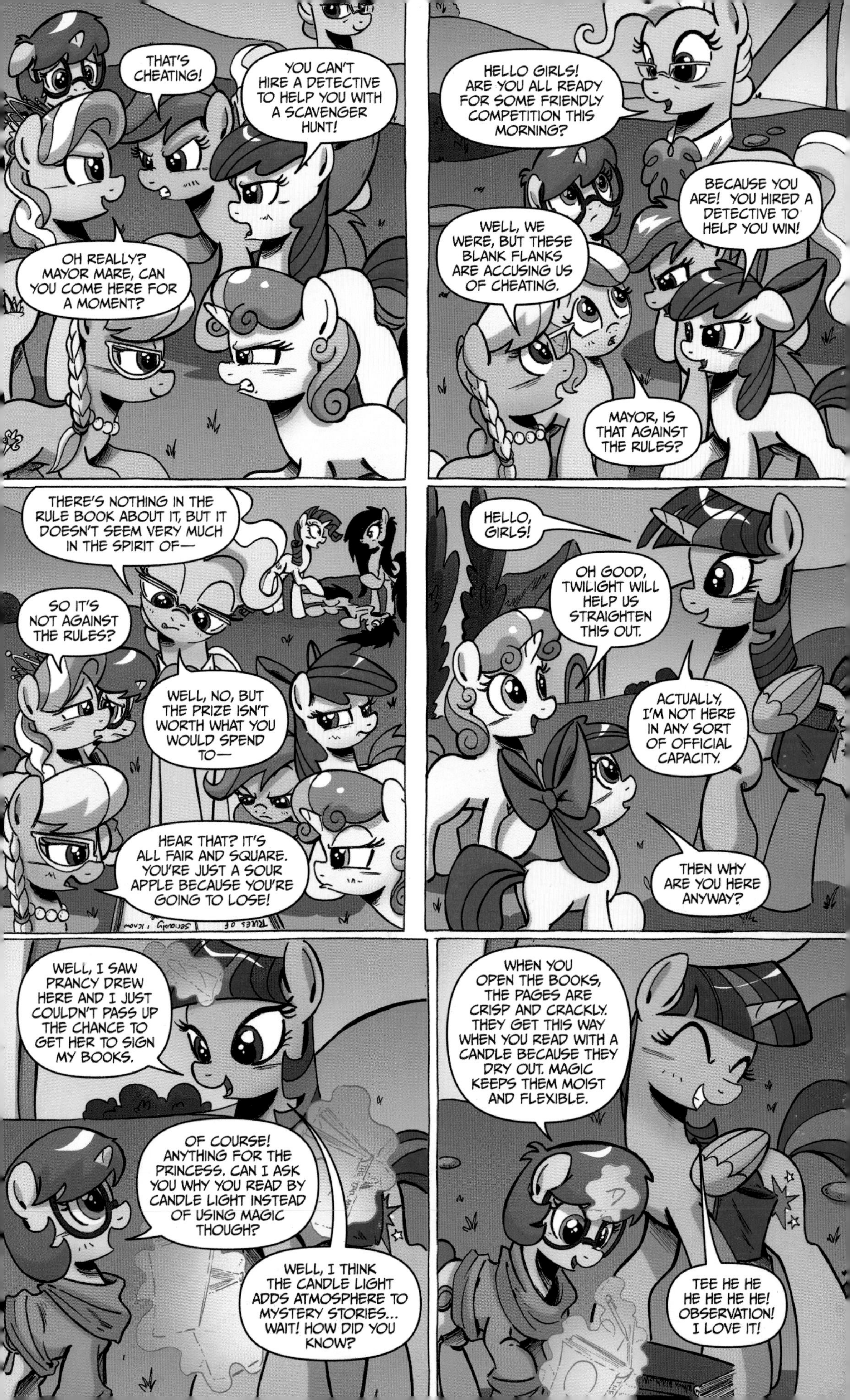
THAT'S CHEATING!
YOU CAN'T HIRE A DETECTIVE TO HELP YOU WITH A SCAVENGER HUNT!
OH REALLY? MAYOR MARE, CAN YOU COME HERE FOR A MOMENT?
HELLO GIRLS! ARE YOU ALL READY FOR SOME FRIENDLY COMPETITION THIS MORNING?
WELL, WE WERE, BUT THESE BLANK FLANKS ARE ACCUSING US OF CHEATING.
BECAUSE YOU ARE! YOU HIRED A DETECTIVE TO HELP YOU WIN!
MAYOR, IS THAT AGAINST THE RULES?
THERE'S NOTHING IN THE RULE BOOK ABOUT IT, BUT IT DOESN'T SEEM VERY MUCH IN THE SPIRIT OF—
SO IT'S NOT AGAINST THE RULES?
WELL, NO, BUT THE PRIZE ISN'T WORTH WHAT YOU WOULD SPEND TO—
HEAR THAT? IT'S ALL FAIR AND SQUARE. YOU'RE JUST A SOUR APPLE BECAUSE YOU'RE GOING TO LOSE!
HELLO, GIRLS!
OH GOOD, TWILIGHT WILL HELP US STRAIGHTEN THIS OUT.
ACTUALLY, I'M NOT HERE IN ANY SORT OF OFFICIAL CAPACITY.
THEN WHY ARE YOU HERE ANYWAY?
WELL, I SAW PRANCY DREW HERE AND I JUST COULDN'T PASS UP THE CHANCE TO GET HER TO SIGN MY BOOKS.
OF COURSE! ANYTHING FOR THE PRINCESS. CAN I ASK YOU WHY YOU READ BY CANDLE LIGHT INSTEAD OF USING MAGIC THOUGH?
WELL, I THINK THE CANDLE LIGHT ADDS ATMOSPHERE TO MYSTERY STORIES... WAIT! HOW DID YOU KNOW?
WHEN YOU OPEN THE BOOKS, THE PAGES ARE CRISP AND CRACKLY. THEY GET THIS WAY WHEN YOU READ WITH A CANDLE BECAUSE THEY DRY OUT. MAGIC KEEPS THEM MOIST AND FLEXIBLE.
TEE HE HE HE HE HE HE! OBSERVATION! I LOVE IT!

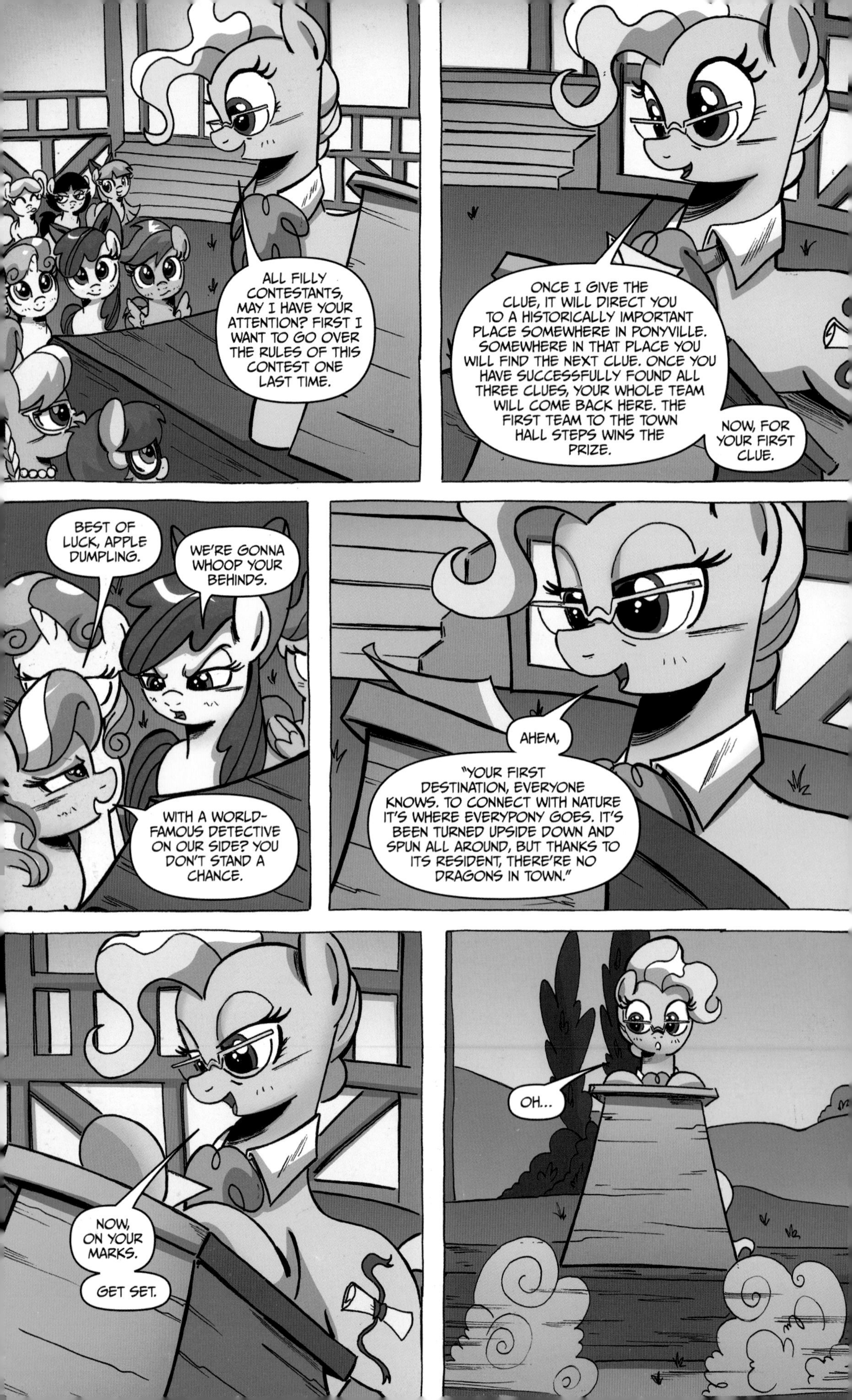
ALL FILLY CONTESTANTS, MAY I HAVE YOUR ATTENTION? FIRST I WANT TO GO OVER THE RULES OF THIS CONTEST ONE LAST TIME.
ONCE I GIVE THE CLUE, IT WILL DIRECT YOU TO A HISTORICALLY IMPORTANT PLACE SOMEWHERE IN PONYVILLE. SOMEWHERE IN THAT PLACE YOU WILL FIND THE NEXT CLUE. ONCE YOU HAVE SUCCESSFULLY FOUND ALL THREE CLUES, YOUR WHOLE TEAM WILL COME BACK HERE. THE FIRST TEAM TO THE TOWN HALL STEPS WINS THE PRIZE.
NOW, FOR YOUR FIRST CLUE.
BEST OF LUCK, APPLE DUMPLING.
WE'RE GONNA WHOOP YOUR BEHINDS.
WITH A WORLD-FAMOUS DETECTIVE ON OUR SIDE? YOU DON'T STAND A CHANCE.
AHEM,
"YOUR FIRST DESTINATION, EVERYONE KNOWS. TO CONNECT WITH NATURE IT'S WHERE EVERYPONY GOES. IT'S BEEN TURNED UPSIDE DOWN AND SPUN ALL AROUND, BUT THANKS TO ITS RESIDENT, THERE'RE NO DRAGONS IN TOWN."
NOW, ON YOUR MARKS.
GET SET.
OH...

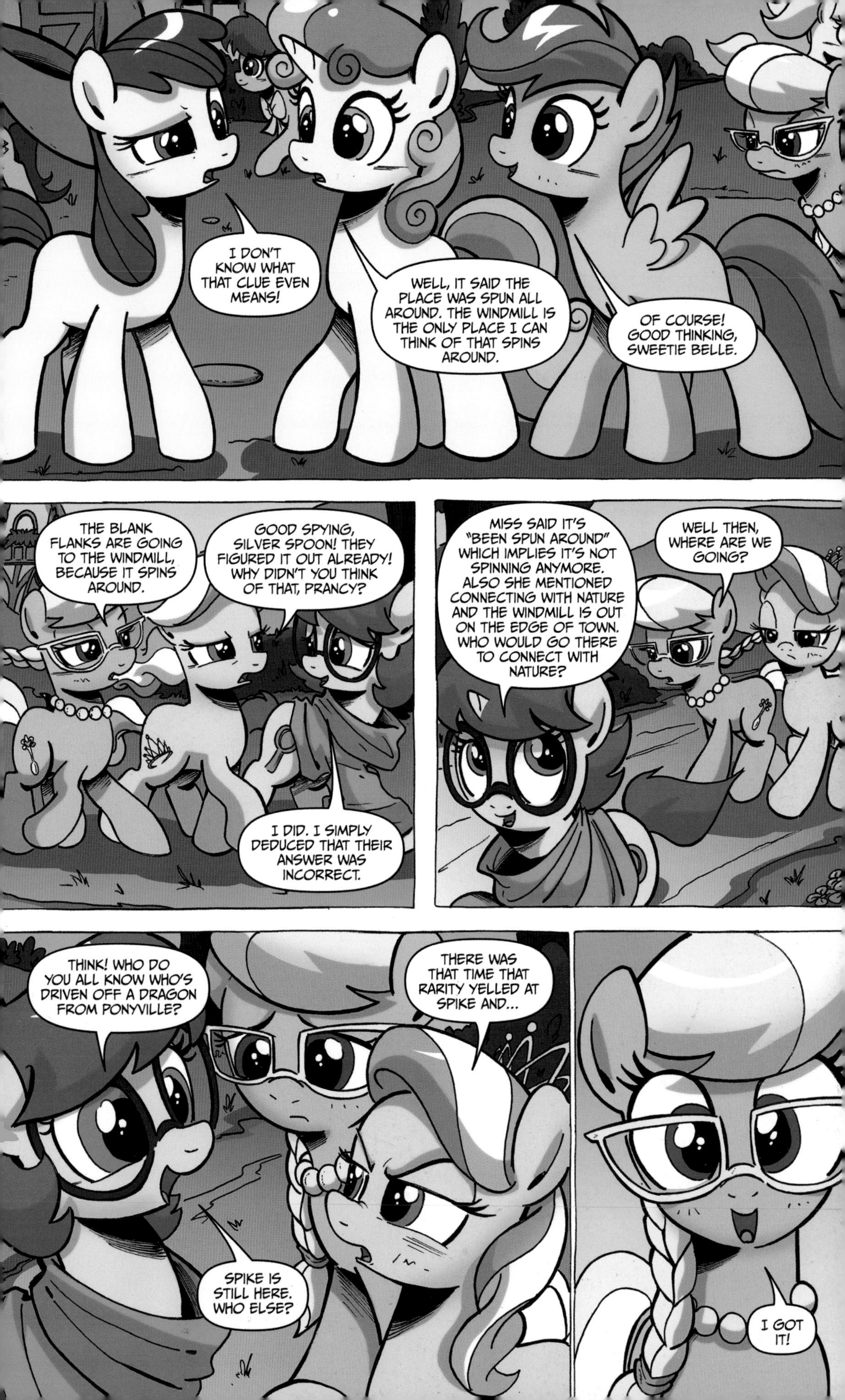
I DON'T KNOW WHAT THAT CLUE EVEN MEANS!
WELL, IT SAID THE PLACE WAS SPUN ALL AROUND. THE WINDMILL IS THE ONLY PLACE I CAN THINK OF THAT SPINS AROUND.
OF COURSE! GOOD THINKING, SWEETIE BELLE.
THE BLANK FLANKS ARE GOING TO THE WINDMILL, BECAUSE IT SPINS AROUND.
GOOD SPYING, SILVER SPOON! THEY FIGURED IT OUT ALREADY! WHY DIDN'T YOU THINK OF THAT, PRANCY?
I DID. I SIMPLY DEDUCED THAT THEIR ANSWER WAS INCORRECT.
MISS SAID IT'S "BEEN SPUN AROUND" WHICH IMPLIES IT'S NOT SPINNING ANYMORE. ALSO SHE MENTIONED CONNECTING WITH NATURE AND THE WINDMILL IS OUT ON THE EDGE OF TOWN. WHO WOULD GO THERE TO CONNECT WITH NATURE?
WELL THEN, WHERE ARE WE GOING?
THINK! WHO DO YOU ALL KNOW WHO'S DRIVEN OFF A DRAGON FROM PONYVILLE?
THERE WAS THAT TIME THAT RARITY YELLED AT SPIKE AND...
SPIKE IS STILL HERE. WHO ELSE?
I GOT IT!

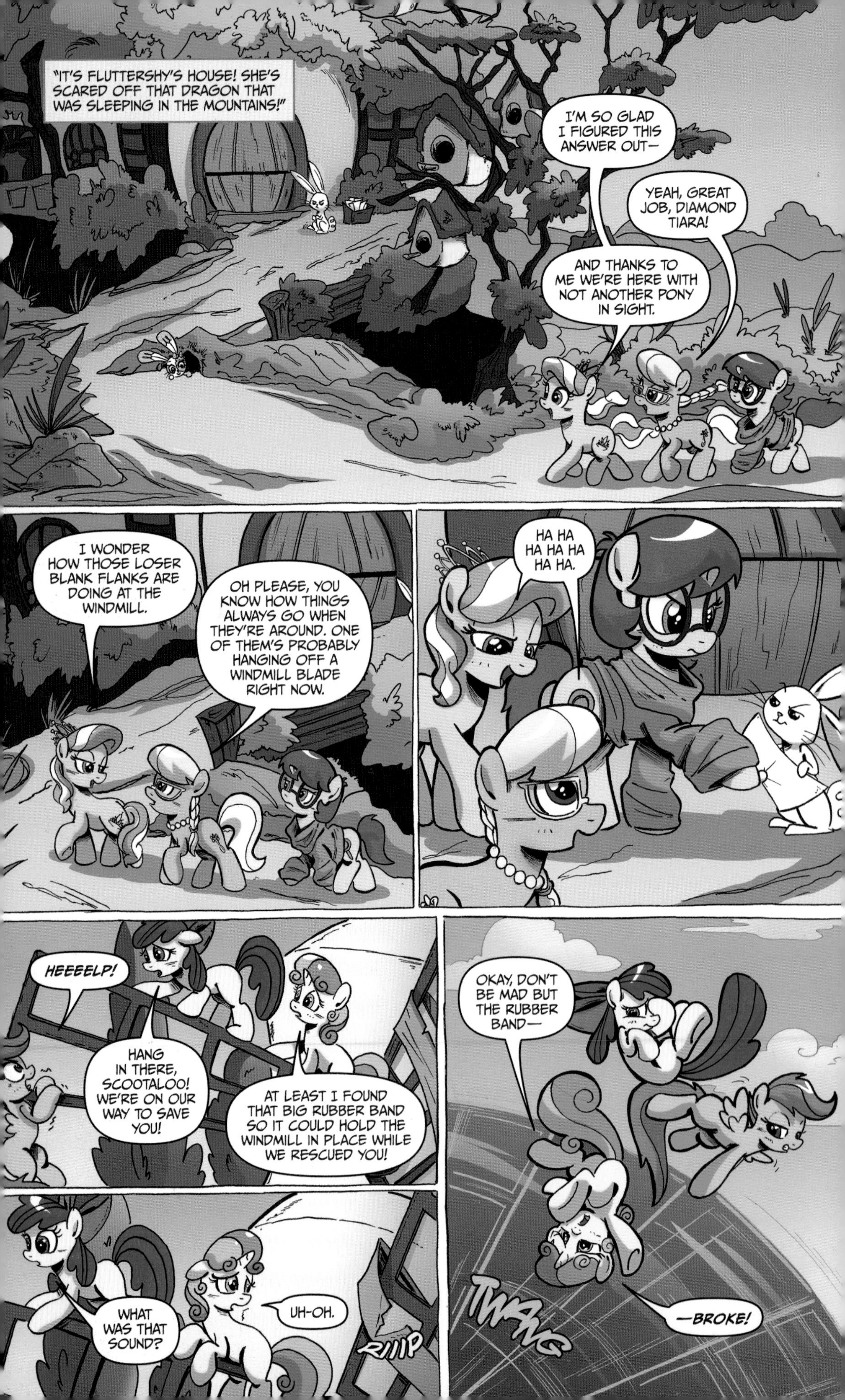
"IT'S FLUTTERSHY'S HOUSE! SHE'S SCARED OFF THAT DRAGON THAT WAS SLEEPING IN THE MOUNTAINS!"
I'M SO GLAD I FIGURED THIS ANSWER OUT—
YEAH, GREAT JOB, DIAMOND TIARA!
AND THANKS TO ME WE'RE HERE WITH NOT ANOTHER PONY IN SIGHT.
I WONDER HOW THOSE LOSER BLANK FLANKS ARE DOING AT THE WINDMILL.
OH PLEASE, YOU KNOW HOW THINGS ALWAYS GO WHEN THEY'RE AROUND. ONE OF THEM'S PROBABLY HANGING OFF A WINDMILL BLADE RIGHT NOW.
HA HA HA HA HA HA HA.
HEEEELP!
HANG IN THERE, SCOOTALOO! WE'RE ON OUR WAY TO SAVE YOU!
AT LEAST I FOUND THAT BIG RUBBER BAND SO IT COULD HOLD THE WINDMILL IN PLACE WHILE WE RESCUED YOU!
WHAT WAS THAT SOUND?
UH-OH.
RIIIP
OKAY, DON'T BE MAD BUT THE RUBBER BAND—
TWANG
—BROKE!

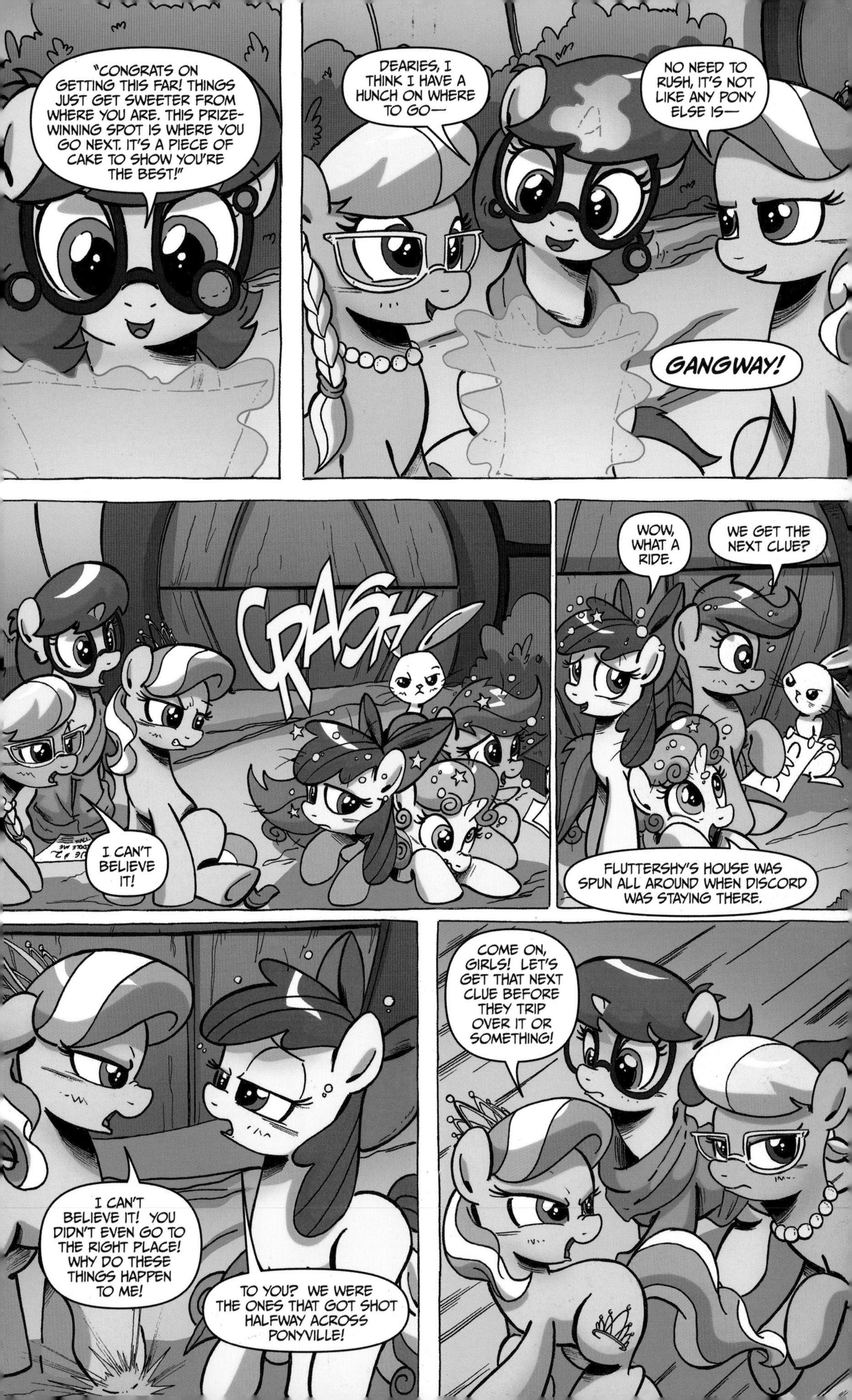
"CONGRATS ON GETTING THIS FAR! THINGS JUST GET SWEETER FROM WHERE YOU ARE. THIS PRIZE-WINNING SPOT IS WHERE YOU GO NEXT. IT'S A PIECE OF CAKE TO SHOW YOU'RE THE BEST!"
DEARIES, I THINK I HAVE A HUNCH ON WHERE TO GO—
NO NEED TO RUSH, IT'S NOT LIKE ANY PONY ELSE IS—
GANGWAY!
CRASH
I CAN'T BELIEVE IT!
WOW, WHAT A RIDE.
WE GET THE NEXT CLUE?
FLUTTERSHY'S HOUSE WAS SPUN ALL AROUND WHEN DISCORD WAS STAYING THERE.
I CAN'T BELIEVE IT! YOU DIDN'T EVEN GO TO THE RIGHT PLACE! WHY DO THESE THINGS HAPPEN TO ME!
TO YOU? WE WERE THE ONES THAT GOT SHOT HALFWAY ACROSS PONYVILLE!
COME ON, GIRLS! LET'S GET THAT NEXT CLUE BEFORE THEY TRIP OVER IT OR SOMETHING!

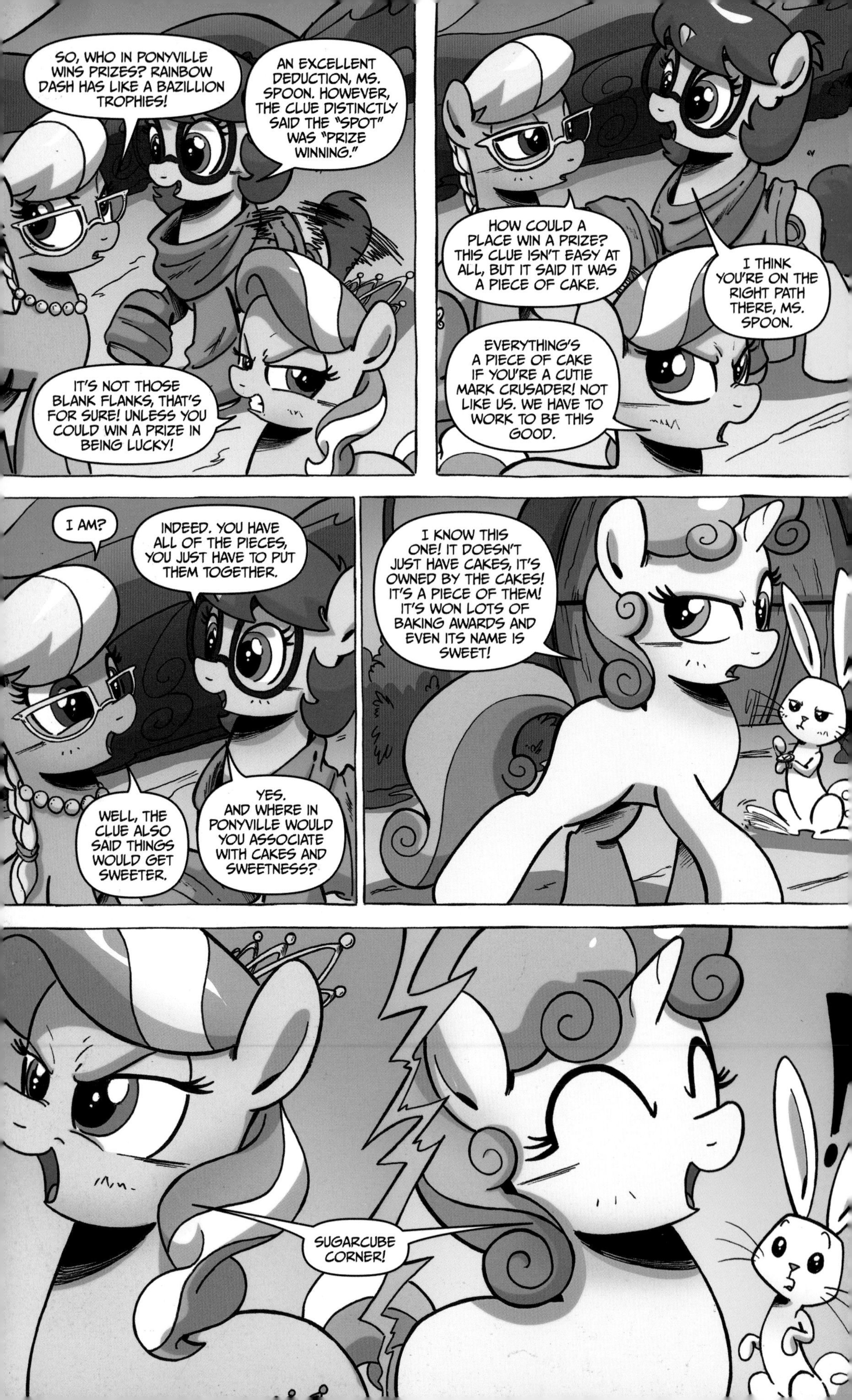

SO, WHO IN PONYVILLE WINS PRIZES? RAINBOW DASH HAS LIKE A BAZILLION TROPHIES!
AN EXCELLENT DEDUCTION, MS. SPOON. HOWEVER, THE CLUE DISTINCTLY SAID THE "SPOT" WAS "PRIZE WINNING."
IT'S NOT THOSE BLANK FLANKS, THAT'S FOR SURE! UNLESS YOU COULD WIN A PRIZE IN BEING LUCKY!
HOW COULD A PLACE WIN A PRIZE? THIS CLUE ISN'T EASY AT ALL, BUT IT SAID IT WAS A PIECE OF CAKE.
I THINK YOU'RE ON THE RIGHT PATH THERE, MS. SPOON.
EVERYTHING'S A PIECE OF CAKE IF YOU'RE A CUTIE MARK CRUSADER! NOT LIKE US. WE HAVE TO WORK TO BE THIS GOOD.
I AM?
INDEED. YOU HAVE ALL OF THE PIECES, YOU JUST HAVE TO PUT THEM TOGETHER.
WELL, THE CLUE ALSO SAID THINGS WOULD GET SWEETER.
YES. AND WHERE IN PONYVILLE WOULD YOU ASSOCIATE WITH CAKES AND SWEETNESS?
I KNOW THIS ONE! IT DOESN'T JUST HAVE CAKES, IT'S OWNED BY THE CAKES! IT'S A PIECE OF THEM! IT'S WON LOTS OF BAKING AWARDS AND EVEN ITS NAME IS SWEET!
SUGARCUBE CORNER!
!

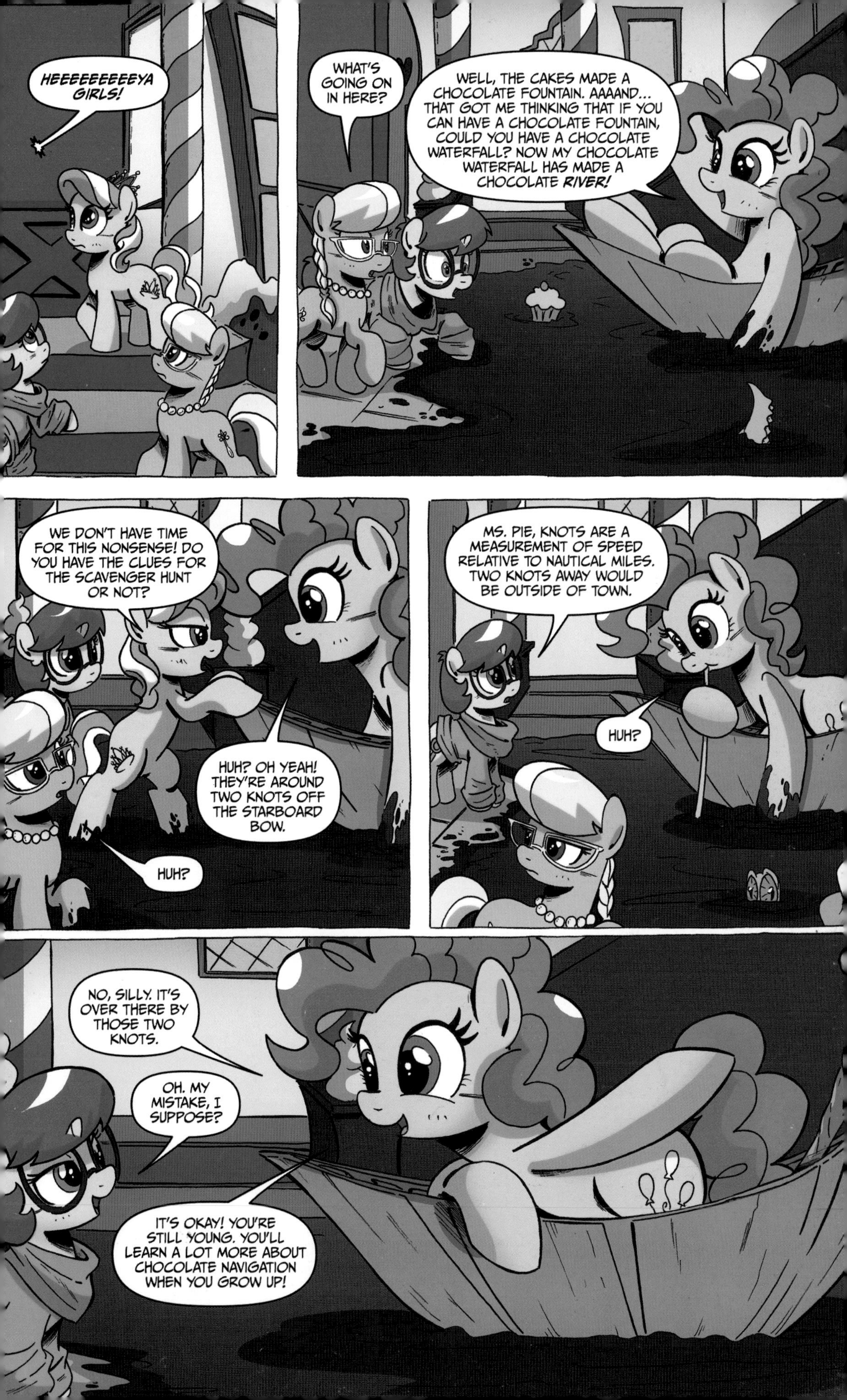
HEEEEEEEEEYA GIRLS!
WHAT'S GOING ON IN HERE?
WELL, THE CAKES MADE A CHOCOLATE FOUNTAIN. AAAAND... THAT GOT ME THINKING THAT IF YOU CAN HAVE A CHOCOLATE FOUNTAIN, COULD YOU HAVE A CHOCOLATE WATERFALL? NOW MY CHOCOLATE WATERFALL HAS MADE A CHOCOLATE RIVER!
WE DON'T HAVE TIME FOR THIS NONSENSE! DO YOU HAVE THE CLUES FOR THE SCAVENGER HUNT OR NOT?
HUH? OH YEAH! THEY'RE AROUND TWO KNOTS OFF THE STARBOARD BOW.
HUH?
MS. PIE, KNOTS ARE A MEASUREMENT OF SPEED RELATIVE TO NAUTICAL MILES. TWO KNOTS AWAY WOULD BE OUTSIDE OF TOWN.
HUH?
NO, SILLY. IT'S OVER THERE BY THOSE TWO KNOTS.
OH. MY MISTAKE, I SUPPOSE?
IT'S OKAY! YOU'RE STILL YOUNG. YOU'LL LEARN A LOT MORE ABOUT CHOCOLATE NAVIGATION WHEN YOU GROW UP!

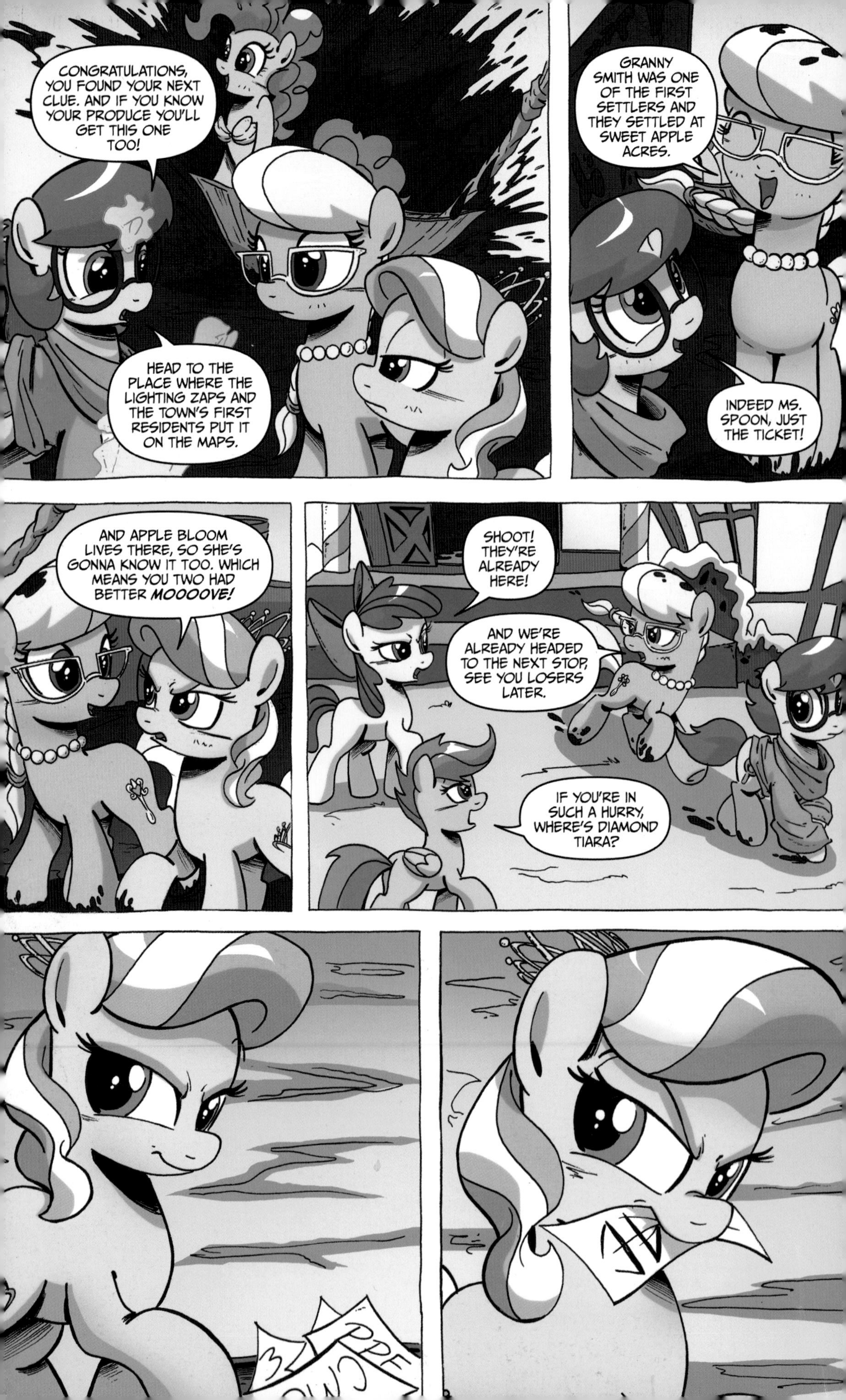
CONGRATULATIONS, YOU FOUND YOUR NEXT CLUE. AND IF YOU KNOW YOUR PRODUCE YOU'LL GET THIS ONE TOO!
HEAD TO THE PLACE WHERE THE LIGHTING ZAPS AND THE TOWN'S FIRST RESIDENTS PUT IT ON THE MAPS.
GRANNY SMITH WAS ONE OF THE FIRST SETTLERS AND THEY SETTLED AT SWEET APPLE ACRES.
INDEED MS. SPOON, JUST THE TICKET!
AND APPLE BLOOM LIVES THERE, SO SHE'S GONNA KNOW IT TOO. WHICH MEANS YOU TWO HAD BETTER MOOOOVE!
SHOOT! THEY'RE ALREADY HERE!
AND WE'RE ALREADY HEADED TO THE NEXT STOP, SEE YOU LOSERS LATER.
IF YOU'RE IN SUCH A HURRY, WHERE'S DIAMOND TIARA?

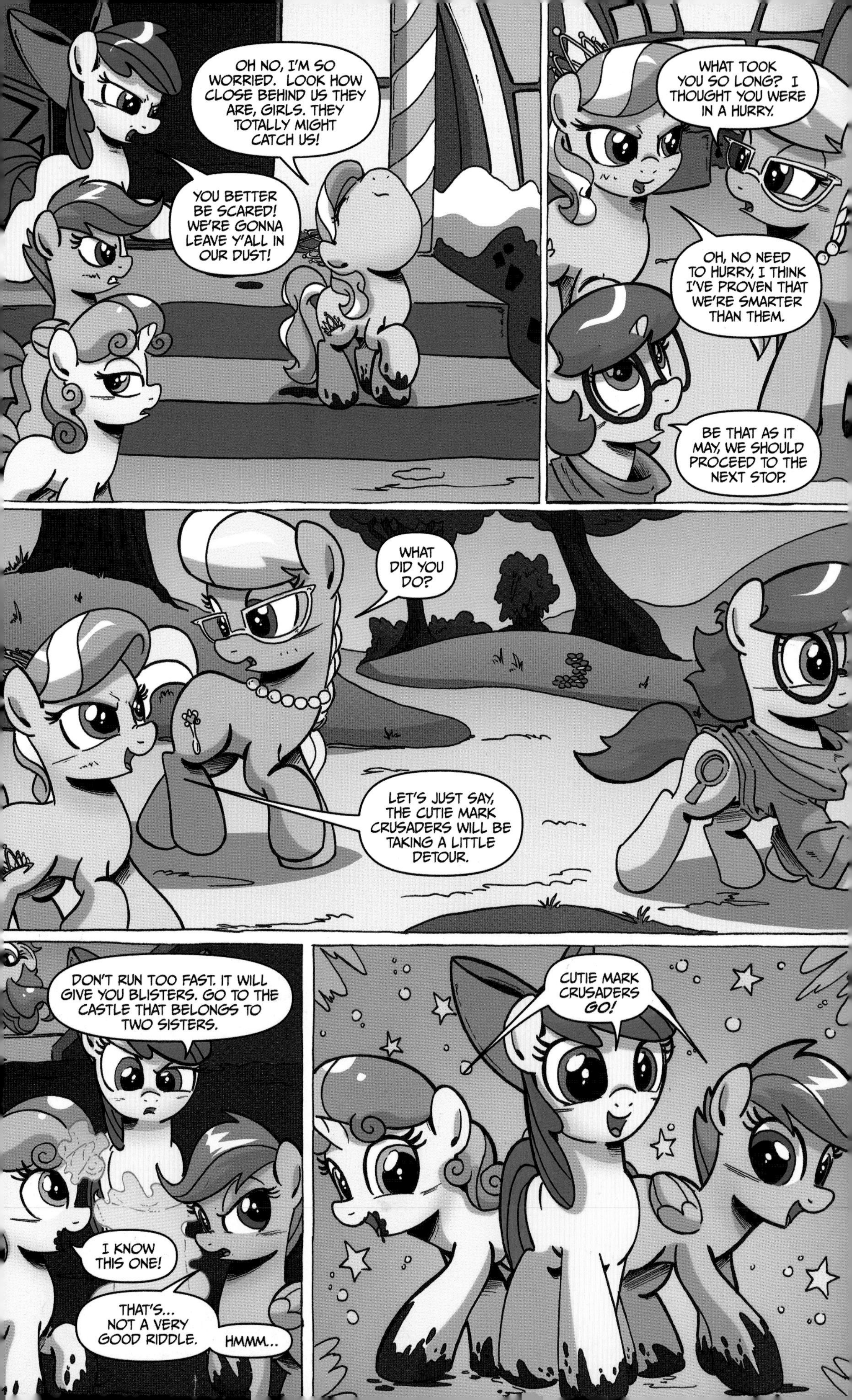

OH NO, I'M SO WORRIED. LOOK HOW CLOSE BEHIND US THEY ARE, GIRLS. THEY TOTALLY MIGHT CATCH US!
YOU BETTER BE SCARED! WE'RE GONNA LEAVE Y'ALL IN OUR DUST!
WHAT TOOK YOU SO LONG? I THOUGHT YOU WERE IN A HURRY.
OH, NO NEED TO HURRY, I THINK I'VE PROVEN THAT WE'RE SMARTER THAN THEM.
BE THAT AS IT MAY, WE SHOULD PROCEED TO THE NEXT STOP.
WHAT DID YOU DO?
LET'S JUST SAY, THE CUTIE MARK CRUSADERS WILL BE TAKING A LITTLE DETOUR.
DON'T RUN TOO FAST. IT WILL GIVE YOU BLISTERS. GO TO THE CASTLE THAT BELONGS TO TWO SISTERS.
I KNOW THIS ONE!
THAT'S... NOT A VERY GOOD RIDDLE.
HMMM...
CUTIE MARK CRUSADERS GO!

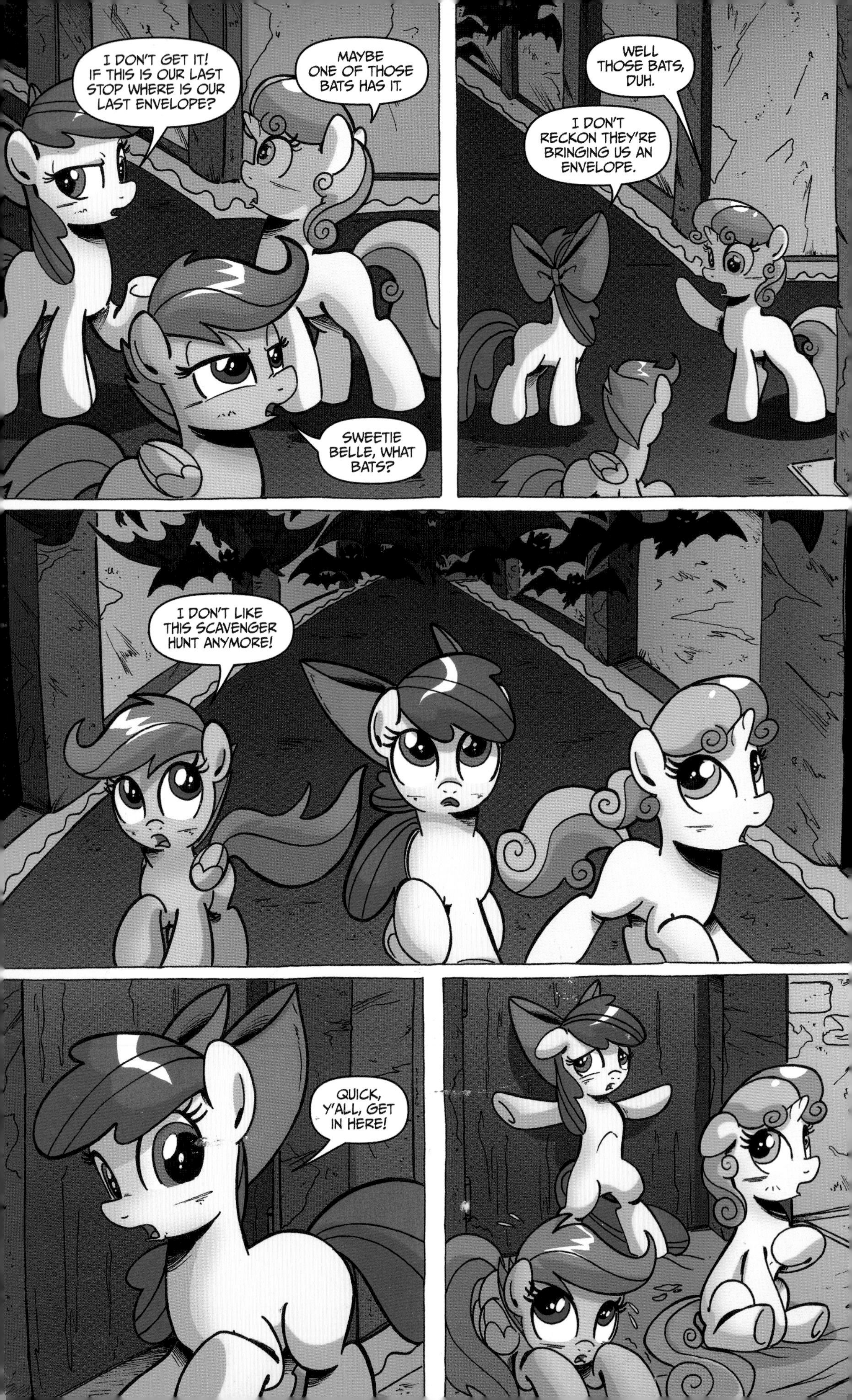
I DON'T GET IT! IF THIS IS OUR LAST STOP WHERE IS OUR LAST ENVELOPE?
MAYBE ONE OF THOSE BATS HAS IT.
SWEETIE BELLE, WHAT BATS?
WELL THOSE BATS, DUH.
I DON'T RECKON THEY'RE BRINGING US AN ENVELOPE.
I DON'T LIKE THIS SCAVENGER HUNT ANYMORE!
QUICK, Y'ALL, GET IN HERE!

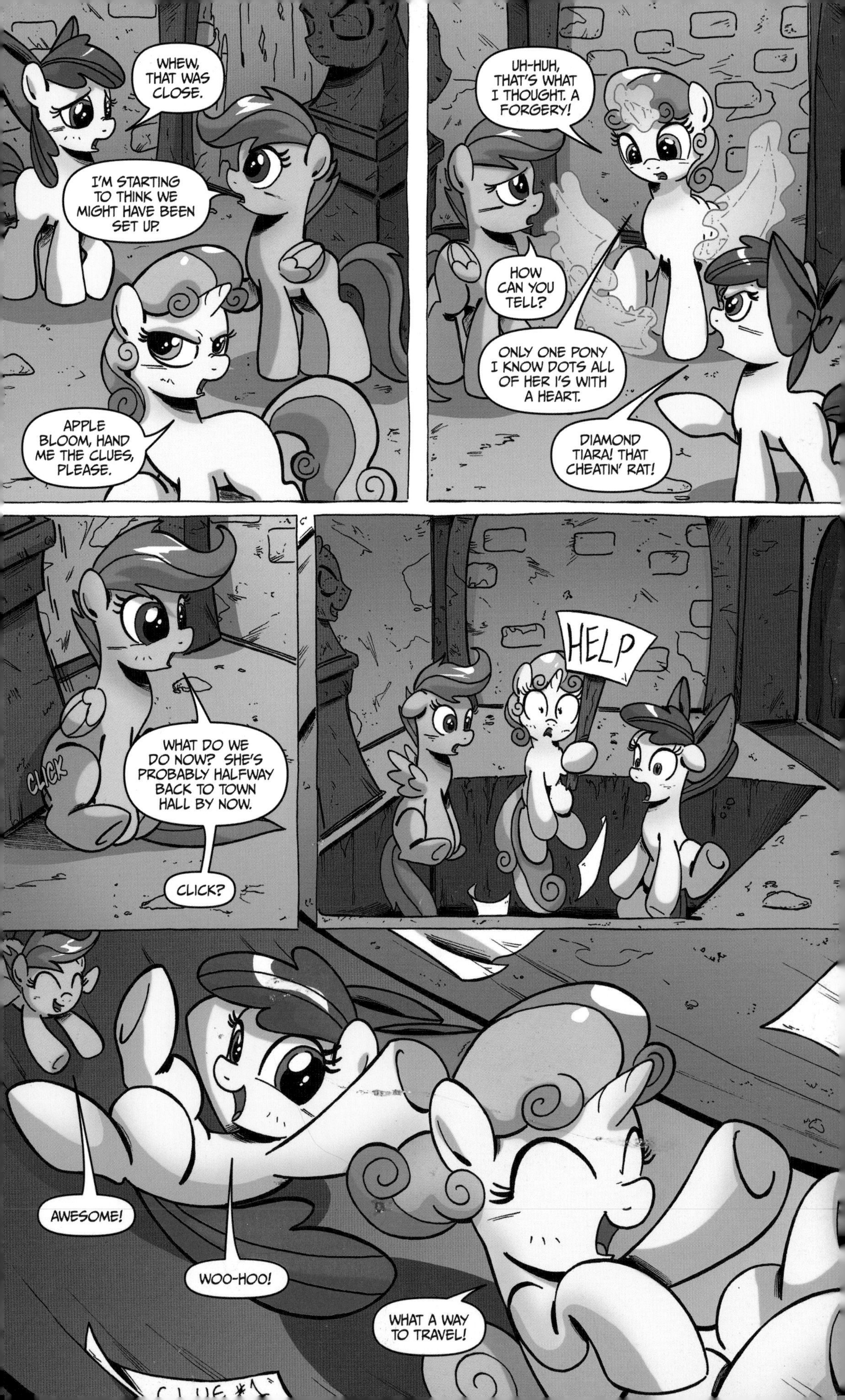
WHEW, THAT WAS CLOSE.
I'M STARTING TO THINK WE MIGHT HAVE BEEN SET UP.
APPLE BLOOM, HAND ME THE CLUES, PLEASE.
UH-HUH, THAT'S WHAT I THOUGHT. A FORGERY!
HOW CAN YOU TELL?
ONLY ONE PONY I KNOW DOTS ALL OF HER I'S WITH A HEART.
DIAMOND TIARA! THAT CHEATIN' RAT!
CLICK
WHAT DO WE DO NOW? SHE'S PROBABLY HALFWAY BACK TO TOWN HALL BY NOW.
CLICK?
HELP
AWESOME!
WOO-HOO!
WHAT A WAY TO TRAVEL!

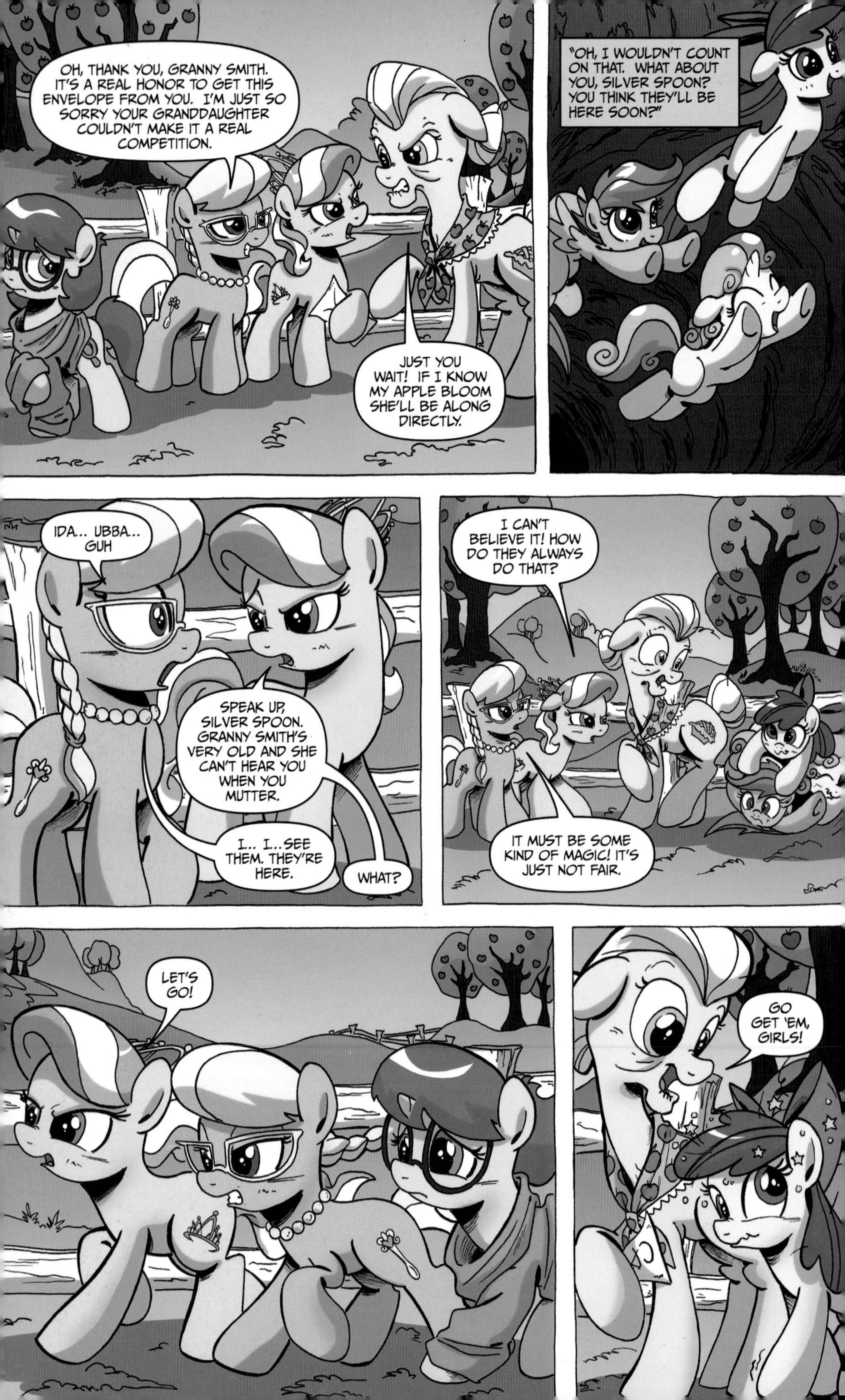
OH, THANK YOU, GRANNY SMITH. IT'S A REAL HONOR TO GET THIS ENVELOPE FROM YOU. I'M JUST SO SORRY YOUR GRANDDAUGHTER COULDN'T MAKE IT A REAL COMPETITION.
JUST YOU WAIT! IF I KNOW MY APPLE BLOOM SHE'LL BE ALONG DIRECTLY.
"OH, I WOULDN'T COUNT ON THAT. WHAT ABOUT YOU, SILVER SPOON? YOU THINK THEY'LL BE HERE SOON?"
IDA... UBBA... GUH
SPEAK UP, SILVER SPOON. GRANNY SMITH'S VERY OLD AND SHE CAN'T HEAR YOU WHEN YOU MUTTER.
I... I...SEE THEM. THEY'RE HERE.
WHAT?
I CAN'T BELIEVE IT! HOW DO THEY ALWAYS DO THAT?
IT MUST BE SOME KIND OF MAGIC! IT'S JUST NOT FAIR.
LET'S GO!
GO GET 'EM, GIRLS!

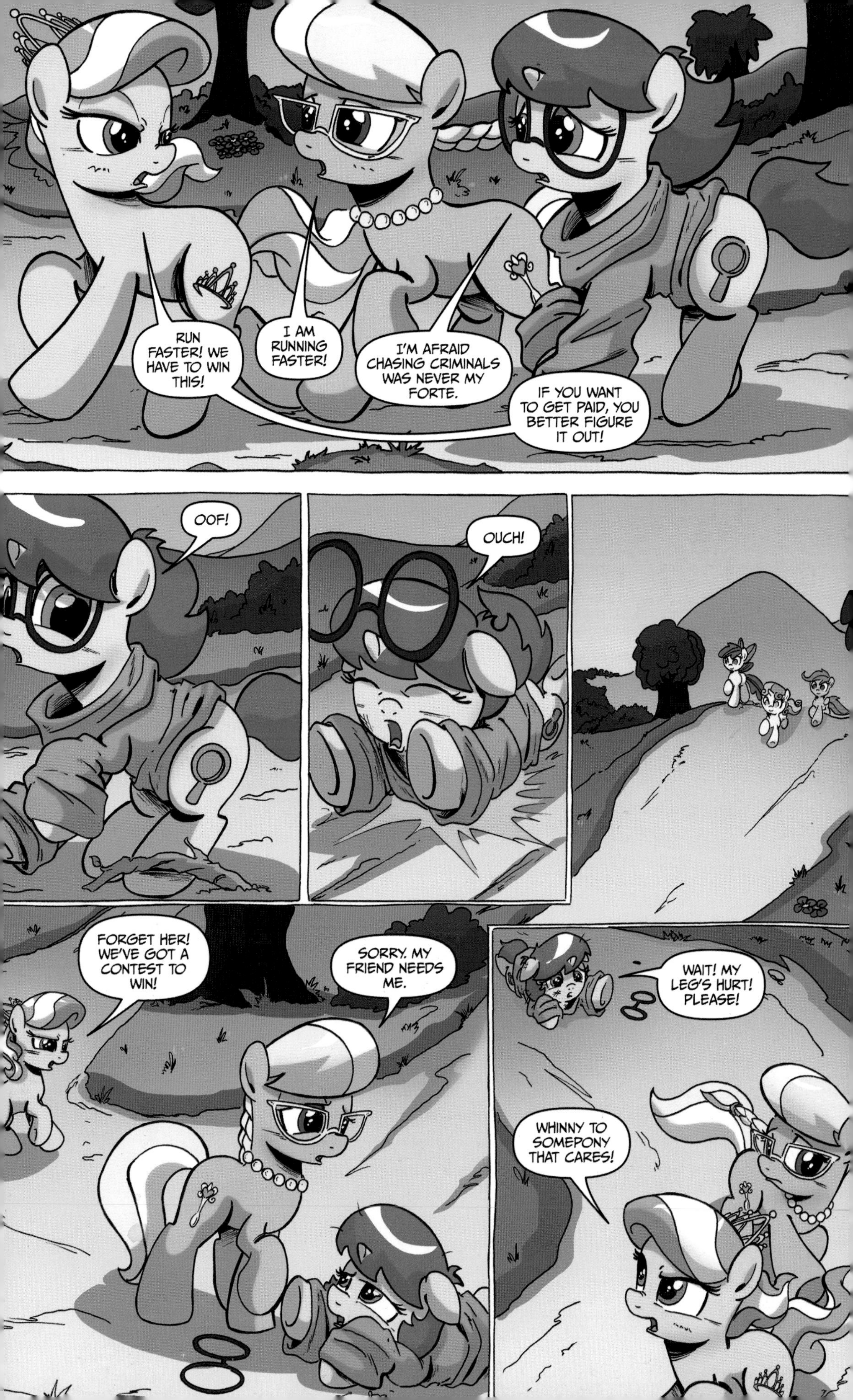
RUN FASTER! WE HAVE TO WIN THIS!
I AM RUNNING FASTER!
I'M AFRAID CHASING CRIMINALS WAS NEVER MY FORTE.
IF YOU WANT TO GET PAID, YOU BETTER FIGURE IT OUT!
OOF!
OUCH!
FORGET HER! WE'VE GOT A CONTEST TO WIN!
SORRY. MY FRIEND NEEDS ME.
WAIT! MY LEG'S HURT! PLEASE!
WHINNY TO SOMEPONY THAT CARES!

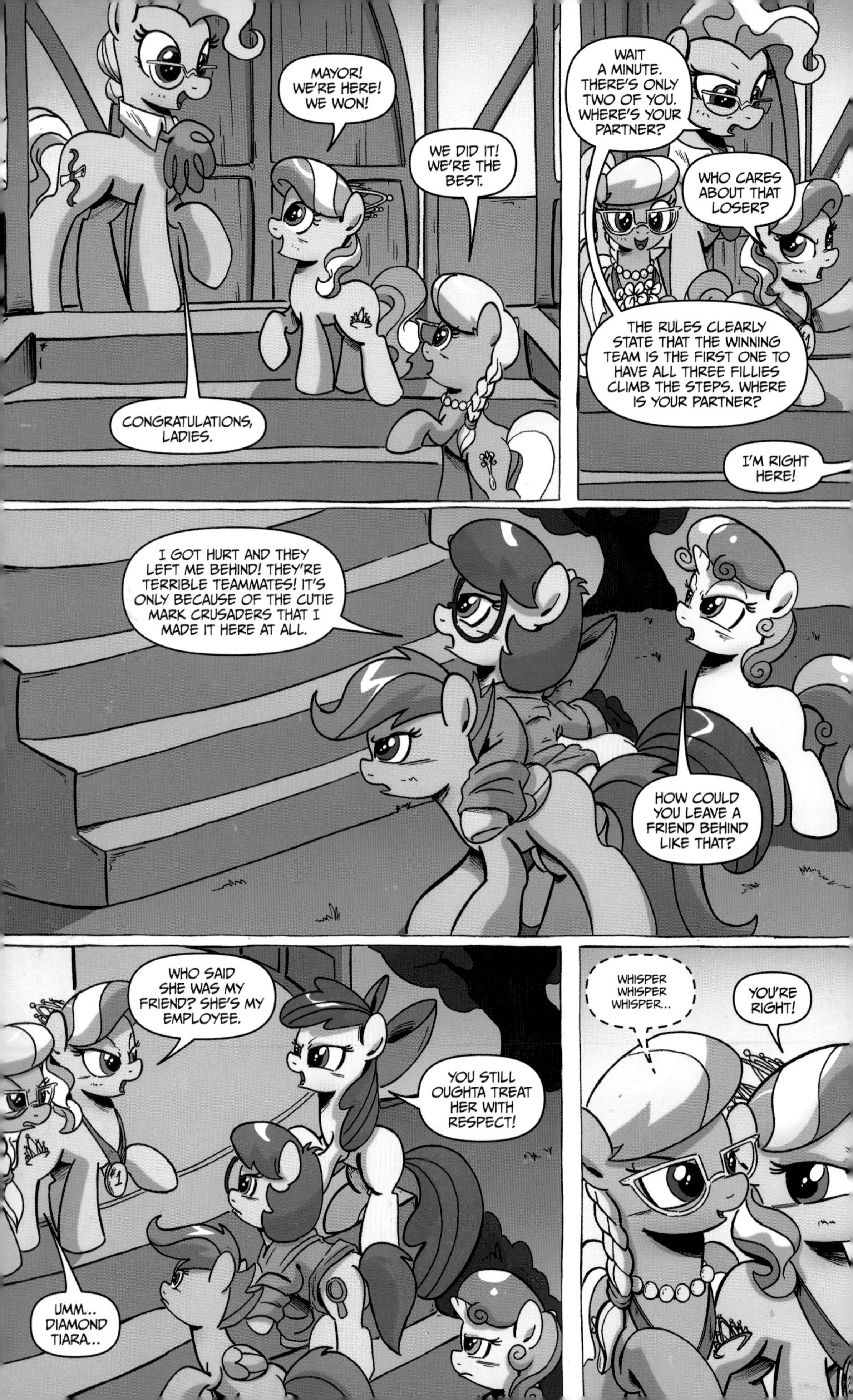
MAYOR! WE'RE HERE! WE WON!
WE DID IT! WE'RE THE BEST.
CONGRATULATIONS, LADIES.
WAIT A MINUTE. THERE'S ONLY TWO OF YOU. WHERE'S YOUR PARTNER?
WHO CARES ABOUT THAT LOSER?
THE RULES CLEARLY STATE THAT THE WINNING TEAM IS THE FIRST ONE TO HAVE ALL THREE FILLIES CLIMB THE STEPS. WHERE IS YOUR PARTNER?
I'M RIGHT HERE!
I GOT HURT AND THEY LEFT ME BEHIND! THEY'RE TERRIBLE TEAMMATES! IT'S ONLY BECAUSE OF THE CUTIE MARK CRUSADERS THAT I MADE IT HERE AT ALL.
HOW COULD YOU LEAVE A FRIEND BEHIND LIKE THAT?
WHO SAID SHE WAS MY FRIEND? SHE'S MY EMPLOYEE.
YOU STILL OUGHTA TREAT HER WITH RESPECT!
UMM... DIAMOND TIARA...
WHISPER WHISPER WHISPER...
YOU'RE RIGHT!

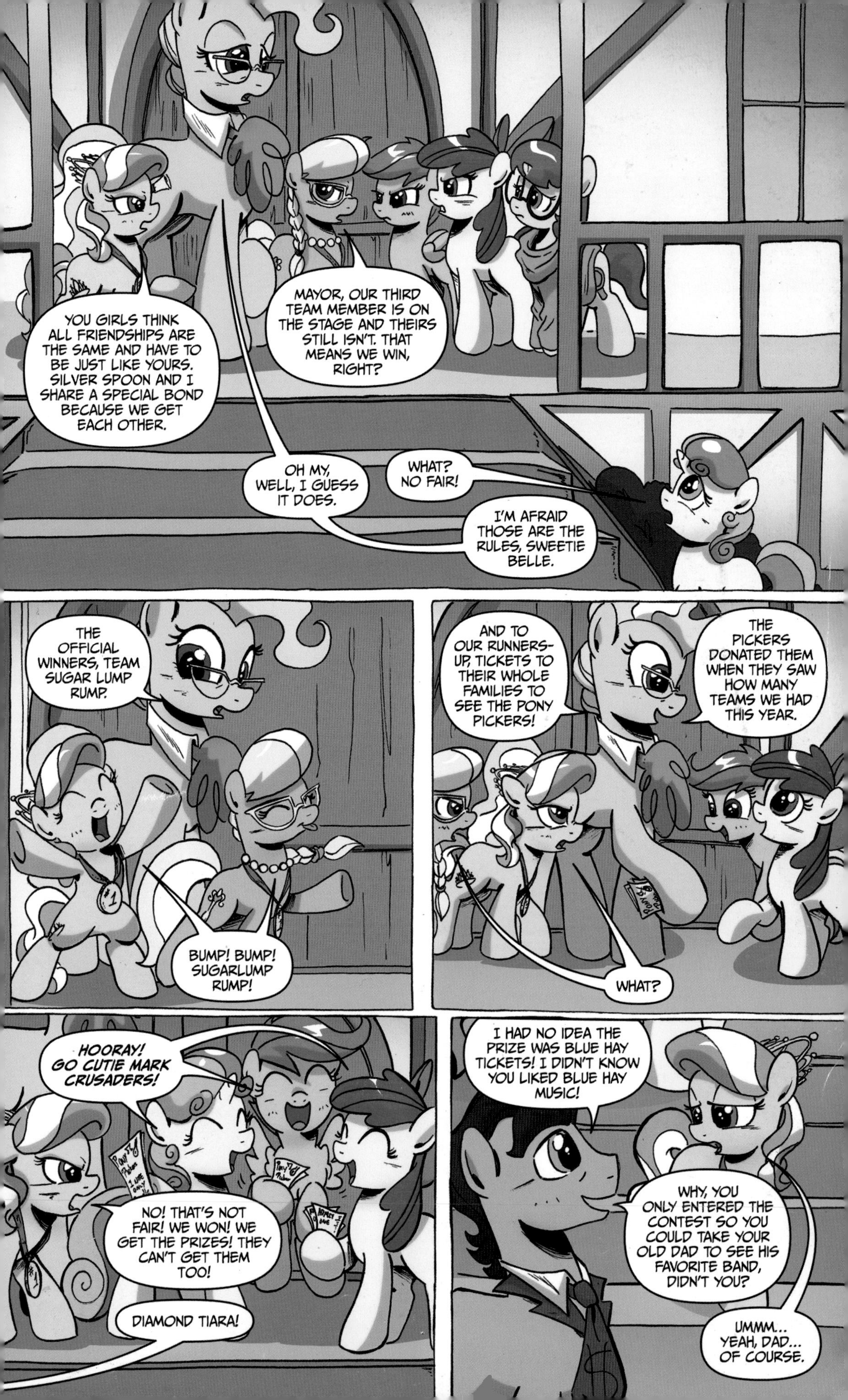
YOU GIRLS THINK ALL FRIENDSHIPS ARE THE SAME AND HAVE TO BE JUST LIKE YOURS. SILVER SPOON AND I SHARE A SPECIAL BOND BECAUSE WE GET EACH OTHER.
MAYOR, OUR THIRD TEAM MEMBER IS ON THE STAGE AND THEIRS STILL ISN'T. THAT MEANS WE WIN, RIGHT?
OH MY, WELL, I GUESS IT DOES.
WHAT? NO FAIR!
I'M AFRAID THOSE ARE THE RULES, SWEETIE BELLE.
THE OFFICIAL WINNERS, TEAM SUGAR LUMP RUMP.
BUMP! BUMP! SUGARLUMP RUMP!
AND TO OUR RUNNERS-UP, TICKETS TO THEIR WHOLE FAMILIES TO SEE THE PONY PICKERS!
THE PICKERS DONATED THEM WHEN THEY SAW HOW MANY TEAMS WE HAD THIS YEAR.
WHAT?
HOORAY! GO CUTIE MARK CRUSADERS!
NO! THAT'S NOT FAIR! WE WON! WE GET THE PRIZES! THEY CAN'T GET THEM TOO!
DIAMOND TIARA!
I HAD NO IDEA THE PRIZE WAS BLUE HAY TICKETS! I DIDN'T KNOW YOU LIKED BLUE HAY MUSIC!
WHY, YOU ONLY ENTERED THE CONTEST SO YOU COULD TAKE YOUR OLD DAD TO SEE HIS FAVORITE BAND, DIDN'T YOU?
UMMM... YEAH, DAD... OF COURSE.

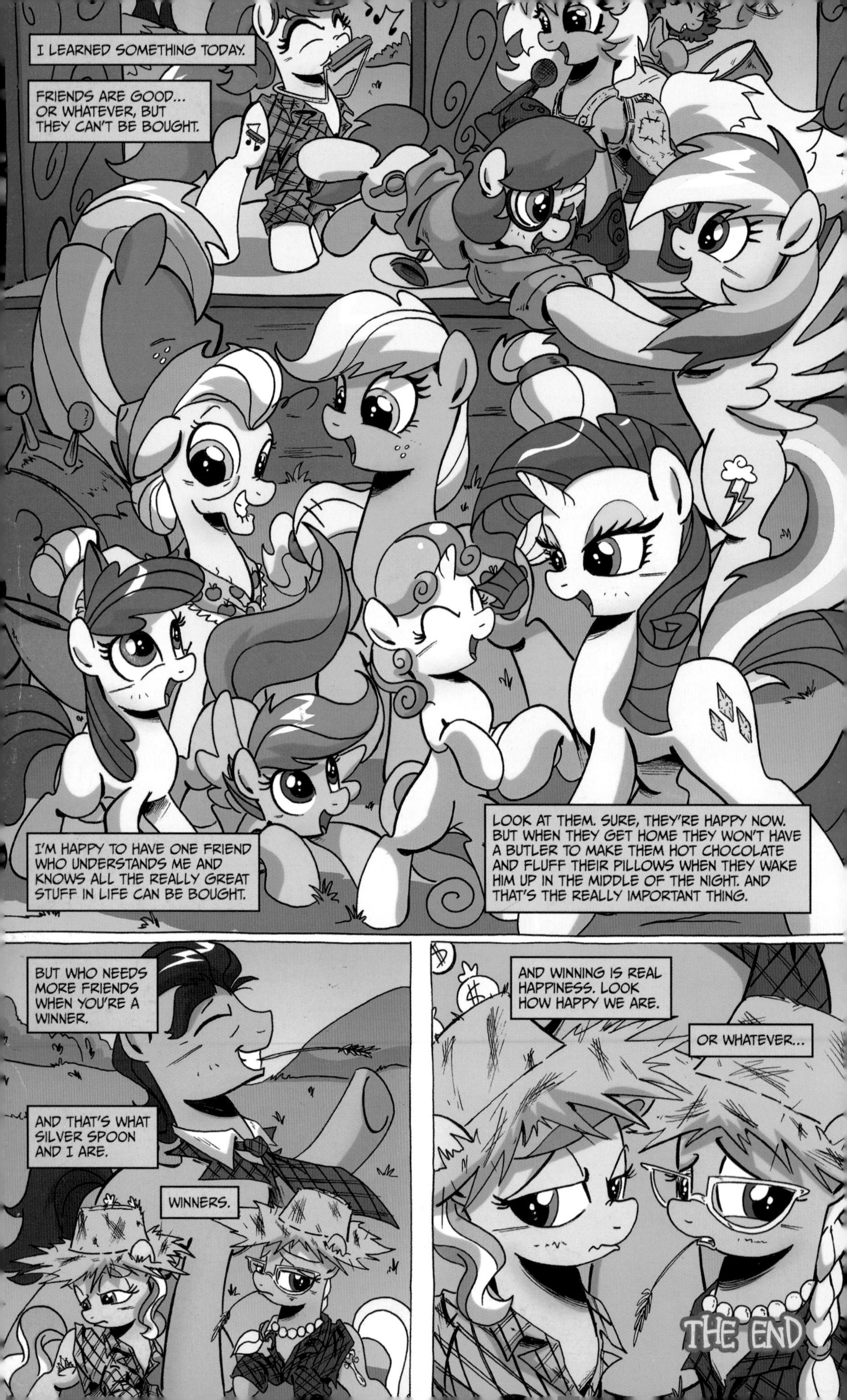

I LEARNED SOMETHING TODAY.
FRIENDS ARE GOOD... OR WHATEVER, BUT THEY CAN'T BE BOUGHT.
I'M HAPPY TO HAVE ONE FRIEND WHO UNDERSTANDS ME AND KNOWS ALL THE REALLY GREAT STUFF IN LIFE CAN BE BOUGHT.
LOOK AT THEM. SURE, THEY'RE HAPPY NOW. BUT WHEN THEY GET HOME THEY WON'T HAVE A BUTLER TO MAKE THEM HOT CHOCOLATE AND FLUFF THEIR PILLOWS WHEN THEY WAKE HIM UP IN THE MIDDLE OF THE NIGHT. AND THAT'S THE REALLY IMPORTANT THING.
BUT WHO NEEDS MORE FRIENDS WHEN YOU'RE A WINNER.
AND THAT'S WHAT SILVER SPOON AND I ARE.
WINNERS.
AND WINNING IS REAL HAPPINESS. LOOK HOW HAPPY WE ARE.
OR WHATEVER...
THE END

my LITTLE PONY

FRIENDS FOREVER

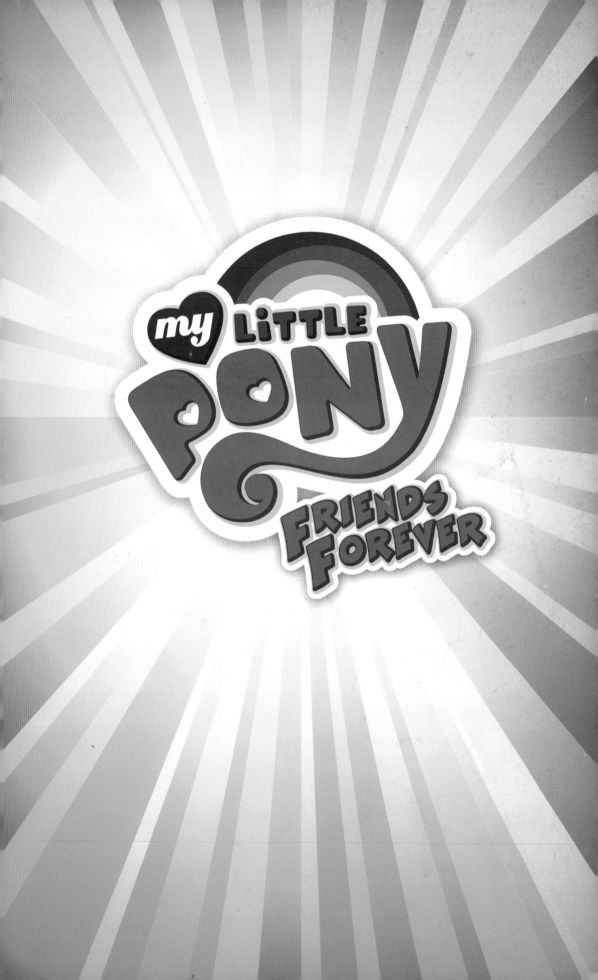

ART BY AGNES GARBOWSKA

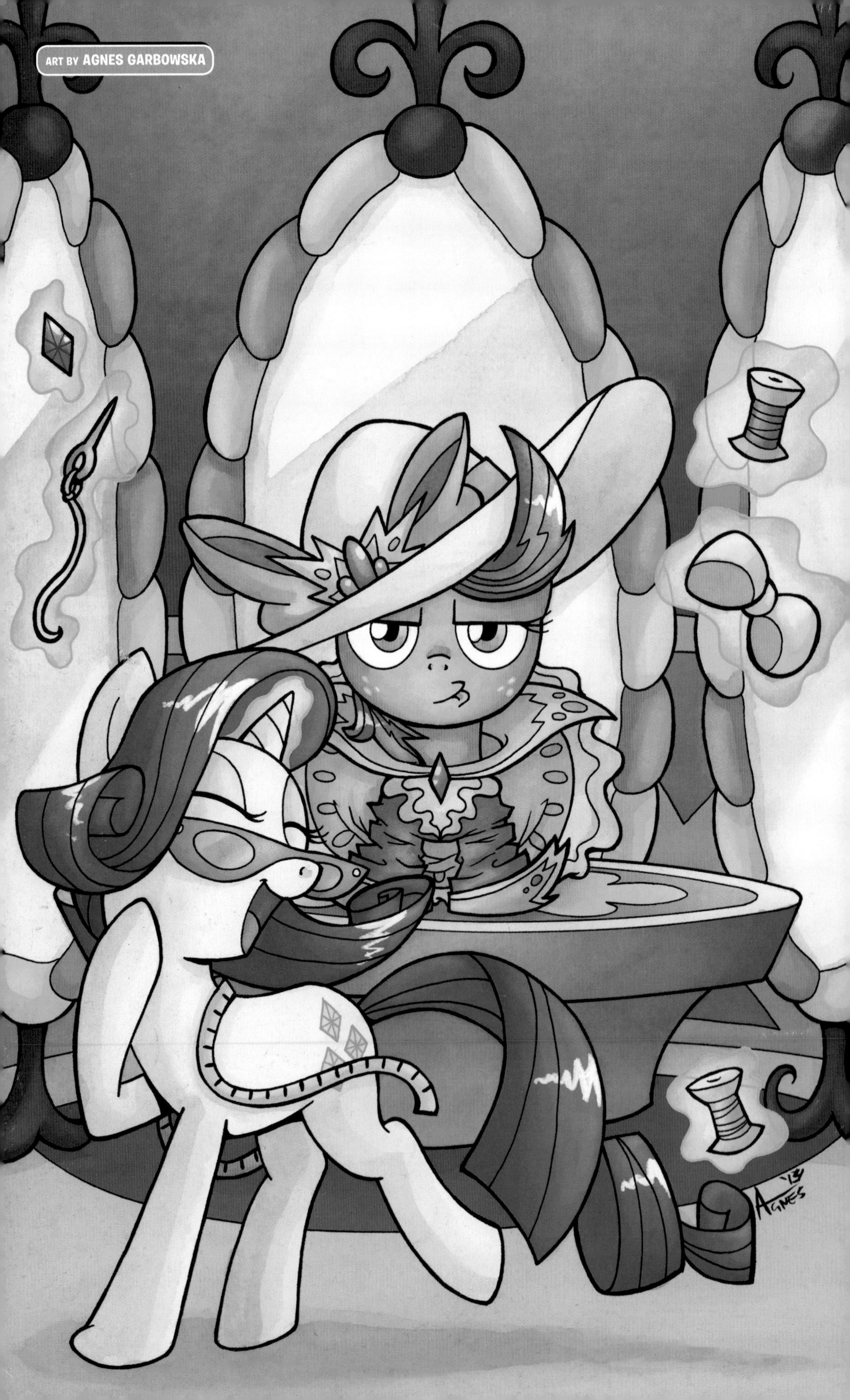
AGNES '13

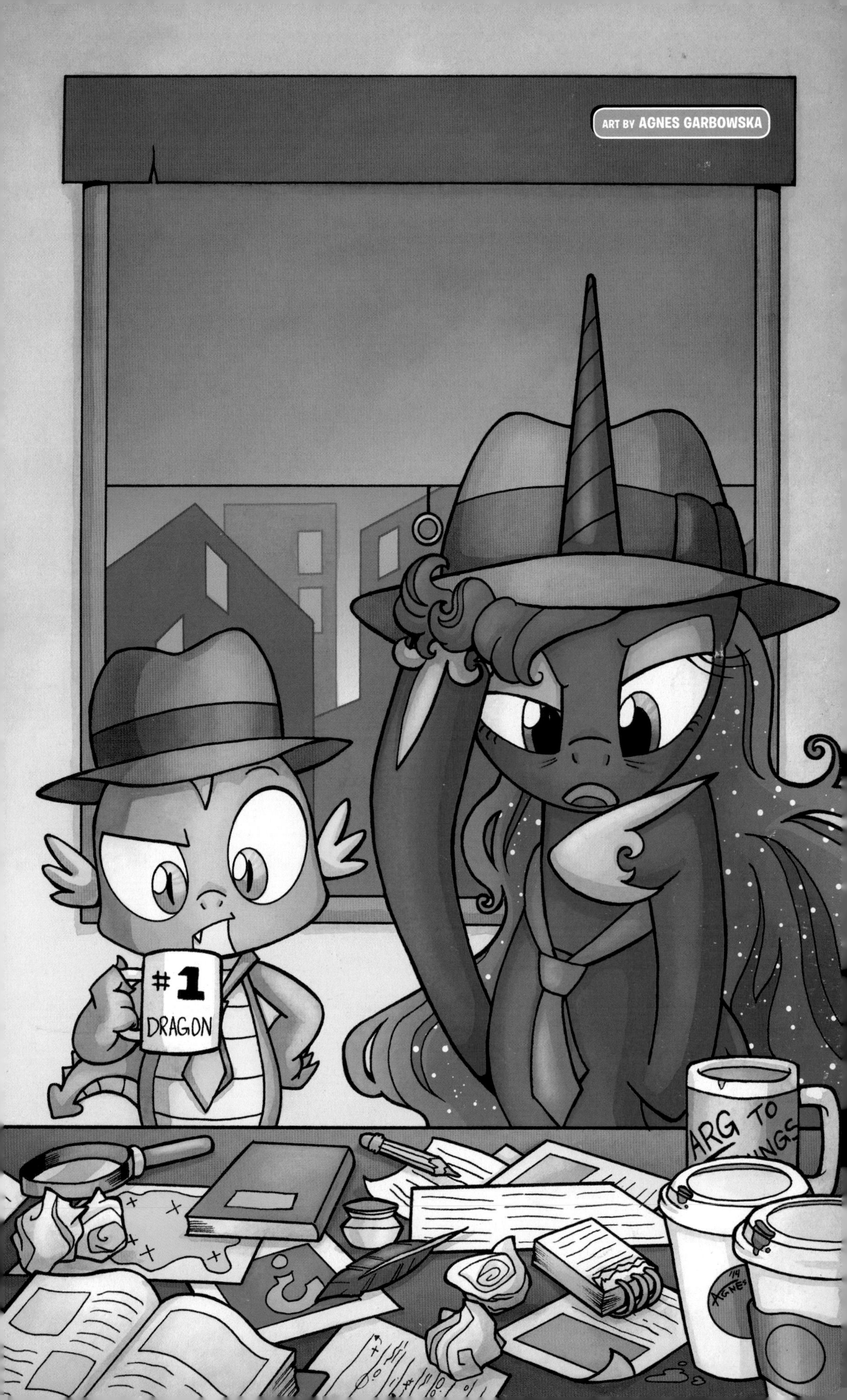
ART BY AGNES GARBOWSKA
#1
DRAGON

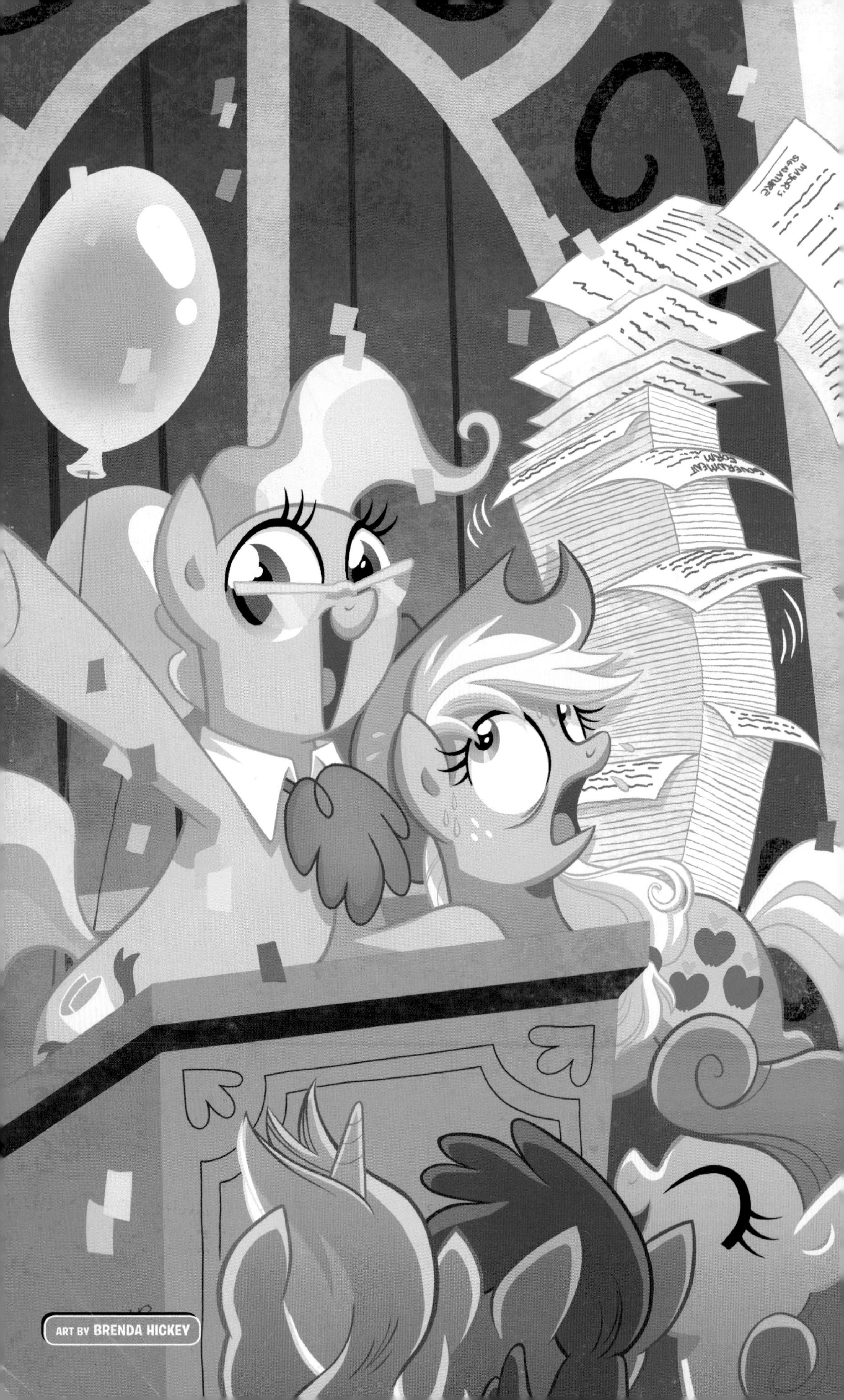
MAYOR'S SIGNATURE
GOVERNMENT FORM
ART BY BRENDA HICKEY

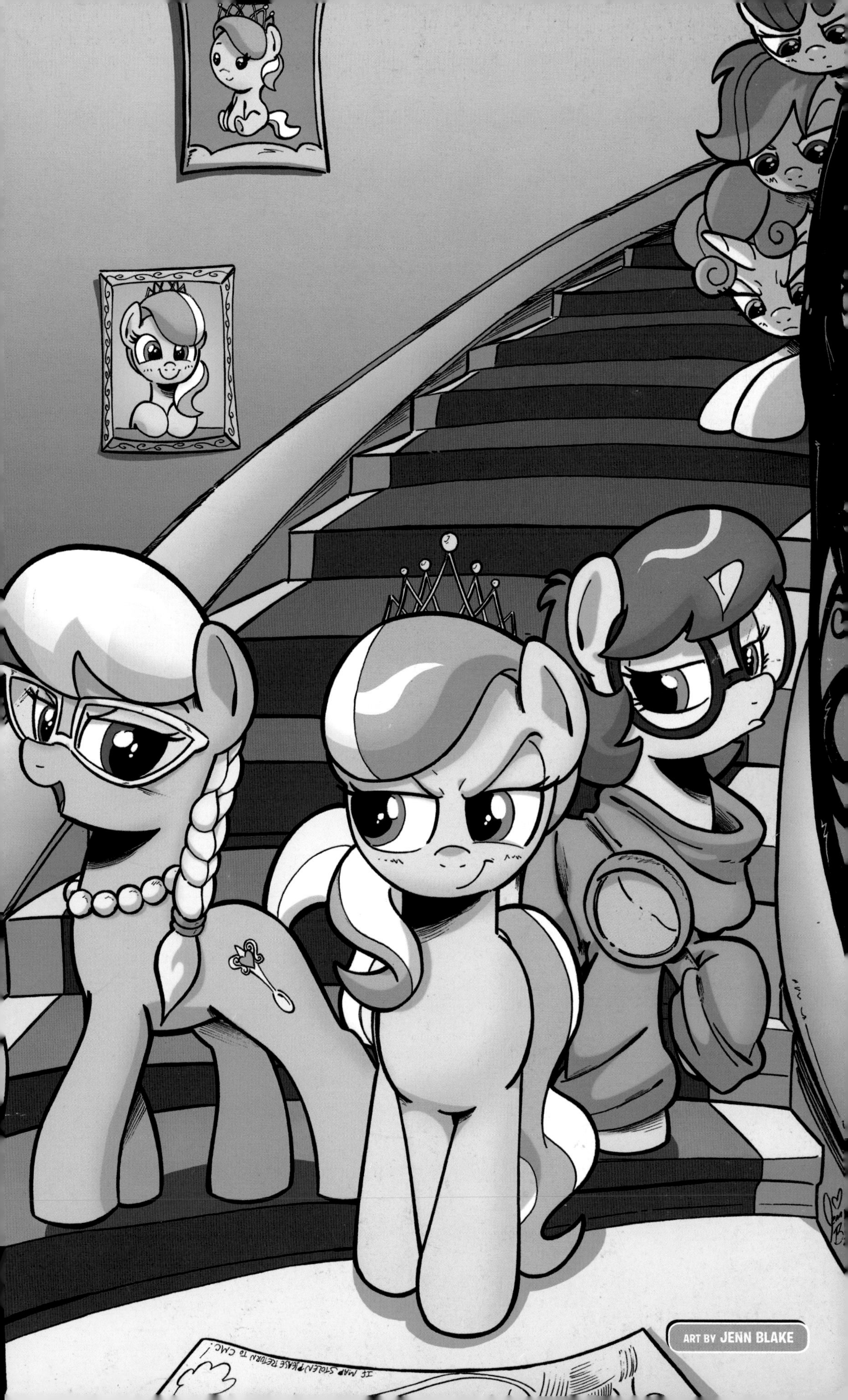
IF MAP STOLEN PLEASE RETURN TO CMC!

ART BY JENN BLAKE

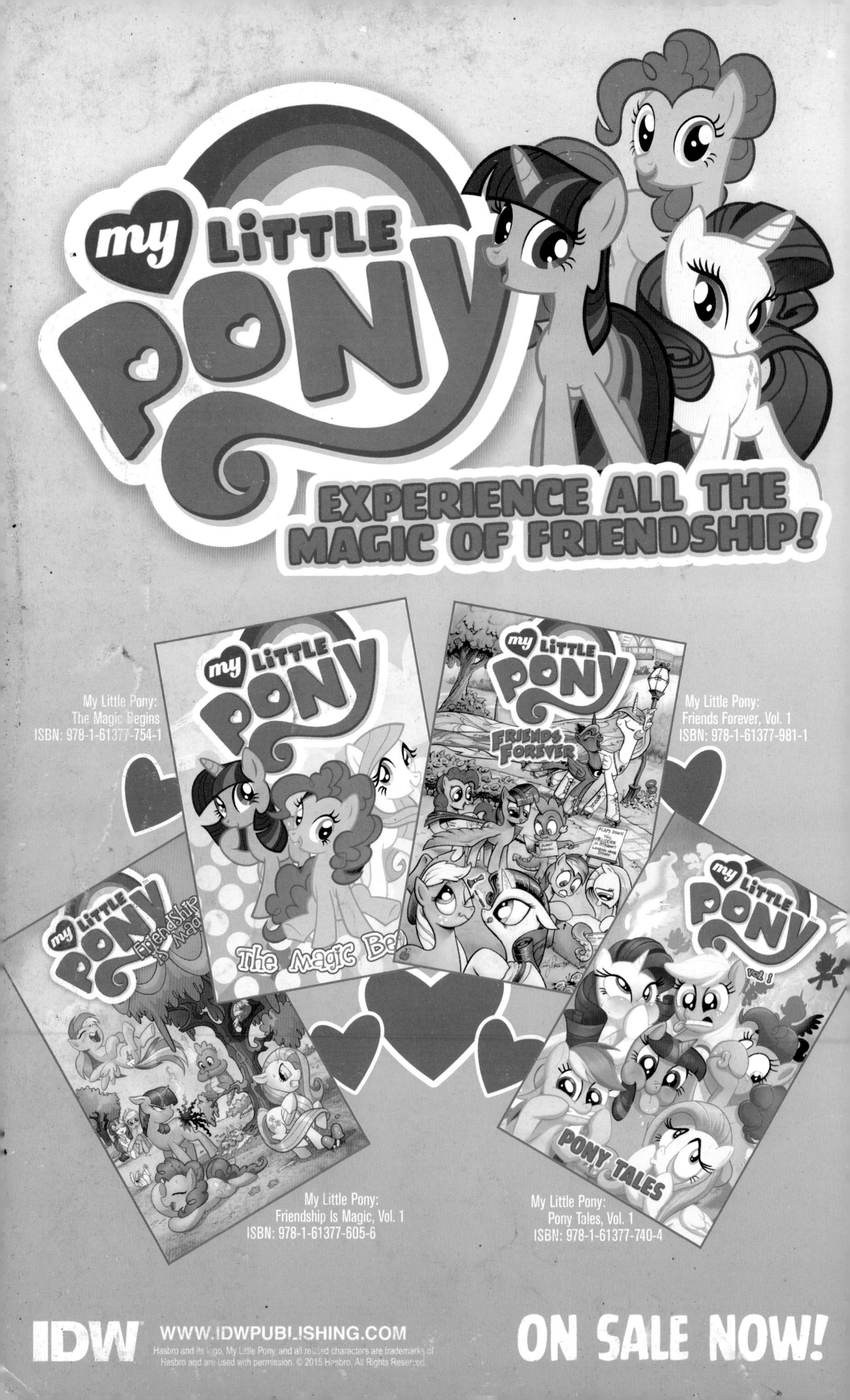
my LITTLE PONY
EXPERIENCE ALL THE MAGIC OF FRIENDSHIP!
My Little Pony:
The Magic Begins
ISBN: 978-1-61377-754-1
My Little Pony:
Friends Forever, Vol. 1
ISBN: 978-1-61377-981-1
My Little Pony:
Friendship Is Magic, Vol. 1
ISBN: 978-1-61377-605-6
My Little Pony:
Pony Tales, Vol. 1
ISBN: 978-1-61377-740-4
IDW
WWW.IDWPUBLISHING.COM
Hasbro and its logo, My Little Pony, and all related characters are trademarks of Hasbro and are used with permission. © 2015 Hasbro. All Rights Reserved.
ON SALE NOW!